GLIMPSE
of
LIGHT
&
GLORY

A GLIMPSE
of
LIGHT
&
GLORY

M.J. WOOD

A Glimpse of Light & Glory
Copyright © 2021 by Makayla J. Wood

Cover Art by Rena Violet
Structural Editing by C.M. McCann
Copyediting by Sydney Hawthorne
Formatting by Zachary James Novels
www.makaylawoodauthor.com

FIRST EDITION published July 2021

Trigger Warnings

Before you proceed, please understand that *A Glimpse of Light & Glory* contains the following things:
- Emotional abuse (parental)
- 1st person experience of anxiety and anxiety attacks
- A store robbery and someone being shot (first chapter)
- Mentions of blood
- Physical abuse (fights between the MC and others his age)
- Mentions of gore (very minimal, only a small amount of times)
- PTSD, and short bursts of self-harm due to an anxiety attack (mentioned, but not a big factor to the story)

Note: Some of these triggers are only mentioned once or twice, but I didn't want to alarm you when you read those parts

A GLIMPSE of LIGHT & GLORY

CHAPTER 01

My lungs burn with each breath but I don't stop. My wet shirt clings to my back and my chest, but I don't stop. I won't stop until he does. His black hair hangs over his eyes, but he still manages to sink every shot.

"Alright boys, we'll call it there for today," Coach shouts from the side of the court. "Hit the showers."

I grit my teeth. Bouncing the ball once more, I shoot it. But Gray flicks his ball at the same time. It knocks mine away and falls straight through the net without touching the hoop.

"Ugh, you would, you freakin' jerk!" I turn to face him with a glare. He cracks a proud smile, chuckling to himself as my teeth grind.

I take one step closer to him before Coach calls out, "Cut it out, you two."

My jaw drops and my heart stutters. "It's not my fault he's such a damn—"

"Sorry Coach. I'll try to keep a tighter leash on him," Gray calls back, sending a sly wink my way before jogging off the court. My fingers ache from clenching and unclenching, my skin burning. Jerk.

"When are you going to give it up?" Milo wanders over to me, his dark curls springy and slick with sweat. His dark skin is flushed, eyes wide with adrenaline. Being the goliath that he is makes Milo a good centre, but he still runs around like an idiot and tires himself out.

"I will when I beat him."

"Then never?"

My temper continues to boil beneath my skin. I crack my knuckles against his bicep, but he just laughs me off. The two of us collect the balls, shooting them into the trolley as the rest of the team runs off to the locker room. Finch Gray isn't *unbeatable*— "I simply haven't found my strength yet."

"Liam, you've tried chess," he curls a finger down as he starts to list off everything I've attempted so far, "spelling b's, checkers, pop quizzes, track, swimming, soccer, weightlifting, basketball... probably others that you haven't told me about." Milo raises his eyebrow with a smart smirk on his lips. "Face it, the guy's essentially Korean Superman."

I shake my head, my teeth gnashing. "I refuse to believe that. There has to be something he can't do."

Milo laughs louder this time. "I get your frustration. Kind of...not really. But you guys are teammates, and if Coach hears you talking like that, he'll bench you. You know how he feels about the team's synergy and all that jazz."

"Yeah, yeah," I wave him off. I brush my hand over my buzzed hair, the fuzziness soft against my blistered palms.

"I keep telling you to stop shaving it," Milo nods to me. "It's our junior year, man. We need to find ourselves girlfriends. And girls aren't gonna look twice when you look like someone straight outta juvie."

2

"It's only for basketball. I don't care what girls think anyway." The only thing I care about is getting to the Championships. *My first step to getting away from this damn place.*

After showering, Milo and I head to the half court near the outskirts of town. The street is busy at this time of the day with students getting picked up or driving home.

I spot mom's silver Mercedes before I see Sawyer skipping towards it, Lemon hot on her heels. As if sensing my gaze, Lemon looks up and catches my eye, waving to me. I stare back, but I don't wave. She slides into the car, giving me one last look before ducking out of sight.

I bounce my worn ball against the pavement as we walk, my other hand buried in my hoodie pocket. Milo yammers on about some girl named Cindy Rose passing a note to him in class that he didn't realize was for someone else when he opened it. He probably assumes that I'm paying attention, but instead I'm thinking of new plays to suggest to Coach tomorrow.

Throwing my backpack down next to the hoop pole, I bounce the ball a couple times. "I have a couple plays I want to run by you. Mind if I try them out?"

"Sure man, go nuts." Milo readies himself, but I move quickly, almost dancing on the pavement. The ball flicks off the tips of my fingers and I sink it. The float of the ball as it flies through the air followed by the swish of the net sends a warm shiver across my skin. Milo tosses the ball back, and I roll the worn surface between my palms.

Would Gray have been able to block that?

Probably.

Milo blows out a long breath as he readies his stance

3

once more. He knows what I'm thinking without me having to say it. It's always written on my damn face. "You and Fin are *both* monsters at this game. You're as good as each other—"

"I'm not as good as him..." I mutter out, my eyes glaring at my old ball. After eight years of playing with it, I've memorized every groove. I know the perfect way to hold it before I shoot, bounce it, throw it. But that doesn't mean anything when Gray could do the exact same thing within the first eight *minutes* of playing with it.

"Talking about me?" I turn towards his irritating voice, the hairs on the back of my neck prickling. Hair stands beside him, his messy ponytail from practice now tied in a tidy bun.

A grunt slips past my lips. "Yeah, about how damn ugly you are."

Finch makes a show of clapping as he bobs his head, a huge annoying smile flashing his teeth at me. My blood boils and my empty hand clenches tight. *Jerk.*

"Wanna play two-on-two?" he asks, his small eyes flickering between Milo and me. Like he can't help himself. Like he has to keep reminding me that he'll always be that little bit better, no matter how much time or effort I put in.

I bite my tongue as Milo raises his hands. "Nah, I'd much rather watch the two of you play. We can't keep up with either of you anyhow." Hair nods in agreement.

I swallow loudly, my eyes narrowing. "That's fine. I can beat him on my own."

Gray whistles, dumping his bag on top of mine. "There's a first for everything, I guess." It's like he can physically see my buttons as he presses them. I bare my teeth and grunt, but I don't fuel the fire. I know that's what he wants. The damn jerk enjoys getting a rise out of me more than he enjoys winning.

I try the play that I ran with Milo, and I score. Gray follows it with a quick three-pointer. When I try the play again in reverse, he's already nailed me. Every time I try to shoot the ball, he shuts me down. He's not as tall as Milo, but he still has an easy four inches on me.

Gray smacks my ball away every time I lean back and shoot, and he steals it when I dribble. He's so much faster— so fast it bothers me to the point where I'm making stupid mistakes.

Black shadows swallow the space around us, a single streetlamp illuminating the court when I finally brace my hands against my knees. My chest is on fire, sweat catching on my eyebrows and dripping down the sides of my face. I'm thankful for the cold evening breeze that passes over my scalp. I wipe the sweat from my forehead, looking around the court for Milo and Hair, but it's just Gray and I.

"They left about an hour ago. Probably bored of watching a one-sided game."

I brush my hand over my wet buzzed hair, my chest tightening at his words. "Yeah, whatever. I'm done."

"You sure? You haven't managed to get ahead yet." The scar on his arm is a bright pink against his flush skin. My stomach twists every time I see that damn scar.

My jaw ticks. "I'm sick of looking at you." *Damn it, I sound so stupid. I sound more and more pathetic the longer I'm around him.*

He bounces my ball to me, and I kick his bag off mine. My mind is racing right now with ways I can counter his

5

counterattacks. He always puts his left foot forward before he jumps. If I fake out and dodge right, I might be able to shoot around him.

I head towards the convenience store at the end of the street to pick up a Hercules on the way home, I need the energy boost. I am so lost in thought about out-manoeuvring Gray during the plays that I don't realize he's following me until he's holding the door open, the bell tinkling above us. "Hey, why the hell are you following me?"

Gray bursts out laughing, wiping his eyes. "You're such an air-head, Liam. You've been muttering about ways you're going to beat me as I walked next to you the entire way here."

My face burns hot and my eye twitches. I grit my teeth. "Piss off."

He laughs again, heading inside ahead of me. I catch the door with a huff, my eyes narrowing on his back. When I enter the store I glance over to the counter, spotting Headphones reading a comic. She glances up when the door slams behind us, her long curtain of hair falling away from her face.

She doesn't take her headphones out of her ears when she responds. "I think there should be one more left in the fridge for you." She nods towards the two fridges they have at the back of the store, where they keep my seemingly exclusive stash of energy drinks. Her eyes glance over to Gray as he wanders the isles silently. "What are you guys doing here together? On a date?" She wiggles her eyebrows at me, her lips pursed.

My nose curls. "Anyone who gets stuck dating this jerk would have to be both deaf and blind."

"So mean, Li-Li. That isn't any way to treat your *date*."

6

He comes up and puckers his lips at me like a fish, his eyes sparkling. I shove him off me and head to the back of the store where the fridges are, scouring the racks for the familiar green can. I catch the shiny green in the reflection of the glass door, and my blood pressure soars.

"Sorry, guess I grabbed the last one. Don't worry, there's still the tropical flavour." The way he smiles always tells me he's not sorry. That he enjoys the anger he stirs in me. I hear the door to the store swing open, but it doesn't take my attention away from the asshole who has my energy drink.

"You don't drink energy drinks. You don't even like the green apple flavour!" I hiss at him, my voice low. I don't want to hear Headphones make another remark about us. "Stop trying to piss me off."

"Well if you didn't make it so easy–"

Headphones lets out a quiet yelp from the front of the store, jerking our attention. Gray and I both spin to see a guy with a ski mask and a brown jacket standing at the counter. Her mascara is already staining her cheeks, her hair sticking to her wet flesh.

"Shit!" Gray curses under his breath. He yanks me down against the end of the shelf hard enough I nearly fall into it.

What the hell? Is someone seriously robbing this place? The two of us can see the guy's reflection in the drinks fridge. He leans closer towards Headphones, his body short but his arms long. She's already shaking. *What the hell is happening?* My mind can't keep up with it. *Am I in danger?* Something suffocating starts clouding my chest.

Finch grabs my arm and yanks me again, bringing my attention to him. His eyes are filled with something hot and dark, and his face is twisted in a way that tells me not to argue. "Don't you dare even *think about it*, Liam." He pushes me back down, his hands shaking against me.

"We can't just—" I try to whisper back through clenched teeth, but his eyes narrow to slits and his nostrils flare.

"This isn't a game. We stay *here*, okay? Stay *out of sight*."

From the way he's looking around, the robber is anxious. Hurried. I guess he would be—he wouldn't want to hang around too long and get caught. But he doesn't seem to have noticed Gray and I hiding at the back. That's good. I can creep around the isle out of his line of sight, throw something to stun him, and then tackle the asshole to the—

I elbow knocks a can of Spaghetti-O's off the shelf, the tin making a loud clanking on the ground before it starts to roll. I reach out and snatch it up, but it's already too late.

"Hey, who's over there?"

My heart drops into my stomach and the can threatens to slip from my sweaty palms and hit the floor again. I turn to Finch and find him already staring at me. His eyes are glossy with fright and his forehead is creased.

Trapped. Trapped here, with nowhere to go. He's probably got a weapon, and we can't get out.

My fault.

This was my fault.

"Hey! Get up and show yourself! *Now!*" The robber shouts again, and my spine presses into the shelf.

I can't move. My body won't listen to my brain as I tell it to get the fuck up. It won't listen as I try to force myself to my feet, because this was my fault, and he doesn't know there's two of us.

He doesn't know there's two of us—

Gray jumps up and raises his hands, his eyes locked on

the robber at the front of the store. He slowly walks down the aisle, away from me, showing his palms. The guy swings his arm towards Gray, leveling a gun at him—*holy shit he has a gun*! *What the hell is Gray thinking?* I look for anything durable to throw. My heart thumps hard in my chest and my palms are sweaty. *Holy shit, what do I do?*

"Hey man, just take a deep breath, and lower the gun..." I have never heard Gray speak with such a smooth voice. He approaches the masked guy slowly, his footsteps short and silent.

"Hey, you stay the fuck where you are, kid!" In the reflection, I see the guy turn his head back to Headphones. "Hurry up already! You're taking too long!" She yelps again, her breathing loud and laboured. I grip the can—the stupid Spaghetti-O's—tighter.

"It's alright. You don't need to wave the gun around." For someone with a shaky gun pointed at him, Gray sounds uncomfortably calm. Headphones looks a little less worried now, like she knows that Gray will take care of it. He'll defuse the situation. Maybe he will. *I'm going to kick his ass for this later. He's not some damn hero.*

It shouldn't be him the gun is pointed at.

"Shut up! Don't tell me what to do. You don't know me, kid!" The guy's voice isn't familiar. I can't...at least I think it isn't.

The can threatens to slip from my clammy hands. I watch the guy in the reflection, ready to pelt the can at him when the opportunity presents itself. I bite down hard on my lip to stop my teeth chattering. It's hard to sit still. I don't know whether that gun is loaded or not, and I'm not willing to risk it on the hope that it's not. My nails cut into the palm of my empty hand, and the air bunches up in my throat.

Think. I need to think.

If I show myself now, it might startle the robber. He'll shoot Gray.

If I throw the can, he might accidently—or not accidently—fire his gun. He'll shoot Gray.

There is a possibility that I would miss him completely, and then my element of surprise is gone. He'll shoot Gray and me.

"I'm not pretending to know you. Just take it easy, no one has to get hurt." Gray's a lot closer to him than before. *What's his plan? Does he even have one?*

"Shut up, kid!"

Gray is halfway down the aisle now, blocking my view of the robber. I can sense the opportunity, only seconds away. Gray's going to get close though to this guy that he'll be able to get the gun away from him. I'll jump in and tackle him to the ground. We'll both pin him down and wait for the police to come. The plan has already formulated in my head.

Until a gust of wind blows the door open and the bell jingles. That's all it takes for shit to fall sideways.

A gunshot shatters the still air, the guy's eyes bulge from his head, and his mouth spits out a curse beneath the mask. My ears ring, but nothing around me shatters. For a moment, I wonder why the glass from the refrigerator didn't explode. He'd been aiming in that direction—

The guy in the ski mask scrambles out the door at the same time I hear a loud *thump*. I think he breaks the door hinge on his way out, but my eyes search for the *thump*.

Close to me. *He's* close to me. He's just lying there. I don't think I've ever seen him lying down. The can finally slips from my hand—the stupid Spaghetti-O's—clunking on the tile floor and rolling away. My knees hit the ground as I stare at him. Just lying there.

He lets out a pathetic sound that has me scrambling forward. Red oozes out beneath him. It's thick but it spreads quickly. *Holy shit. Holy shit holy shit holy shit.*

"Gray..." I choke out. I stare down at him, but I'm not sure what to do. *Is he going to die?*

He moves his hand to press against his torso where there the red spreads across his shirt. He's alive. Holy hell, he's alive. That's all I needed to finally move.

I brush his hands away and press my palms against the wound. His warm blood coats my fingers. I try to keep it all inside him, but it keeps slipping around the edge of my hands.

No, stay in there. Stop. Please stop. Stop, stop, stop.

Something heavy weighs down on my chest, clogging my throat and suffocating me. My eyes burn and my nose itches. I think Headphones says something about calling the police, or maybe an ambulance. He'll be fine. When the ambulance gets here, they'll fix this. They'll know how to stop the bleeding.

"You idiot! You *stupid* idiot! Why would you step in front of a gun? Why would you? *Why*?" I can't stop shouting at him. I'm going to shout at him all the way to the hospital. I'm going to shout at him the entire time he is in surgery. I'm never going to let him forget how angry I am.

His face is sweaty and scrunched up. His inky hair is limp, the longer bits plastered to the sides of his face. He frowns. I don't know if it's at me or if it's the pain. Probably both. "*Stop...*" he rasps out, his breathing laboured.

"I'll never forgive you for this. You're a real jerk, you know that?" I shouldn't be saying these things right now. I should be telling him that it's gonna be alright. That he'll be fine. That the ambulance will be here soon. But every harsh word is spewing from my mouth without thought. My eyes are wide and alert. I don't realise I'm crying until I taste the salty tears.

"You're not allowed to die, do you hear me?" It's only more of what I shouldn't be saying to him right now, but I don't know how to stop it. I won't let him die. Even if he's the same jerk who pushes my buttons every day, I don't want him to die. Even if he's not my best friend anymore, *I don't want him to die.* I press harder against the wound and he grunts louder this time. I think this is how they do it in movies—that's all I have to go off right now.

I don't want him to die.

"I've got to stop the blood." *Why don't they teach you how to treat a bullet wound in high school?*

"*Lia*—" He coughs up blood, the red spattering on his ghostly cheeks.

I...I *can't*... "I'm trying! I'm—" I've got to figure out how to stop the blood. "Stop the blood...stop the blood..." I mutter, my mind crazed. *Is this shock? Maybe it's just the adrenaline.* "*Fucking hell, where is the ambulance? The hospital is ten bloody minutes from here!*" I can't stop cursing. But no other words are coming to mind right now. I don't know what else I should do. I turn back and give him my foulest glare. "You are *not* going to die. *Do you hear me, Finch?*"

I haven't called him Finch since we were kids. I don't know why I did just now. But his pupils pulse. He's lost so much blood, that his skin is turning sickly and grey. My eyes keep staring at the random spots of crimson on his face that he's coughed up, but my heart leaps further into my throat when his eyes start to close.

"*No, no, no*, keep your eyes open, Finch! Hey, listen to me! Don't you close your damn eyes." I don't know whether I'm saying this for him or for me, because I'm not sure how to keep calm right now. I don't want him to die. *I don't want him to die. Please don't die on me...*

His pupils dilate, and suddenly his skin grows warm again. Wait no, it's his blood. But it's hotter now. *So fucking hot.* I pull back from him, wiping my burning hands on my shirt, "Shit! What the hell?" When I look back at him, his body is *glowing*. Like a bloody firefly. His eyes are wide, and his mouth is open, but nothing comes out. His eyes start to glow an eerie white, a weird light shines from his wound. His entire body is glowing now.

My hands burn hotter where his blood touched my flesh, and I try to wipe away as much of it on my shirt as I can, but it's like my hands have been dunked in hot oil. I try to shake it off, but it only gets worse. Crying out, I hunch over them.

Fuck, how do I stop this pain? I can't shake it off as it sizzles and bubbles across my palms. When I finally pry my eyes open, Gray's eyes are closed. But the colour of his skin is normal, and the air around him seems to vibrate.

What...the...fuck? My brain short circuits and I collapse to my side.

I need to stop the blood.

13

CHAPTER

02

My eyes are filled with sand, and my body is numb. Almost like I'm floating. It smells icky and clean. *What could possibly smell this clean?*

Prying my eyes open, the white walls are a stark brightness despite the room being mostly concealed in pale shadows. *Am I in a hospital bed?* I clear my throat and go to call out to someone, but a nurse wanders into my room, her eyes bright. "Good to see you're up. How are you feeling?"

I blink hard to try and clear the last of the fog from my eyes. "Confused." I slur, my head heavy and clouded. "Where's Gray? Is he alright?" *Is he in surgery? Recovery? Where is he?*

She gives me a weird look. At least I think she does. I can barely see two feet in front of me right now. "I'll go and get the doctor." She disappears again, leaving me with the constant beeping of the monitors. I glance down at the hospital gown, my cheeks burning hot. *God damn, someone stripped me and put me in this stupid paper dress.*

When I raise my hands to rub my foggy eyes, they're wrapped with gauze. *What the hell?* I try to move my fingers, but they're bound tight. I can't focus enough energy to try and bend any of my fingers, but they're tingling.

There are multiple murmurs beyond the door, but I can't make out anything being said. A guy in a white lab coat and a clipboard walks towards me, his glasses perched at the end of his nose. Sweat gathers at this hairline, his roots damp and shiny. "Good to see you awake, Liam. I'm Doctor Wallace. How are you feeling?"

I can barely shrug my shoulders. I squint to try and make out a face, but it's all lines and blobs beyond the haziness. "Yeah, I'm fine. What happened to my hands? And where's Gray?" It's a mission to pronounce each word clearly. I'm still not sure I do.

"Gray?" The doctor's eyebrows draw in as he pushes his frames further up the bridge of his slippery nose. *Why is his nose so sweaty?*

Moving—or *trying* to—into a sitting position, I level the doctor with a tired glare. "Finch Gray?" I try to move my arms, but they're so damn heavy. "The guy who got *shot*?" The doctor seems even more confused than before. *Am I speaking a different language or something?* "I was with him at the store that got robbed." I didn't dream that did I?

Now he seems even more confused. "Are you talking about Doctor Montgomery's nephew?"

I nod my head, but it's a struggle to lift it back up. *Who the heck else would I be talking about? "Yes."*

He shakes his head. "He was the one who carried you in tonight. *You* were the one who was hurt."

You *were the one who was hurt.*

He points down to my hands, and I follow his gaze. "Yeah, what the hell happened to my hands?" My throat is scratchy, and coughing doesn't help clear it, but my words are clearer than before. The more I blink, the quicker the fog dissipates, though there's still a haziness that lingers over my head.

"Second-degree chemical burns to your palms and fingers. It will heal nicely as long as you take care of the burns and ensure they don't get infected. You'll have to keep them wrapped for a couple weeks, so no strenuous activity. The longer you allow them time to heal, the less they will scar."

My heart hammers loud in my chest, but my body is too sluggish to respond properly, "Chemical burns?" My mind tries to piece together what happened—how I could have ended up with chemical burns to my damn hands—but everything is white and blinding. My head starts to thump hard. "How?"

The doctor looks down at his clipboard with narrowed eyes. "There isn't much in the report for when you were brought in. It says that Doctor Montgomery's nephew carried you in on his back but disappeared when you were loaded up onto a gurney."

He disappeared?

There is no way he could have carried me here. "Can I at least get changed back into my clothes? This paper-thing feels like crap." I need to talk to Gray. I need to figure out what the hell happened. Because nothing is lining up right now.

"No can do. Your clothes were also affected by the same acid that burned your hands. You will be staying overnight, so there is really no urgency to change."

A loud groan rumbles in my chest. "God damn." I finally

manage to lift my arms and rub my eyes with my fingertips, which only causes my hands to twinge with pain. My vision barely clears. I know it's because of whatever painkillers they've given me, but my hands don't *feel* burned. Just stiff and uncomfortable.

There's a knock on the door, and my head rolls lazily to the side so I can see. The Sheriff, Gray's uncle, stands at the door in his police uniform, his puffer coat doing well to mask how built he truly is. Like a damn tree.

"Doctor Wallace, I was wondering if I could have a moment alone to speak with Liam?" he asks, his voice low and his eyes hard. I swallow, and for a moment I wonder if I'm in trouble.

The doctor rounds the bed and nods to the Sheriff, clearing not looking to intervene with police business. "If you need anything Liam, just press the buzzer on the remote beside your bed."

I don't nod or smile as he leaves. I stay silent as the Sheriff steps further into the room and the doctor closes the door behind him. He takes off his large brown hat and stares at it for a moment, and I try to sit up straight. Dad always said to sit straight. That it's a show of strength.

Strong men always win.

My father's voice echoes in my head like a broken record as the doctor asks in a rumbly tone, "How are you feeling, Liam?" His square jaw is tight, but his eyes are softer than they were when the doctor was in the room. Now it's just the two of us, and the silence is palpable.

"I don't know...I think I'm okay..." I look down at my hands again and my heart starts to hammer. *The doctor said they'll be fine. But what about basketball? What about the*

17

game in two weeks?

I lean back into the pillow when my head throbs louder. My vision starts to flicker so I squeeze my eyes shut and breathe through my nose.

"I know that you only just woke up, but I need to ask you a couple questions about what happened tonight." His voice is gravely, like someone died and he's trying to figure out how to tell me in the nicest way possible.

"Is Gray okay? Did they manage to stop the bleeding?" I quickly ask, my eyes pinched tight. My voice still slurs, but it sounds clear enough to me.

Doctor...I've already forgotten his name...he said that Gray *carried* me here. But I'm sure—I'm *certain* that he was shot.

So he's lying. He *has to be* lying.

I open my eyes when the Sheriff doesn't respond, and find his head tilted, his gaze narrowing slightly. The shadow of his beard casts a dark glow over his sharp features. "What do you mean, 'stop the bleeding'? What do you remember, son?"

Son. Son...

I press my head further into the pillow. Hard enough until I feel the stiff mattress against the back of my skull. "What do *you* mean 'what do I remember'? He was *shot*." I breathe in, but it catches in my throat. "I can't forget something that—"

Blood.

So much blood.

Lia—

I squeeze my eyes shut again, but the image doesn't disappear. Gray's *voice* doesn't disappear. If anything, it blows up right behind my eyelids, like a terrifying loop in my mind.

"*Liam?*" The Sheriff's voice is far away. Underwater. Wait, I think it's my head that's underwater.

When a sudden weight presses down on my shoulder and squeezes gently, my eyes snap open and the Sheriff is standing much closer than before. The sound of my panting breaths rage in my ears, and the Sheriff watches with careful, minding eyes.

He smiles at me. It's not a big smile or a happy smile. More like a smile you give someone when you don't have words for them, but you're there to listen to their words, whatever they might be.

"It's okay, Liam. You're safe. All of you are safe." He says. He squeezes my shoulder again and I wince. It doesn't hurt, but it's strange to have someone standing so close.

Close, close, close.

"Headphones?" I ask.

I peek up at him again, and his eyebrow is quirked. "Headphones?"

"The girl that works there. Her name's..." I don't remember it. She's just always Headphones.

He nods, and his eyes seem more relaxed than before. "She's fine."

I nod slowly, but my skin's starting to itch. I still don't understand how I'm the one who ended up here. I turn to face the Sheriff, my mouth open to speak when a voice travels through the door.

"He's in this room, ma'am." It's the same nurse's voice from earlier, followed by near-silent footsteps.

"What's wrong with him?" A faint, feminine voice asks.

My chest squeezes and pulls.

What's wrong with him?

Mom walks in, her normally well-kept bob strangely messy and her doe-eyes wider than normal. Her clothes are clean, and dressy, her handbag tight against her side.

"He sustained second-degree chemical burns to his palms, so—" the nurse starts, but mom interrupts her.

"Chemical burns?" Mom's voice raises an octave, her eyes glassy. When her gaze lands on me, her lower lip shivers. Her eyes drift to where my bandaged hands lay on top of the sheets. "What did you do, baby?"

My shoulders tense, and my eyes shift to my lap.

The first thing...that's the first thing she asks.

What did you do, baby?

Before I can answer, her gaze drifts to where the Sheriff stands beside me. I shrug out from his grip and slide down the bed. My chest is tight as I watch her flat eyes tighten. "Dean." Her tone is perkier than it was two seconds ago, but she's still dull at the moment. Her eyes are puffy and red, her nose pink at the tip.

"Evening, Marnie. It's good to see you again, although I'm sorry that it's under such unfortunate circumstances." He says, his smile sad. Can smiles be sad?

Mom nods her head, but she doesn't say anything as she steps closer.

"I'm sorry Marnie, but I still have some questions I've got to ask—"

"I'm sure it can wait until tomorrow, can't it, Dean?"

My shoulders hunch when I hear my father's voice. I don't raise my head, but I know he's standing in the doorway with his shoulders pulled back and his hands buried in the pockets of his slacks.

The Sheriff turns towards my father's voice, his smile strained this time. "You know I've got to question him, Jasper."

My father strides into the room and around the other side of the bed, his hands still tucked away into his pockets. "I understand completely. But Liam has just suffered an incredibly stressful altercation, and I'm sure he would like nothing more than to sleep it all off."

Sheriff blows out a quiet breath and nods his head. He knows he won't get any more answers out of me while my father's here. Not even the Sheriff is willing to step on the Mayor's toes.

"Alright. I'll check in on him tomorrow," the Sheriff says, the two of them speaking as if I'm not situated right between them. I move to sink further down into the paper sheets but when my father cuts me a look from the corner of his eye, I freeze.

Strong men always win.

The Sheriff reaches out again to give my shoulder a squeeze, and my neck strains from keeping so still. It's almost impossible not to shift from under his grip. But my father's here. And it'll only be so much worse if I did.

"I'll come by sometime tomorrow. I'll check with the nurses that—"

My father interjects again. "Oh, no. Liam will be coming home tonight."

My shoulders hunch slightly, and I stare at my bandages as something starts to buzz in my head.

Don't move. Stay quiet. If I stay quiet, he might not look at me. He might walk out with the Sheriff and leave me here.

Stay quiet, stay quiet, stay quiet.

I don't see the Sheriff's face because I'm still staring numbly at my bandaged hands, but his makes a suspicious humming sound before he says, "The doctor's said he—"

"I've spoken with the doctor," is all my father says. Because he doesn't *need* to say more. No one will question him. No one will stop him. Not him.

Stay still, stay still, stay still.

The Sheriff hums quietly to himself before patting his hand on my shoulder and nodding his head in farewell to my parents. The three of us wait silently until the door clicks closed behind him. The air is thick and toxic, suffocating me as I stare holes into the white cloth binding my hands.

"I'd like to know how you managed to receive chemical burns in a *corner store*, Liam."

I shrug my shoulders, keeping my droopy eyes low. I've been waiting for him to ask. The first moment he spoke, I knew this was coming. The minute mom walked in, my chest grew tighter. She says nothing next to me. "I don't really remember." I lie, because I'm not sure if it's actually a lie or not.

He hums, his fingers curling around the bed railings. Close. *Too close.* "You *don't really remember*...you witness a robbery and end up with chemical burns to your hands, yet *you don't really remember*."

Angry. So angry. At the situation? At me?

Of course it's at me.

"Don't do this here, Jasper," Mom mutters, her eyes low as well. Her fingertips brush against my forearm gently, absentmindedly.

"I'll do what I damn well please, Marnie," he cuts back.

22

My insides clench and my jaw snaps. "Try harder." Dad's presence turns suffocating when he takes a step closer. He casts a dark shadow over me, my mind sinking.

Answer him. "I'm trying. But everyone's saying confusing things." I shift my head to rub my eye with my shoulder, staring at the bandages. The bandages are the first confusing point. It's still difficult to breathe. Difficult to see.

He moves mom to the side. He isn't harsh or forceful, but the same strange tightness settles in my chest just like every other time I see him touch her. My throat burns with things I want to say to him. Tell him not to lay a hand on her. Tell him to get out.

But I choke.

Every time.

Strong men...

"What *do* you remember?"

I look at mom. I ask her without words to make him step back. To make him leave. I don't want him standing so close. Looming. But mom's fading away into the background, her gaze locked on my face but not meeting my eyes.

"Look at *me*." Dad's tone is like ice, sending a chill across my skin. The hairs on the back of my neck spike as goosebumps fizzle up my arms. When my eyes meet his, I wish they hadn't. It's been a long time since I've met my father's stare. And it's the same emptying feeling that sucks everything out of me when I do.

Look what you did.

Stop crying.

What's wrong with him?

He stares back with a hard bent brow, his dark eyes watching my face closely. He's looking for any indication that I'm lying. There shouldn't be any, but I never know what he sees when he looks at me. It's never been something he likes seeing.

He has me pinned down with his glare and I can't look away. My tongue is thick in my mouth, and my fingertips start to tingle. I can't lie, but I don't know what's true anymore. And saying I don't remember isn't enough for him.

"I thought that...well, the robber had a gun, and he shot...I thought he shot Gray." I stumble out each word, my tight throat threatening to suffocate me as I try not to mumble the words.

Don't look at me.

Don't look.

His brows furrow deeper. The lump in my throat is larger than a bowling ball, like I can't remember how to breathe for a moment. Mom watches with droopy eyes, but she doesn't step in to stop him interrogating me. "Are you talking about the Sheriff's nephew?" I nod, my teeth chattering in my mouth. I'm not cold, but my insides are frozen. Gray's name is never absent in our house. "The same kid who carried you here on his *back*?"

Of course he doesn't believe me. Why is he telling me the same story? Finch was shot. *There is no way he carried me here. No way.*

"Marnie, go sign the discharge papers." Mom flees the room before dad's even finished dismissing her. The moment my father turns to leave, air rushes back to my burning lungs. My eyes itch, a dull throb pulsing from my hands. The doctor from earlier, Doctor Sweaty, walks in before my dad can leave, a frazzled look on his face. My father pauses, his shoulders bunching under his suit jacket.

I bite my lip to keep myself out of it. If this guy wants to try and refuse my dad, it's his funeral.

"I'm sorry sir, but your son's injuries are quite severe. I need to keep him here overnight—" I keep my gaze settled hard on my bandaged hands. I can't come to the doctor's defence. Dad wouldn't listen to me even if I did.

"Who are you?" My father interrupts him, his eyes narrowed. Only my father is capable of belittling someone in three short words. The doctor shifts like he's been dealt a physical blow. He *must* be new here.

"I'm your son's doctor." He says it more like it's a question than a statement. "His burns are still-"

"Thank you *very much* for your hard work, doctor," my father cuts in again, his smile strained and the tips of his ears turning pink. "But my wife would very much like our son to be home tonight." With that, my father strides out of the room, leaving no room for discussion.

"It's alright, doc," I mutter, pushing myself up further with my elbows. I wince when the skin of my hands tugs.

The doctor shakes his head, his eyes still darting back to the door every few seconds. He's not the first person my father has intimidated into his decisions. That comes with his position as Mayor. Or maybe it's just him. "I would really have liked to keep you overnight... I want you to come in next week, so I can check in on your recovery." He hands me his card with his number on it.

I nod my head and take it. "Sure." As the nurse comes back to unhook me from the machines, the doctor explains how to take care of my hands and how to clean them carefully. After going over the last of the dos and don'ts, he slinks out of the room, leaving me with my dizzy thoughts.

No contact sport or physical activity.
Shit.

Mom sneaks back into the room with my school duffle bag slung over her shoulder. The wide black strap looks silly against her small pink frame, but I silently thank God that I now have a change of clothes.

She drops it onto the end of the bed as I spin my legs off. It's awkward without using my hands, but I make it work. This is gonna be a long few weeks.

"Sheriff Montgomery gave it to me when your father was speaking with him. Do you want me to help you get changed, baby?"

I can't even remember when I dropped it. I shake my head. "Definitely not. I'm not there yet, mom."

She nods her head, her droopy eyes falling back to my bandaged hands. She doesn't ask about what comes next. She probably doesn't want to know any more. I'm sure that I'm going to hear about this later.

Walking through the hospital is tedious. Each step is agony, and my entire body is shaking, but whenever mom reaches out to help, I lean back. *Too close. She's too close right now.*

Dad doesn't say a word as mom and I climb into his Bentley. The drive home is equally as silent, until he finally says, "Next time you worry your mother like that..."

I don't ask him what 'next time' entails. I don't want to know. And I don't ask him to stop at a drug store so I can pick up my pain-killer prescription. Neither does mom. I'll just get it on my way to school tomorrow. Even though mom told me I should take the day off and rest, I can't.

I know what I saw. Gray was shot. Then he started

26

glowing. I might be doped up on pain meds right now, but I'd bet my life on it.

When we pull up the driveway, two shadows move in front of Sawyer's window. I groan when I remember that Lemon's probably still here.

Mom grabs my bag before I can, and dad makes sure I see the eyebrow he raises at her. My jaw clenches but I don't ask for her to give it back. My grave is already deep enough. The moment we step inside the door, Sawyer's voice booms from the top of the stairs.

"What the hell, Liam? Mom couldn't take Julia home because of you!" I don't look at her, but I know she has her hands on her hips and she's pouting. When I glance at the hallway clock, it only reads nine thirty.

"Whatever." I mumble, staring at the ugly foyer rug.

"I'll bring your bag up for you," Mom mutters too quietly for my father to hear.

I shake my head. "I'm fine, mom." Dad walks straight past me without a word, but the tension pollutes the air. I nod my head as I struggle to swallow the same bowling ball from earlier. She slips the strap onto my shoulder and I mumble, "I'm gonna go to bed."

"You don't want something to eat first?"

I shake my head again, my gaze focused on the puke yellow carpet lining the staircase. Sawyer doesn't say anything more as I pass her.

"Hey Liam..." June...Wait no, Julina...Ugh, I can't remember what Sawyer said—*Lemon* mumbles from around the corner. I nod, but I don't turn to her. She follows me to my room a couple steps away. "Fin wanted me to ask how you were if I saw you."

Just like that, my blood is boiling, burning behind my eyes. *The stupid jerk was shot, yet he is asking me how I am? Like I can't handle some burns.*

"I'm fine," I bite out. Sawyer tries to tell me off for being rude, but I shut my door before she has the chance, dropping my bag against the wall. My arm from my fingertips to my elbows throbs. Loud and *painful*. My forehead breaks out in a sweat, and my eyes start to cross. But I take a deep breath.

I can handle some burns.

Sitting down at my desk, I wrangle my laptop open with just the exposed tips of my fingers. It pulls on my skin in a sickening way that has a nauseating shiver turning my stomach, but I don't stop. I move my hands slower now and I open up my web browser and type in 'glowing skin'.

Gray was shot. I *know* he was. *So what the hell is everyone talking about?*

CHAPTER

03

My eyes are drawn like a magnet to the convenience store as I cross the basketball court on the way to school. I can make out the yellow tape lined up and down the shop door. *I wonder how Headphones is doing.* When I finally make it to school, quiet whispers are buzzing in the air and a few wide eyes glance my way. I'm sure everyone knows about the robbery. I hide my hands in my hoodie pocket and ignore them.

"Liam!" Milo's voice echoes across the yard, but I don't stop. I just want to get inside, away from all these nosy bastards. "Hey." He catches up. I barge through the entrance to the school building with my shoulder, but he turns me back to face him. His normally dark skin looks pale, like he's seen a ghost.

"What are you doing here, man? I heard about what happened yesterday..."

I shrug. "Yeah, well someone has to tell Coach I can't practice for the next few weeks."

"*Weeks?*" His eyes bug out of his head and he rakes his hand through his curly hair. "What the hell happened, man?"

I give him a pointed look. I don't want everyone to know what's happened. *I* don't even know what happened. All I *do* know is that Gray's blood cooked my skin somehow—it's a ridiculous theory, but it's the only possibility there is—and I'm not going to speak to anyone else about this before him. He and I are going to straighten this out.

Milo nods, taking my silence for my answer. "Where's Gray?" I ask.

He gives me another weird look. "Dude, he's probably trying to deal with what happened to you guys! I'm surprised you're even here, man!"

I shrug again. "No good in staying home."

If he supposedly wasn't *shot, then why the hell wouldn't he come to school? What's he hiding from?* I'll wait until that jerk comes. And then we're gonna talk about what the hell happened last night.

I keep my hands in my pockets for the most part, but they're starting to get sweaty. My palms are burning a lot worse today than they were last night, like I'm holding them too close to a flame.

My feet drag along the floor, my shoulders hunched and my palms splitting with pain. The day drags on, everyone staring and whispering, that by the time I find Coach at the end of the day, I'm about ready to tell them all to go to hell.

"What do you think you're doin' here, Rice?" he barks from across the gym as the rest of the team run sprints up and down the court. The squeaking of their shoes screeches in my ears, and a heavy weight settles over my shoulders. *This is going to suck.*

I glance around the room. "I need to talk to you Coach."

"I already heard 'bout last night. At least take a *day*, would you?" He jabs his thumb towards the main doors. My jaw clenches as I ignore his order and approach him, my hands still tucked away in my pockets. He raises a brow as he watches me approach.

"It's kinda something else, Coach." When I'm close enough, I lower my voice, "Can we talk in your office? I don't want the guys to know yet..."

Coach's brow dips low this time, his lips pursing as his forehead wrinkles beneath his faded blue cap. He points to those on the team who have slowed down, and shouts at them to get back to work. I keep my eyes averted from the team, like I have all day as each of them have tried to approach me about what happened last night.

I follow Coach into his office, shouldering the door closed as he leans back against his desk to face me. "What is it, Liam?"

Something sinks hard in my stomach as I pull my hands from my pockets. Coach's eyes land on the bandages and he sucks in a sharp breath. His face turns pink, then red, then purple before he breathes again. "What the hell happened to your hands? I thought it was a *robbery*."

I breathe out a stuttered sigh. "It was. The doctor said it's a chemical burn. I haven't seen them yet...but he said I can't practice or play for a couple weeks, and that's if they don't get infected."

Coach mutters a curse under his breath, his face turning a light pink. "This have something to do with why Gray ain't here today?"

I shrug. "Don't know why he isn't here. Apparently he wasn't hurt."

"*Apparently*?" His narrowed eyes focus on my face now.

"I mean I haven't seen him, so I don't know. The doctor's told me that he wasn't injured, but I won't believe it until I see it." *I won't believe anything until I see him.*

Coach nods with pursed lips, his forehead still creased. He blows out a big breath, causing my insides to clench. It's never good when he's silent.

"I'll be good as new in just a couple weeks, Coach. Please don't pull me from the line up...I've worked hard to be on that court."

He raises his hand, his forehead creased. "Hold on a sec, I'm not gonna pull you from the line up." He gives me a hard look. "But you're not getting back on that court until you're one hundred percent, alright? I want the doctor's approval first."

I nod, my stomach unclenching. My palms continue to ache, sending sharp tingles up my arm. "Thanks, Coach."

He flicks his head to the door. "Get going, then. You better go check on Gray."

When I hesitate, Coach gives me a stern look. "I figured I would see him when he shows up at school."

Coach's face doesn't change. "I shouldn't have to tell you to check up on him, Liam. He went through the same thing you did. You don't know what's going on in that head of his, and yet you're probably the only one who does."

I blow out a silent breath. Finch Gray is not my problem. I can't get anything about last night out of my head. But I can't know for sure. Not until I see Gray for myself. "I'll check on him, Coach."

He sends me a grim smile, shooing me out of the room. "Good, get going then."

I hitch my bag up higher on my shoulder before slinking out of his office. So that I don't have to pass by the team, I take the back exit through the locker room and cross the football field. I don't want to lie to Coach if he asks later, so I head towards Gray's place.

I'm surprised I remember the way on foot, considering how long it's been since I last stopped by his house. What would usually be a boring twenty-minute walk if filled with thoughts of everything that happened.

I'm positive I didn't imagine anything that happened last night. I'm *sure* that Gray's blood burnt my hands. Even though blood is warm, it doesn't cause chemical burns. But I know I touched his blood. He was shot. I didn't imagine what I felt last night.

That tight panic in my chest. The numbness in my veins. The suffocation in my throat. The warmth of his blood on my cold skin. The blood splatter on his face.

Lia—

There's no way I imagined that.

My cheeks burn as I remember everything I said. *Jeez, what was I thinking? Gray even saw me crying. Why the heck was I crying in the first place?*

Shock. If he asks, I can say it was shock.

Standing outside his house is suddenly a lot more daunting when I see the two cars parked in the driveway. The pale blue paint makes my eyes dizzy the longer I look at it. Too many windows. You can see inside. My reflection stares back through the windowpane.

My eyes...they don't look the same.

A car door slams across the street, and my spine seizes. My throat clenches up and my vision flashes.

33

He's in front of me.

The mask.

The gun.

He's—

I stumble back, the house in front of me warping, the barrel of the gun closing in. How did he get so close? What is he doing here? What is he *doing here*?

"Liam?" There's a voice...far away. The harder I strain my eyes, the clearer the colours become. "Liam? Are you okay, hon?"

I gasp out, the air suddenly rushing in. My eyes burn as my mind finally snaps back. I spin around and see a lady across the street helping her kid out of the back seat. She slams the door closed as the kid rushes up to the front door ahead of her. The sound has my entire body flinching.

"Liam?"

I turn back to Gray's house and find Doctor Montgomery staring at me from the top step of the front porch. Her blonde hair hangs past her shoulder, swaying in the gentle breeze. My head jerks from side to side, but the masked man is gone. He's nowhere. When I look back to Doc, her eyes are downcast.

"Are you okay, hon?" she calls out, moving down a step. Her bright-coloured clothes have my eyes squinting. What just happened?

Taking in a deep breath, the pressure slowly starts to subside. She's watching me like I'm crazy. I'm not crazy, am I? "Hi Doc." I choke out. "I'm sorry to drop by unannounced, but I—"

I don't even remember why I came here. I stare back at her, not sure what I should say. I don't know what happened just now.

Her lips pull down in a sad smile. "Did you stop by to check on Fin?"

Did I? My mind is still foggy. I swallow but don't respond. Doc doesn't miss the way my hands are stuffed in my pockets. She nods to them. "Would you like to come in and I can show you how to change the bandaging?" My shoulders hitch, touching my ear lobes when she mentions the bandaging. "Julia told me about your hands."

I nod, clearing my throat. "It's fine. I can manage."

She shakes her head. "Come inside, Liam. It's not so easy to do on your own."

I try to tell her no again, but she steps away from the wide-open door and walks further into the house. I glance back down the footpath towards the street, but the street is clear again. Releasing a long breath, I step into the foyer and elbow the door closed.

Their house is different from mine. Warmer. Inviting. There're so many family photos lining the walls and entry table. Pictures of Noodles, Lemon and Gray from when they were kids. It's before Gray got that scar on his arm. He looks too much like his mom for the three of them to look like they're actually cousins. There's pictures from competitions, and the holidays, and fishing trips. That one time we dared Lemon to suck a lemon. Her face is so sour, but Gray and I are laughing in the background. There's a picture of Doc and Gray's dad when they were younger. For a moment it's difficult to tell who is who. Gray's entire family is so close. They're all—

"Liam?" My head snaps in the direction of the kitchen, finding Doc standing in the doorway a few feet from me. I didn't even realise I'd stopped following her.

"Sorry," I mumble, my eyes drifting back to the picture. Although Gray shares a lot of his mother's features, he still has the same brawniness as his dad. I wonder if it still upsets him to think about them. It's been so long since they passed.

"It's alright." She wanders over to where I'm standing and presses her hand against my bicep. "It's crazy how much time has passed since a lot of these photos were taken."

I jerk my head away, pursing my lips. "I'm sorry, I shouldn't have—"

"It's *alright*, Liam." Her tone is wispy and soft. She pats my arm again and leads me into their big kitchen. I can't even begin to remember when I last stepped foot in this house. Probably that day I said I wouldn't be Gray's friend anymore—

"How are you feeling, hon? Did you go to school today?" She points to the bar stool at the marble island. I plant my butt and let my bag slip off my shoulder.

"I'm fine," is all I say. My hands hurt like *hell*.

She tucks her hair behind her ears. It's a lighter shade than Lemon's, and longer. When she slaps a medical bag down onto the counter, I swear my blood pressure spikes. Holding out her hands for mine, my throat clogs up and my heart hammers. My chest clenches as I remove them from my pocket for the second time today. My nose pulls up when I glance down at the white bandaging from yesterday, now replaced with a yellowish green.

Gross.

"Oh dear, this is going to be messy." Her laughter is light when she sees my horrified expression. "Don't worry. Take good care of them and they should heal up nicely."

36

I just nod my head, swallowing my tongue as she starts to unwind the damp binding. The wrap starts to tug at my sensitive skin the more she unravels, and soon she is peeling it back from the slimy skin of my burnt palms. My eyes bulge when I see the spongy puke yellow flesh and bile rises in my throat. A rancid smell floats up through my nose, and I gag.

"Don't look, hon." Too late for that. I bite my lip as I force back the bile that heaves in my stomach. She walks off to dump my bandages in the trash and points me over in the direction of a powder room. "We need to rinse them under cool water. Don't rub them together, just let the water run over them. It will hurt, but it will help with avoiding infection."

Taking a deep breath I follow her, forcing myself to stay as still as possible as she turns on the water. My shoulders tense, the water sends painful spasms up my arms. Pressure builds in my forearms as the burning pain rips through my palms, but I don't make a sound. With soft movements, she pats my hands dry. It's harder not to show how painful *that* is.

My skin's uncomfortable and achy, and I want to dunk them in buckets of ice to cool them off, but I know nothing other than painkillers will help. Doc leads me back to the barstool and sprays some antibacterial before she starts to redress my hands. I watch her carefully so that I know how to do it tomorrow.

"Thanks for doing this, Doc."

She snorts, her teeth showing with the corners of her lips pulled up high. "Just call me Alice." I nod my head—*Alice*—silent again as I watch her tuck the end of the bandage in, securing the binding. I'm not sure I'll remember that. But I'd like to. She's always nice to me. My hands are comfortable now, but still hot. The bandaging is itchy against my palms, but I won't complain to her about it after she just did me a favour.

"So what's wrong with Gray?"

She gives me a sideways glance as she starts to pack away her medical kit. "He's been locked away in his room since he got home last night, and he hasn't spoken to anyone. I thought it would have something to do with what happened..." She watches me with sharp eyes. It's the same look dad gave me at the hospital.

But I shrug my shoulders. Carefully, I slip my hand under the strap of my bag, sliding it gently up onto my shoulder. "Do you think I could talk to him?" I try, but the second I've asked and I see the look on her face, I know it was a pointless effort coming here.

"I don't think today is a good day, hon."

I nod and try not to show how irritated I am. "Thanks for..." holding up my re-bandaged hands, I nod my head again. She flashes her shiny teeth at me once more.

"Anytime, hon. If you need help with it, you're always more than welcome to stop by."

I head towards the door just as Lemon walks in. Her eyes bulge when they land on me. "Liam? What are you doing here?" She glances upstairs for a moment before coming back to me. I shrug, about to answer when Doc moves to stand behind me.

"I was re-bandaging his hands." Doc places a gentle hand on my shoulder blade. I take the gesture as an indication to leave, so I move towards the door again. But right when I try to slip past, the Sheriff walks in with Noodles, shrugging off his ugly brown police coat. When the Sheriff's gaze lands on me, his eyebrows rocket to his hairline.

And when Noodles sees me, his eyes bulge out of his skull. "Hey Liam!" He races forward, his bag rattling on his back until he's right in front of me. He's gotten so much bigger since the last time I saw him. I don't even remember how old he is now, but I think he's in middle school now. He's already staring at my fresh bandages. When he goes to say something, the Sheriff quickly clears his throat.

"Liam." He looks at Doc over my shoulder for a short moment before his eyes are on me again. My shoulders tense and my fingers curl on reflex, causing me to make a pathetic noise when sharp pain splits through my palms. I hold them against my chest, my eyes wet and my mouth set when I meet his gaze again.

"Hi Sheriff," I mutter, because I don't know when I'm not supposed to call him Sheriff and I don't remember what his name is even though I should. But he doesn't seem bothered, as he reaches out to hang his coat on the stand near the door. "I was just leaving—"

"I planned on stopping by later tonight when you were home, but if you have the time, I have a few questions I need to ask you about last night." His eyes watch me like a cat does a defenceless, weak little mouse.

Doc blows out a loud sigh behind me. "Right now, honey? You just walked in the door, and Liam is on his way home."

Sheriff gives her a look that has her throwing her hands up, a strange smile on her face. The Sheriff raises his eyebrows and tries to smother a smirk of his own, but he winks at her as he takes off his Sheriff's hat. I glance between

39

them.

They're so different from mom and dad.

My skin starts to itch when the Sheriff turns back to face me. "You up to answer a couple questions, Liam? It won't take long."

I peek over my shoulder at Doc and see she's drifted back off into the kitchen, but Lemon and Noodles linger at the bottom of the staircase, both of them watching me. I clench my jaw and turn back to the Sheriff, nodding my head without a word.

Following him into the living room, I take a seat on the sofa when he points to it. My spine is stiff as I sit, my toes tapping on the carpet as I hold my throbbing hands close on my lap. The Sheriff watches me for a moment, but I don't meet his eye.

Strong men always win.

"How are you feeling today, Liam?" He asks, his fingers interlocking as he leans forward over his knees. His police shirt stretches over his arms, his badge shining under the ceiling light and catching my eye.

I nod my head. "I'm fine." I try to think of anything other than the moment when I looked at my reflection. Because I *was* fine until that. As fine as I can be. *Stop being stupid, Liam.*

He watches me closely, his eyes crinkling at the corners. "Can you run me through what happened last night? Whatever information you can give could help me catch this guy."

I've barely even thought of the robbery. It wasn't what ruined my hands. It isn't what keeps echoing in my head every time I close my damn time.

Lia—

I clear my throat loudly and blink *hard* as Gray's broken voice strangles me. That terrified look in his eyes. The blood sprinkled on his white cheeks—

Get out of my head, damn it.

Out of my head.

Get out, get out, get out.

"I walked in with Gray. I don't know what time it was, but it was dark. We were the only ones in the store apart from Headphones." It's harder to get the words out than I thought it would be. My hands are shaking in my lap, so I lean forward to hide them from the Sheriff's sight. I think he sees it anyway.

"Where was she when you both walked in?" he asks, his voice balanced and patient. The Sheriff is still as stone as he watches my every move, his eyebrows furrowed and his eyes squinted.

It's hard to think of where she was because there's only Gray taunting me with the can of Hercules in the reflection. His smile as he riled me up. His narrow eyes sparkling in the most annoying way they do when I snap back. When he grabbed my arm and yanked me down.

"I knocked a can off the shelf." Spaghetti-O's. *Fucking Spaghetti-O's.* "I knocked it, and he knew we were hiding."

He leans forward an inch. "Who were you hiding with, Liam? Was it Finch?"

This isn't a game. We stay here, okay? Stay out of sight.

"He said to stay hidden, but then the jerk jumped out and he wasn't hiding anymore, and it should have been me 'cause *I* knocked that stupid can off the shelf. But he jumped out, and the guy saw him, and he—"

Lia—

My shoulders hunch, and my eyes pinch. My gaze flickers to the Sheriff. I shake my head, telling him I don't want to continue, but he unlinks his fingers and balls his hands into fists.

"Liam, I'm sorry something like this happened to you. And I'm grateful that you three got out of that situation alive." I can see there's more in his expression. He needs more from me. I haven't given him enough. "But I need to ask you what the robber was like." He pauses for a moment, waiting for my reaction. I don't say anything as I stare at him. "As much as you can think of."

Rocking back and looking towards the staircase, I secretly wait for someone to come and interrupt us. Anyone. I listen for footsteps, but it's uncomfortably silent.

I half expect Gray to walk down those stairs at any moment, but I know he won't.

"Short. Wait, no, probably around my height. And a bit chubby." I swallow loudly, the Sheriff attuned to my every word. "He was wearing a ski-mask, so I couldn't see his face." I can tell that the Sheriff isn't satisfied with my description. I squint my eyes. "Weren't there any security cameras in the shop?"

Sheriff blows out a loud breath and leans back. "There were. We're still waiting on the footage from the security company."

I nod, and my jaw sets in a hard line. My hands are shaking up to my elbows now, and my head is throbbing. My palms are throbbing. Everything is throbbing.

Strong men always win.

My father's voice in my head pins my shoulders back and

straightens my spine. The Sheriff leans back further, and his eyebrows raise, but he doesn't say anything when I stand. "Sorry, Sheriff, but I should get home."

Sheriff stands as well, reaching out to grab my shoulder and gives it a tough squeeze. Telling me that he's still the stronger man. He was doing it last night as well, when I was in hospital.

Strong men always win.

"Do you want me to drive you home?" I'm already shaking my head before he finishes his question, and he breathes a loud sigh. "Well, if you think of anything else, don't hesitate to call—"

"Will do," I mutter as I head for the front door. I don't turn back as I fumble with the door handle, or as I try to tug it closed behind me. I keep my head down and I rush towards the footpath, out of reach of them. Of *everyone*.

I head straight for the nearest drug store and give them my prescription, anxious for something to kill the pain. The box is awkward to grab with the padding around my hands, and it slips across the counter a handful of times before I finally wrangle it into my bag. But I'm past being shy about it and don't hesitate to ask the pharmacist to pop the capsules for me. He gives me a grumpy look with narrow eyes but does it anyway.

Another day passes with still no sign of Gray, and now my frustration is at breaking point. The Maverick game is just around the corner, and that jerk has been a complete no-show.

I have every damn right to be angry at this point. *That stupid jerk is avoiding me. He has to be. I don't know what the hell is going on, but I know he was shot that night. I'm certain of it. And for some reason, everyone is hiding it. Why else would he be staying home?* Milo said the Sheriff caught the robber after Headphones picked him out of a line up—even *she's* back now.

So where the hell is Gray?

My jaw clenches as I march up the footpath to his front door. Cutting school early was the only way I would get here before Lemon or Noodles or Doc.

Or the Sheriff.

Banging on the door with my elbow, I grit my teeth as a dull pain throbs across my palms. After a couple minutes of waiting I bang again, but it's still silent inside. Glancing up and down the street, I sneak around the side. Wrangling the side gate open with no hands takes longer than I would have liked.

The wooden gazebo that covers the balcony doesn't fit with the rest of the house, and it looks relatively new, despite the vines weaved between the diamond-shaped holes, but it keeps me concealed from any nosy neighbours. I peep through the glass door like a creep, but I don't see Gray. A hiss slips between my teeth, my eyes catching the second story window to his bedroom. My eyes glare around the back yard in search of something to prop myself up on or throw at the glass, but there isn't a damn thing. Staring through the holes of the wooden gazebo above me, my eyes roll to the back of my head.

Of course I'll have to climb up there.

Swinging my bag up onto the gazebo near the window, I try to flex my fingers. I shouldn't be using them to climb up a damn picketed awning—it's an incredibly unnecessary and irrational idea—but I'm fuelled by my frustration. *I need to know what the hell is going on.*

I try to use my fingers more than my palms but tensing them still hurts. The wood groans louder than the hissing between my teeth, shaking under my movements, but once I reach the top it rocks less. It's awkward as heck to crawl across the flimsy landing on my elbows, but somehow I manage, probably looking like a damn idiot in the process. Glancing down through the gaps in the gazebo, my heart rate hammers hard in my chest.

"Why couldn't the jerk just come to school?" I mutter.

I crawl across the gazebo slowly to lessen the groans of the rocking wood. When I finally make it to the house, I stretch up on my forearms and peek over the windowsill.

The throbbing in my hands is intense now, my skin burning all over.

And Gray's just lying on his bed. His hair is plastered to his forehead, and his skin is covered in a sheen of sweat. On top of the covers in only a pair of basketball shorts, his chest is completely exposed.

There's...nothing.

The bullet wound—all the blood that I have burned into my memory—is non-existent. Not a single inch of his skin is scarred. I look at his arm. Even that scar...the one he got when we were younger...it's *gone*. I strain my eyes, pressing my face against the glass. "What the hell?"

I probably look like a huge pervert right now, peeking in on a half-naked guy, but I'm past the point of caring. And I want to know why he doesn't have a hole in his damn body anymore. I *didn't* imagine that. There is *no way* I could imagine something like that. I can still remember the heat of his blood squishing between my fingers, and my stomach rolls at the memory.

Lia—

Raising my elbow to the window as quickly as I can—while still keeping my balance on this stupid, rickety gazebo—I bang on the window. The sudden noise rouses the jerk from his sleep, his eyes groggy and his mouth hanging open. When his gaze focuses on me, his eyes widen.

"Liam?" His voice is muffled through the windowpane.

"What the hell are you doing? You jerk," I call back. He opens the window for me to crawl inide, and I reach back out to grab my bag, hissing when the burns on my hands pull sharp. Gray's eyes drop to my bandaged hands. His gaze is trained on them, his stare unwavering. I slip them into the pockets of my hoodie, out of sight, but his eyes remain on my pockets.

"Should you have climbed up here?" he asks, palming his face. His hair is always such a mess.

I breathe out a frustrated sigh. "Shouldn't you be asking why I was up there in the first place?"

"You were checking up on me." His voice is hollow, but his words have my teeth biting down on the inside of my cheek.

My eyes narrow, because of course the jerk would like to think that's why I'm here. "I wasn't *checking up* on you. I'm just trying to find out what the hell is going on." I take a step closer, and he takes one back, his lips pinched tight. "You were shot. I *saw* it."

His cheekbones tense and his eyes wander off lazily. "I wasn't shot, Liam."

This time when I step forward, he holds his ground. Standing less than a foot away, I take him in. He doesn't look like he's been shot. Physically, there is no evidence on his body that shows he ever could have been.

"Then how do you explain these?" I pull my hands out of my pockets again, holding them up to his face, because they're the only tangible form of evidence I have. His brows knit together, and his nostrils flare in response. "I didn't imagine it. I *know* I didn't."

He clears his throat. "Look at me, Liam. I'm fine." He indicates to his stomach, where there should be an ugly line of stitches keeping his skin together. But it's all smooth.

"Why did you point to your stomach?" My eyebrow shoots up to my hairline, and my eyes narrow to slits. Gray shrugs.

47

"I didn't. I was gesturing to all—"

"I know what I saw, Gray," I mutter, looping my arm through my bag strap and hitching it up onto my shoulder. "I don't know what the hell happened after, but I don't believe for a second that I imagined that. I couldn't—" my lips press together tight, and I look away. That much blood was *sickening*. Nobody sane could imagine something like that.

Lia—

He goes to raise his arm, but I turn away. "I'm leaving. And I ain't going back down that damn gazebo. If you're fine, then hurry up and go to practice."

He doesn't say anything as I leave, and he doesn't try to stop me.

"Julia wanted me to ask how your hands are doing." Sawyer stands at my bedroom door with her phone in one hand and the other propped on her hip. I only glance at her for a moment before my eyes drift back to the ball spinning on my finger. The pressure pulls my skin horribly, but I just need to touch it. This is the longest I haven't been able to practice.

"Tell her they're fine." is all I say. I think she's talking about Lemon.

Her name's Julia, right?

"Should you really be doing that?" Her top lip twitches, and her eyes darken. Her sickly perfume wafts into my room, and I gag on the overpowering mist.

"Geez, did you drop the entire bottle or something?" I pull the collar of my shirt over my nose. She frowns over at me.

"Fuck you. It's Chanel."

"Did she drop the bottle?"

She throws her hands up, rolling her eyes. "Ugh, why do I even bother with you?"

The words sink in like a familiar knife.

Why do I even bother with you?

Try harder.

What the hell, Liam? Mom couldn't take Julia home because of you.

Because of you.

Try harder.

What did you do, baby?

Whatever it is, it's his problem to deal with.

"Liam!"

My head snaps up and my family's voices fade away. I look back up at Sawyer, her eyes following my basketball as it rolls across the ground. "What?" My voice wavers, but my tough gaze doesn't let her question it. Sawyer rolls her eyes, lowering her phone to her side. Her hair hangs low, the ends touching her ribs. I finally notice what she's wearing. "You're a cheerleader, now?"

He flips her hair, the long wavy strands floating over her shoulder. "Obviously."

Turning to reach for my ball again, my eyes droop slightly. These pain meds have been perfect for knocking me into a dreamless sleep.

Sawyer's gaze is making my chest tight, and I don't like it. She's got our father's eyes. The same eyes.

"Fin's coming back to school tomorrow."

I don't turn to her as she speaks this time. *He damn well better be at school tomorrow. That jerk.*

49

"Julia told me he's been really sick, but he's better now." She starts to twirl her hair around her finger and fiddle with the tiny cheer uniform skirt.

I don't comment. I don't want her to say anything else to me. I just want her to leave and go back to her own room.

Just leave me alone.

When I don't bite, she scoffs and storms out, slamming my door behind her. When I hear my father's voice just beyond it, my chest burns loud and hot.

"Congratulations on making the squad, sweetheart," his voice is muffled through the door, but I hear every word. "I'm so proud of you. Are you going to be cheering at every basketball game from now on?"

"Yeah! The captain really liked me, so she wants me on the floor for the game next week." Sawyer's voice passes through the door with the sole intention for me to hear. My chest tightens, a vice wrapping itself around my throat.

I'm so proud of you.

My hand scratches at the place in my chest that aches. *So that's what those words sound like...*

"You tell me the time and day, and I'll be there."

I'll be there.

Stepping away from my desk, my basketball forgotten, my heart aches as I lay down on my bed. I stare at the wall beside the door, waiting for the emptiness to pass, but the hollow space in my chest doesn't fill.

CHAPTER 05

My teeth grind as so many people flock around Gray like he's some damn idol.

He's a lying jerk, is what he is.

"I can't believe you stood in front of a guy with a gun! That's so badass, man!" One of the only guys I've ever seen that's taller than Gray—I think he's on the lacrosse team— claps him on the back, his nose flat like a blobfish. I lean against my locker as I watch them, my bandaged hands locked in the heat of my hoodie pocket. My fingers twitch, my blood throbbing through the centre of my palms.

Milo appears beside me, clapping my shoulder without a word. I don't look at him when I say, "He's not a damn hero, he's *stupid*. He didn't know if the gun was loaded, he didn't know how crazy that guy was. That guy could have turned him into a damn *colander*." Milo raises an eyebrow, but he doesn't say anything. For the first time, his silence bothers me. "What? You think he's a hero too? You one of his *groupies* as well?"

"I never said that," he mutters, his lips pinching. Milo's hair is loose and curly today, instead of the tightly groomed hairdo he usually wears.

I blow out a long breath, watching with narrow eyes as Gray and his new fan club wander past. I know he sees me there, but he doesn't look in my direction. For the first time, I'm making him uncomfortable. Because he knows that I know he's lying.

Strong men always win.

I have to bite the inside of my cheek from calling out to him as he keeps walking. *I won't let you win. No way in hell. You're not as smart as you think you are, you jerk.*

"How long do you think his newfound fame will last?" Milo hitches his bag strap higher on his shoulder, his eyes wondering over every girl that passes us on their way to class. He winks at one of them.

"Who the heck knows? With him, I'm sure he'll milk it as long as he can." I shoulder away from my locker and head towards physics.

He's gonna slip up again. Whatever the heck is going on with him, it's new. And he won't be able to control it. And I'll be there when he messes up.

Sitting on the stands sucks—*a lot*—but I'm not letting Gray out of my sight. The bastard's been obvious in his attempts to shake me, but I won't let him.

Coach said I could sit and watch as they run drills. Gray's making a point of not looking my way, and I know it isn't a coincidence. He won't stop riling me up on a normal day, yet the jerk hasn't said anything or even looked in my general direction this entire time. *He's hiding something. And he knows I'm going to figure out whatever it is. It's only a matter of time.*

Because no matter how resilient *he* is, I won't let this go. Not until I get an explanation. Not until I know what the hell happened to my hands. He's the reason I'm not playing ball right now.

Stop crying.

It wasn't my fault. I was trying to help.

Try harder.

No, I was helping...

Whatever it is, it's his problem to deal with.

My problem to deal with. Always my problem to deal with.

Lia—

My throat swells. *Stop. Something else. Think of something else, damn it.*

I rub at my eye with my shoulder. *Something else. Think something else. Should I let my hair grow out? It's not like I'm playing ball for the next few weeks. I can just shave it again when I come back.* My blurry eyes start to refocus, the sound of squeaking shoes and thudding basketballs filtering back in. The air starts to pass through me easier.

When I look around, I spot Milo watching me, his brows and mouth drawn in a line. He gives me a thumbs-up with a questioning look on his face. He always seems to know when something's up, but he never pries. I don't mind when he's around. I nod back, and he regroups with the team when they form a semi-circle around Coach.

"Game time. Shirts versus skins." His voice booms through the now quiet gymnasium, his eyes glancing between his clipboard and the team. He starts to point out everyone on the shirts side, then goes through everyone's positions. Milo, Gray and the rest of the skins team strip off their sweaty shirts, tossing them to the side of the court. My eyes narrow in on Gray's torso where he was shot. He looks at me, as if sensing my accusing stare. His lips pull in a tight line for a moment before he winks at me, a cheeky grin spreading across his face.

Freakin' jerk. I'm not a damn girl or something.

The guys line up on either side of the court, some of them bracing their hands on their knees. Gray's eyes are locked on the ball in Coach's hand, but they occasionally stray to where I'm sitting. He looks away as soon as he sees I'm still watching him. His chest is shiny, his hair is plastered to his head and his nostrils flaring. I purse my lips. He's not usually worn out this early into practice. But he looks like he is about to pass out. His angular eyes are crossing slightly, lids shuttering.

Coach blows the whistle and throws the ball up. Gray's focus snaps back as the ball comes down, and his eyebrows draw in. The ball passes around the court quickly, but Gray keeps himself on the outside. Milo has to handle the ball more, as Gray keeps himself guarded. He's not playing normally, and Coach notices it as well.

"Why the heck are you hidin', Gray? Get in there and get the damn ball!" he bellows, his face turning red. His bushy eyebrows are burrowed down and his wrinkled mouth is set in a grumpy sneer. Gray nods, pounding his temples with his palms.

What is he doing?

Maybe he's still sick. But he's had an entire week off—even though he *apparently* wasn't shot. So there should be no reason—

When Spanner spots Gray making an opening, he

passes. Gray holds his hands up to catch it, but the ball rockets into his face. But it didn't slip between his hands, it went straight *through* them. If I hadn't been watching him so closely, I can guarantee I would have missed it.

Gray hits the ground hard, his hands cupped around his nose. And I don't know how I missed it, but the jerk stripped off the rest of his clothes. My shoes squeak against the waxed floors as I sprint towards where he's lying *naked* on the ground. The team gathers around him, so I barge through with my elbows, but they all stand back to let Coach in.

"Shit, you alright man? Why the fuck did you take your pants off?" Hair bends down, clicking his fingers over Gray's face when his eyes cross.

There's blood spilling out of his nose around his fingers, and my heart seizes in my chest for a moment. It might be in my head, but I'm certain I can feel the heat of it from here.

"Everybody get back!" My sudden demand has them all taking a step back, and I try to pull Gray up using my wrists, but it's awkward and he's too disorientated to help me.

"Shit, Liam! What the hell happened to your hands?" Speedy asks, pointing at the bandaged hands I didn't realise I had taken out of my pockets. My chest tightens and my throat swells up.

Whatever it is, it's his problem to deal with.

"Don't ask."

No one is allowed to know what happened to me until I know what happened to Gray. And right now, the weirdo is naked with a nosebleed. I fumble to grab his shorts from underneath him, his head still lolling from side to side. He's hissing between his teeth and my palms are screaming in pain.

55

"Is that why you aren't playing?"

"Are they broken or something?"

"Did that happen that night at—"

"I said don't ask!" I turn on the nosy bastards with a foul glare, and it shuts them all up. I notice thin puffs of steam rising from Gray's face and I shove him hard until he sits up. He sways like a bobble-head, and his pupils pulsate.

"Rice, take him to the nurses office." Coach mutters, pulling his cap off and running his hand over his bald head. "And get his damn pants back on."

"I'm fine, Coach. Just need to go clean this up," Gray mumbles, indicating to the blood on his face. It's definitely steaming. His narrow eyes pinch at the sides, so I shove him again. I drop his pants onto his lap to cover him, and he quickly slides them up his legs single-handedly.

"Sure thing, Coach." I mutter. This guy isn't going anywhere without me. My reply has everyone turning to me with a strange look. It isn't often—or ever—that I offer to help Gray. Hair steps forward and helps me lift Gray to his feet, and I watch every drop of blood to make sure it doesn't touch us. I wince when the wet flesh of my hands tugs tight, ripping beneath the bandages. Biting the inside of my cheek, I start to lead Gray out of the room.

"It's okay, I got him." Hair nods his head and leaves Gray's weight on my shoulder.

Trudging down the corridor, Gray stumbles barefoot beside me. *Why did this jerk take his shoes off as well?* He blinks hard, his hands fumbling to catch all the blood dripping from his nose. There's still steam—or maybe it's smoke—floating around Gray's face, where the blood is touching his skin. The sizzling sound echoes in my head, the stench of melting skin searing my brain.

He's annoyingly silent as we approach the nurses office. Now even closer to his face than before, I can see his blood bubbling. The skin under his nose is charred, and his hands are black, everywhere the blood has touched.

My palms itch, irritated and hot. "Since when can't you catch a ball?"

He grunts, and his hair falls against his eyebrow. "My hands were sweaty."

I nod. "I saw it pass through your hands, Gray. You have a Ghost-Mode now or something?"

Gray leans towards the men's room as we pass by, slipping out of my hold. He shoves the door open with his shoulder and dives in, so I follow hot on his heels. The usual smell of piss lingers in the air, despite the bathroom being empty. He's skin is red and sweaty as he washes his hands in the sink, but a sharp crack echoes through the tiled room when his blood touches it.

"Shit!" he mutters, his hands frantic to fix whatever is broken. But blood drips from his nose into the sink, and another crack follows. This time, the front half of the sink starts to leak water down the huge chip in the porcelain.

My jaw drops. When I look back to Gray, I can see his face in the reflection; his narrow eyes are wide and his jaw clenched tight. He turns off the faucet and wipes his nose with his palm again. Most of the blood on his face is gone. But when he absentmindedly wipes his hands on the hem of his shorts, the fabric starts to *disintegrate*.

"*Shit!*" He runs his hands under the tap again—I'm assuming so that he doesn't accidentally wipe it on anything else—but the porcelain is at its limit. The front half of the bowl drops away, shattering on the ground into dozens of huge chunks at his feet. His now clean hands pull through his inky hair, his eyes bulging and a vein popping at his temple.

I stare back at him, my mind at a complete loss for words.

What...what the hell just happened?

Gray turns to me, his nostrils flaring. His burnt top lip pulls up at the corner when he faces me again. "Liam...*don't*." His sharp tone cuts through my daze. I shake my head, drawing my bottom lip between my teeth.

"You can't hide whatever the hell is wrong with you. Just admit that you're lying."

I watch his face, the black beneath his nose slowly changing back to his normal skin colour. His top lip returns to its normal shape, and his hands stop smoking. I raise an eyebrow. I don't even know *what* to ask him right now.

"Liam, this is serious. Pretend you didn't see anything just now." He wipes his forehead with the back of his hand, his eyes unfocused.

I scoff. "See *what*? I don't know what the hell I just saw."

"Good," he mutters. "Keep it that way. Don't ask—"

"I have a right to know, Gray." My bandaged hands shake at my sides. This...this *jerk*. "My hands are all messed up because of..."

Whatever it is, it's his problem to deal with.

I take a loud breath in through my nose. "Look, whatever is going on with you has affected my season," I hold up my bandaged hands as evidence. "So I'm asking you to stop lying to me about what happened. Nothing you say will make me believe differently, so just tell me the truth."

He rakes his hands through his hair, tugging the ends hard, his face bright red. "Fuck off, Liam! I'm trying to figure this all out, okay?" His eyes drift to my bandaged hands for a short moment before snapping back to my face. His mouth forms a hard line, and his hands tighten into fists at his side.

"Is that your version of a confession?"

His thin eyes are darker now, but somehow still brown. "Just leave me *alone*, Liam." He tries to push past me, but I hold my arm up, pressing my elbow against the bare skin of his chest. Only my hoodie sleeve touches his sweaty skin.

"Not how this works, Gray. You don't get to have everything your way every time," My lips pull back from my teeth. "This might be hard to hear, but the world doesn't revolve around what *you* want." I wouldn't be surprised if Gray could hear my teeth grinding. His eyes narrow to slits as he shoves my arm away and storms out, his shoulder blades taut and his back stiff.

CHAPTER

06

It's been two freakin' days, and *nothing*. I nearly punch something when Milo confesses that Gray's back to skipping practice again.

That jerk gets off scot-free whilst my hands are butchered and burnt, and he doesn't even *show up* to practice? I'll freakin' kill him. *If he doesn't play in the Maverick game, I can kiss the Championships goodbye.*

The cold continues to bite at me through my hoodie. Strolling past the corner store down the road from the half-court, my skin starts to burn. When my eyes lock on the building, the same suffocating tightness seeps into my lungs.

No matter how many times I've tried this, it's not getting any easier.

I turn my back to the shop, but the suffocating weight hovers in my chest. *Not like it ever truly leaves.* But now it only grows heavier whenever I'm near the court, and my skin becoming itchy.

I only have a handful of safe places, and now one of them is ruined.

I spot someone walking down the road, and immediately

recognize Gray. My eyes lock on him. He's dressed in all black, with his hood pulled over his head. *Is he trying to be discrete? Because if anything, he looks more suspicious. Doesn't he know how to be sneaky?*

Gray looks distracted as he walks; he doesn't even notice me standing across the road. When he turns a corner that doesn't lead to his house, I follow him in the same direction, careful not to let him see me. *Where the heck is he going?*

I manage to jump a couple short fences and duck through some back-yards, keeping Gray in my sights. When he starts to wander out of town, I frown, sticking to the tree line as I follow him. But he barely passes the 'Welcome to Franklin' sign before he turns down the dirt road directly in front of it. It's not like he would be going for a swim at this time of year. I watch my feet closer than I watch Gray. If I snap a twig or fall in a ditch, it's game over. I won't give him the opportunity to try and avoid me again.

When the trees start to thin out, I linger further back. Gray stops at the edge of the lake, the grass brushing his ankles. The setting sun hits the still water, casting a blinding light over the shimmering surface. It's been so long since I've been here.

Gray bends down to reach for something, but he starts throwing his fist against the ground. What the hell is he doing? I step forward, ready to confront him. He can't escape me out here—

"Useless! Figure it out! Just figure it *out!*" he shouts, his hair flopping around his ears.

Useless.

Figure it out.

Try harder.

A buzz fills my ears. *Why can't my eyes focus?*

Try harder.

Look what you did.

Whatever it is, it's his problem to deal with.

I shake my head again. *I'm not leaving this. I was there that night as well.* Gray's knuckles crack loud enough for me to hear. He shouts a few curses at the ground, clutching his fist to his chest. Something definitely broke just now.

"Hey, don't go injuring yourself before the Maverick game! You can't play if your hand's busted, you jerk!"

Gray turns to me so fast, I'm surprised his neck doesn't crack as well. When he rises to his feet, his small eyes bulge. The dark rings under his eyes are unfamiliar on his face. "*Liam?* What the hell are you—?"

I definitely didn't expect Gray's clothes to suddenly slide off his body. I'm not sure he did either. They just...*fell* off him. *How does that happen?*

He quickly drops his broken hand to his dick and covers it from my view. I look up at the sky, my cheeks burning hot. This is definitely not the first time I've been face-to-face with Gray's junk, but it's the first time I've seen it outside the locker room.

"What...just happened?" *Maybe I'm dreaming.*

"Nothing! I don't know! Can you just leave?" His tone is hysterical, but when I glance back at his face—*extremely* careful to not look anywhere else—his jaw is clenched, and his skin is bright red. He reaches down to gather his pants, slipping them back on.

"Your clothes just—"

"*Fuck off*, Liam! Just leave me alone."

I lean back, my brows touching my hairline. *That's very*

unlike him.

His fingers fumble to do up the button of his jeans. His hands are shaking like crazy. His entire body is.

"Gray—"

"I told you to leave me alone, Liam!" He comes back with fire in his eyes, his nostrils flaring. "I told you to stay away from me. Why the heck did you follow me here?"

My head falls to the side, my brows drawing together. "*You* don't leave *me* alone. What makes you think I would listen to you?"

"Because this is different, Liam!" He throws his hands in the air and stares back with burning eyes. His hand doesn't seem broken. When I start to advance, he takes a step back. "What're you—"

"Your hand." I grab his wrist and yank it forward—hard to do with just my fingertips—so my eyes can inspect every inch of it. He tries to pull it back, but my nails dig in. My blood pulses beneath my raw skin, sending violent shivers up my arms. He could pull harder, but he probably suspects it would hurt my hands more if he did so he doesn't.

The pale pinkness of his knuckle tells me all I need to know, but I press down on it with my thumb. When he doesn't respond in any other way than trying to pull it out of my grasp, I know I have my answer.

"So what are you, the freakin' Wolverine now?"

His lip curls as he squints at me. "What?"

"I heard you break something in your hand. And now it's healed."

When he pulls again, I let go. He rubs his thumb over the pink knuckle. I point at the remaining pile of clothes, an existing form of evidence. "You can't lie that away. I saw it with my own damn eyes, Gray."

He doesn't say anything yet. I can see the wheels turning in overdrive. He's trying to think up a lie I'd believe, but nothing can make me unsee his clothes falling to the ground without him even *touching* them.

"There's nothing—"

Ugh, that's it.

I throw my entire body weight at him, shoving him off his feet. He hits the ground, his nose scrunching up. He sends me a foul look, one I've never had the pleasure of receiving until now.

"What the hell, Liam? What's your—"

"Problem?" I shout, my eyes burning when I refuse to blink. "What's my problem, Gray? I've been telling you what my problem is this entire time! Tell me the truth already!"

"No!"

I jump on him. When I try to land a hit to his stupid lying face, my club-like hands are blocked. When he grabs my other wrist, I dig to knee into his side, but the awkward movement throws me off balance. Using my falling momentum, Gray rolls us over and pins my arms down. My chest tightens and my nose starts to itch, but I give him the meanest glare I can manage.

"Why the hell not? Why the hell *not*, Gray?" I shout back.

The same kid who carried you here on his back.

Try harder.

Strong men always win.

Always, always, always.

"You don't understand what I'm going through!" he pants, his pale skin flushing.

"You don't even have that scar on your arm anymore!" My eyes narrow as I watch his reaction. He blinks hard, his lips pinching together. "Don't think I didn't notice, Gray. It was the first thing I saw."

Liam, hurry up. Pedal faster!

Everyone's stupid voices won't get out of my stupid head. *He was the one who didn't see the rock, that day. He was the one who fell off his bike.*

What did you do, baby?

What's wrong with him?

Whatever it is, it's his problem to deal with.

My head starts to ache and my chest tightens in a different way. It's familiar, just different from before. *He's too close. I need space.* I shove hysterically with my elbows, but he pushes down until his entire weight pressed down on me.

Get out of my space. Out of my space.

Get out, get out, get out.

Try harder.

Why do I even bother with you?

His problem to deal with.

When Gray realises I'm struggling to breathe, he falls back. My chest heaves as I watch him through narrow eyes. "What's wrong? Are you alright, Liam?" He inches closer, but I throw my shoulder forward between us and turn away. *Don't look at me, damn it.*

Try harder.

"Not gonna work," I mutter, turning back to glare at him when I have a steadier control of my breathing. "I'm not an idiot, Gray. I can see *something* is up with you, so why won't you admit it?"

It's hard for my eyes to focus; my vision is distorted, and my chest continues to tighten. Gray stares back silently, but he doesn't say anything for the longest time. He's looking for something. Or maybe he's waiting for me. I scratch behind my ear as I sit silently. I have plenty more to say, but not until he fesses up. *I'm not leaving here until I have his confession.*

He rises to his feet, brushing the dust from the back of his jeans. He isn't looking at me anymore. I can tell he's still trying to figure out a plausible lie.

"I wonder what would happen if this kind of information reached the *wrong* people..." It's a risk. A gamble. But I'm sick of him avoiding me like I'm not a threat.

Maybe I'm not. But that doesn't mean I won't go to whatever lengths I need to.

He's looking at me now. It's another look that I've never seen before. I'm not sure that this is the same guy that I've known my whole life. Nothing about him is what it used to be. "*Don't*, Liam. *Don't* threaten me."

I shrug and glance out over the lake. The sun turns the water gold as it starts to set on the horizon. "What is there to threaten, huh? If I'm making all of this up, then what difference does it make?" His jaw clenches and I wonder if he's about to lose his temper with me. Does he do that? Lose his temper? Get *mad*? Using my elbows to help me stand, I stare up at the freakin' stupid giant. "Well?"

He throws his hands up, huffing at me. "Why do you need to know so badly? Why won't you just leave it?"

"Because if you don't play in the Maverick game, then I can't play in the Championships. And I'm *going* to play in the Championships." *I don't care what I have to do, but if it gets him to practice, I don't care. I'm not missing out. If I can win the Championships, eyes will be on me. Scouts will take notice, and I'll be one step closer.*

I need to win.

Gray shakes his head, apparently unsurprised by my answer, sweeping up his shirt from the grass. My eyes are on his hand, waiting for the fabric to pass straight through his palm, but his fingers curl around it before he pulls it over his head. "So what if there is something?" He raises an eyebrow, his lips pinched. "What does telling you solve?"

It's my turn to give him a weird look. "Why does it have to *solve* something?"

He steps closer, his small eyes narrowed. "How do I know I can even trust you with this?"

"Gray, you're not pregnant. Don't act like it's such a big deal."

His eyes bulge from his head, and his mouth drops open. "It *is* a big deal!" he shouts loud enough to bust my eardrum. His face turns pink. "I keep moving through things like a freakin' *ghost*, Liam! It's a *big fucking deal*." My arms cross over my chest, and I stare at him pointedly. His eyes squint at me again, his nostrils flaring like a bull. "What the hell is that look for?"

"You finally admitted it."

The cold wind blows through me, but I'm not willing to leave yet. Even though he finally confessed, I don't know enough. I don't know *everything*. I wave my bandaged hands between us. "Explain."

Gray clenches his teeth, baring them at me. He runs his hand—the one that I was sure he broke earlier—through the front of his hair, pulling hard. He looks out on the lake as the wind blows a mist of icy water at us. We've been standing here so long, the sky is bleeding from gold to vibrant pink.

"Fuck it," he mutters, his eyes settling on me again. He steps up until we are nearly toe to toe, his eyes sweeping the tree line behind us. I roll my eyes but leave it. Bloody paranoid jerk. "I can't control it, but my body keeps...*ghosting*—" he bites out with a sour face, "and my clothes...fall off..."

I can only hope that my expression translates just how unsurprised I am by his words. "No shit, Sherlock." I pinch the fabric of his shirt between my fingertips and tug it away from his skin. "I want to know about *this*," I poke my finger into the exact spot I know he was shot. Pain flares through my palm, but I don't show how much it hurts.

Like the over dramatic jerk that he is, Gray takes in a deep, *loud* breath, his hand drifting to the same spot I just pointed to. I bite the inside of my cheek so I don't roll my eyes at him again. "I heal quicker now...a *lot* quicker."

"So you *were* shot? I just want to reiterate that I was right." I don't really understand it, but I don't doubt him. He doesn't have any sign of the eight-year-old scar on his arm—or any scars for that matter—and yet I know he was shot almost a week ago.

Gray stares back for the longest time, before he finally blows out a loud breath. "Yes, Liam. I was shot. Are you happy now?"

I shrug my shoulders. "Happy that I was right? Of course I am. But just to confirm, you haven't *always* healed quicker?"

He shakes his head, furrowing his brows and biting the inside of his cheek.

Frowning, I glance over to where he had been punching the ground—like the moron he is—but there are only a couple rocks. Some have black steaming spots, but there is a distinct mark where his fist hit the dirt. "What were you doing before?" I nod towards the rocks, my eyebrow raised. Gray blushes a pale shade of red, his eyes squinting as his lips part for a moment.

"I was trying to pick one up. I've been coming out here, trying to figure out how to...control it. Away from where anyone would see me."

I pluck one of the pebbles from the ground and weigh it on my fingertips. As if knowing what I'm about to ask, he holds his hand out for me, and I drop the pebble into his palm. I watch with focused eyes as it bounces once in his palm, his skin damp and dusty.

"Interesting. So you don't know how to turn it on or off?" I mutter, my eyes focused on his hand. Gray shakes his head without a word. "Who else knows?"

He looks away again. "Just you. But I'm worried my family will realise something's up. It's becoming increasingly difficult to cover it up."

I raise an eyebrow. "What about your uncle?"

He nods, his face strained. "He's asking a lot of questions. He saw the security footage yesterday."

"What did he see?"

Gray shrugs his shoulders. "I don't know. He's had a weird look on his face ever since he saw it. I don't know how much he *could* see. I was down an aisle, so only the gunman would have been in view." As if suddenly realising something, his eyes bulge. "What have you told him, Liam?"

My eyebrows furrow as I try to recall the conversations I've had with the Sheriff. I haven't seen him since he questioned me the other day I was at his house. "I told him you were shot—"

"*Liam!*" he shouts.

"Hey! I had no idea what was going on! I was freaked out and trying to piece together what had happened. He might not have even believed me."

Gray runs a hand through his hair and blows out a loud, dramatic breath. "He knows. Or he will figure it out. My uncle *hates* when he can't explain something." He glances around the lake, his forehead creasing. "He's going to figure it out. I won't be able to hide it much longer. He's going to catch me."

I hold my up hands to stop him. "Hold on a second, just calm down. No one else has any idea, and it's a pretty far-fetched conclusion to come to. We just need you to get this stuff under control, and he won't suspect a thing..." I trail off, because the look on his face says there's something he hasn't told me yet. "What?"

Gray scratches the back of his head, his face pinching. "The ghosting stuff has been the hardest to control when I'm sleeping. So I keep...falling through the floor and landing on the kitchen island...naked..."

That was not the response I expected. I almost laugh at how outrageous the idea of that is. "You...fall through the floor? *Naked?*"

I must sound sarcastic, because Gray's jaw tenses. "I'm not joking, Liam. I haven't been getting any sleep because of it. My uncle keeps trying to talk to me about what's been happening, but I keep dodging him."

"I don't even know what to make of that." Falling through the floor? Hell, I just wanted him to admit that he was shot, not that he's got some freaky superpowers. "Also, avoiding your uncle would only make you look more suspicious. You need to think of a plausible lie to tell him."

His eyes narrow on me. "Why the hell are you taking this so well? I'm telling you that I have these weird powers now, while you're just nodding your head and giving me advice like everything is *normal*."

I shrug again, my eyes averting when he continues to hold my stare. "Because shit like this doesn't happen, but *of course* it's something that would happen to you."

Strong men always win.

Gray is silent after that. I finally calm down enough to

71

ask. "Have you tried sleeping downstairs?"

He rolls his eyes. "Of course I have." I raise my eyebrows when he doesn't continue. He looks away, biting the inside of his cheek. "But I would wake up under the couch."

I rub my eye with my shoulder. *What the hell is this conversation?*

"Alright," I say when I take my hand away, holding out the rock again. Gray watches me with tired eyes, but he holds his hand out anyway. "Why don't you fall through the ground?"

"I just told you, I—"

"No, *the ground*. The second story of a house is not what I'm talking about. I'm talking about what we are standing on right now." *Why doesn't this jerk use that annoyingly smart brain of his when he needs to?*

"I don't know..." I watch his face change, like he hadn't considered the fact that he hasn't fallen through to the Earth's core yet.

"It could be a natural blocker of some kind or something," I mutter as I test dropping the rock into his palm again. It makes a soft pat on impact. He clenches his fingers around the rock for a moment, before he lets it slide off his fingers.

"It comes and goes. I don't know how to control it," he murmurs, his eyes lingering on the rock.

I nod. "This is weird."

He scoffs, nodding his head as well. "Yep."

"But you can't keep missing practice, jerk."

"And I can't risk copping another nosebleed like last time." His nose scrunches at the thought.

"Yeah, what's with your blood?" My hands twitch when

72

I mention it.

Gray looks away, his lips pinched in a tight line. "It's like acid now. Whatever it touches..." he doesn't finish his sentence. He doesn't have to. I know first-hand what happens to whatever it touches.

I blow out a short breath and glance in the opposite direction. "Yeah, we're gonna need to figure that out as well. Cause there is no way you are getting out of playing the Maverick game."

Gray shakes his head, his eyes drifting down to my hands. "How are your hands feeling? You don't seem to have any problems whacking me with them."

Whatever it is, it's his problem to deal with.

"They're fine." They're not though; I can see the red peeking through the white. They burn as hot as they did that night at the corner store, and I can feel sweat gathering along my hairline. When I look back out over the lake, it's morphed into an unwelcoming black. It's a lot darker now, but the few slashes of pink still streak the sky. I turn back towards the dirt path, assuming that Gray will follow. He quickly falls into step beside me.

"You're not going to tell anyone, right?"

I make sure he sees my eyes roll to the back of my head. "I'm not an idiot, Gray. I know how dangerous this is. I won't say anything." We're both quiet as we walk home. The awkward silence hangs between us, until I've finally had enough. "Do you think it was a magic bullet or something?"

He's silent for a moment longer, before he finally answers. "You sound ridiculous."

My shoulders drop. "Of course you would get shot with a magic bullet." I wonder if I could talk to the robber. I assume he'd still be in a holding cell at the police station. *Would he have more bullets like those?*

When Gray stops walking, I stop and turn to see what he's doing, but he's just staring at me like a bloody weirdo. "What?"

He clears his throat. "Whatever you're thinking, stop it."

I lean back. "I don't know what you're talking about—"

Suddenly he's crowding me—does he have super speed too?—his eyes narrowed to slits. "Don't lie to me, Liam. You're stupid enough to do it."

I push back, not giving him an inch. "'Stupid enough to do what, huh?"

"Go looking for that robber." I shrug, but he shoves my shoulder. "I'm serious, Liam. Don't even think about it."

Strong men always win.

"What, so you get to be the only superhero?" I bite out.

His lips pinch. "I'm not a superhero, Liam. Whatever's wrong with me has ruined *everything*."

"Yeah, yeah, drama queen." Waving him off, I turn and continue back home. He follows, his shoes scuffing the rubble and kicking up dust.

We reach my place first. This is the most time I've spent with Gray in years, and it's been weird as hell. He's like an entirely different person right now. But I guess everything is different now. I point my finger at him—he can only see the tip of it, though—and level him with a hard glare. "Try not to fall through the floor tonight." I raise an eyebrow, a smirk threatening to crack my stoic glare.

He purses his lips and shakes his head. "Jerk."

"Actually..." I pause, before turning back to face him. "I have an idea. I'll be over tomorrow, after school."

He doesn't look pleased. My eyes drift over to my father's car, and my stomach seizes. I can feel Gray's eyes on me as I head up the steps, so I force myself to grip the handle without hesitation.

The locks haven't changed...the locks haven't changed.
Marnie, what happened to changing the locks?
The knob turns, and air rushes back in.

CHAPTER

08

"Liam...why?"

"I told you I had an idea. Noodles helped set it up." *Yeah, there was no way I was getting this up when my gauzed hands are bigger than the size of the mallet head, so it was a good thing Gray's younger cousin was hanging around.* "I told him that you lost a bet and now you have to sleep outside for two weeks. I don't think he believed that you lost a bet though."

Gray shakes his head, apparently more concerned with the tent. "So tell me, *why* have you set a tent up in my backyard?" He jumps over the shallow steps from the patio, his face pinched.

"Because you don't fall through the ground." I thought that was the obvious answer. Maybe only obvious to people who don't have stupid superpowers.

His brows don't raise from his set frown. "So, you expect me to sleep outside?"

My laughter bubbles up, sounding as sarcastic has I hoped it would. "I don't expect you to do anything. If you don't want to, that's your prerogative." But if this jerk doesn't get his shit handled, he's not gonna be able to play Maverick.

And without him—as much as it bothers me to admit—our chances of making it to the Championships are slim.

Whatever it is, it's his problem to deal with.

"I'm just trying to *help*. You would only need to sleep out here until you have better control of whatever the hell it is that's wrong with you. I need you to get a handle on this." After a long moment he nods, ruffling his hair as he glares at the tent. The dark rings under his eyes are prominent today, so I assume he didn't sleep well last night either. I peel back the nylon flap to reveal the gloriously tiny living space. "Home sweet home."

Groaning, he peers into the small room. "I'm not gonna be able to fit my mattress in this thing!"

For a brief moment, I'm stumped. "You've camped out before, right?"

"Of course I have." I watch his nose twitch slightly.

I nod my head, but mutter, "Liar."

Turning away, Gray heads back towards the house. "Whatever. I'll get my stuff."

"No mattress."

He grunts in reply. Following him inside, my eyes sweep the kitchen. "Where'd the rest of your family go?" His cousin was just here helping me set up the tent.

Gray shakes his head. "Jules is at your place, Dawson's gone down to the game store with Aunt A, and my Uncle is still at work."

I hum in response, my eyes following the wall full of family pictures. My eyes are drawn to them like a magnet, glancing over each of them slowly. *It's weird to be here again after staying away for so long.* The same picture of Gray with his late parent's hides at the back. Present, just out of sight.

His parent's death has always been an uncomfortable topic. Something I was never brave enough to ask about.

It seems that some things haven't changed.

"Just wait here, I'll go get my things," Gray points at me, pulling my attention away from the photographs.

I scoff. "I've seen your room, Gray."

His eyes roll back, a weird smile tugging at the corners of his lips. His cheeks bloom a pale pink as he rolls his lips between his teeth. "Do you *want* to come to my room?"

"Don't be weird." I scrunch my face at him. "Be grateful I'm putting up with your ass right now."

He wriggles his eyebrows at me. "Thinking about my ass?"

"God, you're such a jerk." But that's something he would have said before everything happened. Before he got shot. *Maybe things aren't so different with him.*

The damn jerk.

He laughs, his hand on the banister as he swings around to climb the stairs. "Admit it, I've got a pretty good—" He suddenly falls forward, completely phasing through the stairs and disappearing—well, *Gray* disappears. His clothes are left in a pile on the steps. Even his shoes. There's a thump from beneath the stairs when he disappears.

I glance around to be sure, but I don't see him anywhere. "Gray?" I call out to him, moving closer to the wall. I look for the landline to call his cell, but then I realise that his phone will be with his clothes.

A sudden banging on the wall tells me that he's at least alive. Pressing my ear to the wall, I can barely hear his muffled words. I cup my hands around my ear and listen again.

"This is a fucking joke..." I catch, his voice vibrating through the dry wall. There's another loud bang from the other side of the wall again, startling me.

"I'm right here, idiot!" I shout, frowning at the wall.

"What do I do? I can't see anything!"

And you're naked. But I won't add insult to injury by pointing that out right now.

"Just calm down. Unless you plan on busting a hole through the wall, you need to phase through it."

"Phase?"

I shrug, then I realise that he can't see me. "I did some googling last night when I got home."

"Dude! What if—"

"Don't get your panties in a wad. I was incognito and I erased my browser history." I don't know if the government would really care what I'm searching on the internet, though. Searching superpowers is kind of nerdy, but it's not uncommon or out of the ordinary for some people. "What are you thinking about when it happens?" I shout loud enough for him to hear. *He's probably cold as hell in there*.

"If I knew what triggered it, don't you think I would have better control over this?" He calls back. He must be pressing his mouth against the wall now, because it's suddenly much easier to hear him.

"Well, I don't know...just relax?"

"Relax? How do you expect me to relax? I'm trapped under the fucking stairs with no clothes on!"

Tapping my foot, I debate whether I should just smash the wall. *It's probably pretty freakin' scary in there*. He thumps on it again, and my heart spikes. *What the hell do I do?* "Give me a minute." My face starts to burn and my lungs seize up. *Get him out. I need to get him out.*

Try harder.

Think, dammit! How do I get him out? Pressing my cheek against the wall, I call out, "Close your eyes, Gray."

"What the hell is that gonna do? I already can't see anything!"

"I know," I take a deep breath. I need to be calm. "Just do it." It's silent for a moment, and I drag my fingertips on the wall. Tracing *slow* circles, my skin creates a wispy sound. "Keep your eyes closed, and just focus on the sound I'm making. Don't think about anything else, alright?"

"What are you doing?" His voice is quieter now, but definitely still there.

"Meditation. If you *relax*, it might work." It's the only thing I can think of. "Stay pressed against the wall." My hand sweeps the wall in slow motions. The skin of my fingertips starts to burn from the friction, but I make sure to keep at it.

"It's not working, Liam."

I throw my hands up, but again, he can't see me. "I've only been doing this for ten minutes!"

When he bangs hard on the wall, I jump back. "This is stupid! It's not—" Like a ghost, Gray falls through the wall in front of me. His arms swing out to balance himself, but gravity forces him forward until he collides with me. When I hit the ground, his body crushes mine, the back of my head smacking against the hardwood floor.

A groan slips from my mouth as his elbow digs in my side. "Get off me already."

He scrambles off, hands dropping down to cover himself. "This is getting ridiculous."

"You're telling me," I grumble. Using my elbows to prop

myself up, I level him with a dark look. "Only *you* could manage to get stuck in *there*," I nod to the space he fell through, my eyes narrowed on his face. He has the audacity to look shy about it. I scramble up to my feet and head for the stairs. I collect his clothes off the steps with my fingertips and toss them over the banister to him. "How about *I* get your things, and *you* wait here?"

Gray catches his clothes with one hand, still covering his junk with the other. He holds his pants in front of him and nods his head. "Yeah, alright."

His room is a bloody mess today—*how the hell can someone eat so much caramel popcorn?*—but I don't go rifling. I grab the comforter, a couple pillows and a pair of basketball shorts that I see on the ground. It's hard to do with only my fingertips, so I throw most of it over my shoulder, pinching the corners. I toss his stuff over the balcony, and Gray catches it in his arms. I don't say anything as I make my way back down the stairs.

Tossing the last pillow into the tent, I glance back at him. "Is this going to be enough? It's getting pretty cold at night now."

"Yeah, I'll manage."

The evening sky grows darker by the minute, the wind picking up and sweeping icy air through us. The snow is probably going to start falling soon. "I think I'm gonna head home then. You gonna be—"

"Wait, you expect me to stay outside *by myself*?" His eyes widen, glancing back and forth between the tent, his house, and me.

My eyebrow lifts. "You need me to hold your hand for you?"

His eyes roll and his nostrils flare. "I haven't slept outside before."

I knew it. "Get Noodles to stay out here with you, then."

"Noodles?" He gives me a weird look, causing my chest to tighten and suffocate.

His name. What's his name? What's his name?

"Uh, his hair is stringy and curly..." *Like noodles.* I look over his head at nothing in particular. I just can't look at him. Something in my chest won't let me. Or maybe it's in my head.

"Are you talking about Dawson?" He asks, still confused. He looks at me harder, taking a small step towards me. But I take a larger step back, creating distance.

"Yeah." *Dawson. Remember his name, damn it. Remember his name.*

"My family doesn't *know* about any of this stuff, remember?"

I throw my hands up in the air, my brows pinching together. The longer he looks at me that way, the more difficult it gets to breathe. *I need space. Air. Distance.* "You'll be fine. You can call my home phone if anything happens." Though he shouldn't need to. *He would probably call my house just to be annoy me.*

Gray's eyes narrow in a weird way and his head falls to the side. "Can't I just call your cell?"

Too many. He's asking too many questions. My fingers start to itch, my blood thumping beneath the moulted skin. His eyes don't miss the way my fingers fidget. "Just call the landline, *alright*?" I mutter, attempting to leave. But he reaches out with his stupid long arms, wrapping his fingers around my bicep.

"Hey...thanks for this." My eyes follow the way his head nods to the side, and my eyebrow arches.

"It's just a tent..." Gray drops his hand and shrugs, so I leave without a goodbye.

Distance. I need distance so I can breathe again.

It's already a lot colder than I thought it would be tonight. But he'll be fine.

My eyes follow the tips of my shoes as I walk, until the familiar crack in the pavement catches my eye. Glancing up at my house, Sawyer and Lemon are walking out towards the car while mom lingers in the foyer, fussing over something. When Lemon spots me walking up, she stops to smile at me. The wind picks up a piece of her pale brown hair, sweeping it across her cheek until she tucks it back.

"Hey Liam." Her tone is always so soft. "How are your hands?"

Horrible. They hurt so freakin' much. "They're fine."

"I thought you might have been staying for dinner at my house tonight. Fin said that you were over?"

Sawyer whirls back around with narrow eyes. "You were at their house just now?"

I gnaw on the inside of my cheek. "Yeah."

The little point of her nose tips back with her head. "Why?"

I shrug and look over Julia's head, to the front door. "I just was." Mom heads towards the door, fishing her keys out of her bag.

"That's not a real answer, Liam." Sawyer's tone is snarky now. She crosses her arms over her chest, and her eyes narrow. "Were you bothering Finch?"

Were you bothering Finch?

Was I bothering him? I was trying to help...I don't think I was bothering him. I wasn't...

Were you bothering Finch?

Bother.

Why do I even bother with you?

Our father's car isn't here, and mom's about to close the door.

Marnie, what happened to changing the locks?

My throat seizes, my blood running cold and thick under my skin as my father's words filter in. I rush towards the door, almost bowling mom over. "Liam, are you alright, baby?" Mom's voice is soft as well, but it sounds fuzzy. I think my ears have gone numb, because even my movements feel creaky and muffled.

Despite that, Sawyer mumbles, "You're so lucky *your* brother isn't a freak."

I nod my head, the lump in my throat too swollen to speak around. I wave mom off and take the stairs two at a time until I reach my room, slamming the door shut behind me. Pressed against the familiar wood, the pressure in my lungs tightens.

Were you bothering Finch?

Why do I bother with you?

Were you bothering...

Were you bothering...

Sliding down the door until I hit the floor, I pull my knees up to rest my forehead against them. *I was helping...I was.*

I don't move until I stop floating. When I raise my head, my room is shrouded in shadows. It isn't the darkness that makes my chest seize, but the emptiness.

My bandaged hand slides along the wall above me until I finally hit the switch. My eyes pinch against the bright light, blinking hard until they finally adjust.

It's the same ordinary room.

Quiet. Cold. Empty. Always the same.

The jingle of keys dropping onto the hallway table echoes up the stairs in the same moment the phone rings. I struggle to my feet and open the door as quietly as possible, the sound of my father's voice drifting up from the foyer.

"Are you calling to speak to Sawyer?" There is a brief pause, and his foot taps an irritated rhythm. "Sorry son, he's not here."

CHAPTER

09

Milo spots me from across the corridor as I'm walking to History and rushes towards me. "Dude, did you hear?"

The blood freezes in my veins. My mind immediately goes to Gray. *Did that jerk phase in front of someone? Did he bleed all over the damn place?* "Did I hear what?"

"Fin flunked the physics test."

"What?" My eyes bulge. Gray doesn't flunk. Even when he took an entire month off to go to Orlando with his family—the jerk *still* managed to score higher than me on a damn English exam.

"Yeah, apparently he told Mister Harvey he didn't want any special treatment because of what happened. He didn't look surprised about the grade. I think you might have finally beaten him!"

I did really well on that test. My head wasn't in it, but I still managed to pull my shit together to get it done. But despite the point Milo makes, this isn't a win. And I *won't* accept it as one either.

I storm off as Milo looks around for someone else to tell. But I have no idea where to find him. *Where does Gray even hang out?* He's *usually the one to come and bother* me.

There are a few people whispering about it in the halls, their eyes locking in on me as I pass them. *Who are his friends? He's so freakin' chummy with everybody, does he even have friends he hangs out with more than others? Why am I so freakin' lost for answers right now? I've known this guy my entire life. I should know who his damn friends are.*

I spot a few members that I'm sure are from the lacrosse team leaving the locker room, so I corner them before they get too far. "Woah, easy buddy," the biggest one laughs.

It's the same guy that was following Gray around that first day he came back—I can't forget that blobfish sized nose. His beady eyes creep me out, shivers racing down my spine.

"Where's Gray?"

One of the guys beside him gives me a weird look, his oily black hair falling past his shoulders. "Finch Gray?"

I roll my eyes. "Anyone else with that last name go to this school?"

Blobfish purses his lips, his eyebrows dipping in at the centre. "Hey, don't get smart, kid." The guy next to the giant taps his arm, muttering something I don't hear.

My lip curls at the corner. "Do I look like a fucking kid to you?" It comes out ruder than I intended it to. I just wanted to ask them if they knew where Gray was. *Why am I even having this conversation with them?*

Blobfish steps forward, and I nearly swallow my tongue. Maybe I should swallow it—it clearly doesn't do me any favours. "Watch it, Rice. I heard you ain't playing ball for the next couple weeks. I wouldn't go picking fights and *extending* that little vacation."

"I'm not the one picking fights here." *That's not what I'm trying to do, damn it.* "I'm just looking for Gray. You guys were with him the other day, so I just thought you might know where he hangs out."

The other guy—the one with the small eyes and slimy black hair—pinches his entire face at me. "Isn't he *your* friend? Why the hell are you asking us?"

I blow out a loud breath. "This has been the biggest waste of time." I try to turn around, but the giant blobfish reaches his grabby hands out and snatches my arm back. The jerk pulls my hand from my pocket, bringing the stark white bandaging around my palm into view. I hear a few people that had been lingering in the area starting whispering, so I try to snatch my arm back. "Get the hell off me," I grunt, trying to yank my arm away. But this guy has nails like a damn cat and locks on.

"What happened to your hands, huh? You jerkin' off too much or something?" he chuckles.

"Piss off," I hiss, the blood thumping in my palms. When I glance at the bandages, they're still white.

"Looks like you'll need to find some help with that, Rice," he nods down to my pants, "if you can't handle it yourself." Blobfish pulls me up to blow his breath across my face. I almost pass out from the stench alone. Does this guy *own* a toothbrush?

"Is that you offering?" I raise an eyebrow. "Because I'll pass." The guy on his right chuckles into his palm, but Blobfish doesn't seem to think it's funny *at all*. Using his other hand, he grabs at the collar of my hoodie, pulling me up closer. I wrinkle my nose. "You better not kiss me or anything."

I watch his other arm draw back, but I don't think to move before his fist flies and connects with my cheekbone.

The side of my face aches and my tongue fizzles—I can't tell if I bit it or not—but the guy doesn't drop me. A few people have stopped to stare, so I try to cover my hands, but the Blobfish Giant still has my arm in a death grip, and he's gathering my collar back up in his hand again. "I don't care if your hands are messed up. Don't start something you can't finish, Rice."

"I can finish just fine with my own hands, trust me. I don't need your clams," I spit out. *God, why can't I just shut up?*

Before Blobfish can hit me again he's slammed into the lockers, his grip on me falling away. I find my feet and my eyes bulge out of my sockets. "What the hell, Gray?"

With his arm pressed tight against Blobfish's throat, his eyes flicker over to me briefly. His nostrils flare, and his hair hangs over his eyebrows. *He didn't style it today. Wait, does he usually?*

"Keep your damn hands off him, Ray," he grunts, his eyes narrowing in on the guy's big nose. He brings his hand up to try and ease Gray's arm off his throat, but Gray just presses down harder, his eyes sparking.

"Hey man, Rice started it," Clumpy Hair grumbles, standing awkwardly to the side. He doesn't seem overly invested in getting between these two giants.

"Don't care," Gray mutters. "Just stay the fuck away from Liam."

Almost everyone in the corridor is staring now. I blink hard, trying to wake myself up. Because this can't be Gray right now. He doesn't fight, or get angry, or threaten people.

Not ever.

Gray shoves away from Blobfish, cutting him one last scathing glare before pushing me down the hall. Those lingering in the halls all press back against the lockers as we pass them, their eyes wide and their phones out.

"What the hell was that? I can fight my own—"

"Shut up, Liam." His tone has a finality that I don't care to oblige.

"You're being more of a jerk than usual." I watch him, my ears burning hot when he meets my stare.

He taps the back of his hand against my forearm, reminding me of my exposed hands. I quickly shove them into my pockets, though I'm sure it's pointless now. "Stop making yourself a target and I wouldn't have to be a jerk."

I turn and shove him with my shoulder towards an empty classroom. *Why does what I do even matter?* I close the door with my heel and pin him with an ugly glare. "I didn't ask you to do that," I snarl. "That wasn't your business, so next time just stay out of it. I can handle myself."

Look what you did.

Look what you did.

Whatever it is, it's his problem to deal with.

He snorts, crossing his arms over his chest. His t-shirt pulls around his biceps, the same colour as his dumb floppy hair. His jeans look similar to the ones he wore yesterday, but they're a lighter blue. "It's not wrong to ask for help sometimes, Liam."

I scoff. "Bit hypocritical, isn't that?"

He moves closer, the brown of his eyes darker than usual. "*I'm* different. I'm not dealing with some asshole, I'm dealing with fucking *superpowers*."

I roll my eyes. "Yeah, isn't that a joke. I finally beat you on a test, and you get shot by a magic bullet."

"It wasn't a magic bullet!" His fists clench in front of him and his face screws up before he takes a deep breath and chills out.

"Uh-huh, sure it wasn't." I turn and open the door, ushering him out. "Ladies first?"

Gray blows out a loud breath before passing me. "Why were you even talking to Ray in the first place?"

I raise an eyebrow when I remember. "Was asking where you were. Heard you flunked physics."

He blinks, right before his annoying laughter breaks through. "You're so desperate for a win, aren't you?"

I purse my lips. "*Jerk*. Have you phased yet?" I whisper. He glances around to make sure no one is withing range before he answers.

"I mean, I woke up naked, but I actually got a full-night sleep."

I regard him with a raised eyebrow. "How are you keeping your clothes on at school?"

His eyebrows furrow like mine do. "I don't know. I don't know what's triggering it, but I guess whatever it is, it doesn't happen at school."

I nod. "Definitely something you need to figure out if you are going to play the Maverick game." I have no idea what class he has now, or why he's following me towards history.

"So where did you go out last night?"

My face burns as I glance over at him. "What do you mean? I was home last night."

His head falls sideways and his eyebrows dip down the

bridge of his nose. "I called your house and your dad said you weren't home."

Are you calling to speak to Sawyer?

Sorry, son, but he's not here.

"Oh. Yeah, I went for a walk." From the corner of my eye, I watch him. He nods his head, like what I said makes perfect sense. "What did you call for? Did something happen?"

The purple circles under his eyes are a lot lighter today, and his skin seems brighter. He probably still woke up naked and cold, but the tent must have helped. "Nah, nothing happened. Just wanted to bother you some more." He scratches the back of his head, his nose twitching.

Bother.

Why do I bother with you?

Were you bothering Finch?

"I've got History." I take off ahead of him, ducking into the classroom without glancing back.

Don't bother him.

I'm not bothering him.

When I walk into Chemistry, Gray's sitting in the wrong spot. "*Move*, Gray. That's my spot."

His smile is annoyingly blinding. "Don't worry, I'm willing to share." He pats his knee, winking at me.

My bruised cheek aches when I clench my jaw. "No. Go back to your desk."

He leans forward to rest his chin on his open palms, his elbows propped up on the bench. His narrow eyes are smaller than usual, and his face is bright. "Well, since Monica and I switched partners, this *is* my desk."

I turn my eyes to Curly, but my partner is too busy peering up under her eyelashes at Gray's partner. Her curly brown hair is an even bigger frizz ball today. "She can't just *swap* partners."

"Miss Colin said it was fine." He leans in closer, his eyes drooping. "I don't think that she wants her favourite student to fall behind, so I suggested she pair me up with her *second-best* student to help me catch up on the things I missed."

I turn and head towards Miss Colin's desk, my lips pursed. *We can't change. We can't. It doesn't just happen like this. And he wasn't even gone for a week. There's barely anything for him to catch up on.* But she stares back with an annoying smile on her lips, like she had expected me to object the change. "Thank you for helping Finch catch up, Liam," she coos before I have the chance to say anything. Her hair's pulled back in its usual tight bun, but she looks even more intense than usual today.

My aching hands shake at my sides as I frown down at her. "I don't want a different partner."

Her raises her thin eyebrows at me. "I'm sorry Liam, but Monica has been asking me to swap partners for a while now, and Finch said he's willing to work with you."

Willing to work with you.

Is it hard to work with me? Has Curly always felt that way? We never really spoke, but she never... "I didn't realise that she had a problem being my partner."

Miss Colin's eyes soften somewhat. "That's not what—"

"It's fine."

I wander back to my seat, my eyes lingering on the frayed ends of my shoelaces. I take the seat next to Gray—Curly's old seat—and open my bag without a word. My skin burns beneath the bandages, the pain-killers barely doing their job, but I just bite my tongue. Gray doesn't say anything either, tapping his pen on the desk.

"We start labs next week. You can use my notes to *catch up*." *I guess it doesn't matter now if people see my hands.*

"How's your face?" He nods to me, his eyes lingering over the bruise.

I bite the inside of my cheek and balance my pen between my fingertips. "Fine."

"Are you going to be home tonight?"

My shoulders tense, but I don't look away from my notebook. I flick through the pages as I answer, "Don't know."

"Boy, do you love playing hard to get." He bumps his shoulder against mine, laughing quietly between us. I can't even be bothered to try and understand what he's talking about, so I slide my book across the desk without a word and rest my head on my arms.

Just breathe, Liam. Switching partners isn't a big deal. I didn't like Curly anyway. She doesn't paid attention, and she always skips class, and she has never been any help on the assignments. So really, she's doing me a favour. This is a favour.

Soon enough, my voice isn't the only one circling around in my head.

Try harder.

Look what you did.

Monica has been asking me to swap partners for a while now.

Try harder.

Why do I even bother with you?

What's wrong with him?

My eyes burn, so I bite down on my tongue. My nails are burrowing into my bandaged palms, the ache morphing into violent pain, when I feel Gray's fingers uncurling them. Jerking back, my wide eyes land on his face. He stares back at me with tired eyes, showing me his palms as he pulls away from me. "Hey, if you don't want to be partnered with me, I can just—"

Why do I even bother with you?

Look what you did.

Look what you did.

"It's fine, Gray." My tongue is thick in my mouth as I try to speak, so I lay my head back down on my arms.

His breath blows at my ear when he leans in closer. *Bloody jerk.* "How do you expect me to read any of this? Your handwriting is terrible."

I narrow my eyes at him. "Don't sit so close to me." I scoot my seat away from him, but Gray only laughs.

People are watching us. When I glance around, I catch some turning away, but not before I see their pulled brows and dropped jaws. The bandages around my hands grow damp, and I worry they're infected because of the burning that itches and pulls at my skin. I might need to stop in at the hospital—

What did you do, baby?

What did you do?

Whatever it is, it's his problem to deal with.

I'll just...change them when I get home. They'll be fine.

95

CHAPTER 10

I finish off the test and lean back, watching Gray from the corner of my eyes. His shoulders are tight as his head whips across the page like he's lost. I cock my head as I watch him for a moment longer. His forehead is creased, and his hair is starting to brush past his eyebrows. *I don't think I've ever seen such a confused look on his face.*

There's a knock on the door, and when it opens, the Principal is standing there.

With the Sheriff.

I send a swift kick to Gray's shin, and he yelps. When his head snaps up to glare at me, I give him a pointed look towards the door. When he spots his uncle standing there, he immediately shrivels. But the Sheriff is looking between us, his eyebrow raised when Gray starts to lean back. I kick him again.

"Sorry to interrupt, Miss Colin, but I need Liam Rice to come with us. The Sheriff has some questions he needs to ask." The Principal glances between Miss Colin and I, his round glasses slipping down his nose and his bald head shining under the ceiling light. My heart hammers in my chest, and when Gray's head snaps back to me, I'm worried it's because he can hear it.

Miss Colin nods in understanding and turns to me, along with everyone else in the class. My cheeks burn from the unwanted attention, and I slowly slide my chair back from my desk. I glance at Gray again, telling him with my eyes that I'm not going to blow his secret.

For some reason, he doesn't look reassured in the slightest.

Everyone watches as I fumble my bag onto my shoulder and head towards the front of the classroom. I don't turn back to look at anyone—especially Gray. The Sheriff watches me as I approach, his eyes flickering over my shoulder, probably to Gray again, before he steps back to let me pass.

I keep my head low as I follow them into the hall, then down to the Principal's office. No one says a word as we walk the halls, and my hands are shaking again, blistering hot and aching. When we finally reach the office, the Principal says something to the Sheriff before closing the door and leaving us alone.

"Take a seat, Liam." He gestures to the two chairs in front of the Principal's desk. I hesitate for a moment before sitting down. The Sheriff sits in the seat beside me. "Thank you for coming, this won't take long. How are your hands feeling today?"

They hurt so fucking *much.* "Fine."

I peek up at him as he nods.

Strong men always win.

Straightening my shoulders, I raise my head. *I'll look suspicious if I avoid him. Think of a lie. A lie.*

"I'm sure you heard that we caught the robber," he says,

watching me carefully. I meet his eye for a moment, before glancing around the room. There's a laptop on the Principal's desk, the screen facing us, an image frozen on the screen.

It's the corner store.

I hold my breath as I stare at the paused footage. The robber is at the centre of the image, pointing the gun at Gray. But like Gray thought, you can only see half of his head, the rest of his body concealed by the high shelves. You can see me peeking out from the end of the aisle, my head caught in the very corner of the screen.

"If you caught him, then why do you—"

Lia—

The gun is fuzzy on the screen. Everything is fuzzy. Pixelated. But I see it in perfect clarity. I remember every single second.

"I'm still trying to piece together what happened that night," is all the Sheriff replies. I drag my eyes away from the screen, my vision blurry.

Strong men always win.

He put this in front of me on purpose. Trying to make me weak again.

Weak, weak, weak.

"Why?" My voice is stronger than I anticipated, and my shoulders straighten further when I hear the firmness in my tone.

The Sheriff raises his eyebrow, his lips pursed and his cheekbones tightening. "Why am I trying to investigate a crime?"

"But you caught the guy? Isn't that the end of it?" Sweat tickles my forehead. The Sheriff presses a button on the keyboard and the video plays. My eyes are glued to the screen as the scene unfolds. No sound plays from the computer speaker, but it all rings in my head in sequence.

Gray's head moved and I know he's saying something. The robber's arm shakes as he waves his gun around. Headphones is crying, Gray says something else. I know what's coming. I know.

I know I know I know—

I flinch when the gun-shot echoes in my head at the same time there is a small flash at the barrel of the gun. My eyes are stuck on Gray as the robber escapes out the door. From the corner of my eye, I see when I stand up when Gray disappears from view. I move slowly, before I drop down out of sight as well.

I don't want him to die.

I've got to stop the blood.

Lia—

I'm trying!

Stop the blood...Stop the blood...

You are not going to die. Do you hear me, Finch?

"This is the part that has me confused." The Sheriff's voice pulls me back from where I was leaning forward into the computer screen. But I don't look away, because suddenly a bright light starts to glow from out of sight, until it suddenly flashes, and the screen goes black.

I stare at the screen, waiting for the image to come back. But it stays dark.

The Sheriff lowers the screen, but my gaze stays rooted in place. I don't know *how* to look away.

"Can you tell me what happened in that aisle, Liam?" The Sheriff's voice is deep and rumbly again. Like it was when I woke up in the hospital. Strong. *Really strong.*

Strong men always win.

"Nothing happened."

The lie slips off my tongue easily. *Don't think about what happened. Just lie.*

You're not going to tell anyone, right?

The Sheriff shifts beside me, drawing my attention. I keep my shoulders back. *Strong men win. I know what he's trying to do. I won't let him do it.*

"There is a giant section of the floor in that aisle that has completely *eroded*. I assume it was the same chemical that burned *your* hands. Can you explain that?"

I shrug. I'm assuming he's referring to where Gray's blood spilled out onto the floor, but I can't answer.

I can't.

His brown hair falls to the side from where he has it loosely slicked back, his stubble longer than the last time I saw him, but still just stubble. His eyes narrow on mine. "When you woke up in the hospital, you said that Finch was shot."

Is Gray okay? Did they manage to stop the bleeding?

What do you mean 'what do I remember'? He was shot.

"The doctor said I was on a lot of pain meds. I don't even remember that conversation."

Lie, lie, lie.

I don't know what I show on my face, but the Sheriff's doesn't change. He keeps a close eye on me, his jaw pulsing as he tenses. His fingers curl into fists on his lap, uncurling and curling again.

"Liam, if something has happened to my nephew, you need to *tell me*." His tone is hard, but not dominating. Not controlling.

Strong, but different. It's not how dad would speak about me.

I shake my head. *Keep lying.* "He was surprised by the gunshot, and he fell over. There's nothing else to tell."

Still, he watches me for *long*, silent moments. My head is pounding louder than a drum when finally nods his head.

CHAPTER

11

"He knows." Gray says as we walk home. I shrug, because I've already told him so many times—

"He *doesn't*. He believed me."

Gray throws his hands up. "What do I do? Do you think he'll call the government? Will they send people to take me away? To *experiment* on me?"

I kick him, and he lets out a yelp, but he *finally* shuts up for a moment. "He won't call the damn government because he *doesn't know*. And calm down, would you? We can figure this out." Even though I went over what happened in the Principal's office, Gray's won't shut the hell up.

He spins to face me, his face pinched. "How the hell are we gonna do that?"

I send him a scathing glare. "I don't know. I'll figure that out."

Gray takes a deep breath and nods his head, his lips pursed. I stare at him for a moment longer, until finally I ask, "Do you think you'll be alright for the game next Friday?" *He'll need to have control of this phasing thing by game night.*

He rakes his fingers through his soft hair. "I don't know.

I can feel when it's about to happen, but I still don't know how to stop it or control it."

"What does it feel like?" My fingertips fiddle with the edges of the bandages. I followed him the long way home, so we'll reach his house first. I think he wanted me to be here if his uncle tries to corner him.

Gray rubs his lips together, peeking at me. "It's like...a sheet."

My mouth pulls in a straight line. "A sheet..."

His jaw ticks. "I don't know. It feels like a sheet is being ripped off me. It feels like a tugging at first, and then a breeze of cold air, and that's when I lose my clothes."

This is definitely going to feel like the dumbest thing I've ever said. "Have you tried holding onto the *sheet*?" I tried not to sound sarcastic, but I don't think it worked.

He rolls his eyes, shoving his hands into the pockets of his jeans. "Obviously."

I tilt my head. "Physically, or mentally?"

Gray peeks at me again, his brows furrowing. "What do you mean?"

I shrug, hitching my bag higher onto my shoulder. "In the movies, sometimes it's a mental thing. It might be a physical ability, but it's all triggered by whatever is going on up here." I point to my temple, giving him a thoughtful look.

He nods slowly, contemplating my question. "I haven't really noticed what I'm thinking about when it happens."

"What were you thinking about when you tried to catch the ball in practice that first time after what happened?" I ask. My eyes follow him as he runs his hand through his hair again. It keeps falling back in his eyes. *Was his hair always that long?* The sunlight is catching on each inky strand. *It's really shiny today.*

"I was worried I wasn't going to catch it. That's why I was avoiding the ball." He rubs his hands down his face as he looks ahead.

I hum. "What about when I caught you at the lake?"

"Well, you scared the shit out of me. I didn't think anyone would follow me there." He shrugs.

My head shakes. This idiot. "It wasn't that you were surprised. You were scared you got caught."

"So?"

Is he really this dumb? I lean in closer and flick his forehead with the exposed tips of my fingers. Pain rears up through my forearm and I hiss out the breath in my lungs. "You were *scared*, dumbass. It's most likely your fear that's triggering it."

"Fear?" Gray thinks over the possibility. "So I just need to...not be scared?"

I scoff at him. "You can't always control your fears. You just have to get better at controlling how your fear triggers your phasing." He nods slowly, finally understanding. "That being said, if your phasing is a result of fear, then what were you scared of when you fell through the stairs the other day?" When he's silent for too long, I look back at him, surprised by how pink his face is. "What? Scared I would see how much of a pig you are for that popcorn?"

He scratches the back of his head, glancing away. "Uh, yeah."

"I don't understand how you don't have rotten teeth."

He laughs, kicking a stray stone out of his path. "You can talk. You guzzle those energy drinks like water."

My hands grow itchy beneath my damp bandages again,

and the hairs prickle on the back of my neck. "I actually haven't had one...not since the robbery." Haven't looked at my reflection since that day I thought I saw the robber in front of his house either.

"Oh." He looks like he's about to say something more, but I stop in front of his house and his jaw snaps shut. I look over to where Doc is grabbing grocery bags out of her trunk when she spots us on the sidewalk.

She stops short, her eyes flickering between the two of us. Lemon pops out from around the other side of the Mercedes, smiling when she sees me.

"Hey boys," Doc calls to us. "Fin, could you come and give us a hand?"

"Sure." Finch clears his throat and heads towards his aunt. I breathe a little easier when I don't see the Sheriff's cruiser out front of the house.

"I'll see you tomorrow—" I start, but Doc is already back to smiling her big smile at me.

"Why don't you stay for dinner, hon?"

Gray grips my wrist before he gets too far away and nods his head. "You should stay for dinner." I raise my eyebrow. He's probably still too nervous to be caught alone with his uncle. *The jerk probably needs me to hold his damn hand, too.* The look on my face must say I need some more convincing, because Gray quickly adds, "We can invite your family as well."

My mood immediately sours and my eyes droop.

No...don't...

Thankfully, Doc looks down at her watch and says, "It's a bit late notice to be organising *that*." Doc nods to me. "But you're welcome to stay for dinner, hon—since you're already here."

The corners of my mouth pinch, but my eyelids don't lift any higher. *It would be rude if I refused her now, right?* "Sure."

Gray releases my wrist to go help carry in the groceries, and the sudden cold air makes my skin shiver. *His skin was so hot.* I follow Doc into the house to where Lemon has already started unpacking the groceries.

"Want any help?" I offer even though my hands are throbbing at my sides. My forehead has broken out in a sweat from how painful it is.

Lemon turns with a kind smile on her face. "Thanks, that would be great."

She points me to where some things go, but the rest of it is pretty easy to locate on my own. I've gotten pretty good at using the tips of my fingers for things, but the uncomfortable tugging of my raw flesh is impossible to avoid. She starts pulling some random ingredients out for dinner, so I watch silently. I don't think my aching hands would be much help in the kitchen right now.

"You and Fin have been spending a lot of time together lately."

Have we? I mean, I think it's the same amount of time, we're just spending it differently now. And I wouldn't say it's been a lot *of time together.* I hum, not sure how else to respond. I don't want to give her any ideas, but she seems to be making her own assumptions anyway.

"Are you guys friends again?"

My mouth fills with something bitter. *Friends again? He would have plenty of friends. He doesn't need me. I just know his secret.* "Don't know..."

She switches subjects when I don't continue. "It's nice to

have *you* here for a change."

I nod. "Yeah."

"You know, you don't need an invitation. You can come over anytime."

You can come over anytime.

No I can't.

What did I tell you about bothering the Montgomery's?

My spine seizes. The air is suddenly thinner, and my lungs burn for oxygen when his voice echoes in my head.

Marnie, what happened to changing the locks?

Try harder.

The hairs on my arms start to prickle. I catch Lemon's head tilt from the corner of my eye. "Liam—?"

"I'm fine, Lemon," I choke out, forcing my jaw to relax. When Gray walks into the room with another full bag, the temperature spikes. My t-shirt sticks to my back where my skin breaks out in a cold sweat.

I try to busy myself, but my movements are awkward and stiff. I sense his gaze shortly before he asks, "You okay, Liam?"

My jaw clenches again. "I'm *fine*," I bite out.

He doesn't get to see me like this. I don't want him to see this.

I walk to the back door and yank it open, wincing as pain spasms up through my palm. The cold air hits my damp forehead first, sending icy shivers down past my shoulders. I roll them back, taking a deep breath as I stand outside in the silence.

Pull it together, Liam. He'll ask questions. I don't need him knowing. I don't need to add another thing to the ever-growing list of shit that makes him better than me.

Strong men always win.

"Liam—"

"Don't, Gray, I'm fine. I just needed some fresh air." I spin around to head back inside, but he blocks the doorway. His hands ball into fists at his side, his brows furrowing down at me. *Damn giant.*

"Don't lie to me." His stupid inky hair is hanging over his stupid eyes again as he stares back at me. I grit my teeth.

"I'll do whatever the hell I want," I mutter, my eyes narrowed.

"So I have to cough up everything that's going on with me, but the same doesn't apply to you?" He crosses his arms over his chest, his eyebrow raised.

"Exactly." My stomach clenches painfully, and my hands shake. *Just leave me alone, Gray. Leave me alone, damn it.*

Look what you did.

Whatever it is, it's his problem to deal with.

Look what you did.

"Is it about my uncle?" he asks.

"Sure." I shrug because I'm already sick of him asking. I push past him with my shoulder, and I come face to face with the Sheriff himself.

My heart stills in my chest as he stares down at me, his eyebrows almost touching his hairline. "Liam." He says it like a question, glancing over my shoulder to where Gray stands behind me. "Fin." He looks back down to me. His hat is gone, as is his coat. "I didn't know you were here for dinner tonight."

I shrug, my shoulders stiff. He steps aside so that I can go inside, and Gray follows close behind, right on my heels.

Thankfully, the Sheriff doesn't follow us up to Gray's

bedroom. But that only seems to make Gray more anxious.

"*He knows*, Liam. He's so confident he knows, that's why he's not coming up here to question me—"

"Ugh, *shut up*." I grumble, my eyebrows furrowed. "He *doesn't know*—"

"'He doesn't know' what?"

We both whip around, because apparently, he *did* follow us. And like the idiot jerk that Gray is, he didn't shut the door.

My heart is in my throat, and my mouth pops open like a fish. *Holy crap, what do I say? What do I say?* I look at Gray, but he's got the same face I do. He's scared.

I quickly shoot my elbow into his side, and he grunts as he doubles over. I would feel bad, if I hadn't just saved his ass from having to explain to his *entire family* how he phased through the floor and ended up naked in the kitchen.

Because pain is a distraction from fear. Even momentarily. *I can figure out something else next time.*

"This jerk cheated on an exam today." I shrug, my frown deep. Gray leans back, his hands covering his side where I elbowed him. He nods his head, a strained expression on his face. The Sheriff continues to look at us, his eyebrow quirked but his face otherwise expressionless.

"Yeah...I didn't want you to find out I...*cheated*..." he grinds out, his hair falling over his eyes as his nose twitches.

The Sheriff stares for a moment longer, and we hold completely still. My elbow is poised at his side still, ready to ram into his ribs if he freaks out again. We are all silent until he finally shakes his head. "You know your aunt would ground you if she knew that."

Gray leans forward. "Please don't tell her! I won't do it

again." His nose twitches as he bunches the hem of his shirt tight in his fist.

The Sheriff shakes his head again. "I know you've been dealing with a lot these last few days—" I nearly laugh, because the Sheriff has *no idea* how much, "but cheating is never the answer, Fin."

This conversation...

It's like the way the Sheriff was talking to Doc the other day.

Something about it is familiar. But *different.*

So different.

It makes my heart squeeze and my mouth dry up, but I don't know why.

"I know. I'm sorry," Gray says, his lips pinching. The Sheriff nods and turns to me. I don't say anything, but I think there's a weird look on my face as I stare back at him. He doesn't comment on it, and he leaves us on our own to continue down the hall.

Gray rushes forward and closes his door, leaning back against it. "Holy shit, I was about to pass out."

I glare at him. "*No,* you were about to fall through the floor and scare the crap out of your aunt and cousins. *You're welcome,* by the way."

Gray's face screws up. "I don't know if I want to thank you. You have a sharp elbow." I roll my eyes.

The phone starts to ring from the foyer, the shrill sound pulling us from the conversation. Doc sings out that she'll answer it, and Gray is heading towards his bed when I hear a muffled, "Marnie, calm down. It's alright, he's here."

My spine stiffens and my insides start to shake. *I didn't tell mom. She's probably wondering where I am...*

I didn't think to tell her. I never stay out, so I didn't think...

Rushing out of room, I lean over the banister and stare down at Doc.

"Yeah, he's joining us for dinner. Did you not try his cell?" I almost swallow my tongue when Doc asks that. I know without even hearing her voice that mom is stumbling to tell Doc that I don't have one.

Mom had to call. She had to bother Doc about me. Bother. I'm bothering them. I'm the bother.

Always a bother.

I need to leave. Need to go home. I should go home and stop bothering them. Why did I even come over? I should have gone home.

"It's alright Marnie, I'll have Fin drop him home later, alright?" Doc says. But my hands are shaking, and the back of my neck is wet. *I need to go home.*

Look at what you did.

You bothered the neighbours.

Look at what you did.

I stare down at the top of her head as she says a quick goodbye, my teeth chattering silently in my mouth.

"Everything okay, Al?" the Sheriff asks from somewhere downstairs. I hear Gray behind me.

"Just Marnie. She was wondering where Liam was, that's all."

Gray leans forward slightly, his gaze now focused on me. "You didn't message your mom?"

I'm not ready for him to look at me yet. My hands won't stop shaking, the blood thumping loudly in my ears. *I need to go home. I need to go home.*

Why do I even bother with you?

Mad. He'll be mad. Mad that I bothered mom. Mad that I bothered the Montgomery's.

Look at what you did.

You bothered the neighbours.

Stop crying.

Next time you worry your mother like that...

I rush down the stairs and for the front door. *I need to go home. I need to leave. I can't let Gray see me like this. I can't.*

Try harder, try harder, try harder.

What did you do, baby?

Look at what you did.

"Liam, where are you going? Liam!" I can barely twist the handle with just my fingertips, my lungs burning for air. *Why can't I breathe? It's so hot in here.* Finally yanking open the front door, I fall out onto the front porch. The air is colder now. Colder than before. I can feel it passing through my teeth against my numb tongue.

My legs carry me home, but my mind is absent the entire time. Standing in front of the door, my skin erupts in goosebumps. *Please open. Please.*

Grabbing the handle, I twist. The warmth from the house draws me inside, my eyes blurring. My breath labours out of me, my nose stinging and my teeth aching. But it's warm.

I'm inside. I'm allowed inside.

"You had your mother worried sick."

The air is sucked out of me again when I hear his voice. Calm. Collected.

My stomach rolls, and my eyes stay locked on the foyer rug. "I didn't think I was going to stay out that long..." I murmur, turning towards the living room. He sits in his chair by the fireplace, his finger tapping against the armrest in a hypnotic and nerve-racking rhythm, the burning wood barely embers now.

"What have I told you about bothering the Montgomery's?" he drawls. He doesn't turn to acknowledge me.

"I didn't think—"

He rises from his chair, his footsteps muted as he approaches. My shoulders shake as he draws near.

I shouldn't have bothered them. I should never have bothered them.

"Just remember, I warned you." He lingers for a moment longer, before silently climbing the stairs, leaving me at the front door. My stomach hits the floor, and I'm pretty sure my heart is with it. It's not in my chest anymore.

That hollowness is back. Maybe I only thought it left.

CHAPTER

12

My feet drag through the halls, my eyes barely focusing on what's in front of me. The shoes of those walking past me are the only spots of colour against the ugly cream colour tiles that line the narrow corridor. *Is the ringing in my head, or is it the bell? I can't be sure. What time is it?*

My eyes burn as I struggle to move. *Tired. So damn tired. Why didn't I sleep? I should have tried to sleep.*

"Hey Liam." The voice is far away, well above the surface. I peer up without lifting my head and stop when I see someone standing in my way. I sure that I know who it is, but my mind doesn't register a name. *So tired...*

"Hey." Something's off with my voice today.

Whoever it is shuffles on their feet, their brows furrowing. They're silent for a moment, before they ask, "You wanna have lunch outside?"

I shrug my shoulders. I think I reply, but I don't hear my voice if I do. Letting them lead the way, my eyes drift back to the floor. *What was I thinking about? Was I thinking about something? I don't remember...*

They fall back into step with me, clearing their throat.

"So you've been spending a lot of time with Fin lately..."

I shrug again, the ringing in my ears growing louder. It's incessant now, like an alarm that won't shut off.

"Are you feeling okay, man?"

I don't answer. *Do I know the answer?* They're silent as I follow them to the sports field. I don't think I want to sit outside—it's too cold—but I don't want to tell them. *Who is it again?*

I warned you.

A few people stare as we walk by, but no one says anything to us. *Why are they staring?*

The bleachers are empty, so I follow them to the top of the stands. They drop down and pull out their lunch, unwrapping the sandwich and taking a bite before I sit. I lean back against the rails and close my eyes.

Bother.

Were you bothering Finch?

Warned you warned you warned you.

"Coach really liked the plays you thought of. Said he wants to use them in the Maverick game next week."

Can I go home yet? Am I welcome there anymore? I don't...

"Liam," Their voice is faded, the last bites of sandwich hanging from their fingers, resting on their knee. "Hey, if you need to talk about something...I'm always here, man." My stomach clenches.

Whatever it is, it's his problem to deal with.

I nod again. I hope that's the right answer.

They're silent again. I blink hard, my mind still hazed. Their face is still foggy, and my head is still underwater.

"So you think we're gonna find ourselves girlfriends this

year?"

Girlfriends?

I shake my head slowly and stare out over the field. I can't remember how I even got to school. *How long have I been awake now? When was the last time I ate?*

Who cares.

We sit in silence as they do something on their phone. My head won't stop ringing. A moment later they rise to his feet, giving me a weird look when I don't move. They're tall. I know that they're tall, but their face... "You coming?"

"Where?" *Is that my voice? Why does it sound wrong?*

Their face changes shape, but I still can't see who it is. Their skin is darker than mine. "To class. The bell just rang..."

Their mouth is moving, but I don't hear the words. It doesn't reach me. "Right."

Someone steps up out of nowhere, their face plastered with a dumb smile. *What a jerk smile.* "Hey, Liam. Why'd you run off last night?" Their hair is dark. A different kind of dark to before. Soulless. Empty. Familiar.

What have I told you about bothering the Montgomery's?

I try to step around them, but they step in front of me again. "Are you okay? What's wrong?" Their mouth moves without much sound as well.

"Go away."

Leave me alone.

Leave me alone.

Their eyebrows furrow. "What's—"

"*Go away.*"

What have I told you about bothering the Montgomery's?

Look at what you did.

I warned you.

My stomach rolls as the voice echoes over and over, drowning out the constant ringing.

"Liam, what's—?"

"I don't—just..." I don't know what I'm saying. I try to storm off, but they pull me aside, against the set of lockers.

"Liam, tell me what's going on."

My gut clenches at the same time my heart thumps painfully against my ribs.

What have I told you about bothering the Montgomery's?

I warned you, I warned you, I warned you.

"Nothing." My hands are shaking, violent and numb, and my head won't stop ringing. *Loud. So loud.*

I try to turn and walk away again but they grab my wrist and pull me back. They're tall. Taller than me. I try to swallow around the thick ball in my throat, but it's hard. *Really freakin' hard.* "Just leave me *alone.*" *It's exhausting to talk so much.*

Why do I even bother with you?

Were you bothering Finch?

"Liam." Their tone is different now. It's hard to describe, but it's unusual. They watch me for a moment longer, and the last of those wandering the corridors file into their classrooms. I try to pull my arm away again, but they hold tighter.

"Let go." My throat swells and my eyes burn. The air is hot now, it hurts.

They yank me forward, but my heels dig in. Still, the giant has no problem pulling me along. *Jerk. Stupid jerk.*

"I have to get to class." I say even though I can't remember what class I need to get to. They don't answer me as they continue to drag me towards the gym. I tug back on my arm, but they don't release. "*Stop.*"

When the double doors open, they drag me to the edge of the shooting semi and drop my arm. I stand there for a moment, watching to see what they do, my eyes droopy. They head over to where the ball trolley sits at the side of the court, ready for practice this afternoon. They grab a ball out and slam it against their palms. Their toes touch mine when they finally stop in front of me, only the ball separating us. My skin starts to sweat again. *Why are they so close? Are they staring at me? Why—*

"Shoot the ball."

But my hands...I roll my eyes, but my fingertips tingle. "I can't—"

"Shoot the ball, Liam."

My hands are shaking harder now. My blood is screaming through my veins, tightening my muscles. "I—"

"For fuck's sake Liam, just *shoot the damn ball.*"

I snatch the ball from their hand, but only my fingertips touch the rough grip. The constant ringing in my head starts to dull, and my eyes lock on the hoop. My vision domes, and it's all I see; it's the only thing that makes sense in my head.

I raise my arms and toss the ball. I put the exact amount of force behind it, so it flicks off my fingers at precisely the right moment. The pain that spasms along my palms fades away as the ball sails through the air, swishing through the net. The bounce echoes off the walls, the rustle of the net clearing the lingering noise from my head. I stare at it for a while longer as the swaying slows, until it's still again.

But by the time the net stops moving, Gray is standing in front of me with the ball between his palms again. He looks like he always does. His hair is long, so long that it touches his eyebrows. His brown eyes narrow, watching me. He's tall. *So damn tall.*

Stupid tall jerk.

I take the ball without resistance and spread my palms over it. I can't feel it through the bandages, so I put the ball under my arm and tug the bandages away. I'm done with them. I'm sick of seeing the white.

The ball...I need to feel it.

"Wait, Liam—" He reaches forward to stop me, but I jerk out of his reach.

"*Don't*," I grind out. *I'm* done *with them*. My skin pulls, the week old starting of scabs threatening to split open, but the discomfort isn't unbearable. Neither is the pain.

I warned you.

What did you do, baby?

What did you do?

I drop the bandages to the ground and stare down at my distorted flesh. It's mostly healed, but my palms are completely scarred now. The skin is a fresh pink and scabbing in some places, but ghostly white in others. Doc said that I wouldn't feel things the way I used to, but right now the idea of this ball feeling different to how I remember terrifies me.

Gray still watches me, his brows pulling in as I hesitate. "What is it?" His voice is still flooded, but it all reaches me.

When I look back at him, he seems closer. I don't think he is, but I'm sure his breath is touching me now. His eyes seem wider, brighter. They're that same familiar brown. A lump forms in my throat. Why is he looking at me? I don't know what that means. But he's patient. *How long has he been patient with me?*

"It's going to feel different than before."

A slow smile spreads on his lips, and his eyes soften even more. "That makes two of us."

Somehow, an ounce of the pressure that had settled in my chest lifts when he says that. *It is different for him. Everything is different for him. Just like how things are different between us. It's not what I'm used to anymore. It's all different.*

"Liam?" His voice is clear now. I can hear all of it.

Drawing a deep breath, I move the ball between my palms. The contact generates a foreign numbness that spreads across my fingers, the tingle reaching up through my fingernails. But I feel it. Some of it, at least. The rough surface, the black grooves. I spread my hands over it and swallow the hiccup that threatens to burst out.

This is the one thing I get to keep. Basketball is my *only* thing. The only thing that he hasn't touched. That he hasn't *ruined*.

"Think you can play one-on-one?"

Yes. God, yes. It's sitting on the tip of my tongue, but the zapping in my fingers from just *holding* the ball isn't reassuring. I shake my head, lowering my chin slightly as I gaze at the ball, rolling it over my palms.

"I don't think I can bounce it yet." My shoulders deflate, my eyes still lingering on the ball.

"Wanna just shoot some hoops, then?" he asks. His eyes flicker across my face, but I can't tell what he's thinking. Or why he's looking at me so damn hard.

My body fills with fire. Anything. I'll do anything to keep this ball in my hands right now. I give him my answer when

I toss the ball high, sinking it. Every time the ball swishes through the net, a little piece of me slips back into place, like a jumbled puzzle being reconfigured. The pieces are slightly jagged, but somehow, they still fit.

It feels like no time has passed when we suddenly hear the bell ring, signalling the end of the school day. He doesn't seem the least bit bothered that we both skipped the last period. I don't know how Gray knew, but I *needed* this.

He steps closer again, crowding me. I've got the ball between us, but I meet his eyes without glancing away. "Whatever happens, just come right back here. You always have this."

Too close.

Brushing his hand away, my face burns hot. *Why is this idiot in my business?* I watch him, my body still. He stares back, standing close. *Is he closer again? I can't be sure.*

"I..." My hands tighten around the ball. I know that feeling. The disappointment of not getting to play. But he has a chance—he only needs to make sure he doesn't lose his clothing when he receives a pass. Glancing down at the ball again, my lips tighten. If I don't help him—if I don't keep him in the Maverick game—I don't go to the Championships. I won't play for the rest of the season. Things can't get better if I don't win the Championships.

"Whatever," I whisper. It wasn't supposed to sound so quiet, but my voice wouldn't carry the word any louder.

CHAPTER 13

"We're having your family over for dinner tonight," Gray says when he suddenly appears beside my locker. He leans back against the metal doors, watching me. Always watching so damn closely.

When my head snaps to him, my neck cracks. "What?" Now that it's finally the end of the day, all I can think about is going home and sleeping.

His head tilts as he stares back. "You're coming too, *right*?"

My elbows creak as I clumsily swap my books out of my locker and into my bag. *Can I go? If it's just mom and Sawyer that are going to be there, then it'll be bearable. But if my father's coming...* "Maybe."

He shakes his head. "I already told Aunt A that you were coming back with me. And don't worry, she told your mom."

I breathe out a loud breath, my palms tingling. "*Jerk.* Don't just assume I wouldn't have plans tonight."

He laughs, propping his elbows against the lockers. The sun is starting to set now, the bright pinks and oranges bleeding across the sky. "You make it sound like your attention is in high demand. And even though I know you're lying, I still don't like it," he pouts, his brows furrowed. "You have to give all of your attention to *me*."

"You're such a baby," I mutter. *What's with him saying weird stuff like that?*

"You should stay over tonight, since it's the weekend."

My eyes bulge. Gray is still watching me, completely focused and alert. He's studying me. "Why do I need to stay over?"

He purses his lips before he flashes his teeth in a grin, like he anticipated my question. "Do you have a reason not to?"

I stare back at him as I slam my locker. "Just because I know your secret, doesn't mean we're friends again, Gray," I mutter, my eyes narrowing. *Has this jerk suddenly forgotten that?*

Strong men always win.

Always win, always win, always win.

Which means weak men always lose...

Gray claps his hands together, rubbing them. "Irrelevant! You ready? Let's go." He pushes off the lockers and heads towards the school entrance, his shoulders stiff. I blow out a frustrated breath and follow behind him, because apparently my night has been decided for me.

We walk in silence as everyone gets into their cars. "How come you haven't been driving to school?" I ask when I finally realise that he's been walking home all week.

Gray shrugs. "I was a little anxious about driving my car and phasing out of it," he explains like it's an obvious answer.

But I shake my head. "You are such a paranoid jerk."

My eyes wander over to the corner store as it draws near.

Gray follows my stare, his shoulders bunching. "Have you been in there since that night?"

A lump forms at the back of my throat. "Of course not."

I can see Headphones' dad through the window. He rubs his forehead, his eyes pinched together as he glances around his shop.

"Have you spoken to her?" Gray asks as if reading my thoughts. My chest tightens and my palms start to sweat.

"No. I haven't seen her around school."

I haven't been looking. I saw her that first day back, but when she avoided me, I assumed that it was too much too soon.

The rest of the walk is silent, apart from our scuffing shoes and our uneven breathing. It's not long before Sawyer's voice booms from up ahead. "Hey Fin!"

"*Shit*," he mutters. Gray leans behind me slightly, but still returns her wave. She skips over from mom's car, leaving Lemon at the car door. Lemon waves at me, her lips pulled up in a friendly smile.

"Did you hear that I'm on the cheer squad?" Her eyes are wide and shiny, and her hair hangs long past her shoulders. It looks more blonde than brown today. *Has it always been that long? It looks smoother than normal, too.* Gray scratches the back of his head again, his mouth pulling into a tight smile.

"Congratulations," he says, his eyes flickering between his house and me. *Is he expecting me to do something?*

"I'll be cheering for you *on the court* now," she smiles, her eyes glittering. She moves closer, her hands swinging forward at her sides, nearly touching him.

I usually wouldn't interfere—it's not my problem if my

sister likes him—but something weird floods my chest. It's slimy and gross, and it throws my body between the two of them.

"We have to study," I mutter out the lie without a hello. She didn't even look my way until now.

"Study?" Her tone says that she doesn't believe me, but Gray wraps his arm around my neck and pulls me in close to his side. His entire body is warm—*really* freakin' warm—and he stinks of sweat. But somehow his hand smells like salty caramel. *This sweet-toothed jerk needs to stop eating that crap.*

"Right! Liam's gonna help me study for my make-up exams." He follows the lie. I can't see his face from the way he holds me.

Sawyer's eyes narrow, her head tilting. "Why would you need *Liam's* help?" Her gaze flickers over to me for a moment, then back to Gray. The sticky feeling inside me spreads, and my teeth grind.

Were you bothering Finch?

Were you bothering Finch?

Gray pulls away from me, his eyebrows furrowed. "Why wouldn't I? He's the second-highest ranking junior. He's the *best* person to help me."

He's the best person to help me.

Why would he say something like that?

He's the best person to help me.

She snorts. "As if."

My palms start to sweat and my skin itches. I try to pull out from under Gray's arm, but he keeps me tucked into his side. *Bloody jerk.*

Gray's frown deepens, the brown in his eyes dark again.

"He scored a fourteen-fifty on the SAT's, and he has an IQ of one-thirty." My lips pinch and my cheeks burn. *How does this jerk know my IQ rating?*

Sawyer's wide eyes flicker to me. "You never said anything about your scores."

I shrug my shoulders, glancing up at the house. I want to be as far away from this conversation as possible. "You never asked."

Why would she know? Why does it even matter? It's not like my IQ is worth anything. I still can't beat him.

Before Sawyer can comment, Gray pulls me towards the house. "Study time!" he shouts as we leave Sawyer standing on the front lawn by herself, Lemon following us in.

It's warm when we get inside. They don't have a fireplace, but it's cosy. Welcoming. Gray still has his arm wrapped around my shoulder, dragging me along with him. I would slap him away from me, but a lot of the pleasant heat that I'm feeling seems to be emanating from him. And something in my core is feeding off it.

"You wanna study in my upstairs bedroom or my downstairs bedroom?" he laughs. I roll my eyes, pointing upstairs. We almost have our first foot on the stairs when Doc appears in the foyer, her eyes locked on the arm Gray has coiled around my shoulder.

"Hey Liam." Her smile is soft, her eyes creasing at the corners. "How are you?"

"Good," I nod. I should apologise for running out last night, but the words aren't forming.

What have I told you about bothering the Montgomery's?

Doc points a slender finger towards me. "They're feeling better?"

My eyes drift down to my exposed palms and move them behind my back. "Yeah," I mutter, my eyes straying back to her a moment later. She nods slowly.

"We're going up to my room to study," Gray cuts in.

"Dinner will be ready soon." Doc's gaze narrows on him, but her smile remains.

"No worries." His arm drops from my shoulders and his fingers clench around the sleeve of my hoodie. He gives it a tug, telling me to follow him up the stairs. I haven't seen mom yet, but I don't go looking for her. Gray drops my sleeve when he sees I'm following a few steps behind.

His room isn't as messy as last time. But my eyes don't miss the trashcan full of empty popcorn packets in the corner. Gray heads straight over to his desk, pulling his textbook out and dropping his things down onto the floor beside his bed.

The skin on my hands tingle and zap as I fish around in my bag for my own things. A lot of things feel different now. But as long as I can still play ball, I can live with it. "I still don't understand how you flunked physics."

He gives me a pointed look. "My attention has been on other things, so I haven't had the chance to memorize the chapters from my textbooks."

I stare back at him, my eyebrows raised. "I knew you had to have a photographic memory or something. You *are* a cheating jerk."

Gray laughs at that. He laughs so hard, he hunches over, clutching his stomach. When he comes back up, his eyes are squinting and his teeth—I can see his tongue—are showing. His smile is different. It's unfiltered and genuine. Not like every other time, when he's being a jerk. His eyes are sparkling. "It's not cheating. I just happen to be gifted—in more ways than one, it seems."

I nod my head, my lips pushed out. "Is that why you failed and kept falling through the floor?"

"Whatever." He laughs again, but it's calmer. It sounds warm—can things *sound* warm?—and settled. When he drops down to the floor, he flicks open his books.

My eyes sweep the bedroom, taking in everything. I've been in here a couple of times now, but both times had been an in-and-out experience. This time I get to see his space.

His basketball posters line the walls, ranging from pros to our own home games. There are photos of Gray and Hair standing next to each other on the court, as well as a picture of Gray and me. At least I think it's him—the figure to the side is slightly blurry. In the photo I'm poised to shoot, my eyes trained on the hoop.

"You gonna help me or what?" He draws my attention back to where he's tapping the end of his pencil against his book. I roll my eyes and drop down next to him.

"You don't even need my help."

He snorts, leaning over the books he's spread out and shoving my shoulder. "Whatever."

He takes his time looking over my notes. I spot his basketball sitting at the foot of his bed and I reach over to swing it up into my hands.

I spin it on the tip of my finger, watching it with focused eyes. It's only been a couple weeks, but I've missed playing. Missed practice. Missed being completely absorbed in something I enjoy. Something that calms me and excites me at the same time. The sound of a camera snapping has my head turning to find Gray lowering his cell phone, his eyes plastered to the small screen.

"Did you just take a picture of me?"

He scoffs, his nose twitching. "You wish. I was taking a picture of your notes."

I continue to spin the ball on my finger, watching it turn. "You nervous for the finals?"

Gray drops his phone to his lap and looks up at me. "Obviously."

Letting the ball fall into my palm, I meet his stare. "Why are you nervous?" He gives me a look that asks if I'm joking, so I shrug my shoulders. "Well you only phase when you're scared, right? So, don't be scared about doing it, and you won't do it."

He shakes his head and laughs, the sound airy and sarcastic. "Right. Just don't be scared that I could drop my clothes in the middle of the game like some streaker."

"Why would you take your clothes off during a game?" My heart's in my throat when I see Noodles standing in the doorway. His brows are furrowed, probably trying to figure out what kind of conversation we were having.

"I wouldn't. It's just another bet," Gray quickly lies, his nose twitching. *He's been doing that a lot lately. Is he sensitive to dust or something?*

Dawson nods his head slowly, his glasses slipping down his nose. "Well don't lose *that* one. Mom would get *so* angry if you did that." He laughs his kid laugh, and I breathe a sigh of relief. "I was just coming to tell you guys that dinner's ready."

"Great!" Gray claps his hands and clambers to his feet. He strips his shirt off to change it for a clean one and throws his thumb up towards the door. "Let's go."

Following him down the stairs, my mom's voice travels up from the kitchen, loud and hyper. "I'm sorry if you felt obligated to invite us over tonight, Alice..."

Gray and I both slow down, hesitating near the top of the stairs. Noodles stops behind us as well, but I can hear Lemon and Sawyer's voices from down the opposite end of the hall. Gray leans over the railings slightly, but I can't see his face.

"You know that's not why I invited you guys, Marnie. Your family is always welcome here," Doc responds, her tone soft.

"I didn't mean to worry you last night. I just didn't know where Liam was. He's always home, so when he wasn't, I..."

I don't recognise my own mother's voice. I know it's her speaking, but something in my mind is shutting it out. Trying not to familiarise myself with her words.

"Why don't you give him a cell phone? Even just for your own piece of mind..."

Mom must be panicking right now. She's probably shaking her head, trembling like a leaf. I don't have to hear her say it. I know why I'm not allowed to have one.

"Jasper thinks it could take his focus away from basketball."

My lips pull into a tight line. *What a ridiculous excuse. Does she think anyone would buy that? It sounds like complete bull—*

"—shit." Gray finishes my thoughts, stomping down the stairs.

My fingers strumming the air at my sides as I follow behind Gray. The tension lingers as we enter the kitchen, where Doc and mom are dishing up the dinner plates. Doc raises her head, a bright smile on her face when she looks at me. "Liam, would you like to help Fin set the table?"

Would you like to help...

Help...

I nod. "Sure."

Mom comes over to give me a quick kiss on my cheek, but her lips are cold. Or maybe it's because my cheeks are burning hot. "Your father called me. He said he can't get away from work, so he can't make it tonight."

He can't make it tonight.

CHAPTER

14

"You're cheating," I grumble as I throw my cards down in front of us. Gray laughs, leaning back. His eyes crinkle at the corners as I scowl at him.

He holds his hands up, showing me his cards. "Trust me, I'm not. You're just not very good."

"Piss off." *It's so damn cold in this stupid tent. Why the hell did I think a tent was a good idea? Why the hell did I even agree to stay tonight? This is something* friends *do.*

The only source of light is the lantern-style flashlight beside our pillows. *It's so damn claustrophobic in here.*

"Do you wanna go another game? Or do you want to play—"

"I swear, if you try suggesting mah-jong one more time, I'm going to throw the board at your damn head." There isn't enough warmth in this stupid tent. I pull the blanket tighter around my shoulders, thankful I've at least got my hoodie on.

Gray laughs, his shoulders shaking. My eyes linger on them. *How the heck isn't he shivering? How is he wearing a t-shirt when I'm freezing my damn butt off over here?*

"Someone's a sore loser."

I cross my arms over my chest. "Well if somebody didn't cheat, I wouldn't—"

"I'm not cheating. I don't think you know how to play Gin Rummy." He laughs again, his eyes crinkling. *Damn jerk.*

"Fine! One more game." Collecting all the cards, I shuffle them.

Gray rolls his eyes and breathes out a loud sigh, leaning back on his palms. "What are we playing this time?"

"Old Maid." *There's no way he can cheat at this. Maybe he doesn't even know how to play.* He nods his head, a sneaky smile on his lips. His hair hangs over his eyes, the tips brushing around the bottom of his ears. It's as black as a raven at night, but it always looks lighter in the sun.

"That brings back memories," he mumbles, his eyes focused on my hands as I deal the cards. I make sure to slap them down on the covers so that he can't peek at them. *Damn cheater.*

"What does?"

"Playing Old Maid." His head tilts when I stare back at him, his eyebrows quirked upward. *Am I supposed to know what he's talking about?* "When we were kids? You taught me how to play when you got a pack of cards on your birthday. We spent all day playing it."

"We did?" *What birthday is he talking about?* Gray leans closer, inspecting my face. Probably trying to figure out if I'm lying. I stretch away, my eyes wide. "What?"

He's slow to respond, his eyes flickering across my face. "How could you forget? We played for an *entire day*. You even told me not go easy on you just because it was your birthday."

An entire day? What is he talking about? I wouldn't forget something like that. My hands fall to my lap as I think back. *There were always games. I was always trying to beat him. We've played it before? Why don't I remember that?*

Something pinches at my temple, and I grunt. *Why would he make up something like that? Did I really forget?* My skin breaks out in a cold sweat, shivers rushing up my spine. *It's cold.*

So cold.

Cold, cold, cold.

"Liam, are you okay?" Gray's voice is thick and foggy, his words cycling in my head. He reaches for me, but I swat his hand away.

"I'm fine. I remember." I lie. He watches me for a moment longer before gathering his cards and sorting out the pairs. I do the same, keeping a close eye on his moments as I breathe deep.

I've never played this with him. I'm *certain* I haven't. So if that bastard tries to cheat, I'll catch him. His forehead is creased, and his eyes are barely focused.

"Liam...are you alright?"

Were you bothering Finch?

Gray's eyes watch me carefully, flickering over my face.

What did you do, baby?

What did I tell you?

I warned you.

"I'm *fine*." I snap. Tossing my cards down and falling back against my pillow, I throw my arm over my eyes. The silence between us stretches on for too long, making my skin crawl. His gaze is heavy, but I don't move my arm. I don't want to hear whatever else he has to say, so I won't look at him.

Were you bothering Finch?

What have I told you about bothering the Montgomery's?

Whatever it is, it's his problem to deal with.

Damn it, leave me *alone.*

What's wrong with him?

Wrong with him wrong with him wrong with him?

I hear him shuffling under his covers, my own skin erupting in goosebumps. It's so damn cold, but I don't want to move. He flicks the lantern off without a word, the silence slowly eating at me. *Is he angry with me? Did I make him angry?*

"I—" I choke, my fingers twitching. *I should say something, but what the hell do I say? He's always pushing me. He's too nosy. Why does he want to talk all of a sudden? He's never wanted to talk before. We're not friends.*

He breathes a loud, tired sigh. "It's alright, Liam. You don't have to talk to me."

You don't have to talk to me.

Were you bothering Finch?

"I know that, jerk," I bite out, my eyes peeking under my arm. I can barely see him in the faint moonlight shining through the tent. He's staring up towards the sky, the whites in his eyes visible. *What is he even looking at?*

It's silent for a moment longer. I'm about to say something—I'm not sure what—when he suddenly comes out with, "I never said I'm sorry."

My arm flops away from my face, hitting the covers. I turn to face him, but he continues facing forward, his eyes blinking slowly as I ask, "What the hell do you have to be sorry for?"

135

He frowns. "I'm the reason you can't play in the Maverick game," he chokes out, his eyes shiny under the pale light. My chest tightens, and my fingers rub at the itchy scabs on my palms. "I ruined your hands."

"I don't blame you for that," I say. The moment I say it, a strange relief floods my chest. I *don't* blame him. Maybe I did, back before I knew the truth, but this wasn't his fault. It wasn't his fault he got shot, or that he developed these weird powers because of that stupid magic bullet. But he's gone silent again. I sit up on my elbow and stare down at him. I can't see well, but I know he isn't looking at me. He averts his eyes to the side, further in the opposite direction. "I'm not lying, Gray. I don't blame you for any of that—"

"Why the hell not?" he barks, his nose scrunching. His sharp tone has me leaning back, my eyes wide. Finch never snaps at me. The last time he did was in the bathroom at school when he destroyed the sink. Before that...I can't remember a time before that. *Why is he so upset about this?*

"Because you had no control over it. It all just *happened*—there's no way I can blame you for that, even if I wanted to." My jaw creaks and my pulse thuds in my ears. *Why is it so embarrassing to say?* My cheeks burn and the back of my neck tingles. I fall back down against my pillow and pull the blanket over me, hiding from the cold, thankful that Gray can't see how red my face is right now. "Gray, if I blamed you, you would know. I'm not here to spare your feelings—trust me."

He scoffs. I roll my head in time to see him rub hard at his eyes with his palms. "Man, do I know it." I watch as his arms fall back to his sides and he closes his eyes, chest rising and falling with each slow breath.

I want to say something, but I'm not sure what more I can say. "I never said thank you."

He doesn't miss a beat. "What the hell do you have to *thank me* for?" His voice is strained and unsure.

I shrug, even though he can't see me do it. "You took me to the hospital that night. I'm sure my hands would be a lot worse than they are if you didn't."

Gray swallows loudly, his breathing louder than before. "You don't have to thank me. You *shouldn't* thank me. I don't—"

"Well, I am, so shut up about it," I mutter. "Just because I'm thanking you, doesn't mean where friends, *alright*?"

"Why do you keep telling me that?" he asks, his tone soft, his words almost inaudible.

I open my mouth to explain. To tell him that it's because he keeps forgetting. *Him. He does. He keeps thinking that we're friends again, and we're not. We're not friends.*

But nothing comes out. It's quiet for a long time. So long, that I think he's fallen asleep, until he randomly blurts out, "Do you ever think back to when we were kids?" His voice is gruff, and his bottom lip is drawn between his teeth.

Rolling onto my side, away from him, I pull the covers up to my chin. "Why would I?" He's silent again. My heart is pounding so loud, I bunch the covers over my chest. *Surely he can hear it. I wouldn't be surprised if the jerk had super-hearing.*

"Do you ever think about what it would be like if we had stayed friends?"

If we had stayed friends...

If he wasn't so stupidly amazing at everything...it wouldn't be so hard to be his friend. I can't be friends with

*someone like him. He's way out of my league. He deserves to
have friends that are as smart as he is. As strong as he is.*

Strong men always win.

Which means weak men...

He doesn't need a worthless side character like me.

"No," I mumble, squeezing my eyes shut.

Don't ask such ridiculous questions, you jerk.

CHAPTER

15

It's finally game day. *Finally.*

As I wander towards the locker room's outside entrance, I spot some of the Maverick team arriving on a school bus, some in their own cars. A few of the players catch me inspecting them. We've played these guys before—I can't remember when—and they seem to remember me. One of them nods in my direction so I give him the finger.

More than half the team is already in the locker room when I wander in. The parking lot is already starting to fill up, but there is still over an hour before the game starts. I know that my family is already here—Sawyer said something about having to get here early to practice the routine—so I'm not hurrying to the stands just yet.

Spanner and Hair are talking near their lockers but look up when I enter. The two of them smile our way, their foreheads already sweaty. I search for Gray, but he's not here yet. I didn't see even his car outside. *Maybe he came here with his family—*

Gray appears in front of the locker room door leading to the gym, his eyes shiny and his nostrils flaring. *Maybe he* can *read my thoughts.* My heart starts to hammer in my chest. His skin is washed out and sweaty. "Gray, what's—"

"I don't think I can play tonight." I'm the only one who hears him, but the team sees the look on his face, and the atmosphere plummets. My jaw clenches as I grab the collar of his t-shirt. *This bastard better have his damn uniform with him.* The guys don't comment as I drag him along behind me. Even Gray is silent. When I have him outside, the cold air bites at my now burning cheeks.

I don't drop the grip I have on his shirt when I turn to face him, even as it sends painful spasms up my forearms. I pull his face close and give him a mean stare. "Get your shit together, or you're *really* gonna find out how sharp my elbow is." It was supposed to come out reassuring, but it definitely sounded more threatening than anything else. "You aren't allowed to bail, Gray—*I won't let you.*" I lean back. "I told you I'd be watching you. If I see anything that looks dangerous, I'll figure something out, *alright*?"

Gray's standing close now, very incredibly in my space—or maybe I'm in *his* space. He nods his head after a moment, like he's snapped out of whatever trance he's in. *Good, because I was close to slapping him.* Someone hollers from the carpark, and I know it's those losers from Maverick.

"Something happened today, though...something weird," he mumbles, his gaze flickering towards the noise. I watch him, taking inventory of his shaking hands and tense shoulders.

"What happened?"

He takes a deep breath, his eyebrows drawn together. "I think there was someone else in my head."

I stare back at him for a moment, trying to process what

he just said. "Huh?"

His head tips back, his eyes staring up at the sky for a moment, "I think I heard a voice...in my head..." I hum in response. *He heard a voice... In his head...* I hum louder, until he suddenly shoves my shoulder. "I'm being serious, Liam."

"Well, what did the voice say to you?" I ask.

He scratches the back of his head. "It was telling me an address, I think."

"Did you search the address?"

He nods. "It's some random building in Chicago."

My eyes narrow. "Do you think it could have been your imagination?"

Gray pulls his hair back from his face, giving it a hard tug. "I don't know. I could have just imagined it..."

I don't believe it's a coincidence. Or his imagination. But I don't want him freaking out right before the game. He can't afford to be getting scared right now.

"When did you hear it?"

"This morning."

I clench my fist, tapping his arm with my knuckles. "Why didn't you say anything until now?"

He shrugs. "I didn't know what it was at first. I wanted to try and figure it out myself." He blows out a loud breath, running his hands down his face.

I bite my tongue from saying something I shouldn't, and instead go with, "I'm sure it's nothing." The lie leaves a bad taste in my mouth, and when I clap him on the back, zaps of pain shoot through my palm. I don't like the pressure that's building in my chest from brushing this off. Whatever he's hearing is probably connected to these weird powers he has. But hopefully whatever it is can wait. We need his head in the game tonight.

Coach is already rallying the team around him, going over the plays once more. I slip out of the locker room when Gray focuses on Coach's instructions, making my way over to the stands. But when I see my father sitting on one of the middle benches, mom fussing over something in her bag beside him, I make a sharp turn and head for the food stall.

I grab a Hercules—I'm actually surprised that they have the apple flavour—and when I see the red and gold striped popcorn bag, my hand reaches for it without thought. When I turn back towards the gym after I've paid, I bump into a short girl. Her curly electric blue hair is a damn statement if I've ever seen one. She stumbles back slightly, her eyes droopy and her dark skin flushed. A ginger kid throws his arm out to brace her, his eyes narrowed on me.

"Sorry, didn't realise you were behind me."

When the girl glances up at me, I think she is going to say that it's fine, but her eyebrows frown and her nose scrunches. "Yeah, well how about you be a bit more aware. Just because you're good looking doesn't mean you get to barge into people."

I stare back at her. "What?"

She wags her finger at me. "I'm on to you, mister. You're not getting my number, so just forget it."

Who the hell is this chick? She must be here to support the Maverick team, because there is no chance that I wouldn't have seen her around school. Her neon blue afro curls bounce as she thrusts her hip to the side, the ginger-haired guy behind her smiling like he has seen all of this before. My reaction must be a common one.

"Uh, okay." I try to walk around them, but the ginger

throws his arm out in front of me.

The girl takes a step towards me. "Since I've got you here, stud, I've got two questions for you."

Who calls people 'stud'?

I breathe out a sigh and point down the hall. "Bathrooms are that way," I flick my finger to the gym hall, "and the gym is that way."

The girl rolls her eyes. She has really long eyelashes. "Not my question." A shiver runs through her body, and she hunches forward. *She looks ready to hurl.*

I take a step back, my nose curling. "Seriously, restrooms are just around that corner."

She waves her hand at the ginger when he leans towards her with his hands out. When she rights herself, her eyes narrow on me. Her dark skin is washed out now, and her forehead's sweaty. *I swear, if this girl pukes on my shoes—*

"Do you live in this town?" she strangles out.

I give her and the guy an eyeful. "Why do you ask?"

She peeks up at Ginger before glancing back to me. "Because it has to do with my second question."

Usually I would just walk off without answering or tell her to shove it. But the only place I have to go is the stands, where my father is waiting.

"Yes, I live here," I breathe out a loud sigh.

She nods her head, her blue curls bouncing. "Then, have you seen anything...*strange*...around here lately?"

My heart clenches. I don't mean for it to, but something must show on my face, because Ginger's eyes narrow on me again. "Lots of strange things happen all the time. You'll need to be more specific." They look young—probably my age—so they couldn't be dangerous. *Could they? I didn't think this would happen so soon. I was hoping it wouldn't happen at all. But the fact that these strangers are asking questions is too coincidental.*

Blue didn't catch whatever look I had on my face that Ginger did, and she watches me with slightly unfocused eyes. "Strange as in...supernatural?"

My throat constricts as I squint at them. *Who the hell are these two?* "Sorry, nothing *supernatural* in Franklin." I make a point of mocking her before I calmly shuffle past, the skin on my hands tingling. He already suspects me, so I don't know if insinuating that they're crazy did much for myself. "Game's gonna start soon, so if you want a good seat, I suggest you head in." I don't want them asking others about 'strange supernatural' things and raising awareness, but if I linger it'll seem suspicious. *I'll have to keep my eye on them tonight as well.*

With the popcorn tucked under my arm, I crack open my drink and walk towards the stands. I don't look back to see if they're still watching me. The way Ginger was staring had my palms sweating. I can't rule out the possibility that they might be here searching for Gray.

Mom waves to me from the stands as my father glances down at his phone, pointedly waiting for Sawyer to come onto the court with her squad. I move slowly, my body is tense.

"Liam! Wait up," I turn to find Noodles rushing towards me. His bugged-out eyes shine behind his thick glasses as he smiles, his curly brown noodle hair bouncing on his head.

I wave, slowing down for him to catch up. I lock eyes with Doc and Sheriff behind him, and wave to them as well. The Sheriff hasn't brought up the robbery again since that time in the Principal's office, so it's been easier to breathe when he's around. Noodles bumps his shoulder against my side, nodding his head down at the popcorn tucked under my arm. "Did you get that for Fin?"

My face burns. "No. This is for me." I almost choke on my words. *Why can't I just tell him it's for Gray? Wait, why the heck did I even buy this? That jerk doesn't need to eat this trash. And we're not friends. How many times do I have to tell him?*

Noodles laughs as he walks in step with me. I watch my mom from the corner of my eye as she signals for me. My father still hasn't looked up from his phone, so I pretend I don't see her as I take another swig of my drink, following close to Noodles. My chest tightens as I walk past mom and dad.

Tonight is an important night, so I need to keep a close eye on Gray. I promised that I would be there if anything goes wrong. I need to keep my head on straight, but the heaviness in my chest doesn't dissipate no matter how many steps I take.

The Sheriff claps his hand on my shoulder. "Hey Liam. How're you going?" He has a smile on his face, but his eyes are tense for some reason. He's not wearing his uniform, but his regular clothes are too normal. Like he's happy just being a civilian sometimes. *Dad wouldn't wear something like that, even when he's home.*

He's standing close. Too close. Closer than other people get to me. Why is he in my space? Am I in his way?

"Yeah, good." Noodles is already halfway up the stands when I reply. Sheriff nods as he pulls Doc under his arm. The two of them stare back at me, their smiles matching.

Doc steps towards me and latches onto my elbow, her eyes clear and her smile brightening her face. "Let's go find some seats."

I hesitate, but her grip tightens. "It's alright if I sit with you guys?" My rub my palms over my face as I glance away. I shouldn't have asked. *I shouldn't have asked.*

What have I told you about bothering the Montgomery's?
What did you do, baby?
What did I tell you?
What's wrong with him?

Her head tilts to the side and she spins me towards the stairs, nudging me forward. "Of course, hon. You don't have to ask, Liam, you can sit with us whenever you want to."

Whenever I want to?
What have I told you about bothering the Montgomery's?
You don't have to ask, Liam.
What does she mean by that? Does she not want me to ask?
What have I told you about bothering the Montgomery's?
I won't ask again.

When we finally managed to shuffle through to the seats Noodles snagged, my eyes roam the crowds. I don't spot Blue or Ginger. I'm sure they won't pose much threat, but I can't ignore the risk.

Gripping my knee to stop my foot from tapping, I drop the popcorn and my drink at my feet. When both teams finally emerge from the locker rooms, the crowd rises to their feet and hollers as loud as they can. My gaze locks on Gray without meaning to look for him, finding his eyes sweeping the stands. When they finally land on me, his shoulders drop, and his smile beams a bright light at me.

Ugh, what is wrong with him? Why is he so damn bright all the time? What happened to the scared guy I pulled aside earlier?

I flick him the finger, which only makes him smile wider. *Jerk.*

As soon as the teams are lined up on the court, Gray's shoulders bunch up again. My eyes don't stray from him—not for a single second—as he sizes up his opponent and shakes his hands out at his sides. We're sitting higher up on the stands than I'm used to, but I'll jump over every head in front of me if I need to. I need to come up with a contingency plan in the meantime.

From the corner of my eye, Coach paces up and down along the bench, his hands gripping the clipboard behind his back. He worries his hand over his bald head as the teams get into their positions. The referee steps forward with the ball, Spanner and that smoker-guy from Maverick poised at the centre.

The crowd goes eerily silent for the seconds leading up to the ref tossing the ball. They erupt into deafening cheer when the shrill blow of the whistle sounds and Spanner swats the ball to Milo. My eyes don't leave Gray as he weaves between the guys on the court.

Watching him play is an entirely different experience to playing beside him. I'm calculating where he will move right before he does, studying the fluid way his body bends around others on the court.

He doesn't make an avid play for the ball, but he's always nearby. Coach is shouting—I can see his arms waving the clipboard around—but I can't hear him over the crowd. Gray starts to move faster, and it takes him until halfway through the first half to pull forward in front of his partner. *I can't let him get caught. I can't.*

Lia—

Pinching my thigh, I pull myself out of it. *Not here, not now.*

Don't think of that shit now.

Gray calls for the ball, but he's moving too slow, and his guard blocks the pass. His guard is glued to him, and our team's getting frustrated. Winning this game will take us to the Championships, and Gray is bombing our only chance.

Milo tries passing him the ball again, but he doesn't even hold his hands up to catch it, and it sails right past him into the other team's hands.

I'm already shoving pasted Doc and the Sheriff, and everyone else sitting in our row. I don't bother with my manners as I break onto the side of the court. *He's gonna start freaking out. He'll drop his clothes any second now if he continues to spiral.*

"Coach, call a timeout." I pant out, my eyes following Gray. He's disorientated, fumbling around on the court, and Spanner's shouting at him to get his shit together.

Coach turns to me, his frown deeply embedded deep on his face. "What?"

"Call a timeout!" Coach doesn't need to ask why I'm telling him to pause the game, and he doesn't waste time deliberating his decision. Holding his hands up to form a 'T', he hollers to the ref. The whistle blows and I take off across the court towards Gray. He watches me as I approach, his eyes bright red. I hear mumbles across the court and the stands as I latch onto Gray's arm and yank him towards the locker room.

"Liam, *I'm sorry*. I—"

"Just come with me," is all I can scrape out. My heart is in my throat and my nose burns. *What if someone saw him phasing? I saw it happen because I knew what I was looking for, but what if someone else noticed as well? What if those two from earlier saw? I couldn't see them in the stands, but they might be watching from somewhere else.* He stumbles behind me as I drag him out the back door towards the car park. The icy air cuts through my chest, and my skin prickles.

"Liam, what are you—?" I drop to the ground and grab a handful of dirt before slapping it against his skin, rubbing hard. He tries to swat me away, his nostrils flaring. "What are you—?"

"It's the only thing I can think of right now." I try to lift the shoulder strap of his uniform and rub in the dirt that I have left in my hands, but he grabs my wrist. His eyes are hard as I stare back, and his lips are drawn in a tight line.

"Liam, why are you rubbing *dirt* on me?"

I sigh, glancing up at the sky as I take in a long breath. "You don't phase through the ground."

He nods slowly. "Yeah, so?"

"It's not like you don't phase through flat surfaces, otherwise you wouldn't fall through your bedroom floor. So it has to do with the earth or something."

He nods slowly, his mind trying to make sense of it. "So you think rubbing *dirt* on me will stop me phasing through things?"

"I think it *might*." I squeeze my eyes shut as I take another deep breath. *Why the hell is my heart pounding so damn hard?* "You're freaking yourself out on that court, but you can handle it—this is just a precaution." I drop the handful of dirt and grip his shoulder, leveling him with a hard stare of my own. "Whenever that ball comes your way, you will *catch it*, okay? You're not allowed to think that you won't, or you can't. Just picture my voice in your head, okay? *You will catch it*."

CHAPTER
16

"I don't know what the hell you did, but you saved our asses," Coach mutters, his eyes wide as we follow Gray's movements. He's playing like normal now—no, he's still playing differently. *Better* than normal. He's got a drive in him that's not usually there.

"Just gave him a good dose of reality." *Kind of.* I don't know why, but watching his pupils dilate when I was touching him stirred something weird in my chest. It was all weird, but thinking over it more and more, it didn't feel like a *bad* weird. Despite that, it seems to have worked. He's playing a lot more confidently now.

I peek my head up at the stands, and I find the Sheriff is still watching me. So is my father. But while the Sheriff looks like he's trying to piece something together, dad looks *angry*. The terrifying kind of angry that has me turning back to the game.

What did I tell you about bothering the Montgomery's?

Well, Gray isn't technically a Montgomery—

Were you bothering Finch?

Not now. Don't do this now.

Coach nods his head, his lips pushed out as he stews over something. "You two are gettin' along better."

I shake my head, my hands shaking at my sides. I quickly tuck them into my hoodie, out of sight. "He's still a jerk."

Coach rolls his eyes. "Yeah, yeah."

The last eight minutes of the first half fly by as I watch him play, only stopping when the whistle blows. Gray's hair brushes forward and back, covering his eyes then falling past his ears. His mouth is parted as he rakes in every breath, and his skin is shiny. *Has he always looked that good playing ball?*

Definitely not. That was a weird thought.

Gray manages to close the point gap, leaving Maverick only three points ahead. But they're fired up as well now. The smoker from the Maverick keeps glancing at me throughout the half, so I flick him the finger when I catch his eye. He starts towards me, his face so red I think he might explode, but someone from his team grabs his arm and pulls him towards their Coach.

The team surrounds us, grabbing their bottles and spraying the water into their mouths. They stink like nothing else, and they're sweating buckets as they try to catch their breath. My fingers drum against my side, itching to feel the rough ball in my palms. Gray bumps his shoulder against mine when he catches me making evil eyes at the red-face Maverick player. "That guy's a dick."

I stand close, my eyes watching his shoulders rise and fall. *Why the hell am I staring at his damn shoulders?* I tap the back of my hand against his, glancing around to make sure no one is listening. "How're you doing?"

He nods, his smile wide. "It's working. I haven't phased through anything."

It was a fluke idea, but I'll take it. *If it helps keep his head on out there, I'll lather as much dirt on him as I need to.*

"Listen up, boys," Coach brings them in to form a circle around him, and Gray pulls me with him when I try to step back. My cheeks burn, but I let him drag me in without a fuss. "Whatever happened at the start of the game..." If looks could kill, Gray would be six feet deep from the glare Coach shoots his way, "is behind us. You guys have made a great come back. Now close that gap and take the lead. You're all much better players than those losers." The team laughs at Coach's pep talk. I'm not sure if he's supposed to say that. "Hands in."

The team puts their hands in the centre, and once again Gray grips my fingers and thrusts my hand into the centre with his. My entire face is hot now. *Why is he holding my hand? Why the hell are his fingers so soft?*

"Franklin on three," Spanner shouts, his eyes sweeping the circle of the team. They are all dripping in sweat and excitement, their eyes wide with adrenaline. When his eyes meet mine, he gives me a nod. He counts us in, and we all shout "*Franklin!*"

The ref toots his whistle and both teams flood back onto the court. My eyes follow Gray, drifting over his sweaty shoulders. I move to tell him but catch myself at the last second. If I don't tell him the dirt's gone, maybe he won't notice.

He bends his knees, his eyes locked on the ball. He's in game mode again. And I've seen that look before. Out of the corner of my eye, I see Coach's mouth pull up in a sick smile.

The ref blows his whistle loud and long this time, throwing the ball up between Smokey and Spanner. This time Red-Face tips it, smacking it to their side of the court. But Gray already predicted it. He intercepts it and dribbles the ball to the hoop before Maverick has even realised, they didn't snatch the ball after all.

Gray is a menace on the court. He doesn't stop, he doesn't slow, and he doesn't phase. He catches every pass and makes every basket. The team is buzzing as they pass the ball. They're all taking bolder shots on the hole, spurred on by Gray's tenacity.

Maverick's getting desperate now as they make any play for the ball. Their technique is out the window at this point, and their coach is screaming for a time out. The ref blows his whistle, and Maverick huddles up around their coach, but our team stays out on the court. Gray gives everyone a clap on the back, his narrow eyes wider than normal as he draws in loud, laboured breaths. His mind is nowhere near the stuff he's been dealing with these past few weeks. He's completely absorbed in the game.

Maverick doesn't carry any confidence as they walk back onto the court. A lot of them are muttering to each other, their eyes on Gray, probably planning on shutting him down.

Idiots. It's not like he's not the only great player on our team.

As I thought, the ref's whistle blows and everyone lingers around Gray, all guarding him unnecessarily. So I watch as Gray lingers back, and the rest of the team take centre stage. The team are sweating buckets, but they don't relent. They steal the ball, they shoot threes, they carry it to the hoop.

I can tell the guys are enjoying the applause. It's deafening now, almost busting my eardrums. But it has my skin tingling and my scarred palms sweating. We're going to the Championships.

My eyes catch Red's gaze. He spoke to Gray earlier, but whatever Gray said seemed to have pissed him off. Glancing up at the score board, we're almost twenty points ahead now, and there are only seconds left on the clock.

We're going to the Championships.

I almost can't hold myself back from the court before the final buzzer sounds. The crowd *screams* our victory, and the team runs at each other with huge smiles on their faces. Coach laughs behind me as I run in and jump on Milo's back.

"We're going to the Championships!" I holler, and they shout back their glory. My face is hurting from smiling so damn hard. *When did I start smiling?* It feels more like I've been smiling for hours. My eyes sweep the team as they huddle in, their faces sweaty and red and relieved.

The team huddles around Spanner and make absolute fools of themselves by trying to lift him up. We might be strong, but that guy is pure muscle—he's not getting anywhere off the ground.

When I don't immediately see Grey, my blood runs cold. *Where is he?*

I catch Gray glancing around for something as everyone swarms him. When his eyes land on me...there's something about his gaze that screams '*what the hell do I do?*' and I freeze. *He's blinking fast. Is that supposed to be morse code or something?* He pushes through the suffocating crowd and escapes to the locker room. I slide off Milo's back, giving him a quick bump on the shoulder as I go to follow after Gray.

"Liam!" I turn to the sound of my mom's voice, and my

spine stiffens when I see my father standing next to her. He's giving me a weird look, like he can't figure something out, so I don't make eye contact, instead staring at mom's shoulder. "You didn't sit with us, sweetie..."

The fact that she sounds upset has my stomach twisting in knots. *Is my father going to say something again? Is he going to get mad?* I still don't look.

"Sorry, mom." It comes out as a whisper, but I think she hears me over the ruckus of the audience and the team. "Gray needed me, and I—"

My chest *burns* when my father scoffs at that. That noise. It sounds over and over in my ears like it's stuck on repeat. My heart beats *hard* in my chest. *Is it going to break my ribs? Why is it so hard to breathe?*

"It's alright, sweetie," she quickly adds, her gaze flickering to my father for a brief moment. I don't think she means to dig my grave any deeper.

"I'm gonna celebrate the win with the team tonight," I choke out, my gaze rooted to her shoulder. She nods her head and moves closer to wrap her arms around me. I know she's trying to comfort me, but the embrace feels cold and empty. Or maybe that's me. *Is that my fault?* My arms stay limp at my sides until she finally lets go.

"Mom! Dad! Did you like the routine we did during half-time?" Sawyer comes bounding over with her pompoms, the crispy rubbing sound echoing in my ears. *She performed during half time?*

I don't look—I *can't*—but I know my father's face lights up when Sawyer joins us. "Of course we did, honey. You were amazing out there."

Those words don't sound like something he would say.

They sound fake in my ears.

I don't want to be here. Not here.

I rush off in the direction of the locker room. The rest of the team is migrating there as well, letting the audiences' cheers lull as they start to gather their things.

Noodles suddenly pops out of nowhere, my popcorn and Hercules in either hand. "Hey, you didn't come back for these." His glasses make his eyes look wider than they really are, but the smile reaffirms his excitement. "I can't believe you guys are going to go to the Championships!"

The heaviness in my chest already starts to alleviate when he reminds me. I take the crinkly bag and energy drink, nodding my head. "Thanks Noodles. Can you let your folks know that Gray and I are gonna go out with the team to celebrate?" I assume we are, but I need to go and check on him. *Something was definitely wrong with him before.*

He gives me a weird look. "Yeah, sure. You gonna crash at ours tonight?"

Why would he ask that? I shrug my shoulders, unsure how to answer. "I'm gonna go find Gray." He nods, his limp curls bouncing against his forehead.

I need to find Gray. He looked like he was about to phase.

CHAPTER

17

When I clear the crowd and make it to the lockers, I don't spot Gray amongst the team. They're all hooting and hollering, shirts off and fist-pumping. When a few of them spot me, they pull me in for sweaty bear hugs as excitement continues to explode through the room, their smiles contagious. I'm not sure why I'm careful to keep the popcorn out of their reach.

"Hey, you know where Gray went?" I ask Hair when I catch his eye.

He gives me a strange look as I pull his attention away from the team's shouts of victory. He throws his thumb over his shoulder, indicating to the back door leading outside. "He bailed out the back."

I clap him on the back, the sensitive skin on my hand tingling. "Thanks man. Congrats on the win."

His eyes light up and taps his knuckles against my shoulder. "We'll *all* be playing at the Championships, man!"

We'll all *be playing at the Championships.*

I get to play. I get to play one more game this season.

I'm not done yet.

When I give the rest of the team a shout, they respond with a deafening cheer that has my ears ringing. I push their sweaty bodies out of the way as I head to the back entrance leading out to the carpark.

It's darker now. I struggle to see far in the shadows, the only light nearby is the car park lights. A lot of the crowd lingers around their cars, all shouting about the game. There's heaving panting from around the corner, and I approach without question. My heart pounds hard against my ribs and my throat swells as I find Gray hunched over the brick wall, his arms covering his face from view.

"What are you doing out here? You should—" He reaches out and covers my mouth with his clammy hand and grips my bicep with the other, pressing my back against the brick. His nostrils flare as his chest heaves. He's still wearing his game shirt, his forehead damp. His gym bag sits at his feet, half open.

"I'm—" his voice is rough, like he's been punched in the throat. *What's going on with him?*

"*Do you need more dirt?*" My words are muffled by his palm. He doesn't move it, his head tilting when his eyes drift over my face. His arms are shaking, his grip tightening when I try to shift my weight. When I look back at him, he looks deranged.

"*What's wrong?*" Still muffled. Gray's pupils dilate as he bares his teeth. When he shakes his head, he finally moves his hand from my mouth. The cold air hits my skin where his hand had been, and goosebumps break out across my arms. His skin burns everywhere he touches me. His big hands grip my arms tighter as he moves forward to rest his forehead against the brick wall above me. *Freakin' giant*

159

getting in my space. When I look up, his mouth is pinched in a tight line, the corners of his eyes creasing. Even in the dark, I can see how red his cheeks are against his usually pale skin.

"Are you going to hurl?" Gray shakes his head, the skin of his forehead scraping against the rough wall. "What's up? Why are you—?"

"Thank you for earlier," he mumbles under his breath.

This jerk has a really weird way of showing his appreciation. "It's fine. Gotta make sure you keep your clothes on in front of an innocent crowd." I joke.

He's silent for a while. He doesn't move, and his breathing doesn't really settle. "I promised myself I would do something if we won...promise you won't hate me for it."

I tilt my head when Gray moves back to stare at me. He has a confusing look on his face, I can't tell what he's thinking. His breath is warm as it blows across my face. Something inside me is warming the same way it did when I was over at his house the other night. Like *he's* warming something inside me. "I won't hate you any more than I already do."

He laughs at that. It's a quiet laugh, like he expected that response. It rumbles in his chest, sending vibrations through his hands into my body.

Does he have a new power or something? That felt...different...

When he doesn't move, I tilt my head back to get a better look at his face. *I swear if this jerk throws up on me—*

He tugs me up, and my body goes stiff when he swoops down and captures my mouth with his. The side of his nose brushes mine. His hair flops forward, tickling my forehead. My heart melts into a slush of magma, incinerating my insides. I'm not sure if I'm breathing right now.

Gray...he's...

I think I should be freaking out, but instead I'm thinking about how soft his lips are. *They're softer than his hands. Have I noticed that before?* I've certainly never felt them before. But now they're pressing against mine, *hard*.

Why is Gray's kissing me? Is this a new superpower or something? Wait, that doesn't make sense. His lips move, and I try to suck in any air that I can, but he presses closer. *Why do they feel softer now? Why am I not freaking out?* I definitely should be.

Gray presses me back against the bricks, the coarse stone catching on the threads of my hoodie. The scratching sound echoes in my ears, making everything else loud as well. *Holy crap, he's breathing loudly. How is he breathing? Why can't I breathe but he can?*

Bracing my forearm against his chest, I shove him back. I stare at him with prickling eyes and tingling lips. His sleepy eyes follow me, his mouth red. *Why am I looking at his mouth?*

"Wh-What are you d-doing?" *Why would he kiss me? Why would he? I don't get him.* Leaning forward against my arm, Gray stares back with hard eyes. *Has he always looked at me that way?*

No, I've never seen that look before.

"Kissing you."

"Why?" *Kissing...you kiss people you like. People that you want to—*

"Because I want to."

Because I want to.

I don't...What does that even mean, coming from him?

"Liam..." He leans forward again, his inky hair flopping over his eyes and I just stare back at him because he said my name and I don't know what to say back. I stare because what the hell else am I supposed to do?

He's so close, and when I don't turn away, when I don't tell him to back off, he presses his lips to mine again. Slowly. Softly. Giving me the chance to stop him. But I don't. I'm stuck there, rooted in place, my eyes wide as I try to figure out why. And in a split second, he's sucked all the air back out of me.

This is weird. Definitely weird. But it's weirder that I don't hate it. Is this what kissing a girl would be like? Somehow, I don't think a girl's lips could be this...nice. Gray always has to be better at everything, probably even at kissing.

His lips move slowly, prompting me. *Is he showing me that he's the better kisser between us? Is that what he's doing? Of course it is, the freakin' jerk.* I push my head forward and try to move my lips. *He's not going to be better at this than me too.*

He must know what I'm doing because he doesn't back down. Pushing back, Gray's lips move faster against mine, yet still just as slow as before. My heart pounds loudly in my chest. My fingertips throb as I breathe into his mouth. I open my mouth against his, but he surprises me when something wet touches my tongue. I try to jerk back, but Gray moves his hand to the back of my head, holding me steady.

My hands are shaking between us now. I'm not sure what to do with them. When his tongue touches mine again, my fingers latch onto his uniform, scrunching the material. My lungs are burning for air again, my mouth gasping like a fish out of water. His air fills my chest, setting my insides on fire.

When he pulls away, my lips go cold in an instant. My mouth is numb, tingles spreading over my face. His breath brushes against my top lip, blowing hot air against the swollen skin. When I open my eyes, he has that sleepy look on his face again. He's panting now, hands clenching tighter around my arms. *Has he always been this close to me? I swear it didn't used to be like this. He's in my space. He's too close. Why is he so close?*

Were you bothering Finch?

I don't—

"Why weren't you breathing?" Gray's voice is rougher than before. His lips are slightly parted, his brows frowning down at me.

I clear my throat, my brain fuzzy. *He's too close.* "Cause you weren't letting me, jerk."

"Breathe through your nose."

Oh, yeah.

His laugh is breathless, careful not to break whatever bubble we're in right now. I'm hyper-aware of every sound. Gray releases his hold on me, and my arms drop down to my sides. When he closes his eyes for a long moment, whatever spell he had me under is broken. I blink hard and take a long breath, my chest burning. *That has to be a superpower or something.*

What is he thinking right now? I'm not looking at his face anymore, my eyes locked on his uniform number. The silence between us is deafening. *Why isn't he saying anything? How does he have nothing to say right now? Does he not know what to say—*

"Liam, look at me."

I can't. Why would he do that? Doesn't he think—

Were you bothering Finch?

Why can't I breathe? He's too close. He's still too close. Taking up all the air.

Because I want to.

Were you bothering Finch?

Has he done that before? Does he pull others aside and kiss them because he wants *to?* My skin still tingles as I bite down hard on my lip. My blood is pumping through my ears so loud I wonder whether he can hear it. *He doesn't have that superpower, does he?*

"Liam." His voice is different now. I squeeze my eyes shut when they burn, dropping down into a crouch and covering my head with my hands. *I can't breathe, damn it.*

Can't breathe can't breathe can't breathe.

He didn't. He didn't want to. He was grateful, grateful that I helped him. That makes sense. I helped him, that's why. He's grateful. That's why he's so close, why he kissed me. Why he's looking at me like that.

Were you bothering Finch?

Look at what you did.

Stop crying.

Look at what you did.

"Shit. Liam, *look at me.*"

"I can't." *Is that my voice? I don't even remember now. He's too close.*

Close, close, close.

"I'm sorry."

My heart stills for a moment; the same moment that the air lodges in my throat. My skin freezes over and my nails bite into my scalp.

He's sorry. He didn't mean it.

Were you bothering Finch?

Look at what you did.

What did I tell you?

"I'm sorry, Liam. I won't do it again—I promise. Please calm down. Just *breathe*." His hands try to tug mine away from my head. He's sorry again.

I won't do it again.

I won't do it again.

I'm sorry, Liam. I won't do it again.

It's still there. The tingling on my lips. It's a constant buzz now. *Why won't it go away?* My head's getting dizzier, my lungs screaming for air.

"Listen to my voice, okay? Count with me, *alright*?" His voice cuts through the fog. I pull back, my eyes blurry as I try to focus on his face. *He's still too close. So close...warm...he's warm. His hands...they're holding my face. When did he—?* "One..."

By the time he reaches nine things are clearer. My lungs are on fire, but the cold air fills my chest. My muscles ache and seize, my shoulders hunching slightly. Gray's smiling now. His eyes aren't sleepy anymore, they're dark and squinting. His hands are warm against my cheeks.

Every sound starts to dull, and the blood slowly stops thumping hard in my ears. He keeps smiling, his shining eyes almost black. "That's it." His thumb moves against my cheekbone, the heat from his hands soaking into my skin.

My eyes move to my hands, clutching at his forearms. I stare at them, willing my fingers to uncurl, but their grip doesn't break. *Why can't I move my hands?* They're aching so badly from how tight I'm holding onto him.

"Let go," I mumble, but he hears me. His smile falters and his eyes droop, but he drops his hold and my hands fall away. Gray leans back, his eyes trained on me as I focus on calming my racing heart.

"Liam?" I don't look up when he calls my name. I don't think I can ever look him in the eye again. My body's sapped, and my head is heavy. I just want to go home and sleep. "Liam, are you—?"

"*Don't, Gray.*" *Forget this. Forget what just happened. Don't stare at me with that pathetic look. Don't pity me. Don't.*

His eyebrows drop down, his forehead creasing. I've nearly got my bearings when he steps closer. "Don't '*don't*' me, Liam. I'm not letting you—"

"I said *don't*, Gray!" I shout, my heartbeat pounding in my throat. *Leave me alone. Don't look at me.* I climb to my feet, my legs wobbling, and shove my hands inside my hoodie pocket when I notice how badly they're shaking. *Get it together, Liam. Get it—*

Look what you did.

Were you bothering Finch?

I won't do it again.

Whatever it is, it's his problem to deal with.

Home. I should go home. I try to walk away but he reaches down and snags my wrist. He scoops up his gym bag with his other hand, the popcorn bag sitting on top of his gym towel—I don't even remember when I dropped it—and starts pulling me away from the building in the opposite direction.

"*Let go.*" He ignores me.

My mind is still trying to play catch up as he leads us to

the car park, pulling me towards his car. He fishes around in his bag for his keys as he asks. "Is your family expecting you home tonight?" I shake my head, so Gray continues to drag me towards the passenger door of his car. When he drops his hold on me and rounds the car to the driver's side, he notices that I've made no effort to climb in. He presses his palm against the roof of the car. "Liam, get in the car."

When I look up at him, his eyes are narrowed and shadowed by his hair. His lips are pulled in a tight line, his jaw tense. I shake my head. "No."

He presses both hands against the roof now. "*Liam*—"

"I'm going home." I turn away from his car, finally noticing how empty the car park is now. I don't see mom or dad's car. *I'll walk. I just need to*—

"Please don't go yet."

I hesitate. My heart hasn't stopped thumping since Gray kissed me. *Why can't I calm down? And why hasn't my damn mouth stopped tingling?* When I turn back, there's something different about him. Something sincere, and raw, that's afraid of something.

Please don't go yet.

So many voices in my head. *I'm sick of them. So sick of them.*

"I won't touch you. I won't ever touch you again, if that's what you want, if that keeps you here. I'm sorry, I didn't mean to scare you..." He yanks his hair back from his forehead, his eyes red. He looks away as he takes a deep breath, before he focuses on me again. "I promise it won't happen again."

Turning slowly, my eyes finally meet his over the roof of the car, and my heart leaps into my throat. *He'll never do it again...*

Nodding my head, I turn back to his car. *"Fine."*

The smell of salty caramel violates my nose as soon as I climb inside. Peeking over into the backseat, I find a hoard of empty red and gold striped popcorn packets. *This guy has a real problem with this stuff.* I don't know where he's driving me when he takes a different turn, but the car is warm, so I won't complain just yet. The cold always makes me so damn tense.

"Do you want me to turn the heat up?"

My fists clench. "Why?" *Was he reading my mind just now? The bloody jerk.*

He keeps his eyes on the road, both hands on the wheel. He's gripping it tightly, his knuckles pale. "I know you hate the cold."

I glare at him. "Since when did you start caring about that kind of stuff?" Thinking about the time we've spent together, I try to pinpoint when things started to change. *When what he said actually started to matter to me. We haven't been friends for years, so why does all of this matter now?*

When I turn to look at him, his eyes are narrowed, and his brows are low. His gaze flickers to me very few seconds, but he keeps his focus ahead. "I've always cared."

This jerk. "I don't expect you to know *anything* about me, Gray. Don't tell me you have always cared." *Why are my fingers numb?* "You don't get it because you live with a perfect family. Your aunt and uncle are awesome, and your cousins don't over-shadow you. They don't think you're pathetic, or a *bother*. I just need to get out of Franklin. Then things will be different..."

They will. When I'm gone, things will be better.

My jaw aches from how hard I'm biting down on

nothing, "But then you go and develop freakin' superpowers. How the hell can I compete with that?" My chest heaves hard, my eyes and nose burning, so I lean back against my seat and cover my face with my arm. "You are the most frustrating person in my life, you know that? Because of you, nothing I do is worth anything."

"Liam—"

"Shut up! Do you know how annoying your voice is? Even your voice is so freakin' perfect. And how the hell am I supposed to grow any taller than you? You're a stupid giant!" *I'll never be taller than him. The jerk.*

"Liam, enough."

I drop my arm back down to my leg and glare at him. He's shifted to face his body towards me, the collar of his uniform shirt hanging low on his chest. *What the hell? Why is it so low? Is he trying to seduce me or something? That's how a guy would do it, right? Wait, why do I think he's trying to seduce me?*

Were you bothering Finch?

Whatever it is, it's his problem to deal with.

Not Finch's problem. I'm not Finch's problem to deal with.

"We're *not* friends. So just pretend none of it happened, *alright*?" It's a struggle to get the words past the enormous lump in my throat, but I manage to sound stronger than I feel.

Not friends, not friends, not friends.

He leans back into his seat, nodding. "Yeah, let's do that." The word sounds weak. But when I look up at him, he's teeth flash down through his hesitant smile. "Let's go get something to eat. I'm dying for a burger."

Something inside *me* is dying too.

CHAPTER

18

My heart is still beating erratically in my chest as we climb out of his car. It's been a long time since I've been to the diner.

"I think the last time I was here was when I was ten," I murmur, my eyes staring up at the big neon sign. My eyes droop as I struggle to stay awake. *Did he suck all the energy out of me or something? Does he have a new superpower?*

Gray's head tilts to the side, his mouth stretched out in an unhappy line. "How is that even possible? I see your family here *all* the time."

Something in my chest zaps again. It's like they live a life completely separate from mine. I shrug my shoulders, but his face crumples. "Liam—"

"Just *stop*." I whisper as I follow him into the diner, my gaze falling where Cook's sitting at the bar. When the bell above the door rings, his wife, Happy, glances up from her notebook, her eyes locking on Gray and me. A huge smile pulls her red lips back, flashing her large teeth.

She squeals, throwing her arms up. "Congratulations on the win, honey buns!" She rushes around the counter to give

Gray a big hug and a kiss on the cheek. "You little giant, you! Your team has already done the rounds of informing those who couldn't get the night off." She gives him one last squeeze, before her eyes swivel to me. "Liam Rice, that you, hon?"

I nod slowly, my eyes half open. "Yeah. Hi, Happy."

"Nuh-uh, none of that, honey! I know you have trouble remembering names, but you still remember mine. It's 'Georgie', or you walk right back out that door." She shoves Gray aside and pulls me in for a bone crushing hug, the warm smell of pastries and black coffee flooding my nostrils as she cushions me against her plump body.

She knows? How does she know? My fingers pluck at the skin of my thighs. *Why would she...*

When she pulls back, she's still smiling. So *happy*. "Let me get a good look at you, now." She grips my biceps and twists my body from side to side, my face burning from the scrutiny. Gray watches the two of us, the same weirdness in his eyes. "Hmm, you grew up nice and strong, didn't ya' hon?"

Strong? I stare back at her. *I'm not strong. I'm not...*

Her smile softens around the edges. "You look like you need a little lovin'." She turns on Gray, pointing a menacing finger his way. "You better be takin' *good* care of him, Finch Gray."

Him taking care of me? What is that supposed to mean?

My mind flashes back to when he kissed me against the bricks of the school building, and my face burns even hotter than before. The tingling on my lips morphs into a buzz.

We're forgetting about that. Pretending that nothing happened.

I'm sorry, Liam. I won't do it again.

He won't. He won't do that again.

"Working on it, Georgie." Gray winks at me, earning a chuckle from Cook.

My eyes flicker over to the old man to see he's spun around in his chair to face us. He nods his head in our direction. "Heard about the game. Good job tonight, kid." He beacons Gray over, pulling him in for a hug and a clap on the back. His dark skin is wrinkled from years of running this diner, but his spirit is as kind and lively as I remember. Georgie's eyes are surrounded by age lines and spots, but her smile hasn't faded either.

"Thanks, Maurie. Is it okay if we sit in my booth?" Gray throws his thumb over his shoulder, his eyes flickering to me.

Georgie nods her head, patting my back gently. "Go ahead, hon. I'll be over in a sec for your order." She smiles as she nudges me in Gray's direction, so I follow him to the booth at the end of the diner. It's a quiet night, but I assume it's because everyone's celebrating somewhere. Spanner is probably hosting a party in honour of the win.

Sliding into the bench seat across from him, I pick up the menu. "Do they still do those stuffed triple stacks? I got a craving for something sweet." I all but stare a hole through the menu. In the car, Gray couldn't watch me like he is now. I'm pretty sure he hasn't blinked yet.

Gray stares at his hands on the table top, his eyes wide and strained. "I think we need to talk about what happened—"

My stomach clenches. *What happened to pretending nothing happened?* "Anyway, there were some suspicious people who came up to me before the game tonight."

Don't talk about it.

He breathes out a long sigh. He knows what I'm doing, but it doesn't argue his point. "What do you mean suspicious?"

"Her hair was bright blue, and his was ginger."

He stares back, not fully understanding where I am taking this conversation. His top lip pulls up at the side. "The colour of their hair doesn't make them suspicious, Liam."

"They asked me if I've noticed anything *strange* going on..."

Gray perks up at that. "What?"

I nod. "It was a bit *too* coincidental, given everything that has been going on these last few weeks with us."

With us.

With him. Him. I meant him. Everything that has been going on with Gray.

"What did you say?"

I shrug, covering my flaming cheeks with the collar of my hoodie. *Why won't my heart just slow down already?* "Told them that I didn't know what they were talking about, but I'm not sure they believed me."

"Do you think they're bad news?" His nails tap anxiously on the tabletop. Without thinking, I rest my hand on top of his to stop the sound echoing in my ears. He jerks back when he feels the rough blisters of my scorched palms, and the pressure in my chest bears down. I curl my hands into fists and move to pull it back, but he grips my wrist and says, "Wait, I'm sorry, I didn't mean to do that."

Slowly, he turns my palms face up, his fingertips tracing over the raised lines of my scars. They're still fleshly, but they aren't raw anymore. *They're probably going to look like this for the rest of my life.*

My heart stutters at his touch. He trails his fingers over the marred skin, his eyes following. I gnaw at the inside of my cheek as his fingers clench around my wrist a little tighter. I clear my throat. *Not a big deal, Liam. Guys touch. It's okay. It's normal. We're still not friends.* "I couldn't be sure. The girl didn't seem intimidating, and the guy didn't say anything, but he was observant. He knew something was up the minute I hesitated."

He's watching me closely now, his finger still brushing circles into my palm. "It's alright, Liam. I'm sure it will be fine." I pull my hand back when I hear footsteps approaching, my head spinning. *What's wrong with me? Why am I letting him touch me so much? Why is he touching me so much—*

Didn't happen. We're pretending it didn't happen.

Happy stops at the end of our booth, her smile sweet as she holds her notebook out with her pen ready. "Alright honey-buns, you want your usual?" she asks Gray, who replies with a nod. When she turns to me, her eyes shimmer. "And what can I get you, sugar?"

I glance down when she holds eye contact, instead staring at the pen she's holding. "Uh, if you still do the triple stack—"

"Stuffed with strawberry sauce?" She chuckles behind her notepad. "You and your sister are like two peas-in-a-pod."

Something bitter slides over my tongue. "Is that what Sawyer usually orders?"

"Only every Sunday morning your family stops in for

breakfast. It's nice to finally see your face around here, sugar. You gonna stop being so stubborn and join them for breakfast sometime soon?"

Stubborn? Me? Join them? My vision starts to dome, before stretching again. *It's so hot in here.*

It was an innocent question. She just wants to know. It wasn't supposed to hurt. Not this much. "Maybe," I scrape out. *I won't. He won't bring me with them. They never do. They never will. I'm—*

"He'll be coming here with me from now on," Gray tells her, a tight smile on his lips. I try to breathe past the suffocating lump in my throat.

He'll be coming here with me from now on.

Were you bothering Finch?

I've always cared.

"That's good to hear. You better be spoiling him, Fin, or else this mama bear's coming for you." She points to her eyes and then at Gray. "Got ma' eyes on you, honey buns. I'll be right back with your orders, boys." She flutters away, yelling something at Cook about putting his hand in the pie display.

Gray directs a sneaky smile my way. "Well, you heard it from the mama bear herself, I need to make sure you're spoilt."

I snort, the tension in my chest slowly ebbing. "You wish, pervert." Gray is about to say something, but his eyes flicker over my head when the bell rings above the door. I turn in my seat as some of the players from the Maverick team waltz in.

Red—who isn't too red-faced anymore—leads the group, sucking his teeth as he glances around the diner. When his eyes rest on Gray and me, they widen slightly. His lips curl back in a sick smile, before he follows his team to one of the empty booths down the other end of the diner.

"I gave that guy the finger earlier," I remember, shrugging my shoulders. When I turn back, Gray's lips are pinched.

"Why?"

I shrug again. "He was giving me a weird look."

Gray shakes his head at me, rubbing his mouth. I think he's trying to hide his smile. "Doesn't mean you give him the finger."

"Doesn't mean I don't."

He nods. "Touché." The other team's obnoxious laughter floods the diner, but I don't turn to look. I don't want those ugly mugs imprinted on any part of my brain. Gray glares something menacing, though.

"Hey," I snap my fingers in front of his face, drawing his attention back. "Who cares what they're doing. They lost— that's the end of it."

Gray sends another dark look in their direction, blowing out a long breath. "They're just giving me a bad feeling. Why the hell are they hanging around Franklin?"

I shrug again. "Don't know, don't care." Gray pulls out his phone to check the time, his eyes squinting. "So are you back inside yet? Or are you still falling through the floor?" He gives me the finger right as Happy wanders over with drinks. She places two glasses of soda in front of Gray and I, her eyes catching mine before I can remind her that I didn't order a drink.

"Hope you still like Cherry Coke, sugar." Her smile is warm like it was before, but it's different. I can't put my finger on why, but it has my chest tightening.

"Yeah." My voice comes out thick and wheezy. "I do."

"Anytime, hon." She reaches out to pat my cheek, her hand hot against my skin. "It's good to see you, Liam."

It's good to see you, Liam.

Good to see you, Liam.

Good to see you.

She wanders off, leaving me to figure out how to breathe again. *Why would she brother remembering that? Why would she—*

"Liam, are you alright?" Gray reaches his hand out to mine, but I pull them back onto my lap. *Don't touch me right now. I can't...*

"*Fine*," I strangle out, my eyes pinched shut. The sound of the fizzing soda is the only sound that comes from our table for a long moment as I try to steady my breathing. The air is warmer in here. Sweeter. When I open my eyes, Gray's still watching me. There's no special way that he's looking at me. He's just staring. Probably trying to figure out what's going on inside my head.

"I'm fine, Gray." I reach for the soda and take a sip, my face pinching from the sweet taste. My eyes are drooping, but the soda is helping to perk me up.

"If I asked you to call me Finch again, would you?"

The base of my spine tenses. *Why did that feel so expected?* Glancing up under my eyelashes, I find him watching me again. His straw sits between his lips—*why the hell am I looking there again?*—as his gaze flutters over my face, his hooded eyes wide and waiting. He looks like he's just stepped on a landmine, and he's waiting for it to blow his legs off.

"We're not friends, *Gray*."

His head tilts to the side. "Even if we're '*not friends*', you can still call me by my first name."

I'm silent for a moment as I try to come up with an excuse. But I can't think of a single relevant reason. "I don't know." I shrug. "I guess."

He smiles, his eyes crinkling. "Go on then."

My nose scrunches up. "I'm not gonna just say your name randomly."

"You used to call me Finch when we were kids."

I frown at him. "We're not kids anymore."

He rolls his eyes, his lips pursed. "It's often considered male etiquette to refer to your *enemies* by their last names."

"You are my—" My tongue swells, yet Finch's smile doesn't falter. But he's the reason I never win. *He's*—

We're not *friends*.

Cook suddenly appears at the end of our table, a plate of sticky sweet pancakes in one hand, and a mammoth burger with fries in the other. "Order up." He places the plates in front of us before squatting down to our eye level. "So Liam, it's been a long time. It's good ta' see ya', kid." Cook flashes his wonky smile at us, the way he always did when I was a kid. I remember being convinced he was a pirate when I was younger.

"Yeah, thanks Cook." I try to control my breathing, but it's difficult when I'm not given a second of reprieve.

He laughs. "Still have trouble with names, huh?" My cheeks burn and my eyes flicker to Gray. He's already looking at me, and the strange look is back. But before he has the chance to ask what Cook and Happy have been talking about, Cook asks, "So what's this I hear about you movin'?"

My entire body seizes. The muscles in my arms coil and tighten, snapping back and aching.

Moving?

"What are you talking about, Maurie?" Gray's gaze flickers between Cook—*Maurie*—and me, his mouth drawn in a straight line. I'm frozen in place.

I warned you.

"The Mayor was saying just the other day that you're going to live with your grandparents in Toronto soon. But won't that mess with your game?"

Going to live with your grandparents.

The Mayor was saying...

Try harder.

My entire body is frozen stiff, my fingers numb. *My father's...telling people...I'm...*

What did I tell you...

Look what you did. You bothered the neighbours.

I warned you I warned you I warned you.

The walls creep in closer, squeezing the air out of my lungs. *Close. Too close.* I scramble out of the booth and fly through the front door before I even hear Gray call my name. My eyes don't raise from the ground as I yank the handle, my body falling out into the icy cold night. *Where am I going?*

Look what you did, you did, you did.

Marnie, what happened to changing the locks?

I warned you.

I'm going to be sick. The acid's crawling up my throat, burning my nose. *Did he change the locks? I need to go home. I can't breathe.*

The rough brick scrapes against my sensitive palms, my nerves frayed, bringing me back to the surface of whatever thickness is suffocating me. I grind my sensitive palms harder against the brick, the blood rushing back to my head.

My head is pulled gently to my side, and my ear presses against something warm.

"Breathe, Liam...just breathe..."

It's...*Gray*.

At least, I think that's his voice. I can smell the lingering dirt I rubbed on him during the game, and I know it's him. *What is he doing? Why is he so close? Stop. I can't...*

His heartbeat thumps in my ear, my nose stinging. My vision starts to focus again, and the white streetlight eventually turns yellow. *Where...What happened?* His hand is brushing my head, his fingers running over my ear. He's making a sound that reminds me of waves. *Why is he so close?*

"It's alright, Liam. You're alright," he murmurs quietly, his tone soft and slow. I want to throw him off me. At least sixty percent of me does. But the other forty percent wants to grab his shirt and hold him here just a little longer. *He's so warm*. "I've got you."

I've always cared.

I need to make sure you're spoilt.

Just breathe.

I've got you.

I don't know how much time passes before my breathing is calm. My head finally stops spinning. I lean away from Gray and stare at him. His eyes have colour, and so does his skin. His cheeks are red, and his mouth is pink. His small eyes are wide, and his hair is hanging over his eyes.

I draw in a long, loud breath. "I'm—"

"You always say that you're fine," he says, his eyes sad.

"But I'm here anyway."

I nod, swallowing the lump in my throat. *Why does this keep happening around him? He keeps catching me in these moments. It's his fault. It's his fault that I'm staying out late. That I'm making my mom worry. That I'm making my father...*

Gray swipes his thumb against my eye, catching any moisture that had gathered. The gesture wipes my brain completely. "How about I go and get the food boxed and we go back to my place? You can crash in the guest bedroom."

I swallow and nod my head, slowly, my eyes staring at the hand he used to wipe my eye. *Why did he do that? Why is he—*

"I'll take you to the car first." Gray offers me his hand, giving me the choice. My stomach clenches as I glance between his hand and his face. He waits patiently, eyes soft. He's not pushing me to take his hand. He wants me to, but there's no expectation. I don't know how, but I know that's what he's telling me.

You always say that you're fine. But I'm here anyway.

I grab his hand and let him help me up, my legs wobbling under my weight. I'm so damn *tired*. He reaches out to grab my elbow and steady me, but I shake his grip off. "I can stand." The words don't come out as strong as I would like, but he doesn't coddle me. As we walk back to Gray's car, he tugs on my sleeve and hands me the car keys.

"Sit in the car and wait for me, I won't be long." He doesn't look thrilled to leave me on my own, so I wave him off. *Just because I'm tired doesn't mean I need a babysitter.*

"Yeah, yeah," I mutter, pulling the passenger door open and falling in. I rip my hoodie off when I realise how clammy my skin is and toss it into the back seat. My eyes close, but my mind refuses to give in to sleep. Instead, it's running over every word Gray has said to me tonight. His footsteps fade away, and my body grows achy and fatigued.

Footsteps accompanied by a bunch of loud mouths approach the car. There are a handful of cars parked near Gray's car, the lights turning on as the loud mouths unlock them. When I pry my eyes open, my gaze lands on Red, surrounded by five of his buddies. He spots me at the same time, his mouth pulled up in a dark way. A shiver runs down my spine at the gross look he's giving me.

"What happened to your boyfriend, huh?" He calls out, his eyes thin. His hair is greased back like someone out of an eighty's movie. *What decade does this guy think we live in?* I give him the finger because that's apparently the way I communicate with this guy. *Gray and I aren't even friends. What a ridiculous taunt.* His eyes narrow to slits, his tongue smacking as he sucks his top teeth. *Gross.* "You got some nerve, Rice. You don't even in play tonight's game and yet you keep getting smart with me."

My jaw ticks. The aching in my body all but evaporates as I climb out of the car. "Sounds like something a *loser* would get upset over." I pause before adding, "And he's not my boyfriend."

A few of the guys turn to glower at me, suddenly interested in this altercation. All five of them turn away from their cars and step toward me, their hands twitching at their sides.

Ugh, I'm too tired for this shit.

CHAPTER

19

"Have any of you heard of a shower? If you're going to stand that close, at least put some deodorant on."

Red sneers at me, taking another step closer. "You're gonna try and trash talk us after doping up your boy *mid-game*, you fucking *cheater*?"

My eyes narrow to slits. "You think I'd let that jerk do that shit?" Enhancers can ruin your damn life. Anyone with a single brain cell knows that. "He doesn't *need* to be doped up. He's that good a player on his own merits."

Red shakes his head, and one of his friends mutters *bullshit*. "You really think I'd believe that? I saw the difference in his game. Why else would you have taken him out of the gym, huh?"

I bite the inside of my cheek. *I can't tell them why.*

"He *wasn't* doped," is all I say.

He shrugs. "You're just as pathetic as he is, alright? You two are gonna be *destroyed* at the Champs. And I'm gonna be sitting in the crowd, watching as they wipe the floor with your asses."

I don't realise until I glance around that Red's team

mates have me surrounded. They sneer and grunt at me like they're damn animals, and my lip curls in disgust even as my chest clenches. *They're too close.*

Too close too close too—

"Get the fuck away from him." I glance over Red's shoulder to see Gray approaching with a plastic take-away bag in his hand.

Red turns to the sound of his approach, his eyes narrowing as his lips pull in a tight smile. "There's the cheater himself."

"I told you, he didn't dope," I breathe out, but he ignores me. My strength is waning as each second passes. I can't get a full breath of air in.

"You got a problem, Harvey? If so, then you settle it with me." Gray pipes up as he storms towards us. My hands clench and unclench at my sides. *His name's Harvey? He doesn't look like a Harvey...*

Harvey's gaze flickers back to me for a moment, his eyebrow raised. "Just wondering why you're not out *celebrating* with your team?" He doesn't sound bitter as he says it, only curious.

"None of your fucking business, asshole," I bite out. My hands start to shake as Harvey grabs the collar of my shirt, pulling me closer. He stands a good head above me, but I don't cower.

"Don't fucking touch him." Gray steps forward, but one of the players shoves him back.

Gray's face changes for a split second, and in that moment, he doesn't look sane.

"You got a smart mouth, Rice, but I don't believe I was talking to *you*," Harvey sneers down at me, his top lip curling back.

My lip curls back from my teeth as I grind out, "Still doesn't make it any of your business *asshole*, so get lost."

Gray shoves forward, but two of the players grab his shoulders and pin him back against one of their cars. My heart thuds hard and my palms tingle.

Fuck this. I launch his knee into Harvey's gut, knocking his grip away as I watch him curl over. Before he has time to collect himself, I swing my fist and collect the side of his face with my knuckles. He hits the ground with a loud thud, and I cradle my knuckles into my chest. *Fuck, that hurt.*

"You heard him," I pant out. "Don't touch me." I barely get the words out before one of the other guys tackles me to the ground. We hit the gravel hard, I swear my head *cracks* from the sudden splitting pain.

There's an immediate temperature drop when I hit the ground. One minute it's cold, and the next it's frigid. When I hear Gray grunt and I manage to look back at him, he's shaking. Wait, no. It's like the air around him is *vibrating*. It's trembling like a mirage. His eyes are black—completely black, no trace of his usual brown—and his teeth are bared. He looks angry. No, angry is definitely not the word; it's worse than angry. He looks *feral*.

I don't know where he gets the strength, but he *launches* the two guys off him, sending them *flying* over their cars. I watch them hit the pavement with collective groans, then my eyes snap back to Gray. His shoulders are hunched, and his breathing is heavy. He looks like a damn *monster* right now.

"What the fuck?" Red mutters, his eyes widening. It wouldn't surprise me if he pissed his pants. Gray advances on him, his movements almost a blur. He grabs Red by his arm and swings him around, flinging him against the building before either of us take our next breath. The guy who tackled me scrambles to his feet, anxious to get away.

What the hell's wrong with Gray? He's definitely not acting like himself. But he said there weren't any new powers. This has to be some kind of power, right?

Gray's eyes snap to the guy rushing away from me, and he pounces. The guy hits the ground as Gray sweeps his legs out from under him, a loud snap echoing through the carpark when the guy lands on his shoulder.

Holy shit...

But Gray either doesn't hear it or he doesn't care. He lands on top of the guy and wraps his hands around his throat.

Holy shit! "Gray!" My palms scrape against the rough ground, adrenaline pumping through my blood. *What the hell is he doing?* I clear the distance and jump on his back, wrapping my arm around his neck and pulling back. "Gray, *stop!*"

My pulse thumps so damn hard against my temple that my vision blurs. His hands loosen from around the guy's throat, leaving him gasping for air. Gray rises to his feet with me dangling on his back.

He turns his head, his shoulders tensing when he sees me. His black eyes—freakin' *terrifying* right now—are soulless and empty. Like there is no light left inside of him. He doesn't even look like the same person from two minutes ago. The way he's holding himself...it's everything Gray *isn't*. When my arms are too weak to hold on any longer, I drop to the ground, staring up at him in shock.

His shoulders shake when he turns back to the guys who tried to jump me. He runs for one of their cars, grips the fender and flips the *entire car* onto its roof. The loud crunching of metal has me covering my ears, but my eyes don't move from him. Seemingly unfazed—despite the fact that he just lifted *two tons of metal*—he runs off towards the road that leads out of town.

"Gray!" He doesn't turn back as he disappears into the shadows. I scan the broken and bruised bodies of the Maverick team before landing on Gray's car. I could drive after him, but I don't know how to. "Fuck!"

Crawling to my feet, my legs wobble. *Get it together, Liam. I need to go after him. I need to make sure he's alright. He might hurt himself. He might hurt someone else. I need to figure out what's wrong with him.*

You always say that you're fine, but I'm here anyway.

CHAPTER

20

I don't even know if I'm going in the right direction. He could be anywhere. The sudden rain falls like ice pellets, battering my hyper-sensitive skin. *Why doesn't everything hurt so damn much?*

Following the same path I took when I followed him to the lake, my eyes sweep the edges of the woods. It's hard to see through the rain at this time of night, but I don't have a light or an umbrella. There's nothing I can do about it.

Try harder.

My head is heavy, and I can barely lift my feet off the ground. But Gray needs my help. *No one else knows he's out here. No one else knows.*

I've always cared.

Because I want to.

You always say that you're fine, but I'm here anyway.

I'm going to find him. We need to figure out what happened back at the car park. One minute he was fine, and the next he was going *crazy. And what the hell was with that random burst of strength? He flipped a freaking car. He hasn't been able to do anything like that before. It was only the blood, and the healing, and the phasing. He didn't have this monster strength before now.*

The ice rain falls harder now, and my clothes cling to my skin. My shoes are squishy, slapping against the path as I try to keep my eyes open. But it's so cold, my entire body numb. I squint through the rain, and water dripping from my eyelashes.

Where is he? "Gray?" I call for the hundredth time, my voice croaky and weak. I've been calling for him for so long. I bite down on the inside of my cheek. "*Finch?*"

Nothing. He probably didn't even go this way—

My head jerks to the side when I hear a branch snap, and I take off running. The muscles in my legs seize up and my heart pumps hard in my chest, but I don't stop. Even when I trip and stumble over rocks and branches and huge tree roots, I don't stop. It could be an animal, or it could just be a branch falling from the heavy rain.

Or it could be him.

I wheeze with each struggling breath, and the rain hits my already raw skin harder than before. My jaw chatters as I run, and I worry I'll bite my tongue. Another branch breaks, much closer this time. My head whips from side to side when I stop, but I can barely see two feet in front of me.

"Finch?" I try again, but I still don't see him. I move closer to where I heard the sound, stumbling over fallen tree trunks and brush. My toes probably have frostbite now considering how much it hurts to move my feet. Maybe my entire body has frostbite. "Finch?" My eyes squint as I sweep the area, but it's too dark to make anything out.

Then I see him. At least I hope it's him. It's a big, dark figure lying on the ground. *We don't have bears in this area, do we? I seriously can't remember.* I scramble over the last of the protruding rocks and sticks, latching onto his shoulders. *It's him. Definitely him.* Rolling him over to his back, my eyes pinch as I look over his entire body. I can't see much, but I don't think he's hurt—

His hands are a different colour to the rest of his exposed skin. It's dark, and thick, and it has my heart sprinting in my chest.

Holy shit, is that blood?

He doesn't even flinch when I pick up his hand. It's still sticky despite the rain. Even though his clothes are soaked through, the hem is drenched in the same darkness as his hands.

My heart clogs my throat, and I quickly peel his shirt away from his body. *Don't be hurt, don't be hurt.* Flashbacks of the night he got shot race through my mind, and my chest burns and clenches.

Not again. Please not again.

My eyes land on his stomach, and it's covered in the same colour. But when I run my hand across his skin—holy crap, his skin is *burning* hot against my near-frozen fingers— there's nothing there. No puncture wound. No cuts. *Did he get hurt, then heal? Wait, his blood isn't like this anymore. It burns like acid—*

"Don't worry, it's animal blood."

I whirl around at the sound of someone shouting over the pouring rain, and I make out the girl with blue hair from the game earlier. But her hair's flatter now—wet from the rain—and she's only got an oversized t-shirt on. I quickly avert my eyes when I notice a lot of skin.

"Who the fuck *are* you?" It doesn't sound menacing

because my teeth are chattering like crazy. Ginger stands next to her, shirtless. His jeans are dark and wet, but he doesn't have shoes on. At least I don't think he does. The girl glances up at Ginger, who nods his head. I move in front of Finch, my eyes narrowing.

Blue points to Finch. "We're like *him*."

That wasn't what I was expecting.

"Wh-...What?" My eyes are crossing, the two of them are merging together. Now that I've stopped moving, the fatigue is catching up. My body sways, so I brace my hands on either side of me, my fingers submerged in the cold mud.

"Come with us. We all need to talk." Ginger finally speaks. They both move towards me—or is it just one of them? I can't tell anymore—but I raise my hand to stop them.

"*Don't*. Don't come any closer..."

Blue's lips pinch tight and her finger points to Finch again. "We need to get him out of the rain."

"I can do it on my own." *I'll do it. I'll get him home. Gray is my responsibility.*

Whatever it is, it's his problem to deal with.

He's my problem to deal with...

He's mine to deal with...

Mine...

You always say that you're fine, but I'm here anyway.

Turning to lift his arm over my shoulder, I heave him onto my back. *Bloody hell, he's heavy.*

But he's mine to deal with.

My knees buckle as I try to stand, but the ground is muddy and slippery, and my body doesn't have the energy to lift him any higher. He's dead weight right now, but I just grip his arms tighter and push up. My knees nearly give out, but I *don't let them*.

"Just let us help you—"

"*I said don't touch him.*" I turn my dark glare on them, and they take a step back. I clench my chattering teeth, my head pounding. The heat that emanates from Finch is scorching against my frozen skin. But that only makes my fingers tighten on him. *I've got to get him somewhere safe.*

"At least come with us," Blue shouts over the rain, her eyebrows furrowing. "We won't touch him, I promise." She holds her hands up and takes another step towards me, my legs quivering in response. I glance away again, my eyes locking on Ginger. He watches us with cautious eyes, like he's expecting an attack.

"*Fine,*" I chatter. I need to figure out what these guys are up to. I don't know how much they know about Finch, but she said they're like him. *Does that mean they can phase through things as well?*

The girl turns, but her eyes don't stray from me. I glare down at my feet, willing them to move. One step, then another. I barely lift my mud-caked shoe off the ground, but I get it in front of me.

I make sure Blue and Ginger stay in front of me as I follow them back towards the main road. *It'll be easier when we get there. All flat. No rocks or tree roots or mud. I'll be able to carry him better there.*

Glancing up at the two strangers, my mind burns with questions. *How did they end up here? How did they know about Finch in the first place? What do they mean when they say they're like him?*

But none of the words make it to my chattering lips. And

the rain is coming down too hard for them to hear me. So I follow them with the giant jerk unconscious and bloodied on my back while trying not to panic.

My head is filled with noise when I see a streetlight in the distance. *Nearly there. So close.*

"Are you sure you don't want—" Ginger lingers behind, his forehead creased as he shies away from the rain.

"I said *don't*." I send him the darkest glare I can muster, which probably isn't much. But he stares at me for a moment longer before he turns and continues towards the road. I draw in a deep breath, nearly choking on the rain as it runs into my mouth and force my body to keep moving.

I can do this.

You always say that you're fine, but I'm here anyway.

Damn it, get it together, Liam!

It takes too long to reach the main road, but I nearly cry when we do. *He's too damn big. Why the hell is this jerk so damn big?* I can barely keep my hold on him while keeping my legs straight. *If I let them bend, I don't think I can get back up.*

"That way," I nod to where the 'Welcome to Franklin' sign is posted. Blue and Ginger keep ahead of me, glancing back every so often to check that I'm still there. As if I'm not making enough noise trying to carry this giant on my back.

My fingers are struggling to hold on to him. I can't even feel them anymore. My vision is hazy, and icy cold water keeps rushing down my face, but I *keep going.*

I can't stop. If I stop—

Lights.

A pair of lights move towards us, the yellow orbs blurry from the rain. But I see them. And my heart jumps into my throat as I try to figure out what the hell to do.

We're on banks of the road right now, visible but not at risk of being run over. But whoever it is will still see us. *What if they do?*

The lights grow closer, and the two in front of us seem to be caught in the same panic. They turn to me, their eyes wide. "What should we do?" Blue asks, her trembling lips almost as dark as her limp hair.

I don't even have the energy to glare at her. I don't have the energy for words. I barely have the energy to *stand*. And the lights are getting closer. And closer. And I don't know what to do. And I don't have the energy to even *worry* about that.

Closer, closer, closer.

The car comes skidding to a halt in front of us, and everything but the rain is silent for a moment.

The door opens.

He's so heavy.

"Liam!"

I lift my gaze to the person climbing out of the car door, and I don't know whether to be happy or horrified. I don't think I can keep my eyes open anymore.

"*Sheriff.*"

I don't know how I get inside the car. One second the rain is hitting me hard, freezing every inch of my skin, and the next my ears are ringing from how quite it is inside the cab. The creaking sound of doors slamming jolts me.

"Alright Liam, enough games. *Explain yourself.*" The Sheriff's deep baritone shakes me too my core. Or maybe I'm still cold.

Definitely still cold.

I cling to Finch, shielding him with my body as I avoid the Sheriff's hard gaze in the rear-view mirror. I try hard to keep Finch out of sight from where Ginger shares the back seat with me, rubbing his hands up and down his arms. *Why are they in the car?* My teeth are still chattering, and my vision is blotchy, but Finch's heat is *soaking* my skin the same way the rain was.

"I *can't*," I mutter, my eyes meeting his in the mirror. The Sheriff looks back at me, his eyes narrowed.

"I find you on the brink of hypothermia with my bloodied, unconscious nephew on your back, and you *can't tell me why*?"

When he says it like that, it sounds like I'm being unnecessarily difficult.

Blue clears her throat, turning in the front seat to face the Sheriff. "Officer, if I may—"

"You *may not*," he cuts her off. "I'm not done with him yet. I'll get to *you two* soon." His eyes flash to Ginger, who leans back into his seat. Blue faces the window again, her shoulders stiff. The Sheriff meets my gaze again, his eyes hard. His clothes are soaked from the rain. *When did he get out of the car?* "Liam."

I peek up through my wet eyelashes, my shoulders shaking as my fingers spasm around Finch's shirt. The heat from both inside the car and emanating from Finch's body is sending mine into shock. "He asked me not to," I whisper, resting my head against Finch's temple. "He asked me not to...he asked me not to..." It keeps slipping off my lips, and my eyes won't focus on anything in front of me.

The Sheriff stares at me for a moment longer, but I turn away.

How the hell did he find us?

CHAPTER 21

I think my head might be swollen. It's pounding so damn hard. I reach up and rub my eyes, groaning when I try to open them. It's like sand's been poured over them. I rub them again, coughing when I try to breathe.

"Easy, Liam. Easy." I know that voice. At least I think I know that voice.

When I finally manage to pry my eyes open, everything's blurry for the first few seconds. I keep blinking until everything is clear again, and I gaze around the bedroom I'm in. It smells familiar. Clean. Soft.

The Sheriff steps into my line of sight, and my chest tightens.

He found us. On the side of the road.

Shit.

I sit up, my head screaming at me, but I don't see Finch. I open my mouth to ask, but the Sheriff raises a hand to stop me, sitting down in a chair next to the bed.

"Fin's okay. He's asleep in his room right now." He watches me as I lean backwards, catching myself on my scarred palms. Everything is warmer now, but my entire body is still aching.

"Where are they?" I croak out.

Sheriff nods, his eyes locked on my face. "They're downstairs. Alice is keeping them occupied."

My spine stiffens. "You shouldn't leave her alone—"

"It's okay," he interrupts me. "I've already spoken to them."

I lower my head, my eyes pinched shut. *He knows.*

He knows.

The Sheriff is silent as he watches me bring my legs up to rest my forehead against my knees. I sit there and try to think. Think past the pounding. Think past the exhaustion. But he hates me now. Hates that I lied to him. Lied about everything.

Liam, if something has happened to my nephew, you need to tell me.

Didn't keep him safe. Didn't keep him safe.

"It's alright, Liam," he says, leaning forward on his knees to watch me closer. "I know you were protecting him. I'm not angry."

I'm not angry.

I still can't look up. Because he's lying. *He is angry. I didn't keep him safe.*

If I see anything that looks dangerous, I'll figure something out, alright?

Didn't keep him safe.

What did you do, baby?

Strong men always win.

"I'm sorry," I whisper, the words bubbling out past my lips, my eyes wet and my shoulders shaking. *Didn't keep him safe. Didn't keep him safe.* "Didn't keep him safe..."

The Sheriff moves so suddenly I don't have time to get out of his way. But he wraps his arms around my shoulders, pulling me forward into his warm chest. I choke on the air as it's squeezes from my lungs, but not because his hold is strangling.

It's *unexpected*.

"You did good, Liam." He strokes my head with his large hand, brushing the wet fuzz. My chest burns, but I don't move. I can't. I don't know how to. "You did good."

You did good, Liam.

Good, Liam.

"I—" My voice cracks and I try to tell him he's wrong. *He's wrong. Finch wasn't—*

He squeezes me tighter, his warmth seeping into my skin. "I'm so proud of you, son."

His words make me jerk.

I'm so proud of you, son.

My stomach rolls and clenches and spins and pinches and flips and I'm sure I'm going to be sick but I know I'm not. My head is lighter than before even though the pounding is *fading*. I still can't get a deep breath, my lungs are squeezing so damn tight.

There's a knock on the door, followed by a quiet, "Dean?"

Dean.

His name, it's Dean.

Dean pulls back slowly, his eyes watching me differently from before. My face is wet when I don't mean for it to be, so I quickly rub my cheek with the back of my hand. He pats my head again, and something unknown yet strangely familiar floods my chest for a moment. Dean walks over to the door, opening it to let Doc look inside. When she sees me, her eyes smile.

"Hey hon, how're you feeling?"

I sniff. "I'm fine." My voice is croaky, and I'm too anxious to look at either of them.

I'm proud of you, son.

What do I even do with those words? Do they even mean anything when it's not your own father who says them?

Strong men always win.

What did I tell you about bothering the Montgomery's?

"Finch is still sleeping. It seems you guys partied a little *too* hard." She gives me a disapproving eyebrow, but her lips are twitching at the corners.

Partied? I turn to look at the Sheriff and he's nodding to me without actually moving his head. I can see in his eyes that he's given her a different story to what really happened.

"Yeah. Went too hard too fast," is all I say. Doc laughs and leans into Dean for a moment.

"The kids downstairs are nodding off, love. I think it's time to take them home."

Dean nods and turns to meet my gaze. "Would you like to come for the drive, Liam?"

I'm already throwing the blankets off my legs. He's giving me the opportunity to find out who they are. I need to find out as much as I can about whatever this magic bullet shit is.

"Are you from the government?" I ask as soon as the doors close. I'm riding in the front with Dean this time. I turn and lean between the seats to glare at them with tired eyes. But

199

I need to know if they're safe. Blue just snorts at me and Ginger chuckles under his breath.

"Do we seriously *look* like we're from the government?" Ginger mutters, his eyes trained on my face. His clothes are dry now, his shoulders tense as he wrings his hands in his lap. When he reaches up to scratch behind his ear, I notice the clear plastic his hearing aids.

They seem like ordinary teenagers, but that doesn't mean their presence here isn't suspicious.

"We spoke before the game. Did you know that I knew something when you approached me?"

The girl shakes her head, her blue curls starting to bounce again. "That was a coincidence."

"Was it?" I glance between them. "Was it also a 'coincidence' that you ended up at the same place I found Finch unconscious?" Dean is silent beside me. I don't know what questions he's already asked them.

"We aren't going to hurt him or anything."

My lip curls. "Tell me how you guys ended up in Franklin."

Ginger shrugs, his t-shirt hanging loosely over his chest. "No idea, man. I just follow my sister. She has a nose for sniffing others like us out, it seems. She leads, and I follow."

What the hell is this guy even talking about?

Wait, did he say sister?

I take another long look at the two of them. Blue's skin is darker, her vibrant hair drying into a large head of tight, frizzy curls. Ginger is pale with orange hair and a dozen freckles to match. These guys are total opposites. But the same could be said for Finch and his cousins, so I don't comment on it.

"So what do you guys want with Finch, anyway?"

The guy scratches the back of his head. "It's difficult to explain—"

When Blue finally looks at me instead of out the window, her lips are pursed. "We're like *him*...well, I *thought* we were like him, but after last night I'm not so sure..."

My fingers tighten around the seat. Dean is still silent, allowing me to lead this make-shift investigation. My eyes flash to the two strangers. *They look the same age as me.* "How do you guys know that you're like him?"

"Okay, that's enough, Mister Hero. We have questions too." Blue grumbles, crossing her arms over her chest. I lean back slightly, hesitant. *Is she calling* me *Mister Hero?*

Although I've been grilling them for information these last few minutes, I'm not sure I have answers to any questions *they have.*

I'm sure I can make something up.

"Sure," I grunt. I don't know where Dean is driving, but I assume he asked them where they are staying when he spoke to them.

Blue leans forward, her face close. "Did he almost die before he changed?"

I lean back further, my eyes blurry as her question draws out a deep pain in my chest. My hands start to tingle with the memory of his blood staining my skin.

Did he almost die?

Almost die...

Almost die almost die almost die...

Dean's eyes flicker to me and he quirks a brow.

You did good, Liam.

I struggle to swallow the golf ball sized lump in my

throat as Ginger and Blue watch me, their eyes catching everything on my face.

"What happened?" she asks, pushing for the answer. Something squeezes my heart, and it becomes impossible to breathe for a moment. Her eyes scan my face, wide and calculating. I clench my jaw, my teeth grinding *hard*.

Should I tell them? It's not technically my story to tell. I don't know how angry Finch will be with me if I do.

But they already know he has powers. And they've already told Dean, so there's no point in pretending anymore.

"He was *shot*," I say, my eyes focused on Blue. I don't look at Dean, even when his head turns to me. Even when I feel his heavy stare *crushing me*.

Because I won't be able to stomach the look on his face if I do.

Blue's pupils flare, before they're normal again. "Wow." She falls back in her seat, her lips pursed as she rubs at her tired eyes.

I lean forward again, my eyes flickering between the siblings. "Tell me how you ended up in Franklin," I say again. Ginger is silent, his eyes glancing to Blue as he tries to figure out who's going to answer me.

Blue watches me with cautious eyes, her arms crossing over her chest. She's wearing Doc's clothes, the style not meshing with her neon blue frizz. "Because I can sense him."

I roll my eyes. "You can *sense* him?"

She purses her lips. "It's like a radar in my brain. It apparently makes me sick for a couple hours, until I get used to it. But I've felt something strange for a couple weeks, and I convinced him," she throws her thumb at Ginger, "to come with me and find out what it was."

I raise an eyebrow. "So...you can't phase through things?"

Blue's eyes widen, and she launches forward in her seat, but the safety belt jerks her back. I still don't look at Dean. "He can phase through things? That's so freakin' cool!"

"So you're saying you sense people? Is that all you can do?" The car slows, until we come to a stop at a red light.

She huffs and crosses her arms over her chest. "It's not *all I can do*, blockhead."

My eyes flicker to Ginger, whose his lips tug up in the corners. Before I can stop her, Blue unplugs her seatbelt and starts to strip her clothes off. I cover my eyes with my shoulder and look away, my jaw dropping. "What the hell are you doing?" I peek up at Dean, who is looking straight again *very* purposefully.

She huffs again but doesn't say anything as she kicks off her pants. The air around her body suddenly shakes. It's silent for a moment, and I hear Dean blow out a 'what-the-hell' breath. When I turn back, there's a dog where Blue had been. I think it's a golden retriever...but it's fur is bright blue.

What the fuck?

The dog barks, before yapping something at Dean.

"Yeah, that's Cece," Ginger says. It glances at him when he speaks, head tilting to the side, and Ginger shakes his head in response. The air shifts again, shimmering for a few seconds, the blue dogs body stretching in a terrifying way until the girl is sitting in the seat again, completely fucking *naked*.

Ginger reaches over to cover my eyes, and I lean away from his touch, but I keep my eyes closed as my cheeks heat. *Holy crap, I just saw a girl naked. What the hell do I say?*

203

There's the sound of clothes rustling as the girl dresses herself again, before she says, "Sensing isn't *all I can do*."

My tongue is strangely numb, and I wonder whether it's still in my mouth as I try to formulate words. I peek over at Dean again, who sags in relief when he sees Blue's fully clothed again. I quickly turn away in case he tries to catch my eye, the car starting to move forward again. "So...you can turn into a *dog*?"

Her eyes are bright with anger when she looks up at me. My cheeks still burn as I remember her body. *Shouldn't I feel differently, after seeing that? Shouldn't I feel anything other than mortified?* "I don't just turn into a *dog*. I can change into *any* animal I've touched."

I rub my eyes with my free hand when a headache starts to form at my temples. "This is the weirdest conversation I have ever had." *How do I even explain all of this to Finch?*

Ginger laughs. "You're telling me. I thought we were the only freaks."

Blue turns to her brother, her lips pursed, frizzy curls bouncing against her shoulders. "We're not *freaks*, Zeke!"

Dean glances in the rear-view mirror, but I don't know who he's looking at. His jaw is set in a hard line. "I assume you can also do something different, can't you?"

My eyes narrow on Ginger as he slowly nods his head, his gaze switching between Blue and the mirror. Blue shrugs, so Ginger unbuckles his seatbelt as well, shuffling forward in his seat. There's a hard look on Dean's face when he hears the click, and I know it's bothering him, but he doesn't say anything as Ginger reaches between the seats to point to a pair of sunglasses resting in the centre console. "May I?" He looks at Dean as he asks. I look at Dean as well because I forget to not look. But he's not looking at me. He's still staring at the road as we drive, the rain just drizzling now. My skin shivers with each drop I watch racing down the windshield.

"Be quick. And both of you, *seatbelts on*," he grumbles, his voice rumbling in his chest. Blue doesn't bite back, and instead does as he says.

Ginger nods his head and reaches between Dean and I a little bit further, his fingers barely touching the sunglasses before he falls back into his seat, strapping himself in. My lips pinch. *I swear, if this guy turns into a pair of sunglasses...*

When he's sure I'm looking, he lifts his hand from his knee, his finger and thumb pressed together. Flexing his wrist, he flicks his nipped fingers up. There's a quiet scrape as the sunglasses fly between the seats and land in his open palm. I turn back to see that the sunglasses have in fact disappeared.

It takes me a moment to formulate words. "Was that telekinesis or something?"

He chuckles. "Or something. It's more like I create threads. When I touch something, it creates a thread that I can pull on. It only works if I'm close enough though. After some trial and error, we found that it has a distance limit."

My head is about to explode. I turn back in my seat and rest my forehead against my palms, my eyes closing. "This is a lot to take in right now."

There's a short existing silence in the car, where only the hum of the engine and the pattering of rain on the roof fills the cab, before Blue says, "You haven't told us your name, Mister Hero."

Mister Hero?

I turn to Dean, but he doesn't reply. He doesn't look away from the road. Her foot rams into the back of my seat and when I turn to glare at her, she's looking at me expectantly. "Hello? You suddenly hard of hearing?"

Glancing between Ginger and Blue, I lift my lip. "What?"

She raises her eyebrows. "*Your name?*"

When I look at Dean again, he nods his head to me. I don't look at the two in the back seat as I mumble, "Doesn't matter."

My name's not important. *None of it's important.* No here in this car. Not in this moment.

I'm not the one with the stupid powers. I'm not like them. *I'm not like them.*

The girl blows out a loud breath. "Nice to meet you, *Doesn't Matter*. I'm Cece." She waves her hand in Ginger's direction. "This is my brother Zeke."

I nod but stay silent, my hands starting to shake. My palms burn, but I'm not sure why. I clap them together and *force* them to stop, bending forward until I can tuck them out of sight. From the corner of my eye I see Dean turn to look at me again, so I quickly avert my gaze towards the window.

You did good, Liam.

No I didn't. I've haven't done anything *good.*

Not a single damn thing.

But Blue knew what questions to ask. She *knew* that something bad happened to him.

Because he was shot.

It's all my fault. All my fault he's like this now. If I hadn't knocked the can off the shelf, f I had stood up faster, if I had done something—

206

You did good, Li—

Lia—

I squeeze my head between my hands and my insides freeze, everyone's voices echoing in my head like a broken record.

Strong men always win—

What's wrong with him?

Lia—

The air hisses through my clenched teeth, burning hot in my ice-cold chest.

I ruined everything.

CHAPTER

22

"You let me know when you get home, alright? I want to know you made it back safely."

"Is he gonna be alright?"

Stop. Too many voices.

"Drive safe and wear your damn seatbelts."

Too many too many too many.

There's thumping and rain and it's noisy and then it's quiet again and I keep my eyes closed because my head is spinning, and I don't know how to make it quiet anymore.

Because I want to.

What's wrong with him?

Were you bothering Finch?

Liam, if something has happened to my nephew—

I warned you.

"Liam?"

"My fault, my fault, my fault..." I murmur over and over, my lips numb as the words drive a stake further into my chest. He'll never forgive me. *Never.*

Never, never—

"Liam, *breathe*. Easy son—"

"*Don't call me that!*" I shout, my vision flaring as I throw my head back against the seat and meet his gaze.

Dean stares at me with hard eyes, watching my shoulders heave as my lungs pant for air, because I can't remember how to breathe properly. The look in his eyes isn't helping.

"No one calls me that..." slips out before I can stop it. My vision blurs and my stomach twists but his eyes *still* hold me. "*No one calls me...*" I hiccup, my hands shaking harder in my lap.

"Liam." His voice is clearer this time. "None of this was your fault—"

"Damn it, *stop!*" I'm shouting it so damn loud, but he's not listening. "I knocked the can off the shelf! The robber didn't know we were there! But when I knocked it, Finch stood up. But it should have been *me!*" I'm leaning forward over my hands, but they still won't stop shaking. "If it was me, then he wouldn't have been shot, and he wouldn't have these weird powers. He would still be normal and nothing—"

The air is trapped in my chest until it blows out shaky and broken. Dean's still watching me, his body only partially turned in my direction. His hands tighten around the steering wheel, the leather creaking under his grip.

"I tried to stop the blood..." I squeeze my hands tighter, pain flaring up my forearms. The skin burns at the vivid memory of that night. "*I tried to stop it*, but nothing I did was helping. He just *kept bleeding*, and I—"

"Liam," he says again, his forehead creased. His hair is falling forward over his brow, kind of like how Finch's does. We sit there in silence for a moment longer, staring at each other. "Listen to me, alright?" He reaches towards me and I flinch back.

Strong men always win.

He keeps reaching forward despite my reaction and grabs my shoulder in a tight hold. His grip is tough, *unyielding*, and he forces me to look at him. "You did *good*, Liam."

My breath catches in my throat as I stare out the windshield because I don't know where else I should look.

He's still not listening.

I don't talk to Dean for the rest of the drive back. Apparently Blue and Ginger had their car parked at the Diner as well and had been tailing Finch and I from the school after the game. He tells me all of this, but I barely nod my head in response.

What did you do, baby?

What did you do?

Lia—

Please just stop.

I follow Dean up the path towards the house, the rain still drizzling. It's still ice cold, burning my skin where it touches. My footsteps slow as I stare at my shoes, watching each step.

What did you do?

Were you bothering Finch?

Liam, if something has happened to my nephew, you need to tell me.

I shouldn't be here. He knows now. Dean knows, and he'll be able to protect Finch better. He'll be able to figure things out better than I could.

Strong men always win.

Dean's the Sheriff. One of the strongest men in Franklin.

Now that he knows—

"Liam, why are you standing in the rain?"

When I finally look up from my soggy shoes, I find Doc and Dean watching me from the front porch. Doc steps closer to the edge of the porch, her brows furrowed, but Dean grabs her wrist. She stops, and my heart stops.

It's blurry with the rain running over my eyes. But Dean's looking at me, and I don't recognise that look on his face yet it's so familiar it makes my heart split.

Liam, if something has happened to my nephew, you need to tell me.

I lied. I lied about what happened. Now he knows *I lied.*

My fingers curl into tight fists at my side as my heart threatens to break out of my chest. I hope it does, because this hurts way too damn much. *I'm not good. Not* enough. *I can't do anything right. I never win.*

Strong men always win.

I'm the weak man. Always the weak man.

This is why we're not friends.

Why we can't be friends.

I turn away from their house and walk towards the road. *Can't be here. I can't be.*

"Liam! Where are you going?" Doc's voice carries through the rain, but I pay her no mind as I keep walking. The night is dark, barely illuminated by the amber glow of the streetlights, but I welcome it.

I warned you.

There's too much. I just need to go home.

"*Liam!*" she tries again, her voice troubled.

Home.

CHAPTER

23

My head is heavy when I hear my bedroom door open. There's no knock beforehand. I lie under the covers, unsure how long I've actually been asleep—I don't even know what time I got home last night—my eyes blurry and aching as I try to pry them open.

"The Montgomery's will be joining us for dinner tonight." My father says from the door. I sit up faster, my neck cracking when I snap my head in his direction. He stands with his body half out the door, his nose lifting when he glances around my room. His hair is groomed back, his face cleanly shaven and his empty eyes finally narrowing on me.

My chest holds, the air in my lungs refusing to budge. *Why is he in here? He never comes in here—*

"You are not to bother them in their time here," he mutters in a bored tone. "Am I clear?"

*I'm not to...*I open my mouth, but nothing comes out. *Does he know about last night? Why are they even coming over? I can't...* "What do you..."

He raises an eyebrow. The sucking void in his stare as

my gaze lowering to where my scarred palms are gripping the covers in bunches.

My father doesn't give me an answer as he takes slow steps towards me. My heart hammers in my chest with each step that brings him closer, my eyes trained on the covers. Can't look at him.

"Am I *clear*?" Each word is controlled, each syllable punctuated with purpose. He stares down at me from the edge of my bed, and I can't look up.

"Yes," I mumble, my vision blurry. *I won't bother them.* He watches me for a moment longer, before finally breathing a tired sigh and walking back towards the door.

Once it finally clicks behind him, I try to rake in a lungful of air. But there's still pressure.

Can't breathe, can't breathe, can't breathe.

I collapse back on the pillows and stare at the blank ceiling. Empty. It's like *everything* is empty.

Strong men always win.

What did I tell you about bothering the Montgomery's?

His voice thunders in my head, drowning out any other thoughts.

You are not to bother them in their time here.

I won't, I won't, I won't.

Am I clear?

I really won't.

The ceiling somehow seems emptier with each breath I struggle to scrape in.

You did good—

Am I clear?

I pinch my eyes closed, my hands shaking.

When I open my eyes again, they're itchy and sore.

You are not to bother them.

I sit up slowly, my stomach clenching from the movement. The orange glow of the streetlight peeks in from the bottom of my curtains. My room is cold, but my skin is sticky, shivers racing down my spine.

You are not to bother them.

Resting my face in my hands, I lean forward, my breathing shaky. *Get it together. Strong. I need to be stronger than this.*

There's a knock on my door just as I rise from my bed, but I'm hesitant to call out to whoever it is on the other side. My father doesn't knock, so it would be Sawyer or mom. When there's a second, more urgent knock, my heart leaps up my throat.

Strong, strong, strong.

My teeth grind as I shake out the nerves from my fingers and yank the door open. My eyes narrow as I stare up at the stupid giant standing in my doorway.

"What the hell are you doing here?"

Finch throws his hands up, frowning down at me. "Don't you give me that shit, Liam. I've been stressing the fuck out over you, and *I'm* the one with these stupid superpowers."

I shrug, my hand falling away from the door. "Pointless to stress over me, jerk. You should be more worried about yourself."

"I know," he grumbles, pushing into my room. I let him, because I'm sure he has a lot to say after what happened last night. I'm sure he's already spoken to Dean. He's wearing his normal jeans and a plain t-shirt, but he looks...*different*. I can't put my finger on it, but there's something about him that wasn't there before.

He glances around my room, and my cheeks flare. There's nothing special about my room, but it's somehow embarrassing to have him in my space.

Kissing you.

Because I want to.

My skin starts to tingle and an unusual feeling spreads through my centre. I don't like it. But before I can tell him to get out, he's looking back at me and says, "How are you today?"

It's alright, Liam. You're alright.

You're alright.

I've got you.

I shake my head and grit my teeth at him. "I'm fine."

You always say you're fine, but I'm here anyway.

His shoulders drop and his eyes are sad as he stares back at me. *I hate that damn stupid look.*

Hate it, hate it, hate it.

He's so unfamiliar right now. I leave the door to walk past him to my dresser, but he reaches out and grips my fingertips. I barely feel his touch, but it still sends my heart crashing in my chest.

You are not to bother—

I rip my hand away, but I don't look at him. I breathe out a loud sigh, my shoulders hunched.

"Sorry," he says, but I still don't turn to look at him. "I spoke to my uncle, and he said that you ran off last night. I was worried—"

"I told you, just worry about *yourself*," I grind out, my fingers still tingling. *Stop tingling, damn it.* "Like you said, *you're* the one with the stupid superpowers." The words taste bitter. Spiteful. *How can I not be?*

You are not to bother them.

I can see him take a stance from the corner of my eye, and my fingers curl into tight fists. "I'm allowed to worry about you, Liam. You've been weird lately—"

"This is *me*, Finch." I spin around and face him. "We're *not friends*, remember? I'm not the same as I was when we were kids."

What did I tell you about bothering—

He throws his hands up, his inky hair falling over his eyes. "Stop saying that we're not friends, already! I have *always* been your friend, Liam. It was you who stopped being *my* friend." Even though his eyes are shadowed by his hair, he's still watching me with a look that has my heart racing. "You were the one who said you hated me, Liam..."

Everything's your fault, Finch.

I hate you so damn much, you jerk.

I still remember the look on his face when I said that all those years ago. It was the same devastation that I feel every damn time he beats me.

Strong men—

"I *do* hate you," I mumble, but the feeling isn't there. It comes out weak. Pathetic. "You don't *need* me, Finch. You never have. So just leave me alone, okay?" I don't look at him as I grab out clean clothes from my dresser, my gut twisting tighter with every word that spills out. My eyes burn something fierce, so I blink twice as hard. "Don't worry, I won't tell anyone your secret—"

"That's fucking *bullshit*, Liam."

My shoulders stiffen and my fingers freeze. When I turn to look at him over my shoulder, he's standing in front of the now closed door, his hands shaking at his sides.

"I'm sick of you talking about yourself like that! Why do you have to be *needed*? Why isn't it enough that I *want* you?" He pulls his hair back from his face, his jaw set in a hard line. His nostrils flare, and his face is pinker than before, the tips of his ears bright red.

"Why is everything a fucking *competition*? You can't compare yourself to me, Liam. I'm not a unit of measure, I'm a *person*. A person with wants and needs and *fucking feelings* that you have no problems bulldozing because you think I'm better off without you in my life."

He steps forward and keeps stepping forward until he has me cornered against the dresser. My eyes widen as he advances, his gaze is keeping me frozen in place.

"But that's never been your decision to make." His warm breath blows over my face, and my eyelids droop. My heart is calm yet erratic in my chest, in the most strange and relaxing way. It's something that washes over me when he's close, like his proximity alone is something that soothes the tired and blistering ache that never leaves.

"But last night..." I try, but he's already shaking his head, slowly inching closer.

"My uncle already told me how he found us." He's staring down at my, his eyes searching. "I don't know what the hell happened last night, I honestly don't remember *anything* after I left you at the car, but you were there when I needed you. Why do you keep telling yourself that we're not friends, when you are always going out of your way for me?"

"That's not—" *He's not listening either.* "I didn't...I—"

"*Liam*," he takes the final step to eradicate the remaining distance between us, crowding me. But it's not unbearable or uncomfortable or overwhelming. It's just...*warm*. "Stop pretending that you don't care. You're too good a person for me to ever believe it."

You did good, Liam.

Stop pretending.

You're alright.

I've got you.

I drag in a shaky breath, my eyes flickering over his face. But he stares back with an intensity that eases the thumping pressure in my head. His breath warms my face, and I know he can feel mine against his collarbone when goosebumps erupt up the column of his neck.

When I lift my droopy eyes to meet his gaze, my skin tingles and my fingers relax at my sides. He smiles down at me, his eyes barely open. *Stupid giant.* "My aunt and uncle wanted to see how you were today." He nods towards the door, reaching for my wrist.

You will not bother them in their time here.

Moving my arm out of his reach, I shake my head, my eyes shifting to the centre of his chest. "I can't...I'm not having dinner with you guys tonight."

I don't know why my chest tightens when I say that. I don't *want* to have dinner with them. I don't want them to see my father pretend I don't exist. I don't want *him* to know.

He frowns. "What are you talking about? Of course you are. It's *your* family's dinner."

Biting the inside of my cheek, I look away. "Yeah, well, I

have to study."

His frown deepens. "Do you *actually* have to study?"

My silence has Finch's jaw shifting and his nostrils flaring. "That's what I thought." He grabs my wrist and pulls me towards the door again. I stare at his hand as his fingers tighten, dragging me out of my room and down the stairs.

He's done this before. When he took me to the gym and made me shoot hoops. I stare at where his skin touches mine. His knuckles are white around my wrist, but his hold doesn't hurt at all. Why am I even letting him drag me around?

When we join everyone in the kitchen, mom is dishing up some kind of white pasta she's cooked. Everyone except for my father is there, all of them silent as they watch the two of us enter. But only my mom and Sawyer are surprised to see me. Dean and Finch share a look before he suddenly drops his hold on my wrist. My skin goes cold when I lose his touch.

"Are you...*joining us*, baby?" Mom's voice is strained, probably worried what my father might say when he sees me at the dining room table.

"Of course he is," Finch grinds out through his clenched teeth, quickly looking away when Dean cuts him a deathly look. I don't know what is happening between him and his family, but the pressure in my chest is mounting again. *Mom's right. I shouldn't be down here.*

You are not to bother them in their time here.

Am I clear?

Sawyer leans forward, her short tank-top riding high on her stomach. "When did you two become so chummy again? You guys are *always* together." Her tone is sour, but her smiling eyes are locked on Finch.

I step in front of him, sharing my scowl. "None of your business."

Mom continues to dish up the plates, her lips sealed. From the way she is avoiding looking at either one of us, I know she won't interject.

Sawyer leans back, her perfect smile slipping at the corners. She opens her mouth to say something, but Doc walks around the island bench to grab me in a tight hug. "*Liam.*" She barely holds me for more than a few seconds before she's stepping back and cupping my face in her small, warm hands, capturing my attention completely. "Don't you go running off in the middle of the night like that again, you hear me?" she chides me, her brows furrowing. "You had me worried sick."

I...what?

Gawking at her, my mind plays her words over and over again. *What does she mean by that?* I peek over at Dean, but his arms are crossed over his broad chest and he's giving me the same disapproving look. I look at Finch, but he's grinning behind his palm. My skin is cold everywhere, Doc's hand's like heaters against my cheeks.

You had me worried sick.

"Sorry," I mumble, meeting Doc's gaze again. *She wants me to apologise, right?* Doc smiles again, her eyes crinkling at the corners as she nods and drops her hands away from my face. When I glance over at mom, her eyes glassy and her lips are pressed together tightly. She quickly busies herself by plating up dinner, Doc moving around me to help her.

I stare at the two of them for a moment, taking in mom's rigid shoulders and Doc's easy smile. *I don't get it. Why are they so different?*

"Come on, boys," Dean says, glancing between me, Finch, and where Noodles is leaning against the island next to mom. "Let's get out of the way." He nods towards the dining room, and the three of us follow him out. I don't turn back to look at the girls. I don't think I can stomach looking at my mother any longer.

Why are they so different?

Dean takes a seat on one side of the table, but I follow Finch to the other side, hesitating before I finally take the seat beside him. I watch Dean listen intently as Noodles tells him about something he and his friend did today, and my mind reels from everything that's happened over the last twenty-four hours. *How is he so calm after what happened last night?* I glance at Finch and catch him quickly looking away. *How are either of them so damn calm?*

"*Breathe*, Liam." When my eyes focus, Finch is looking at me again, his eyebrows raised. I drag in a deep breath, ready for this night to be over already.

Mom and Lemon wander in with plates, placing them down at each setting. When a plate drops down in front of me, I don't raise my head as I mumble, "Thanks, Lemon." I think she hesitates on her way back to the kitchen, and my spine stiffens when I realise I said that out loud. Finch's gaze burns into my cheek, but I just stare harder at the food on my plate.

Before he can say anything, Sawyer walks in under dad's arm and I shrivel into myself even further.

I know the exact moment he sees me. A cold shiver races down my spine, and my scarred palms become clammy. I don't look up to see his face. I can't look up. *I can't.*

Why did I let Finch drag me to this dinner? My shoulders bunch up as my hands shake in my lap. He's going to say something. Something horrible. Remind me how useless I am. That I'm a bother.

A bother.

"Always good to see you, Dean." He lets Sawyer slip away as he reaches out to shake Dean's hand. Dean takes it in a firm hold, his eyes small as he looks back at my father.

"Jasper," is all he offers in reply. When my father passes Noodles, he rubs his hand against his curly hair and Noodles tries to fix it. Mom and Doc walk in with the last plates before taking their seats. Mom sits between where I sit and the head of the table. Where my father sits. She flutters her hands over her skirt as my father goes to takes his seat. It's not until he tells her she looks beautiful that she finally stops. His smile is strange when he spots Finch sitting on the other side of me.

"Good to see you, son." My throat closes rapidly, the air thin as he strides around the back of our chairs and holds his hand out for Finch to take. My spine stiffens and my insides clench when he stands behind me. I don't know if Finch notices, but he takes dad's hand and shakes it with a dark look on his face.

"*Yep.*"

Finch's biting tone has bile rising in my throat. My heart thuds painfully in my chest, my eyes burning. But Finch's lips form a grim line. When I peek over at Dean, he's already watching me, his square jaw clenching. I quickly look back down at my plate.

Dad moves to his seat, completely ignoring my presence. I lean over my plate, my fingers inching towards my fork. I want nothing more than an escape from this dinner; it's always more uncomfortable when we have guests.

I catch Finch pulling a face out of the corner of my eye as dad takes his seat, so I quickly pinch his thigh. He jumps in his seat, his hooded eyes flashing to me. I shake my head slowly, because I already don't know what to do with myself right now, and I don't need him sticking his foot in it.

"Well, let's eat." Dad claps his hands together and rubs them, and I flinch at the sharp sound. My body is too tense right now. I just need to block him out and eat my dinner, then I can excuse myself.

You are not to bother them in their time here.

Am I clear?

Something curls around my fingers, pulling my hand from my lap. I glance down, finding Finch's hand folding around mine, squeezing gently. My eyes stay locked on his fingers, my mind fritzing until nothing is left in my head. *Why is he...holding...Why's his hand...?*

Dad and Dean talk about politics and the crime rate. Mom asks Doc about work, and Doc starts to yammer on about her days in the hospital. My eyes keep drifting back to wear Doc's and Dean's hands are interlocked on the table. As if reading my mind, Finch slowly weaves our fingers, his strange warmth spreading up my arm and settling in my chest. Mom's eyes flicker to me when I take in a stuttered breath, but she doesn't ask. *She won't.*

I'm terrified to look at Finch's face. I don't know what to expect if I do. *Would he already be looking back? Would he be smiling? Would he be watching me with those dark eyes? His hand is so big, even though we're both guys. Shouldn't we have the same size hands? Why are his so big? And soft?*

Remembering how scarred and ugly my hands are, I try to slip away from his grip, but he squeezes tighter. I sneak a peek from the corner of my eye, finding him doing the same thing. He smiles, his narrow eyes twinkling. *Have his eyes always sparkled? Is it weird that they're sparkling? I can't even remember what they used to look like before now.* Snapping my head back to my plate, I leave my hand in his. *Maybe he's anxious or something. Is this helpful for him?*

The clinking of cutlery on the ceramic plates cuts through any other silence that had been lingering in the air, but it all starts to blur away. Noodles tries to talk to Sawyer about something from his school club, but she doesn't entertain the conversation. Her eyes are locked on Finch, who seems to be making a very obvious point of not looking her way.

"By the way, you were amazing last night, Fin." Sawyer leans forward, and my jaw creaks. Julia's eyes are darting between Finch and I, and for a short moment I wonder whether she knows he kissed me last night. *That happened last night, right? I didn't imagine it, did I? Do I look different now that I've been kissed? I mean, my lips aren't swollen or anything, so I don't look kissed.* But the way she is staring makes me worry she can read minds. *Does she have superpowers, too? Can she tell that he's holding my hand under the table?* My head doesn't move as my eyes drift across the table. Mom isn't holding my father's hand. *Why are they different?*

Will everyone hate us for holding hands? Does holding hands with Finch mean I'm gay? Would they care? Would they hate it?

Finch clears his throat with an awkward look on his face,

nodding his head but keeping his eyes on his plate. "Thanks, Sawyer."

His fingers are clenched tight around mine, and he's blinking hard. Something strange fills my chest. It's so refreshing to see him so uncomfortable. Even if it is due to my sister's unwavering stare.

She twirls the pasta on her plate, bumping her shoulder with Julia. I watch beneath my eyelashes as Julia shrugs back, her face pinched. Sawyer rolls her eyes, leaning forward again.

"So where'd you go after the game? You weren't out celebrating with the rest of the team..."

I nearly choke on my pasta. Finch too. His hand tightens when I try to pull away. Julia's eyes suddenly light up, and a small smile peeks at the corners of her mouth. *How does Sawyer know we weren't with the team?* Something sickening twists in my stomach, and I look to Finch.

I won't do it again, I promise.

I'm sorry Liam. I won't do it again, I promise.

Why does that keep repeating in my head? Why is he holding my hand so damn tightly?

"They came back home," Dean answers, a small smile on his face as he glances between the two of us across the table.

They came back home.

Back home.

"I was really tired after the game," Finch adds in between bites, "so Liam and I bailed early." He doesn't give her any more information and focuses on his slowly diminishing bowl of ravioli. The look on Doc's face reminds me that she was told we had been partying hard last night before we went back to their house, but her confusion isn't aimed

225

towards me. Despite that, something in my stomach starts to unravel and tighten in the same breath.

"That's understandable after the way you carried the team last night," my father comments with a tight-lipped smile, his gaze lifting to Finch. I tense at his side, my mouth pinching. He always says things like this. He wants me to say something, so that he can knock me back down. I know what he's doing, but I still fall into the same trap every time.

"He didn't carry the team, they all played hard last night," I say, forcing myself to slacken my jaw so I don't speak through my teeth. My father's cutlery stills, his jaw clenching, but he doesn't look up. My hand clench around my fork as I avert my eyes before he can return my stare.

Shut up, Liam. Just shut up.

"You all played great last night." Dean says in his gruff tone. My stomach twists in knots so tight that the thought of eating is sickening. Finch is strangely silent beside me, and I can feel his gaze, but I refuse to look his way. Lemon is still watching, and Sawyer hasn't blinked.

"Definitely! It will be awesome for you and Liam to be playing in the Championships in a couple weeks," Doc's hype might have tempted a smile on my lips if my head wasn't starting to swim.

"It seemed to me that the team was more than capable of winning without him."

My father's comment vacuums the air straight from my lungs. A dark pit settles in my stomach. My movements slow and my gut starts to twist up in a ball again. My skin turns icy, and my fingers stiffen.

Capable of winning without him.

Capable...without him.

That's what he thinks. That's what he always thinks...

I warned you.

"Exactly! But there's no way they could have won without you, Fin," Sawyer rubs, her eyes flickering over me before zeroing back in on Finch again. They sparkle as she looks at him, and my stomach churns hot and sickly. *I think I'm gonna hurl.* I clench my fingers tight around his.

Finch drops his fork down onto his plate loudly, resting his wrist against the edge of the table as his other hand grips mine tighter. He has a challenging look in his eyes that has my stomach twisting tighter. "Have you even *seen* Liam play?" His eyes are locked on my father, his lips a tight line and his face a pale pink. The hand holding mine starts to shake. His nostrils are flaring hard, but his breathing doesn't sound laboured or harsh.

Dad returns his look with high brows, gently placing his own cutlery down on his plate. "Excuse me?"

I am definitely gonna hurl.

Please don't do this right now, Finch. Please don't.

Please, please, please...

"I don't remember ever seeing you at any of our games before last night, so I assume the only reason you were there was because it was Sawyer's first Cheer Rally."

"Finch, shut up," I hiss out under my breath, my eyes still glued to my plate as I try to tug my hand from his. My voice is so thick, it doesn't sound like it's mine. *I know that was the only reason he was there last night. I know, okay? I know.*

"What are you trying—" Dad tries to argue, but Finch cuts in.

"Trying to say?" He's getting smart now, his eyebrows high as well. Bile rises in my throat, my head becoming fuzzy and light. "You tell me. I asked if you have ever seen Liam play basketball? It's a yes or no question, not too difficult. Nothing to get defensive over, is it?"

My father looks over to Dean incredulously, his jaw slack. "Are you not going to control your nephew, Dean?"

"He's capable of speaking for himself. And he's not asking anything I'm not wondering *myself*." Dean's eyes narrow on my father, his grip on Doc's hand even tighter than before. My skin starts to crawl, and my father's dark stare flickers to me, probably thinking that I prompted this. But I told Finch to leave it. *I told him not to ask. I told him to shut up.*

I told him, I told him, I told him.

Trying to take a deep breath, my eyes cross as I struggle to stay conscious. *When did the room start spinning?*

Lemon and Sawyer watch Finch with wide eyes, and Noodles' mouth is hanging open.

"You think we were 'more than capable of winning without him', but in case you forgot, we were *losing* that first half of the game until Liam came down from the stands." His hand is shaking harder now, the hairs on my arm standing on end.

"Look here, son, I don't—" Dad's face is bright red now. I don't know whether it's from embarrassment or anger. Probably both. I can't remember the last time he was interrupted this many times.

"You haven't said a single word to Liam this *entire* dinner." Finch snaps, his nostrils flaring. "You haven't even *looked* at him."

It's suddenly so silent that I swear I can hear *dust* falling.

"He was the only one you didn't greet when you walked

228

in. Did you seriously think we wouldn't care enough to notice that?"

"Finch, why are you—?" Sawyer tries to cut in, glancing between our father and Finch, as if she doesn't understand what accusation Finch is making. Mom has her chin tucked against her chest, her eyes planted on her plate. Her shoulders are shaking and her lip trembles, but she doesn't look away from her untouched pasta.

"Is Liam not allowed to have dinner with you or something? Because he seemed quite anxious about dining with us tonight."

Anxious? No, I wasn't. I just...I can't...they never—

Is Liam not allowed to?

I...

"He doesn't like to eat with us." Sawyer rushes out, her wide eyes finding mine. "Aren't you gonna say something?" she asks me, her hard tone hitting me in the centre of my chest. I can't speak. I can't even open my mouth to *look* like I'm going to speak.

I can't.

"Liam and I stopped in at Maurie's last night."

No, Finch...Please don't mention it...Please don't.

My face burns and my throat constricts again. When I peek at him from the corner of my eye, his face is bright red, and his eyes are filled with fire. "Neither of us realised that Liam is moving to *Toronto*. Which is weird, considering Maurie said it was *Liam* who decided—"

"*Finch, stop!*" The words pour out of me like a burst pipe, but they sound far away. I'm surprised the bile lingering at the back of my throat didn't follow. My hands are shaking now, my eyes itchy and sore. Maybe it's me who isn't blinking.

My eyes drift to mom and find her staring at mine and Finch's coupled hands. Her eyes are wide, and her mouth is now stretched out in a grim line. Her nose crinkles, and my heart stops.

I rip my hand out of Finch's hold as I rise from the table and rush out of the room. Something claws at my chest, tightening so hard around my throat that my vision goes blurry. I stumble against the banister when I make it to the foyer, and my stomach twists. *Are the walls shrinking? There isn't enough air in here...I can't...breathe.*

Did you seriously think we wouldn't care enough to notice that?

Did you seriously think we wouldn't care?

Don't. Don't say those things. I can't...

I fumble with the front door, yanking it open and falling outside into the cold. The air is like ice in my lungs; everything's swollen and achy. I only manage a few steps away from the front door before I fall to my knees on the grass. I think it's about to snow. It's wet. Cold. *Is that what it is inside me? Cold?*

"Liam, talk to me. What do you need?" The voice sounds far away, but my hand passing through the blades of grass is loud and scratchy. Something warm presses against my shoulder blade, but all I can hear is the air slicing between my teeth. *Is that my blood thumping in my ears? Can I normally hear that? I think I'm going to be sick.*

"*Come on...*" My arm is pulled up gently, but my entire body prickles. My feet hurt with every step I take, my vision domed and glassy. When I sit down again, it's...familiar. The smell is familiar too. *Last night. I smelt it last night...after the* game. *I know it...*

"Finch." My voice is barely above a whisper. I don't know if he hears me.

Please hear me.

My head turns slowly when something rumbles beneath me, and I watch Finch putting his car into gear and rip away from the curb. The longer I focus on him—on his rigid jaw, his narrow eyes, and his floppy hair—the slower my chest rises and falls. Focusing on something other than the voices in my head seems to make them fade away, until they eventually become nothing.

Sounds start to filter back in. First the growl of the engine, then the jingle of his keys as they swing from the ignition. Finch is quiet, but his hands are shaking. Violently, as they somehow clench around the wheel without jarring the car side to side. As I think that, the car jerks slightly, before he decides to pull over. I don't know how far we've travelled. I haven't looked outside yet. It's still warm inside. He hasn't turned the car off.

Finch clasps his hands together, his shoulders shaking and his face a bright red. My mind is still fuzzy, but I reach forward and wrap his hands in mine. I don't know why, but I know he needs it.

My tongue threatens to choke me when I try to speak, so I stay silent and breathe. When I look back up, Finch is staring down at our hands. His face darkens a deeper shade of red as he strains every muscle in his body, but a few seconds later he blows out a loud, heavy breath. Minutes, or maybe hours pass, as the two of us focus on slowing our breathing. I don't know why he's so worked up, but I can't formulate words yet to ask.

"Liam, I didn't mean to upset you. I thought that was the right thing to do. The way he ignored you, and what he was saying, I couldn't—" He leans his head back against his seat and blows out a long sigh. His body isn't quaking anymore, but his hands are still trembling. Warmth slowly starts to seep back into the cab of the car, and the fog in my head starts to dissipate. I bring my hands back to my lap.

"Why did..." My mouth fills with cotton, and my eyes are itchy.

"Why did I call your dad out on that bullshit?" he hisses, his eyes pinched tight.

"Why did you kiss me?" I rasp out. Finch rockets forward in his seat, his eyes wide open and his lips parted. He furrows his eyebrows at me, searching my face. Something there must tell him that his next words are very important. But I need to know. *I need him to say that it was because he was blowing off some steam. That it was an adrenaline rush. That it didn't mean anything to him.*

Because I want to.

His mouth pops open and his gaze softens. He watches me as I grip my knees, my thumbs rubbing against my jeans. I stare at the fresh grass stains, the denim damp there. His hair flops back in front of his eyes, and he doesn't brush it aside. "Liam, you're..." he trails off, licking his lips and rubbing them together. I wipe the sweat from my palms onto my jeans as I scrub them against my thighs, the sensitive skin tingling from the friction.

"It was random, and we always fight, so I don't understand...why you would—" I look through the windshield, the words rough in my throat.

Finch leans closer, pushing his fingers through his hair,

finally combing it back. "Liam, there is a lot I want to tell you. There's so much that I wanted to say last night, but then everything happened." When he leans his back against the door, he watches me with worried eyes. "Liam, you might not believe it, but you are the *most* important person to me. You...you have been ever since fourth grade."

I blink. I blink again. Though my breathing has evened out my heart seems to beat a mile a minute.

Most important.

He sounds ridiculous. "You've—"

"I kissed you because I wanted to, because it's all I've wanted to do," he whispers, watching me like I'm gonna explode.

Am I going to? Something strange settles in my chest like a heavy, but comfortable blanket. He's tiptoeing right now, trying not to say something I can't handle, but giving me what I seem to need. I don't even know what that is anymore.

The car's warm again. It rumbles beneath us quietly. I nod my head. Then I nod again because I don't know how else to respond. I rub my legs hard, my shoulders tensing as I watch him from under my lashes. He leans forward, resting his hand on top of mine. My hands freeze over my kneecaps. He curls his fingers under my palm, latching onto my rough hand tightly. I turn to look at him head-on, my lips pulled in a grim line.

"Liam, I'm *right here*. I'm not going anywhere, no matter what you say, and no matter what you think about me or about yourself. I am going to be here to tell you that whatever bad things you're thinking are wrong. You're not going to be alone through anything, okay?"

Like something cold has been dumped on the raging fire

inside me, my shoulders slump and my head falls back against the head rest. Everything inside me is burnt and crispy and flaking as I keep my eyes locked on Finch. He stares back, his gaze unwavering. After a long time, with only the thrumming of the car to fill the silence, I nod my head.

"Whatever," I mutter, my throat raw and croaky. My eyes droop and my hands uncurl because his nose didn't twitch. And if he does that every time he lies, like I think he does, then I can relax for now.

"Okay." There is a shift in the car before we're moving again. I watch the streets pass by in silence, and Finch doesn't try to say anymore. My mind is hazy as we drive, until I recognise one of the streets we turn down. I glance over at Finch, quirking an eyebrow at him.

Finch doesn't look my way as he says, "You're staying at my house tonight. And maybe every night after that."

I don't look at him when I ask, "Won't that bother your family—?"

"*Stop*, Liam. You're not bothering anyone."

You're not bothering anyone.

Yeah right.

When he pulls up out front, the glow from the streetlight above us disappears, blocked by the large elm tree at the edge of the Montgomery's yard. Memories of the two of us climbing that same tree when we were younger start to surface, my mind unguarded for a moment. *He's always laughed so damn much. For as long as I've known him, he's had a stupid big smile on his face. Why do I never hear him laughing anymore?*

Because I ruined everything.

When Finch shuts off the car, the clicking of the engine

echoes like a drum.

"Wait, are those the two you were telling me about?" he asks, nodding towards the house. When I turn to look, I spot Blue and Ginger sitting on the porch. Ginger has his arm around her shoulders, his mouth moving fast as he speaks to her. Blue's hunched over, holding her stomach.

I nod, glancing back at Finch. He blows out a loud breath and rakes his hand through his thick hair, tugging it back. We climb out of the car slowly, Finch coming around to my side in seconds, but he doesn't touch me.

When he turns to face the two of them, he doesn't let me put any distance between us. "I'm sorry, this isn't really a good time right now," he says when they're in earshot.

Blue looks like she is about to puke. Her dark complexion is washed out, and her forehead is dotted with perspiration. *Does this girl do anything other than hurl her guts?* Ginger holds her close, his eyes wide and worried.

"We haven't officially met, but we can get to that later then." Ginger looks at *me* now, his lips pursed. "Cece can sense something."

Finch glances at me, and my head starts to pound. My vision is hazy, and I can't get my mouth to work, so Finch asks, "What does that mean?"

Ginger rises to his feet, standing toe to toe with Finch. His eyes are harder now. "She can sense you. That's why we came here last night in the first place – how we were able to find you. We were on our way home when she felt it." He glances back at me again because I'm the one who knows what he's talking about. "She can sense someone *else*."

Someone else?

There's more. More people that are special. More people like them. People that can do amazing things. People that are liked. People that are loved. People that are different from me.

Always different.

"Look, I get that you met Liam and my uncle last night and that you're somewhat like me, but right now is *not a good time*."

Ginger stares at Finch like he's grown a second head. "Dude, this is only the second time she's ever sensed someone else like us. This is a *big deal—*"

"Like I said, *not a good time*." Finch's eyes darken, his voice rough. They both shut up, their eyes wary. Ginger looks over at me, his mouth pops open as if he's about to ask something. I don't see it, but I think Finch cuts him a look that has his jaw snapping shut.

Why is my head so fuzzy? Did I ruin things tonight? With my family? With our families? With Finch? Am I ruining things right now?

"Come on," Finch's voice is softer now as he takes my

hand, and I follow him towards the house with heavy feet.

His hand is warm.

My skin prickles when we step inside, and I breathe in a long sigh. The lights turn on automatically, illuminating the foyer and staircase. I think Finch asks me if I'm hungry, but I don't remember giving him an answer as he guides me up the stairs. He walks at my pace, never tugging on my arm. My eyes follow his heels as we take each step slowly. When I finally look up, we're in his room. I don't know where Blue and Ginger went, but I can't bring myself to care. I've been rung so tight, there's nothing left in me to question it.

I've been in this room a lot recently. *It always smells like that food he likes...which one is it again? Why can't I think of it? It's all he ever eats.*

"Liam." I look up to find Finch watching me, his eyebrows drawn together. "Do you want to talk about what happened at dinner?"

I close my eyes. "Fuck no."

He reaches out and touches my hand. It's a simple, light touch. One that has my heart hammering a mile a minute. "I'm sorry I never noticed what you were going through."

I'm sorry I never noticed.

Swallowing the thick lump in my throat, I mutter, "Not your job to notice."

"I want it to be." He watches me with tight eyes. It's the same look he gave me when I first came here that day after school. When I climbed up onto that rickety gazebo outside his window determined to figure out what really happened that night that everything changed.

I sit down on his bed and lean back, my body all but melting into the sheets. My skin tingles where it touches the covers. The bed dips as Finch lays down beside me. He doesn't say anything for the longest time.

It isn't until my thoughts become too loud that I finally break the silence. "Why didn't you tell me about your powers when you first found out about them? Why did you lie to me?" *Did he not trust me? Maybe he still doesn't.* Seeing Blue and Ginger only reminded me that I'm not special anymore. *They know, and Dean knows.*

He doesn't trust me. Why would he? For the past six years, I've made it my mission to beat him. To be better. Why would he trust me? I've done nothing—

"Because I don't know how dangerous this could be..." he mumbles, his voice rough. "I didn't want you to get hurt by this more than you already were."

My hands clench on reflex. It was his blood, but it wasn't his fault. I don't blame him for what happened to my hands. I already told him that. I haven't for a long time now. But he's been keeping things to himself as well. Prying my eyes open, I turn my head to look at him. He's already staring at me, lying on his back with his hair falling away from his face.

Some part of me, some normal part that Finch *does* know, seeps out. "That's bullshit."

His pupils pulsate, and his lips screw up on his face. *Why does he look good pulling a face like that? The jerk.* "That's how I felt about it, how I *still* feel about it. I don't want you involved in whatever this is, Liam. I don't know how dangerous things could get. We don't even know why I'm like this now."

I lay there, staring at him, my vision doming slightly. His skin is so clear; he doesn't have a single freckle. *How is that even possible?* He's blinking rapidly now, his dark eyes glassy, as if everything he's been bottling up is suddenly pouring out of him like a tap he can't turn off.

"I don't know how to control any of this, and it's fucking *terrifying*. There's a voice in my head that's telling me to go to Chicago, and now there is some *monster* inside me that's triggered by something I can't explain."

I suck in a breath, my eyes narrowing. "It wasn't you." I remember the black, empty void in his eyes and a cold shiver races down my spine. *Definitely not him.*

Finch nods. "I know. Whatever it was felt dark and slimy...so full of hate. I don't remember *anything* that happened. It was like another *thing* was inside me."

"You mean like Jekyll and Hyde?"

Finch shrugs. "I don't know, maybe." His eyes study my face. "I don't know what it was, or how to control it. When I got angry at your dad, it was like something was swallowing me whole. I had no control, and it was getting too close to the surface, but then, in the car, you touched my hand..."

The version of me that he knows is slowly slipping back into place, the more he keeps talking. I didn't know how effective his stupid voice could be. Little by little, the numbness evaporates. "Why are you—"

"I can't control anything you do, Liam. I've never been able to. You care too much, and I don't want you to ever stop caring. I don't want you to look anywhere else but at me." He glances down as he reaches out for my hand. I let him take it, even when my chest tightens. "I don't want you to get tired of me, or ever want someone who isn't me. I feel sick whenever I think about you not being here. Not helping me, or touching me, or calling me a jerk." He's still watching his thumb as it strokes the back of my hand, and my stomach twists into knots.

Why does that feel so nice? Why is it hard to breathe again?

"I want you here with me, *always*. And it's selfish of me, but I don't fucking care." He turns his head to stare up at the ceiling, his forehead creasing. "Why *can't* I be selfish? You're finally looking at me, you're calling me Finch again. Why can't I keep that?" He sounds like he's arguing with himself now.

My lungs seize up, my heart thudding in my chest. *Can he hear it? Surely he can.*

"I'm gonna be more selfish with you, as selfish as I'm allowed to be. Because I don't know when I'm gonna wake up and you'll be back to hating me," he breathes out.

"I never stopped hating you," I mumble.

He laughs this time. It's an I-don't-believe-you kind of laugh, but I watch it reach his eyes. The same eyes as always, but now they look at me differently. Or maybe I'm just noticing that look. Now I know what it means. *When did I start calling him Finch?*

"Yeah, I know," he mutters, his chest puffing up with each breath.

My mind flashes to that kiss. Something changed there. For us. My heart clenches when I remember how warm and soft his mouth was. *Is it wrong to think it was nice? Does that mean I'm gay? Is that bad? I don't know anything about that. Does that ruin things?*

It doesn't with Finch. I haven't ruined it yet.

His smile is bigger now. He reaches his other arm across his body, rolling onto his side as he pulls my head forward, resting his forehead against mine. "You better get comfortable, Liam. Cause I'm not going anywhere."

I roll my eyes, but I don't pull away. I'll blame it on my lack of energy. "Whatever."

I'm not going anywhere.

I want to believe that. *More than anything, I want to believe that.*

I jolt forward, my eyes blankly searching the darkness. My hands rub frantically at my thighs, but the shadows of blood don't wipe off.

No, not again. He's fine. Stop. He's gonna be okay.

"You are not allowed to die, do you hear me?" I mutter. *He has to hear me. He has to know that I won't let him die.*

Don't die, don't die, don't die.

"Liam?" The tired voice nearby doesn't pierce through the haze. It's like wind in the background.

"Stop the blood, stop the blood—" My lungs seize. *He's bleeding. Where the fuck is the ambulance? Stop the blood. It's between my fingers. It's hot, really hot. I've got to stop the blood.*

"Liam, what's wrong?"

Stop the blood, stop the blood, stop the blood.

"You're not going to die..." His eyes are dazed and glassy. *Is he dying? I told him he can't. He's not allowed to. I can't let him. I won't let him. Stop the blood. It's between my fingers. Why are my fingers tingling?*

Lia—

Something warm grabs my arms and shakes me. The motion jerks me out of my daze, my hands freezing in front of me. My sweat is cold now, violent shivers ripping through my body. When I look up, Finch stares back at me, his face illuminated by the streetlight leaking through the window. His brows draw together as his lips pull in a tight line.

Finch.

When I press my hand against his torso he jumps back slightly. But the blood is gone. I choke on my next breath, my eyes pinching. "I'm fine," I breathe out. My shoulders are shaking, but the air is coming easier now, each breath is clearer than the last. The hairs on the back of my neck are on end, and my molars ache from grinding my jaw.

"Liam…"

I drop my hand back to my lap and shake his grip off. "*I'm fine.*"

"Stop saying that." He shuffles closer on the bed, his voice soft.

My hands fist the comforter, and I raise my eyes to the ceiling. "It was just a bad dream. Don't make a big deal about it."

He shakes his head, drawing my gaze. "I remember that night, Liam." My hands bunch the blankets tighter. "I remember everything that happened, everything you said to me. I healed, I know, but I'm still scared sometimes." I look at him now, my gaze drawn to the small smile tugging at his lips.

I nod, the words stuck in my throat as he keeps talking. "I know that it wasn't my fault that guy chose that shop to rob, but it was my decision to step out into that aisle." There is a long pause, until he sighs. "I did it because I know you, Liam. Maybe not as much as I want to, or as much as I thought. But I could see all over your face that you were only seconds away from stepping out into view. There was

242

nothing else I could have done to stop you other than step out first."

"I hate you," I say, my voice weak and croaky. He smiles back, but it doesn't reach his eyes this time. He opens his mouth to respond, but I rush to speak before him. "How is that fair? I watched you get *shot*." I take a deep breath in, and it comes out shaky. "You were *dying*." My breath hisses between my lips. "I didn't know if you would be there the next day. I had no idea what I would do with myself if you died like that."

"It's okay, Liam. I healed—"

"But what if you *didn't*?" I almost shout. "What would I have done then?" A hiccup slips free but refuse to let a single tear fall. "How the hell would I have coped with that? With your blood on my hands and you lying there *dead* because I was too damn useless to save you..."

"Liam..." Finch's eyebrows sit low over his eyes. Collapsing back on the bed, I rub my hands against my face. *Don't cry, damn it.*

"You don't get it, Finch, because you weren't going to be the one who had to live the rest of his life knowing that it was all your fault." It would have been *crippling*.

Dean...Doc...His cousins...They all would've hated me.

Would have wished it had been me who stepped out. Wished it had been me that was shot.

Wished it were me that died.

Not Finch.

Not Finch not Finch not Finch.

"I sound so fucking dumb right now." The bed rocks, and my eyes bulge out of my head when Finch leans over me from where he sits on the edge of the bed. His arms cage me in, his chest hovering above mine. His mouth is relaxed now. *Have I always thought he had a nice mouth?* I'm always looking there. Now that I know how soft it is.

"You don't. Just keep talking to me." His hair's a mess. It's always a mess. He watches me with tired eyes, a droopy smile pulling at the corners of his lips. *Yeah, his mouth never used to look that nice. No way.*

"What do you want me to say?"

"Do I get to choose?"

"Fuck no."

His laughter shakes the bed, drawing my attention to him entirely. "Let's change the subject, okay? I want to ask you something," he mumbles, blinking slowly. I raise my eyebrow, my cheeks burning from the feel of his breath against them. "Right now, this doesn't..." he leans back a little bit, "make you uncomfortable?" I shrug my shoulders and shake my head at the same time. His airy laughter blows his breath over my face. "It doesn't weird you out at all?"

"Weird me out?"

He leans his weight over onto one hand and taps the other against my forehead lightly. "Because I kissed you. And I'm a guy."

Kissing a guy. I can only imagine the look on my father's face. *Would he even care?* The way mom's face curled when she saw our joined hands...

But looking up at Finch's mouth—*it definitely didn't used to look that nice*—those itchy thoughts start to drift off. He promised he would never do it again. I reach up between us to rub at my chest. *Why does it hurt to remember that?*

I shrug again, but my eyes are glued to his. "Does it weird *you* out?"

Finch's eyes narrow. "Why would it weird *me* out?"

"Cause you also kissed a guy." The room is starting to feel warmer again, my skin erupting into goosebumps. I can't tell if it's in response to Finch hovering over me, or if I'm finally starting to settle.

"Yeah, but I've wanted to kiss you for a long time."

My lips twitch. "How long?"

"Too long," he responds as he brushes his hand against my hair. His thumb lingers on the mole above my eyebrow, his eyes flickering over it occasionally.

"Did you mean what you said?"

His brows dip and my heart thuds hard and loud in my chest. *God, I hope he can't hear it.* "What I said?"

When I swallow, the motion draws his eyes to my throat. My hands start to sweat against the covers. It's like a magnet has suddenly been placed in my chest, drawing me impossibly close to him. But it's different. It's not normal for us.

"About never doing it again." My cheeks burn, and my first thought is to look away from his intense stare, but something in his eyes doesn't let me.

About never doing it again.

"I won't do anything you don't want me to do." He leans back. "So if you want me to kiss you, you have to tell me."

If you want me to kiss you, you have to tell me.

You have to tell me.

If you want me to kiss you...

"You can't make me do anything I don't want to do, Finch," I grumble. *I won't let this jerk walk all over me.* But as I lie there, staring up at him, my eyes drift back to his mouth. My entire face burns as I remember being pressed against the rough brick, his hand petting the back of my head, keeping my lips pressed against his. "Say, *hypothetically*, I did want you to kiss me...does that mean I'm gay?"

I can tell he's trying not to smile. "It isn't just black or white, there's a lot in between. Are you attracted to other guys?"

I shake my head, my cheeks hotter than before. "No."

"Are you attracted to *me*?" He studies me closely as he asks.

I turn my head to face the wall, avoiding his stare. "*Jerk*."

My heart hammers so hard in my chest I think it might crack my ribs. From the corner of my eye something flickers across his face. But before I can figure out what it might mean, he's back to smiling down at me with a soft grin.

"Just because you're attracted to me, doesn't mean you're gay. But if that feels like it fits, then that's your choice."

I nod slowly, my eyes wandering away. *I don't really know what that means. Is it a bother?*

Were you bothering Fin—

"Are you feeling better now?" His thumb touches my temple, but he doesn't move closer.

I clear my throat and nod. "Yeah."

"Good." He purses his lips. "I need to ask you to do something."

I lie completely still as I wait for him to continue, staring up at his chin instead of his eyes as I try to swallow past the lump in my throat.

"If I lose control again like I did last night," His chin moves as his jaw clenches, "you get the hell away from me."

There is a long moment where neither of us speak. *Why*

246

would he ask me to do that? "Finch—"

"And that's *not* a request, Liam." When I finally glance up at him, his eyes are softer.

My fingers tighten around the comforter again, my eyes closing. "That's not up to you, Finch. I'll do whatever the hell I want."

"Liam, whatever happened to me last night could happen again. I was *dangerous*. I—"

"I'm the one who found you in the woods, remember?" I bite out, glaring at him. "I'm the one who found you with blood on your shirt and face down in the mud."

"Liam..." He tries to shift into a seated position but falls back onto the edge of the bed when I suddenly sit up.

"*No*, Finch. I'm not going to leave you on your own when you don't even know what you're doing."

You did good, Liam.

I've got you.

His teeth peek through his lips. "It's not *safe*."

"*I don't care.*" *Damn jerk.*

"You don't heal quickly like I do. If something happens and you get hurt—"

"Then that's *my* problem to deal with." I throw my hands up, sick of this conversation.

He leans away, his face crumpling. "You think I wouldn't care if you got hurt?"

Something in my stomach clenches. I don't look at him as I say, "I think it doesn't matter, because in the end it's *my* choice." Finch rubs his palms over his face, nodding his head.

"I'm sorry about tonight," he changes the subject, staring down at his hands in his lap. "I didn't mean to make things worse. I just..." His fists clench tight and his eyes pinch shut. "I *hated* seeing that, seeing the way your family treats you."

I shrug. "It's fine, Finch," I mumble as I lay back down to face the ceiling.

"I thought that if I told your dad where to stick it, you would feel better, now that someone has your back."

I only shrug again.

CHAPTER

25

Light burns my eyelids, rousing me from my dreamless sleep. When I open my eyes, the sun shines over Finch's shoulder, casting a glow around him. A burning ache forms in my chest as my eyes trace every part of him. *Something is different. Something* has to be *different.*

His eyes are closed. His hair is brushed back from his forehead. His lips are parted as he breathes each breath deep and slow. He's so closed, but something in my body keeps me frozen still.

What if I wake him up and everything shatters around me?

My chest starts to squeeze, so I sit up and look away from him. *Why is my chest so tight? It's just Finch.*

I slide out of the bed, careful to move slowly so I don't wake him. I stand at the foot of the bed for a moment, unsure what to do with myself. *Do I stay in here and wait for Finch to wake up? Do I go downstairs?*

I know his family, so I don't understand this nervous coil in my stomach. *Would they think it was weird that Finch and I ended up sharing a bed last night? Was it weird that we did?*

After I woke up last night, he never left me.

I'm not going anywhere.

I'm right here.

I've got you.

I open the door slowly and peek out into the corridor. There's shuffling downstairs, and a delicious smell floats towards me; my nose leads me down the stairs without permission. It's been so long since I've smelt pancakes. I can hear Doc's voice from the kitchen as I descend the stairs, talking to someone. When I slowly enter the kitchen, Lemon and Doc turn to face me.

"Good morning, hon." Doc's smile matches her soft-spoken words, her golden hair like a shiny waterfall as the sun reflects off each strand. She looks like an angel as she flips the pancake in the skillet.

"Morning." My voice is croaky and soft, my eyes flickering between the two of them. *What are they thinking right now? Are they okay that I'm here? I never asked permission to stay last night, and I ran out mid-way through dinner—*

Lemon stands up from her bar stool and wraps her arms around my waist. She rests her ear against my chest and squeezes me gently. My throat tickles in response. *Why is she holding me so tight? Why is she holding me at all?*

Before I can ask, she mumbles into my chest, "I'm so sorry, Liam."

I'm so sorry, Liam.

I'm so sorry.

I'm sorry, I won't do it again.

"Why?" My throat is hoarse as I stare at the island countertop, my arms hanging limply at my sides. *Am I supposed to hug her back? How long is she going to do this? She hasn't even said why she's hugging me. Is there something wrong?*

"Because you don't deserve to be treated the way you were last night. I'm so sorry."

You don't deserve...

You don't deserve to be treated that way.

I'm so sorry.

I hated seeing that.

Seeing the way your family treats you.

I clear my throat loudly, and Lemon's arms slowly drop. My body is cold when she lets go, and I don't look at her when she takes a step back to see my face. *What does she mean by that? Is that why she hugged me? Is that a reason to hug someone?*

Rubbing the back of my head, I nod. I don't know what to say. *Is there something I'm supposed to say?*

I think Lemon smiles at me, but I don't look until she finally turns her back to me and takes her seat at the island again. I watch the back of her head for a moment, trying to figure out what just happened and why. But sensing Doc's stare, I turn and find her smiling at me again as she flips the pancake out of the pan and pours in more of the mixture. Her smile is so soft, so pure. *Why is she smiling at me like that?*

Why is she so different?

My entire body tenses when there's a sudden loud knocking. I glance at the front door, but the solid wood doesn't allow for any indication of who's here. *Why is everyone up so early on a Sunday?*

"Why wouldn't they use the doorbell?" Doc mutters. I

turn back to face her, and she approaches with the spatula in hand. My eyes bulge when she tries to hand it to me. "Can you take over on pancake duty for me while I go answer the door?" She beams at me, her eyes crinkling at the corners.

Why would she smile at me like that?

I nod, my tongue numb as I take the spatula and move towards the frying pan. I stare down at the pale mixture, my mind racing as I try to figure out what I'm doing. I must look as lost as I feel, because seconds later Lemon is at my side pointing at the uncooked pancake.

"When there are heaps of little bubbles, you wiggle the spatula underneath and flip it over." I glance at her when she looks at the pan, and away when she looks at me. I follow her instructions, working the spatula under the hotcake and flipping it onto the uncooked side. Some of the mixture splatters, but it's golden and crispy.

Risking another peek at Lemon, I find her beaming up at me just like Doc had been. "What?"

She pokes my cheek. "You're *smiling.*"

I am? I glance back at the pancake, tempted to touch my face to feel where my smile was, but I don't want Lemon to see me. The tightness in my chest has almost completely dissipated–

"I'm not going to say it again, Jasper. *Get off my porch.*"

My hand clenches around the spatula and my shoulders stiffen.

Jasper.

My father.

I drop the spatula on the counter and rush towards the foyer, my heart in my throat. *Why is he here? Now? Why now?*

"He's *my son*, Alice. He'll come home when I *say* he comes home."

The air falters in my lungs. *That's the first time he's ever called me that.*

Doc's shoulders are bunched up, her hand clenched tightly around the door. He's on the other side of that. *He's here.*

Here, here, here.

"I don't think so. I won't let you hurt him more than you already have," she hisses. I take another step, and my eyes land on him. He's here, standing on the Montgomery's porch. He's wearing that trench coat I hate, and his hair is flipped up the way that always makes my skin crawl. His eyes are sharp and deadly when they find me.

"I understand your confusion, Alice, but you have the wrong idea. Liam," he says. His eyes pierce my skin, his words snaking into my veins. "You need to come home, *right now*. You're making your mother upset."

You're making your mother upset.

I warned you.

Next time you worry your mother like that...

I warned you.

I can't look away. My feet are planted, my chest heaving. Doc looks over her shoulder at me. I think she says something. Her golden hair floats over her shoulder. She's looking at me...

Mom's never looked at me like that.

Are you...joining us?

You don't have to ask, Liam. You can sit with us whenever you want to.

What's wrong with him?

Don't you go running off in the middle of the night like that again, you hear me?

What did you do, baby?

You had me worried sick.

Why is Doc looking at me like that?

She's looking at me, but my father's looking at her. Glaring at her, his jaw clenched tight. When Doc turns back, her spine is straight, her shoulders pulled back.

"If you don't leave, I'm going to call my husband and have him *remove you* from our property." She tries to slam the door, but his hand snatches it before she can, holding it open.

There's something strangling me now. I can't breathe. He's going to do something.

Something, something, something.

Doc tries to push the door again, but my father's hands are shaking now. "No need for such drastic measures, Alice." His voice is snakish and slimy, and my skin itches. "But I won't allow you to *kidnap* my son."

She stands up straighter, her knuckles white as she pushes on the door. "Are you *threatening* me, Jasper?"

Something, something, something.

"'Mayor's Son *kidnapped* by the Head Surgeon of Franklin Local Hospital'. Quite a *defamation*, wouldn't you say? Wouldn't look very good for Dean to arrest his wife, now would it?" His eyes are hard as his lip curls. "I have friends down at the paper, Alice. I can have it in everyone's hands by noon."

Something, something, something.

I know that look. I *know* that look. He's going to do something awful. I know he is. *He's going to hurt her.* I don't even realise I've moved until I'm standing almost toe-to-toe with my father.

"*Please don't hurt Alice.*"

Gripping her wrist and pulling her behind me, my fingers tremble. But I have to keep her there. *I have to.*

Can you take over on pancake duty for me?

I want to stay here. I want to stay here so bad.

"I'm sorry," I mutter, squeezing Alice's wrist once before I drop it and step out onto the porch. My father isn't looking at me again, but I don't pay it any mind.

"Liam, you can stay..." Alice tries, Lemon moving to stand behind her. Her eyes widen when she sees my father standing beside me, and before I can stop her, she takes off up the stairs.

No.

Please don't wake him up.

"I'm sorry for any inconvenience he caused, Alice, but Liam has to come home now." His tone has bite to it, but he doesn't say anything else as he turns and heads for his car, parked behind Finch's. I don't look back as I follow him. I can't look back. *What if she's looking at me differently?*

You don't have to ask, Liam. You can sit with us whenever you want to.

Don't look at me different. Please don't.

I'm not even halfway across the front yard when I hear his voice.

"Liam!"

My shoulders bunch up and my steps falter, but I don't stop. My father turns and raises an eyebrow, but he doesn't say anything. He's mad. He's *so mad.*

I warned you, I warned you, I—

"Liam, what are you doing?"

Not him. I don't want to do this. I can't do this.

"I'm going home." My voice wavers as I stare at my feet. *Get to the car. That's all I have to do. Just get to the car, and he won't hurt her. He won't. He can't—*

"No Liam, you're not!" He's too close. Finch grabs my shoulder and jerks me back. His hand is warm. *Why is he always so warm?*

I hate it. Hate it. *Why can't I breathe?*

"This has *nothing* to do with you, son." My father stops to glare at Finch, his eyes dark and empty. It hollows out my insides.

"You can go *fuck yourself*, you son of a bitch. Liam isn't going *anywhere* with you."

My entire body shaking. "*Finch, don't* ..." I can barely speak louder than a whisper. My knees are buckling and the roaring in my ears is deafening. *Does he hear me? Please don't say anything, Finch. He'll hurt her.*

Can you take over on pancake duty for me?

Finch is beside me now. He's hair is messy from sleep and he has blanket creases on his cheek, but he's wide awake and angrier than I've ever seen him.

My father takes a step closer and I reach out to push Finch back.

No, don't touch him. Not him either.

"Mind your tone. Don't forget who it is you're speaking to." He stands closer again, and my skin prickles, his voice filtered and distant. "This is a family matter. It doesn't concern you."

Don't touch him, don't touch him, don't touch him.

"*I don't care.* Get the fuck away from him, or I'll have my uncle arrest your abusive ass." Finch moves forward again, but I shove him back. *No.*

"*Stop...*" The air is too heavy. Too cold. It's not reaching my lungs.

Don't touch them.

"As long as he lives under my roof, I control him." My father hisses, his voice like poison against my fragile skin. It's gonna break me.

Break me break me break me.

"Then he can live here." It's cloudy, but it's her. My eyes peek up and spot Alice walking down the porch steps, her golden hair blowing in the gentle breeze. My chest seizes and acid fills my mouth.

Don't. Don't be here.

My arm is yanked forward, but I can barely see what's in front of me. The motion jerks me, my eyes burning and my chest heaving. "Stop be so dramatic, Liam." My arm is pulled hard, my bare feet stumbling in the grass. My skin tingles and zaps, aching where something grabs me tight. I'm jerked forward again, but my feet don't catch me this time. My knees hit the grass.

I can't breathe...

Can you take over on pancake duty for me?

Please don't...

"Don't touch him!"

The grip on my arm drops and my body curls over in the grass. My vision falters, the colours changing from green to grey. I can't stop shaking.

"Finch..." *Is that my voice? Why does it sound so muffled?*

How do I remember how to breathe?

"Liam..." Someone says my name, but they're so far away.

Miles away. My fingers clutch at the lawn, each blade like a knife slicing though my skin. He's angry. *So angry.*

I warned you.

What did you do, baby?

What have I told you about bothering the Montgomery's?

I can't breathe.

Someone screams, but it's muffled. There's noise, but I can't see. It's all blurry, *everything is blurry.*

"Now get the fuck off our front yard, and don't you ever even think about coming back. Liam stays *here*."

Only the raging blood in my ears fills the silence. So *loud*. Something touches my back and I spasm, flinching away from the warmth. *I'm gonna be sick. How can I be sick when I can't breathe?*

Can't breathe...

"Holy crap, Fin! I can't believe you just punched the Mayor!"

Punched who?

Someone whispers in my ear. Quiet. Soft. Gentle. *Peaceful.* I don't know what the words are, but they fill my chest with air. Not much, not fast, but slowly, *slowly*, it gets easier to breathe.

"Mom, is Liam okay?"

"He'll be alright. He's strong."

He's strong, he's strong, he's strong.

"Hey." *It's him. I can hear him.* "Liam, can you look at me?" I don't know how long it takes until I can finally lift my head, but I see the outline of him. Of his messy mop of hair. Of his wide shoulders. "Count with me, okay?" Finch takes my face in his hands and stares back at me, not letting me look away. When he breathes, I breathe. "One."

Alice and Lemon watch us silently. He nearly reaches fifty before the outline of him starts to make sense again. Until I can see brown eyes and black hair. My shoulders shake as I look around. There are a few neighbours standing on their front porch's. And my father's car is gone.

"I..." My lungs are exhausted, and my voice is croaky and broken.

"It's alright, hon. You're alright." Alice moves in close and wraps her arms around my shoulders, bringing my head into her chest. *"You're safe."*

CHAPTER
26

Mom hasn't even called to see how I am, or if I'm even alive. To ask why I haven't come home. Not even just to tell me she's *thinking* of me. *No one's thinking of me.* My gut clenches at the thought.

It's not like my father is going to hate me any less the longer I stay away. I haven't seen him since he tried to take me home yesterday. Alice wouldn't let me out of her sight the rest of the day, and Dean wanted to arrest him for assault, but I won't press charges.

I can't. It'll only make things worse.

Walking through the corridors towards my next class, my fingertips rub against each other at my side. *If I stop at home before school lets out today, dad will still be at work. Mom will probably be out shopping. I'll be in and out too quick for either of them to realise I was even home in the first place, I just need to grab a bag of clothes. I don't have to face them.*

The halls are filled with whispers and prying eyes. Everyone is watching, curious, but not brave enough to ask. Rumours have started to pop up that I'm secretly abused at home. The neighbours who saw my father try to force me into his car were quick to pass the story on to their friends. It was already a loud buzz across school when Finch and I pulled up this morning.

I hear Sawyer's voice before she rounds the corner, clutching her bag's shoulder strap tightly. She stumbles to a stop, her eyes wide when they lock on mine. Like those around us are waiting for some kind of reaction, everyone lingering in the hall goes silent, their eyes watching us curiously. Sawyer's mouth gapes like a fish, her eyes wide. My chest tightens at the look.

Were you bothering Finch?

Why do I even bother with you?

He doesn't like eating with us.

She's just like him. She doesn't care. *She's just like him. Just like him just like him just like him.*

I'm not dealing with this right now.

Before she can find the courage to say anything, I storm past her without a word. I stare at the floor, the familiar grooves and cracks guiding me to my next class.

Sawyer doesn't make any attempt to stop me.

"I'm just going to talk to Coach about training," I lie, picking the crud from under my nails behind my back.

"Why can't I come with you?" Finch pouts, his eyes shiny. He stands over me like the stupid giant he is. *So damn close.*

I grit my teeth. "Because you still have to *study* for the retake on your physics test." He shrugs his shoulders, so I blow out a loud breath. "I can do things on my own, okay?

Just, do whatever you do to study, alright?"

Finch gives me a lingering look before nodding his head, taking his seat again. He glances up at me once more as I leave the study hall, but he doesn't say anything else to stop me. *I just need to grab some clothes and catch my damn breath.*

The familiar path home doesn't seem familiar anymore. It's the same path I've walked my whole life, but it's as if I'm walking down an entirely different street. The old lady, Seltzer, is pulling the weeds from her garden, her usual can of seltzer water perched beside her. The old man, Toupee, is roosted on his porch swing, his old dog sniffing at the gate when I stroll past his fence. It's all the same, but there's something *off* about it all.

When the house comes into view, my gut clenches, and my feet stumble before I stop. *No one's home.* I knew that no one would be home, so I don't know why I'm surprised. But it's like there's a shield encompassing the house, warning me away. Telling me that I don't want to go there. *Knowing* that I don't want to step inside.

"I'm not gonna start wearing Finch's clothes," I mutter. *Not a chance, that jerk would like that far too much.*

Pushing past the twisting in my stomach, I fish my keys out of my bag and jog up the steps. In and out, before anyone gets home. Just some clothes and my ball. I shove the key in the lock and twist. I'll use the bag in my—

The resistance in the lock stuns me. It's not turning. *Why isn't—*

Marnie, what happened to changing the locks?

No.

No, he didn't...He...didn't...

My hand twists the key in the lock frantically but each time, it doesn't turn. No click, no movement. Nothing. *It's not working. It's not working. How do I...I can't...*

I can hear every hurried, wheezing breath that slices through my teeth, but the thumping in my ears grows louder. My skin tightens, shivers rushing up my spine as my toes go numb.

When did it get so cold? Is that why I can't breathe? Because it's so cold? Why is it so cold now?

Mom said it was going to snow tonight, didn't she? I should have come back earlier.

This is my fault.

My fault.

He...

Marnie, what happened to—

No no no no no no, he didn't...

My hands are shaking as I try a different key. *I just got the keys mixed up. I can be so stupid sometimes. It was just the wrong key. Deep breath, it's fine.* The keys jingle, the sound scraping in my ears. I shove another key into the lock, but it's the same. *It has to be one of these keys. Why don't I remember which key it is? It has to be one of these keys. It can't be different. It can't be...*

Marnie, what happened to changing the locks?

My stomach heaves, and acid creeps up my throat. *Why is everything swaying?* My knees buckle but the keys are slippery. My fingers are frozen stiff. *Am I twisting the key too hard? Did I break the lock? That must be why it's not working. That's why it's—*

I warned you.

Don't be so dramatic, Liam.

As long as he lives under my roof, I control him.

I control him.

Something zaps my hand and I jerk back. My feet slip and my ass hits the porch hard. My body is ice cold, and my teeth are chattering. The bright sunlight shines on me, but I don't feel it's warmth.

Mom said it was going to snow tonight. Why didn't I listen to her? I should have come home earlier. But I wanted to keep playing...I wanted to win at least one game...

I warned you.

There are noises, and my body moves without direction. *How am I moving?* I can't see anything. I must have closed my eyes. A dog barks, or maybe that's in my head. Everything is muffled now. *Numb. It's numb. So damn cold. Why won't dad let me in? He knows I don't have a key. Why did he lock the door? I'm gonna freeze to death out here.*

Look at what you did. You bothered the neighbours. Stop crying.

I control him.

I didn't mean to, I promise I didn't. I stayed on the porch, like I'm supposed to. I didn't ask anyone. I stayed on the porch. I stayed—

My lungs squeeze, and my heart beats too fast. *Am I going to freeze to death? I think I'm going to run out of air before that. It's so cold. He knows I don't have a key, I can't...*

Something bright flashes in my eyes. The air chokes me, like it's sticky in my throat. *I need air.* My eyes sweep from side to side, but my head is dizzy and I can't focus on *anything. Why I can't breathe?* I think someone is saying my name, but my head is underwater.

Try harder.

Stop crying.
You bothered the neighbours.
Marnie, what happened to changing the locks?
I warned you.

I must have been able to see things before, because now everything's black.

CHAPTER 27

My throat hurts and my eyes are itchy. *Why the hell are my eyes itchy?* When I crack them open, the bright orange light from the sun bleeds through. I know where I am by the smell alone. *What the hell am I doing at the hospital again? Is it my hands?*

"Hey sleepy." My head turns slowly to where Alice is standing near the door. My eyes squint and I rub my hand over my face. It's tingling for some reason.

"Why am I in the hospital?" I croak out. Alice peeks out through the blinds over the small glass window, her eyes sweeping the halls before she turns back to me. She doesn't move away from the door as she replies.

"One of your neighbours, Loraine Morganson, was gardening when she saw you collapse on your front porch. When she couldn't calm you down, she called an ambulance. She was worried you were having a heart attack."

Gardening? Is she talking about Seltzer? Why would she—

Look at what you did. You bothered the neighbours.

Again. I did it again.

You bothered the neighbours.

"Why?" The word comes out weak; my throat is raw and my entire body fatigued. It's like I've been hit by a train.

"Why, what?" The way Alice is looking at me, she's angry about something. *Did I do something wrong?*

"Why would she call an ambulance?" The ache in my chest is only getting worse. It hurts to remember.

He locked me out again. But this time there was no mistaking his intention. This wasn't another 'I forgot you were still at the Montgomery's'. He knew. He knew.

My throat starts to close up. *What do I do? Where do I sleep? I don't have anything...*

Moving away from the door, Alice comes to sit on the edge of the bed. She grabs my scarred hand, her skin hot against my icy fingers. I glance up, and her eyes are filled with the same heat as her palms. She stares back at me, her lips pulled in a thin line.

"Why did you go back to there, Liam?" She watches me, her eyes soft and steady. My tongue numbs as I try to remember how to speak. *Why is talking to her so nerve wracking?*

"I...needed clothes..." I rasp. Her head tilts, and her thumb runs over the back of my hand. *Her skin is smooth.*

"We can always go and buy you new clothes." She shuffles closer, the corners of her mouth turned down. "Tell me what happened."

I can't pinpoint it—maybe it's because she has that soft, gentle, *caring* tone—but something about her cracks something inside me. It's only a small part, but some part of me bleeds through. A sob slips between my lips. "He changed them..."

She grips my fingers tighter, her hair falling like a pretty golden waterfall over her collarbone. Her eyes don't leave me for a single second. "Changed what?" She doesn't ask who. Maybe she already knows. *She would. I'm sure she would*.

"The—" I choke again, forcing back the acid that's rising in my throat. "*The locks*." My chest heaves and my eyes pinch shut.

I don't have anywhere to go. I can't go back home. There's no—

When my eyes open again, Alice is watching me, her gaze soft. "Liam..."

I'm going to be sick. It travels up through my chest, and I try to swallow it back. "I don't have...there's nowhere I can..."

She's already shaking her head, her warm fingers gripping around mine even tighter. Pulling me forward towards her, the crack splits deeper. A heavy sob breaks through it, my chest heaving. And it doesn't stop. It pours out of me, and I can't shut it off. Pulling me forward to rest my head against her chest, she holds me, keeping me close.

Finch held me like this. Her heartbeat thumps in my ear like his did. *She's so warm. Just like Finch. They're both so warm, so close*. It floods forward, and I have no idea how to stop it. I don't know when I fall asleep again, but it's warm when I do.

Everyone is waiting in the foyer when I walk in the door behind Alice. Finch stops pacing and Dean looks up from where he was staring holes into the floor. Noodles looks up from what I assume is homework, abandoning whatever he was working on to rush us.

"Liam!" He throws his arms around me, squeezing my waist tight. "If you went home because you don't want to share a room with Fin, you can have my bed! It's really comfy and you won't have to share it. You could just pretend it's your room!"

I stare at the top of his head as he pulls me tighter, his face rubbing against my stomach. He's so close that he's making my skin feel tight and itchy, but I stare at the top of his head. I stare because I don't know what to say; the words are stuck in my throat, and my hands hover over his shoulders.

When I look up at Finch and Dean, they're watching the two of us with a look of awe on their face. Dean's mouth pulls up in a proud smile as he gazes at his son.

You did good.

You did good, Liam.

Finch stares at me, though. His eyes are glassy, and his bottom lip has been worried between his teeth because it's puffier than usual. His hair sticks up in a dozen different directions, his cheeks pink and his forehead creased. He stares because *he* doesn't know what to do either. He's trying to ask me questions with only the look in his eyes, but I don't want to answer them right now. *I just want to be warm.*

This house is always so warm.

"Dawson, give him some space." Alice says, stepping closer to touch his shoulder.

Dawson.

I reach down and wrap my arms around his shoulders without thought, holding him where he is. "*It's okay,*" I croak out, my eyes blurring. Dawson grips me a little tighter, and my shoulders start to shake.

Dawson pulls away, staring up at me through his small glasses. I rub my hand on his head, his curly hair soft against my ugly scars. "Thanks Dawson, but you keep your bed." It comes out sounding awkward and stiff, but when he smiles up at me, it touches his eyes.

"Alright, you've seen that he's okay. You can go finish your homework," Dean says as he grips Dawson's shoulder, giving it a small squeeze. Dawson nods his head, following Alice and Lemon back into the kitchen. Lemon glances back over her shoulder, questions burning in her eyes, but she doesn't say anything as she disappears out of sight.

Dean steps forward and wraps his big arms around my shoulders, pulling me into his chest. *Warm.*

"You stay as long as you need, Liam. Whether that's a couple days, a couple months, or a couple years. You stay as *long* as you need." His voice is always so strong. I can't see over his shoulder, but I'm sure Finch is watching us. And even though it's embarrassing, my head is cloudy as the warmth seeps in.

My eyes burn as I croak out a pathetic, "*Okay*."

CHAPTER

28

The smell of the waxed floors and the cheap canteen food floods my nose as we enter the small stadium. Jogging in formation towards the centre of the court, the crowd on one side of the bleachers starts to holler. Some rise from their seats and cup their mouths, chanting 'Franklin'. It's good to see that so many people from our town came all the way to Port Loe to watch us play. Slowing down to a walk, Finch comes up behind me and places his hand on my shoulder. He's beaming at me when I turn to face him, his narrow eyes almost disappearing.

"Excited?"

I glance around again, my chest burning with excitement. "You will have to *drag* me off this court by the end of it." I flex my fingers out, observing the stretching scars on my palms. It makes gripping the ball a little harder, but not impossible. *I'll catch every pass.*

"You sure you're ready to play tonight?" Finch's mouth pulls down in a frown as he stares down at my hands. Practice has been hard these last few days, but necessary if I wanted to play tonight.

I clench my fists until he can't see my palms. "I'm not staying off this court *one more game*. It's the Championships, Finch. I'm playing." *This is my chance to be seen. This is where I start.*

He nods. "Fine. Let's start warming up." As we're turning to our end of the court, Finch's family waves to us from the stands. Dawson flails his arms frantically in effort of catching our attention, a huge smile planted on his face. Alice and Dean smile and wave as well, just as Lemon joins them with some snacks. I don't wave back, but I think I smile at them.

The Weston High players walk out onto the court. The other side of the crowd cheers, and a few of the players throw up their hands to encourage a louder applause.

I recognise a few of them from over the years. The skyscraper with the Captain's badge on his shirt walks towards Finch and I with a few teammates at his sides, his ugly face smirking down at us. "Didn't think you two ball freaks would actually make it this far. Did they check your piss for dope this time?"

My eyes narrow. That's what Red said after the Maverick game.

I actually do remember this guy's name. "Looks like *you're* the one of roids, Sith."

His eyes narrow, his fat lips pulling up into a sneer. "It's *Scythe*."

I raise an eyebrow. *Close enough.* "Really? You definitely look like a Sith."

Sith tries to step towards me, but one of his teammates throws their arm out to keep him back. I roll my eyes again. *I'm not scared of an ugly giant like him.*

"Come on, Liam." Finch pulls at my uniform shirt, and I

step back with him. "Don't let him get in your head."

I scoff, my lips thrumming. "As if. I'm not letting that clown ruin my game."

Finch's angular eyes land on something behind me, and they darken further. When I go to turn around, he tugs on the front of my shirt. "Hey, look at *me*." He tries to seem casual, but I can sense the burning rage seeping from his skin like heat waves.

My father's here. I knew he would be. Sawyer's cheering tonight, after all. He can make it to those. "Sure," I mutter under my breath, holding his gaze. When I notice the familiar dark void that tries to suck me in, I focus on stretching. I'm not letting my father ruin this. *He takes whatever else he can, but I won't let him take my basketball from me.*

Everything I've done has led me here. This is where things start to change, this is the game I get noticed. Something fuzzy lingers in my chest as my skin tingles.

This is for me.

Just me.

Coach goes over the game plan, his narrowed eyes lingering on Finch and me. When the referee eventually blows the whistle to line up, we get into position. My eyes sweep the crowd, and when I spot the Montgomery's all looking at us, Dawson and Alice start waving their hands like crazy. I hear Finch laugh, and when I look at him, he's turning to look at me, and there's a moment of calmness. The sounds fade and time slows, and I think about everything that's changed. Everything's warm now.

When the whistle blows, Finch and I blur through the players, both our team and theirs. We steal, we pass, and we shoot before they have any idea we've done it. For the first time in a long time, we're playing *together*.

Now when I see an opening, I pass without thought. The first few passes are filled with anxiety. *What if it phases right through him? What if someone sees?* But the ball hits his palms, and he sinks it every time.

But Sith is glued to me, and he's learning my patterns. His lag time is mere seconds, and he's getting quicker. It's going to be hard for me to be useful soon, and I know that's why he's guarding me. He doesn't say anything as I continue to find ways of outmanoeuvring him, but he's getting frustrated. And his frustration is pushing him faster.

Sweat pours down my face, air ripping through my chest. I'm definitely playing harder than I normally do. Finch and Spanner have noticed I'm heavily guarded and have stopped passing to me. My hands are throbbing at my sides, the blood pumping hard under the fresh skin.

This is the freakin' Championships. I'm not letting this jerk take away any more of my ball time. Making one last attempt to give him the slip, I clear enough distance and call for the ball. Hair sees me and tosses without hesitation, his skin red and his long hair falling loose from the bun on his head.

Sith's enormous hand crosses my vision first. If he were a second earlier, he could have given it a good smack away, but his fingers only tip it. Nevertheless, watching the ball fly off in the opposite direction cracks something inside me. My face burns but my limbs freeze. Milo scoops up the ball after it bounces and takes it to the hoop. My jaw is tight, my tongue numb.

Try harder.

It seemed to me that the team was more than capable of winning without him.

Try harder, try harder, try harder.

The team was more than capable of winning without him.

Sith has an ugly grin on his face. He's under my skin now, and he knows it.

"That won't happen again," I promise.

The team was more than capable of winning without him.

I take off across the court, the fire in me dimming with each step I take.

It seemed to me that the team was more than capable of winning without him.

Sith keeps pace with me for the last minutes of the first half, and I don't try for the ball again. My movements are slower as my feet drag across the court. I've caught Finch and Milo watching me, but they don't have the time to slow down.

Try harder try harder try harder.

Stop. Not now. Please, not now.

The buzzer for half time booms through the arena. Glancing up at the score board, there isn't a great distance between our scores. Weston's only three baskets ahead of us. A painful score to be ending the half on, but we've got time.

It seems the team was more than capable of winning without him.

"Yo, Rice," Sith wanders closer, bending his head towards mine and panting loud into my ear. "You're playing differently to the last time we went up against each other. Since when do you pass to that *gook*?"

My skin tightens as something hot—hotter than a raging fire—ignites in my chest and floods through my veins. My body is suddenly heavy, my scared hands clenching into painfully tight fists.

What the fuck *did he just call him?*

I spot Finch from the corner of my eye, pushing his sweaty hair back from his face as he strides towards me.

It's the first time I've heard someone say something like that about Finch. The slur burns me like acid. Actually, I know what acid feels like. This is hotter. *Angrier*. When I turn, my eyes are dark, and my father's voice seems to thump loud in my ears.

Try harder, try harder, try harder—

Try. Harder.

"I'm giving you one chance to take that back, you son of a bitch."

Sith seems genuinely surprised by my order. He laughs, pulling back to really look at me. "What, you got a problem?"

My eyes narrow further, my teeth baring at him. My hands clench into fists, shaking at my sides. Finch still hasn't made it to me yet. *Don't. Don't come over here.* "Apologise. Or I'm going to make your fucked-up face look *pretty*."

He sneers at me, flashing his wonky teeth. His lumpy, distorted nose scrunches up as he smirks. "What? I'm not wrong. He *is* a gook—"

Even if I had enough control over my fist to stop it from hitting his face, I wouldn't have stopped it. I warned him.

I warned him.

Sith goes down like a sack of potatoes. I hear Finch shout my name. I'm pretty sure he's closer than he sounds, but it's all filtering away slowly, replaced by the loud thumping of my blood in my ears.

I jump on him, throwing another punch at his stupid

lumpy nose. The skin of my knuckles starts to split, my blood cold as it smears over my hand.

I hit him again and again and again because he's *wrong*, before he rolls me over so he's on top of me. He gets a strong hit in, his goliath hand colliding with my jaw and cracking my head to the side. I manage to kick Sith off me, but before I can crawl towards him, an arm wraps around my shoulders and holds me back.

"Liam..." The voice is right in my ear, blowing against the back of my neck, but it's muffled like I'm underwater.

"Liam..." My body's shaking, and I lift my head to look up to the blurry voice.

"Liam." *Finch*. At least I think it's Finch. Everyone's surrounding me, but I can't hear what they're saying. Coach is yelling something, his face is so red.

Have other people said things like that about Finch? Have I ignored it before? That makes me a bad friend, right? I'm a bad friend. I should have hit Sith harder. Maybe I should have let him hit me again. I deserve it. I'm no better than the rest of my family. Pretending to care.

Milo snaps his fingers in front of my face, and my lazy eyes follow the vibration. Sounds are slowly starting to filter back in. Everything is numb and cold, and my hands are still shaking. *I'm a bad friend*. I think my hand is bleeding. There's still an arm around my chest. Coach is arguing with the other coach. They both look really angry. *Coach thinks I'm a bad friend. He's angry with me.*

"Hey, Liam..." It's a whisper now, clearer than before. My hands are still shaking. *What's happening?* Everything seems dull. Colourless. *I could see colours before, right?*

"Liam, talk to me." Finch is holding me. His voice is

quiet, but I hear it. It's not in my head anymore. The air hits my chest like a sucker punch, but I breathe in every bit that I can. Milo's watching me, and the rest of the team's gathered around us. They're blocking Coach and everyone else from view. Finch's arm around me tightens.

"Fin, look at his hands." I'm not sure who says it. The sounds are still jumbled.

"Shit. If Coach sees—"

"Where is he?" Coach's irate voice filters through louder than the rest. Milo stays where he is, crouched down in front of me, but the others step aside so Coach can see me. My eyes lift slowly, my jaw and hands throbbing in time with my racing heart. Colour starts to flicker between grey and yellow. Coach gives me a hard look, but when he meets my stare, his eyes soften.

"Take him to the locker room. I'll handle things here," he grumbles, before grabbing Spanner's shirt and pulling him towards the other team.

"Milo, help me get him up," Finch says, his voice clearer now. His arm is warm across my chest.

I'm a bad friend. I shouldn't touch him.

I'll ruin it.

I'll ruin everything.

Milo grabs my arm and wraps it around his shoulder before lifting me up. I'm like a ragdoll as I'm set on my feet. Finch grabs my other arm and wraps it around his neck, and the two of them walk me off the court. I think there are others still yelling, but I don't turn around.

I don't look at Sith. I don't look over the crowd. I don't look over at the cheerleaders as we pass them, but I catch sight of Sawyer in my peripheral. She takes a small step towards us but stops short, holding her pom-poms close to her chest.

Finch and Milo lead me out of the arena through the same double doors we had entered through...

The game...

"Stop..." My lips are numb as I try to speak, my body limp. *Is that how my voice sounds?* Milo hesitates, but Finch shakes his head.

"No, Liam. Your hands are messed up, I'm not letting you play."

"Stop..." I don't want to beg, but it comes out like a helpless plea. I want to play. *Please don't take me off this court. They need to see me play. I can't get out if they don't—*

It seems to me the team was more than capable of winning without him.

The team was more than capable.

More than capable.

"Stop..."

I dig my heels in, jerking the two of them to an awkward stop. Finch wraps my arm around him tighter and circles his other arm around my back, pulling me forward. *How is he so much stronger than I am?*

"Go tell one of the student medics to be here when we come back out. We'll need them to check his hands," Finch mutters as he and Milo set me down on the bench seat. I lean back against the lockers, my eyes drooping. It's hot in here, but the sweat on my skin is like ice droplets now.

I catch Milo looking me over once more, his eyes creasing at the corners. He looks like he wants to say something, but he disappears from the room without a word.

"Liam, talk to me." Finch shifts closer, crouching in front

of me. His small eyes are soft, calm. No anger or frustration bubbles in the background. His lips are puffy. *Why am I always looking there now?* I stare at them for a long time before I look back to his eyes. Sounds are filtering back in, the fog in my head slowly clearing. "What happened?"

I scoff, my head knocking back against the locker door. The thumping in my ears is dissipating quicker now. After a couple more minutes, I can hear myself breathing again. The tingling in my fingers doesn't disappear. "Sith's a piece of shit," I mutter. "I should have hit him harder."

Finch pinches my thigh softly so that I look at him. "What's going on in here?" He reaches up and rubs my temple with his thumb.

I brush his hand away. "I'm fine. We need to get back out there..." He pushes down on my knees when I try to stand up, shoving me back down onto my ass. Pain is starting to filter back in as well. My jaw aches where Sith punched me, but my hands are *throbbing*.

"You're not going anywhere, Liam. Not until you talk to me."

My eyes roll. "I don't want to talk about it."

The air passes through my lips slower now, and the flurry of dull colours starts to calm. Finch watches me patiently, his mouth pulled into a small smile. "I'm not going anywhere until you tell me what happened. Why did you punch that jerk?" He pins me with a look that doesn't let me argue with him again. His voice is soft. So *soft*.

My lips purse as my lungs take in a heavy breath. "I warned him."

Finch nods his head. "Okay." He doesn't ask me to elaborate. My tongue flicks out to wet my chapped lips, but my mouth is just as dry. Finch notices. "I'll go get you some water, and then we'll head back out. We just need to make sure you haven't broken anything." I nod again and watch him slip out the door. Leaning back, I close my eyes and count my breaths. It helped that time when Finch did it.

I need to apologise to Coach, and the rest of the team. My hands are throbbing wildly. I wouldn't be able to play with them like this, even if I could bring myself to muster the last of my stamina. My mind is so absent and fatigued, I don't even hear the door open.

"That was *disgusting* to watch."

My eyes snap open to see my father standing in the locker room, his hands in his long coat pockets. His eyes don't rest on me for long before they are flickering away. He's making the white walls surrounding us seem very interesting. The puke-green bruise on his face makes him look rougher. Angrier. My heart sits in my throat, choking me. He's wearing the same coat I last saw him in.

He steps further into the locker room, his presence infecting me even from this distance. It seeps in like poison. "Do you have *any* self-control? Or do you enjoy embarrassing me?" His tone is cold, his eyes hard, but his face doesn't change. He still looks as uninterested as when he walked in.

A numb blanket falls over me once more, and my knees draw up to my chest. The air is slimy, and my vision blurs again. "I didn't—" I choke out, my tongue numb.

"You live in *my* house, and yet you have the *audacity* to defy me. You hang out with a complete *deviant*, and you *tarnish* my reputation. You're ruining everything, you selfish brat," he bites out.

281

Do you enjoy embarrassing me?

Yet you have the audacity to defy me.

As long as he lives under my roof, I control him.

I control him.

My mouth fills with something fuzzy, the intense throbbing in my hand and jaw starts to weaken, until my entire body floats.

You're ruining everything.

"How am I supposed to go back out there?" Black dots start to dance in my eyes. *Am I breathing?* "Do you think about anyone other than yourself?" He runs his hand through his hair, his jaw clenching. "After the game tonight, you will be coming home to pack your things. Your grandparents are expecting you."

After the game tonight...

Pack your things...

After the game tonight...

I warned you.

My head's completely submerged. Drowning me.

He's drowning me.

"Dad?"

It's so muffled, I barely hear the words. My eyes don't lift higher than her elbows, but I know it's Sawyer standing there. Her pom-poms are gone, her fingertips rubbing into her palms at the sides of her skirt. Our father turns so sharply I'm surprised his neck doesn't crack. His suit doesn't wrinkle.

"What are you doing in here, Sawyer? Go back out to your squad." I don't hear his voice. I don't think I do.

After the game tonight...

Selfish brat selfish brat selfish brat.

Sawyer's fingers stop rubbing, clenching into tight balls. I can't tell if she's looking at me.

Do you think about anyone other than yourself?

Your grandparents are expecting you.

After the game tonight...

I don't...I don't want to go...

"Why would you say something like that to him?" My head tips back, and I can see her. But she doesn't have a face. Everything's white. *Too bright.* My father has lost his face too.

"Sawyer, I was only scolding him for his ridiculous behaviour."

Her hands are shaking, and I try to unclench my fingers, but they're frozen around my legs, bunched tight. "I heard what you were saying to him!" She sounds hysterical now. "You said such ugly things...Liam didn't deserve any of that." I think she's crying now, or she's about to. I still can't see her face. "And why would you change the locks, dad? Was it so he couldn't come home?"

Can't feel anything. Nothing. Like I'm underwater. Why is everything so dull? And cold? Is he trying to drown me? Why can't I breathe?

"This has nothing to do with you, Sawyer. Now *go back there.*" He points to the door behind her. No one moves. I can't move, my body isn't responding anymore.

That was disgusting *to watch.*

Just leave, Sawyer.

"No! How long have you been treating Liam like this, Dad? You're ruining his life." Sawyer's high pitch seeps through the fog clearer than before now. She's shouting. *Someone will hear her...That will make him even angrier...My* eyes slowly shift between the two of them, tracking my father's fingers as they push back any loose hairs from his face.

"*He's* ruining *my* life." His words are murky in my brain, but they still deliver a sharp knife to my heart.

He's ruining everything.

Everything, everything, everything.

There's a buzzing across my skin, but I block it out.

Don't.

Don't touch me.

"We were never supposed to have him in the first place. If your grandparents hadn't found out your mother was pregnant, we wouldn't have."

Liam, you might not believe it, but you are the most important person to me.

We were never supposed to have him.

Never supposed to have him.

Focus on something else. Anything else— "Please *stop*."

I still can't see their faces, I don't know if they're looking at me. I barely spoke above a whisper, but it scraped through my ears like sandpaper.

Sawyer's long hair is down, messier than normal. She's been pulling at it. Her shoulders are shaking.

Our father's silent now. Terrifyingly silent. I shrink back until my spine touches the lockers, but he reaches toward me.

You're ruining everything, you selfish brat.

Selfish brat, selfish brat, selfish brat.

"*You* don't tell *me* what to do." He snatches my wrist and jerks me off the bench seat. My elbows lock and my shoulders touch my ears, but I don't have the strength in my legs to stand straight. "We're leaving *right now*. I'll drive you there myself if I have to."

Your grandparents are expecting you.

No, don't.

No no no.

I can't go. I can't.

I feel sick whenever I think about you not being here.

"Dad, you can't just *take him*—" Sawyer tries.

"I can, and I *will*. I've had enough of this." Our father's tone is final. My hands start to shake again. Or maybe they never stopped shaking.

I feel sick whenever I think about you not being here.

I can't go. I can't. I can't.

You can have my bed!

You don't have to ask, Liam. You can sit with us whenever you want to.

You're alright.

I've got you.

You're safe.

The locker room door swings open suddenly. Coach stands in the doorway, his arms crossing over his chest when he realises my father is here as well. His eyes flicker between my father, Sawyer, and me. Dad drops his grip on my wrist, and my arm slaps down against my leg.

I can see his face again.

"Sorry to interrupt you *Mayor Rice*, but you ain't allowed in here." Coach's voice is a resounding boom, his eyes narrowed on my father, his face pinched with fury.

Finch towers behind him, his dark glare focused on my father. He's gripping the water bottle in his hand so tight it's about to burst. The tips of his inky hair hang over his eyes casting shadows across his face. I stare at him, waiting for him to look at me. But his eyes are filled with fire as they glower at my father.

Please don't let him take me, Finch.

My father brushes his hands down the lapels of his long coat. "I was simply having a conversation with my son about his misconduct. I think Liam needs to go to the hospital, so I'm going to take him—"

Don't let him. Please, don't let him.

"He's not going anywhere." Finch takes another step forward, but Coach puts his arm out.

Never supposed to have him.

If your grandparents hadn't found out, we wouldn't have.

I feel sick whenever I think about you not being here.

You're safe.

"As his father—"

"He's not going *anywhere*." There's a weird undertone to Finch's voice that sends a shiver down my spine. I see my father shake from it. Finch tries to step around Coach, but still he keeps him back.

Coach's eyes land on me for a second longer. I'm still frozen in place. His gaze bounces back to my father, his forehead dipping slightly. "I'm gonna say it again, cause maybe you didn't hear me before. You ain't allowed in here. Players and their coaches *only*," Coach grinds out between clenched teeth. "I'll speak to the medics about whether or not he needs a hospital, seeing as you ain't a medical professional yourself. But maybe you should have yourself looked at, that looks like a pretty nasty shiner you've got there." Coach says with nasty smirk on his face.

My father clears his throat, patting himself down once more. My shoulders lean away, my skin crawling from our close proximity. "Thank you for your concern, Walter."

"That's Coach Pike to you. And that *wasn't* concern."

I catch the moment my father's jaw tightens. But all he does is nod and move towards the door. Sawyer and Coach give him a wide berth, but Finch stays planted, blocking the way.

Don't do anything, Finch.

Please, don't.

Finch stares back at him for a moment longer, before slowly stepping to the side to let my father pass. He does so without a single glance back in my direction. The moment he's out of sight, the air in the room becomes breathable again.

"You alright, Liam?" Coach calls to me as he steps closer. Finch steps around him, making his way over to me with hurried footsteps. My fingers slowly unclench, aching and throbbing. I nod, but Finch grabs my uninjured hand and jerks my attention to him.

He frowns up at me, and I grip his hand tighter. So tight, I'm worried I'll break his fingers. "Please don't let him..." I whisper, but I can't get the words out. *This room is too small.* Finch squeezes my hand back, shaking his head.

"You're not going anywhere. You're staying right here with me. *I promise.*"

Sawyer is loud with her sniffing. I look over to her from the corner of my eye and find her wiping at her face with the side of her hand as she watches me. *Is she crying because Finch is holding my hand?* I should probably shake him off. But his skin is warming my cold fingers, so I don't want to. *Will Coach think it's weird that we're holding hands?*

Milo brings a medic in, and he wraps my knuckles up in under a minute. It's tight and uncomfortable, but I don't complain.

"Come on. Come watch us finish these bastards off," Finch mumbles.

I nod, blinking hard to stay awake. He pulls me up with his other hand on my elbow, my legs wobbling like jelly. Coach watches me with careful eyes, but he doesn't offer his help. He knows I don't want it. Sawyer stands beside him, her back straight now. Her eyes and face are bright red, but her gaze is harder than before.

With each step I take towards the door, my spine straightens. When we're passing Sawyer, she reaches out and takes my hand. Her skin is colder than mine, damp from her tears. But she grips my fingers tight. I watch her face, and she stares back with a small smile.

"Come on," I whisper to her, tugging her forward. She eventually drops her hand back to her side and follows the three of us back down the corridor. The noise from the crowd starts to grow again, every sound filtering through. When Coach pushes open the double doors that lead into the arena, the crowd hums. Finch's hand is gone now as well, and I'm standing as tall as I had been when we first entered the arena earlier.

That was disgusting *to watch.*

Do you enjoy embarrassing me?

He doesn't matter.

You ruin everything.

Keep walking.

You're staying right here with me.

I take one step, then another.

I promise.

CHAPTER

29

"Don't leave this spot, alright? Stay *right here*." Finch stresses, his eyes locked on mine. When I give him a curt nod, he turns and steps back out onto the court. My eyes narrow on Sith when he steps back onto the court with his team.

He scans our teammates before he finds me on the bench. He sends an ugly smile my way, winking. His lip is busted from where I socked him, but apparently he refused to leave the court.

"Don't even think about going near that kid, Gray," Coach calls out. He's watching Finch closely, his eyes narrowed. "Do you hear me? *Leave it alone.*"

Finch nods with a blank look on his face. "No worries, Coach."

Coach and I both know he's lying, but Coach doesn't say it twice. Gray probably wouldn't listen the second time anyway.

I keep my eyes trained on Sith. He knows Finch is thinking of something, probably everyone on the court does, but he just watches with an ugly smile on his face.

My eyes drift back to Finch as the ref blows the whistle, the shrill sound shaking me to my core. My hands bunch into tight fists, my elbows on his knees as I lean forward. The noise and the smells help to keep me awake. Still, I watch Finch as he moves, weaving between the players without touching them but phasing through them when he gets close.

I blink hard to make sure I'm not imagining it. *He's controlling it*. He's phasing without losing his clothes and without being seen. He hasn't looked back at me yet, but my heart is in my throat each time I watch him shimmer. When he and Hair are close, they slap hands and swap players. Sith doesn't look surprised when Finch appears beside him.

The two of them say something amongst themselves, but it's not long before Finch is racing towards the ball. Sith follows hot on his heels, and when Finch stops abruptly, my eyes flick to where Hair has the ball and I know what he's gonna do and my stomach twists.

Don't risk it, you jerk! What if someone sees you?

The ball phases through his hands, colliding with Sith's face. The sickening, yet *satisfying* crack of cartilage as the ball smashes into his nose rings through my ears and momentarily silences both sides of the cheering crowds. Scythe is knocked back onto his ass, his hands cradling his now broken nose.

He looks up and points a bloodied finger at Finch. "You did that on purpose!" One of the medics rushes over, and their coach is trying to pull his hands away from his bleeding face.

Finch's expression flickers with innocent shame. "Sorry. Sweaty hands."

But when he meets my eye, he winks.

However the moment that ball hit Sith's face, the energy of the game changes. Weston High has a new fire lit, and they're playing even harder than before. I know it wasn't Finch's intention by taking Sith out of the game, but he's definitely paying for it now.

They weren't a team that relied on Sith too much, it seems. And they're all marking Finch now. It's become a lot harder for him to play. He's been trying to phase around them, but he's still conscious about doing it sparingly. Everyone's eyes are on Finch now. Weston High is still ahead, and there is no sign of them slowing down.

I glance across the court to the Weston's bench again, finding Sith glaring back at me with a bloody nose and an ugly sneer. It looks like a tampon's been shoved up his nostril, making it hard not to laugh each time I look at him. But his eyes burn with the same heated fury as mine.

I make a point of not looking in my father's direction. It's not hard to do, but his voice thrumming in the back of my mind isn't as easy to ignore. Sawyer occasionally looks over to me, but her glances are brief. I can't tell what she's thinking, and I don't want to right now.

Coach taps his clipboard against his thigh, his mouth pulled down in a grim line. *I freakin' hate that look.*

I catch sight of Blue's bright frizz-ball of hair from the corner of my eye, almost concealed in the mass of the crowd. Ginger's perched beside her, but his eyes aren't on the game. He's got his arm wrapped around her shoulders. I can't see much from here, but she doesn't look well.

She looks the same as she did the other night when they were waiting out front of Finch's house. She gets this way when she's around others with powers.

She can sense someone else.

Someone else...

My eyes sweep the bleachers as the ball runs up and down the court. Everyone in our stands is watching the game intently, their eyes glued to the ball. They curse when the ball sinks through Weston's hoop, and holler when we make an intercept. I see mom, and quickly turn back around, but Alice and Dean and Dawson and Lemon all catch my eye. Finch's cousins are watching the game, but Dean and Alice are murmuring to each other, their eyes on me.

They see I'm looking, and Alice gives me a thumbs up, the question evident on her face. I give her a brief nod instead of indicating how I actually feel.

When I scan Weston High's side, my eyes latch onto a strange looking blond. In the sea of brunettes and ravens, his white hair is a beacon. Just like Blue. Like he *wants* to be seen.

And he's already staring back at me.

It's like the power of his gaze is what drew my eyes to his in the first place. He has a large mole on his cheek, so large that I can see it from across the stadium, and his mouth is pulled up in a strange smile. I keep my eyes locked on him, and his eyebrow raises in response. Our side of the arena suddenly cheers louder, but I don't take my eyes away from Mole Man to see what's happened.

He glances away, his gaze drifting back to the game. I follow his line of sight, and spot Finch and Hair high fiving under the basket. Like a niggling in the back of my mind, I know that guy is different. There's something raw and deranged about his stare. I can't put my finger on it, but it's there, just below the surface. His mouth pulls up in that same weird smile, his teeth peeking through his thin lips. He rises from the stands and descends with a lithe grace.

"I need to take a leak, Coach. I'll be back in a second." I don't take my eyes away from Mole as I mutter out the first excuse that comes to mind. Coach glances at me from the corner of my eye before he nods.

"Straight back here, Rice. Don't go looking for any trouble now, *you hear me*?"

It's like he can read minds or something.

Nodding my head in response, my feet follow the blonde weirdo out of the arena, into the near desolate corridor. There are a few people mulling around, returning to the arena with drinks and snacks or leaving to get some. I catch sight of the blond disappearing around the corner down the far end of the hall, and jog after him, my legs still wobbly. I hold my busted knuckles close to my chest, my flesh throbbing beneath the bandages. My swollen cheek aches from my jolting movements, but I bite my tongue and keep moving.

When I round the corner, he disappears off around another bend.

"Fuck's sake," slips out, and a mother walking past with her little girl glares at me, hurrying away. Running down the corridor, the noise of the game fades away completely. The air seems to crackle and pop, my muscles tightening uncontrollably. The lights above me flicker like a fucking horror movie, and I debate whether I should continue following the creepy Mole.

"This is usually how the dumb character dies..." I mutter, scratching my head with my fingertips.

"Or how the idiot jackass gets the shit kicked outta him."

I spin on my heals at the same time Sith slugs me. His fist knocks me on my ass, and I fall like a potato sack. When my elbows collide with the hard ground, painful spasms shoot up my forearms to the tips of my fingers. I try to shake it off and kick his legs out from under him, but Sith climbs on top of me and lays another hit into my face. My head whips to the side, my neck cracking and my jaw splitting with *hot* pain. When he plants his fist into the other side of my face, something warm and thick and metallic floods my mouth, dripping onto the ground from the corner of my lips. I swing my bandaged hand at the side of his head, knocking him off me.

"Get lost, Sith." I spit blood at him, spinning on the tiled floor so I can send a hard kick to his torso. "You aren't worth the trouble." I can already hear Coach *and* Finch giving me hell for fighting him again.

Can everyone just leave me the heck alone?

"You think this is some kind of joke, Rice?" he hisses past his wonky teeth. My eye must be swelling over, because one half of my vision is fading.

"I think *you're* a joke," I mutter, climbing to my feet. I send another kick to his stomach, my anger bubbling over and getting the best of me. He got two hits in, so now we're even. He grunts when my shoe meets his gut, curling his body in. "What world do you live in, to think you can say shit like that and get away with it? If I *ever* hear you talk about anyone like that again, you'll regret it." *Don't talk about Finch like that.*

Don't talk about him.

When I turn to follow in the direction of Mole, my

motivation waning, Sith grabs my ankle and yanks. I catch myself on my hands, but not before my chin collides with the floor. Pain sears through my jaw, and my eyes water.

"I don't give a rats ass about that Asian fuck! You tanked my last senior game, you piece of shit. Scouts aren't gonna give me a second glance because of you!" He tugs me back towards him, my shirt lifting as I'm dragged across the floor. My throat starts to seize and my heart hammers in my ears. The pain in my face is near unbearable now, and I'm not sure I can protect myself. My vision sways, my stomach twisting.

Shit, shit, shit.

"At least you've still got your looks." The smartass inside of me doesn't seem to shut off, even when I'm in agonizing pain. Sith's nails—*claws* would be a more accurate description—cut into my skin, and my legs jerks against his grip. He rises to his knees, and I choke on the last breath of air left in my body. His huge body casts a dark shadow over me, the light behind him flickering in tune with my erratic heartbeat. Raising his arm again, he swings it down into my gut. My body lurches forward with the force.

He hits like a fucking train.

The second hit has blood and bile spewing out of my mouth.

"You and that Asian asshole think you're the gods of this game, don't you? Think you're un-fucking-defeatable! But I'll fucking kill you, *don't you dare think I won't.*" he seethes, his anger drawing his words together in a slur.

I can't move my mouth to respond. I can't even move my head to look at him. But god, I want to tell him he's wrong. *He's so fucking wrong.*

Finch is so much better than me.

When Sith fist flies towards me again, I grip his wrist. But he has so much momentum that I can't stop the impact, and his fist drives into my cheek. I raise my legs and wrap them around his waist. I don't have a plan, or any real strength left in me, and Sith takes advantage of my hesitation and launches his other fist into my side. I hear the crack before I feel it splitting my side. I think I scream; I'm not sure. Everything's disappearing, but I can hear my breathing—if that is *my* breathing. It's loud. Everything feels loud. There is too much pressure on my side.

Is that really my *breathing?*

He hits me again. And again. My legs fall away, but my arms fly out blindly, hoping to latch onto something. The pressure and the pain keep mounting. Finch is going to be so mad at me. He'll tell me how stupid I am. Coach told me not to go looking for trouble.

I'm not sure how much time passes before Sith's weight vanishes, but I notice when he disappears. I feel the cold air sweep across my skin, and I realise that my eyes are closed. I think they're swollen shut. My entire face is numb.

"Liam, can you hear me? Li—!"

CHAPTER
30

I groan when I hear an annoying beep from somewhere beside me. *I'm getting sick of waking up here. It's becoming too familiar now.*

One of my eyes refuses to open, the entire left side of my face numb and aching. I'm not as sore as I know I should be. My other eye opens, blinking furiously when it's too blurry. I grunt when I try to prop myself up, but my elbow buckles under my weight and I collapse back.

"Don't move."

I sigh. "You didn't do anything to him, did you?" My ribs are searing hot, but my hands are ice cold. The air hisses through my clenched teeth as I try once more to sit up. Finch's stands to push back on my shoulders, his shove somewhat gentle. I blow out another tired breath, about to growl at him to help me, but the bed hums as he uses the remote on the side table to tilt it forward until I'm sitting up.

Blinking my eye open again, I turn my head to look at him. His narrow eyes are red and sleepy, and his skin is sickly white as he takes the seat beside the bed. Even his normally dark pink lips seem dull. His hair is messy—he's been pulling at it again—and parted in the wrong place. *He'll go bald if he keeps tugging on it like that.*

He looks like shit. But I'm sure I don't look much better. "Did you?" I ask again, my tone strained.

Finch stares back with tired eyes. I keep thinking about how much I like his eyes, even though they're bloodshot and glaring at me. "Doesn't matter."

"I can fight my own fights, Finch." It's hard to talk without panting. *Why is it so damn hard to breathe?*

He blows out a short breath and looks down at his hands. "I got a few kicks in. I'm not sorry about that."

As I watch him, the purple under his eyes seems to grow darker. "Have you slept?" I already know the answer, but I ask to see if he'll lie to me. He shakes his head slowly, and I glance at the empty cot across from me. "Bring that bed over here."

"No."

I roll my eyes. "You can't lie on here with me. You're too damn big, you'll just push me off. Sleep on your own bed." He rubs his eyes and folds his arms beside my legs, resting his chin on top. His eyes are barely open, his pupils peeking through the slits of his eyelids. His pale lips are puffier than normal, and his forehead is smooth. *He's going to pass out any second now.*

"You'll get a bad back if you sleep like that," I mumble, my mouth barely moving. *Everything is so damn numb.*

He shrugs, his eyes drifting closed.

"How did we get here?"

"Aunt A," he breathes, his eyelids fluttering. "The others are out in the... waiting room."

Who are 'the others'?

He rubs his face against his arm, blindly reaching for my bandaged hand and clenching his fingers tight around mine. *He's cold.* I grip his fingers back, trying to push as much heat into his skin as I can. The flesh of my knuckles burns from being stretched, but I pay it no mind.

I watch as his eyelids finally close and his breathing evens out. His hair falls over his eyes, but I don't move my hand from his. *It's still too cold.*

He's wiped out. I wait until I'm certain he's asleep before I draw my hand back. His fingers curl the bedsheets under his fist, but he doesn't stir. I slowly pull the needle from my arm and press into my skin with my thumb when blood pops out of the tiny hole. I already know I'm gonna regret removing that later.

Moving as quietly and slowly as possible, I slide out of the bed. My ribs are numb, but the pain hasn't completely left me. My arm wraps around my torso as I cross the room and yank the blanket off the cot. It's awkward to do quietly, but I manage to lay it over Finch's shoulders without waking him. His mouth has fallen open slightly, his lips chapped.

I pull at the awkward paper gown I've been thrown into and make my way to the door. *He'll be fine if I leave him for a couple minutes.* It's hard to see much in front of me because of my swollen eye, but as soon as I open the door, my eyes lock on blue hair and freckles.

Ginger notices me first and jumps up from his chair. "Liam!" He and Blue rush over and grab onto each of my elbows, helping to take some weight off my legs. "Holy shit, man. That asshole did a real number on you." I hesitate when I spot Sawyer. She rises from one of the chairs, her hands twisting in front of her. She's still in her cheerleading uniform.

Ginger's grip tightens when I try to shake them both off. "I'm fine—"

"Don't try that shit with us, Liam," Blue grumbles, her eyes narrowing. "You got the shit kicked out of you."

I scoff, then curl over when pain vibrates through my core. "You should've seen the other guy."

"We did," Ginger mutters from beside me, his eyes sweeping over my body. "You definitely lost."

I shrug. "I guess he was already pretty ugly, huh?" My ribs ache with every movement, but I try to make sure they can't hear how loud my breathing is. I slowly drop down into one of the chairs they had been sitting in, and Blue takes the seat beside me. I don't look at them when I ask, "What are you guys doing here?"

"What do you mean why are we here? We're your friends, man. Of course we're gonna make sure you're okay."

What does he mean by 'of course'? Am I supposed to know that's what friends do? And when did we even become friends?

"So what happened?" Ginger asks, folding his arms over his chest as he stares down at me, standing at my toes.

I blow out a loud breath. "He caught me out in the corridor. Had an issue with me sabotaging his chances of being scouted." I try to shrug my shoulders, but my breath hisses between my teeth when pain flares up my sides. *He ruined my chances too.*

"Well your mom has gone to take your brother and sister home, but she said she'll be back in the morning. She ran x-rays and said that one of your lower ribs is fractured." *My mom? What he is—*

Alice.

My chest is strangely lighter when I realise he's talking about Alice. My eyes flicker to Sawyer, her lips pulling into a tight line, but I don't correct Ginger, even when I know I should.

His gaze flickers to Sawyer as well, his eyes squinted. "The Sheriff should be back soon. He's interrogating the big guy you got into it with."

Sawyer's eyes are burning a hole in the side of my face, but my chest tightens at the thought of talking to her. *In the locker room...*

That was disgusting to watch.

If your grandparent's hadn't found out, we wouldn't have.

Do you enjoy embarrassing me?

No. I never tried to do that. I never...

After the game tonight, you will be coming home to pack your things.

Your grandparents are expecting you.

You're ruining everything.

My skin turns itchy under Sawyer's stare. The hairs on the back of my neck stand on end, and my jaw clenches. *Fuck, even that hurts.* "You should go home, Sawyer." I don't turn to face her, but I can see her fists clench from the corner of my open eye. Blue glances between Sawyer and I, her eyebrows pulled together, but I keep my gaze low to the floor. Sawyer clears her throat before walking off. She passes in front of me, silent as she leaves without any complaint.

"Liam, are you sure that was a good idea?" Blue mumbles, her voice low. I can't see her—she's sitting on the side of my swollen eye—but I can tell she's not pleased. "She brought some clothes for you to—"

"Did you sense someone else like you at the game?" I

301

change the subject, my eyes lifting to hers.

There is a brief pause before she moves into my line of sight. The two of them glance at each other. "How did you know I—"

"I saw you in the stands. You looked the same way you did when you came to the first game." She nods slowly, her eyes weary. She looks to Ginger again, like she isn't sure whether she should tell me whatever it is she's thinking about. "I think I saw the guy you were sensing." I tell them, glancing down at my hands.

Blue's hands grip my forearms. "What?"

My swollen eye starts to tingle, but I ignore it. "You looked sick, and I figured there must have been someone else triggering it. And when I looked over the stands, there was this guy staring at me."

"A guy?" Blue's frizzy blue curls bounce on her shoulder as she leans forward further.

I nod slowly. "He looked around our age. But he had this really weird look about him. There was a huge mole on his face."

Blue frowns at me, whilst Ginger chuckles into his palm. "Are you saying he looked weird because of a *mole*?"

Shaking my head, I rub my good eye. "No. He looked weird, and he happened to have a goliath size mole. Trust me, you can't miss it." Blue rolls her eyes, her grip loosening around my wrists.

"How do you even know if that was the guy I was sensing?"

"I followed him."

Ginger gives me a disapproving look this time, whilst Blue appears to be piecing things together. "That's why you were in the corridors."

I nod. "He gave me this weird look, like he knew that I suspected something, and when I followed him out—"

"That big guy cornered you."

"That damn asshole," I mutter. I glance between them. "Who found me?"

Blue inches closer. "We did." She rubs at her arm, her eyes flickering over my face. "We were following the guy as well. Well, I was following the *feeling* like I did to find Fin, but I didn't know who I was following. And then we found that guy laying into you."

"She transformed into a bloody *gorilla* and knocked him off," Ginger adds as he shakes his head, his eyes narrowing on her when she chuckles. "You could have killed the guy!" *She can change into a gorilla? That's pretty cool.*

Blue's face flushes. "But I *didn't*. And I couldn't think of anything else to transform into that would be big enough to take that giant on."

"He could have seen you change, Ce!" Ginger is still upset. My mouth pinches, because he's not wrong. *If Sith had seen her, it could have been bad.*

But she risked that to help me. I stare at her for a moment, my vision going in and out. "Thanks," I mutter under my breath.

She pushes her fluffy hair behind her ears, nodding her head. "Any time." She quickly raises her finger at me. "Wait! That's not me giving you permission to go out looking for trouble, Mister Hero! I'm sure Fin would have my ass for that."

I don't understand anything about Finch anymore. He always does the opposite of what I expect him to.

Blue drops her hand back to her lap. "Why do you think that other guy was at the game in the first place?"

I shrug. "No idea. My guess is that it has something to do with you guys..." My body falls forward slightly when I blink, my body sapped of energy. Ginger throws his arm out across my chest, catching me.

"You need more rest, Liam," he says. Breathing out a loud sigh, I struggle to my feet.

"Can you sense anything right now?" I look at Blue. She nods, but her eyebrows are furrowed.

"Whoever they are, they're far away. I can barely sense either of them now." She doesn't look settled though.

I lean back, my jaw uncomfortably tight. "You say that like there were *two* of them."

She glances away, scratching the back of her head. "I don't know why, but some moments feel as though there *are* two of them."

My teeth grind painfully, and my hands tighten to fists. The torn skin of my knuckles tugs when I do. "You can sense *two* others like you?" *Not good. If this guy has some kind of sensing ability like Blue does, then he might have been there because he sensed the three of them together.*

She nods, wringing her hands together. "What should we do if there *are* two of them?" She seems hopeful, despite her anxious tone.

"Well what do you mean '*some moments*'?" I ask as I turn to face her, my legs weak. Ginger wasn't wrong about needing more rest. His foot taps the tiled floor, his eyes flickering between Blue and I.

She shrugs, looking just as confused by it herself. "It's like one minute there is one of them, and then there's suddenly two. It's only for a couple seconds, then there's one again. It's weird."

My head is starting to ache. "I guess we can figure it out tomorrow. Where are you guys staying tonight?"

Blue stands, shaking her hands out at her sides. "We'll drive home—Maverick isn't that far. Tell Fin we'll be back this weekend. The Sheriff has Zeke's number."

I nod but otherwise don't reply. They wave as I slowly stumble back to my room. Slipping through the door, I make my way over to the bed. Finch is still curled up on the side, the blanket wrapped over his shoulders. The dark purple around his eyes hasn't faded, his inky hair hanging over his eyes. *The idiot's drooling. Why does my chest tighten even when he's drooling?* I don't know how long I stand there staring at him like a creep. When I finally slip back into the bed, his hand moves to grab mine.

"Stop running away from me," he mutters, his eyes still closed and his breathing even. My heart seizes in my chest, and my eyes burn.

"Are you awake?"

I don't get a response. His hand grips mine, his nails biting into my skin. But I don't pull away.

CHAPTER

31

"You're a magnet for trouble, aren't you?" Alice mutters when she walks in. The sunlight streams in through the blinds as she winds them up. I rub my eye with the tips of my fingers, my other hand still gripped tightly in Finch's.

He groans and he burrows his face into the blankets. "Too early, Aunt A."

"Open your eyes, Fin. You're not at home," she says as tucks her long hair behind her ears.

When he lifts his head to look at me, his eyes are squinted. They widen when he sees my fucked-up face. "Liam." He lets go of my hand and reaches for me, but I swat his hand away.

"I'm fine," I grumble through my split lip. I obviously couldn't stick the needle back in, so I'm feeling the aftermath of everything this morning. My eye's still mostly swollen shut, and every single part of my body hurts. Finch's eyes turn down at the corners, and his mouth opens slightly. I wave my bandaged hand at him and give him a look. "This really isn't that bad." His face doesn't look any less grim. If anything, he seems more strained by it. I push his shoulder back, trying to give myself a bit more space. He's too close. "Stop freaking out."

"Stop looking for fights and I'll stop freaking out," he bites back.

My open eye narrows on him as Alice moves to stand beside my bed. She checks over the machines but doesn't say anything. "I wasn't *looking* for a fight. I was following..." I glance at Alice. *Shit*. "*Someone*, and Sith came out of nowhere with arms swinging." *That damn asshole*.

"Who were you following?" Alice asks, as Finch glares back at me. He doesn't seem to have taken any interest in the fact that I was following someone.

"I don't remember." My lips pull in a straight line. Alice watches me with observant eyes, but she doesn't ask any more questions. My cheeks burn when I remember Ginger calling her my mom, and I try to change the topic. "Blue said that they were the ones to find me."

"Blue?" Alice looks between Finch and I, confused.

Finch rubs the back of his neck. "He's talking about Cece. The girl with the curly blue hair that came over after the game." Finch offers, rubbing his face with his palms. He still has dark rings under his eyes, but his skin doesn't look as pale as last night.

"Ah, right."

"So you followed after *someone*? You thought that was a *safe* idea? To just *follow* a stranger, after having an attack earlier?" Finch's eyes are hard now. His mouth is set in a hard line, his jaw is clenched tight.

An attack? Is he talking about what happened in the locker room? "Nothing happened..." I start, but he shoots up from his chair, launching it backward and letting it slam

307

against the ground. Alice jumps from the sudden bang.

"Something fucking *happened*, Liam! Your eye is swollen shut and you're bruised all over, you're damn lucky you didn't have internal bleeding. Take this seriously, *please*." He looks desperate now. *Why is he so upset? It wasn't him that was beaten up.*

"Fin, honey, calm down," Alice tries, but he just huffs at her. My lips pinch and bite my tongue. *Don't snap at him. Don't snap. He's just tired. We're both tired. Don't—*

"I'm so damn sick of you pretending that someone hurting you is okay. I'm sick of you telling me you're fine when you're *not*. It's not okay for people to hurt you, I will *never* be okay with it." Finch takes another step forward, his eyes wet and glassy. My chest heaves, the air in my lungs tightening. He sits down on the side of my bed, right next to where my hand squeezes into a fist. Picking it up, he uncurls my fingers without looking away from my face. I let him. "When will you realise that *I'm here?* I will *always* be here. Why won't you lean on me sometimes?"

My mouth gapes like a fish, and my eyes bulge from my sockets. *That is* not *what I expected him to say.* "I...I'm..." *Why can't I formulate the words I want to say? It's like he's erased everything in my mind, and I'm left an empty shell.* But it's not the same cold emptiness that I'm used to. It's warm, and sunlight, and *different*. And I *hate* that I can't stop craving it.

How does he keep doing this? How does he keep bringing out this feeling that I don't know what to do with? With only a look he changes so much inside me. Why him? Why does he have all that power?

"Liam..." Alice steps forward and sits on the other side of the bed. She takes my hand—the one Finch wasn't holding all night—and rests it in her palms as she stares back at me. The blue in her eyes is darker now. "You always have a place in our lives. You are important. We just want to make sure that you are always *safe*." Her gentle tone seeks out that crack in my chest. The same crack she found last time. It's not too deep, but it's there, and it's splintering even more now.

You're not going anywhere.

You're staying right here with me.

I promise.

My throat closes up and my vision blurs. When I can't keep looking at them, I pull my hands away and bring my legs up, resting my forehead against my knees. Taking a series of deep breaths, I feel the two of them waiting for me. Patient, unrushed. Waiting without requirement. Only the sound of my ragged breathing fills the space around us. "I can't...just..."

What did I tell you about bothering the Mont—

"You are coming home with us, alright?" Alice interrupts my thoughts, her tone hard and soft at the same time. When I peek up over my knees, her smile is tugging at the corners of her mouth. "You are going to stay with us until *you* don't want to anymore."

My mouth is dry now. I try to move my tongue, but it's like sandpaper.

You stay as long as you need.

Until you don't want to anymore.

Until I don't want to anymore...

You are going to stay with us until you don't want to anymore...

Damn it, I will not cry in front of this jerk.

CHAPTER

32

The snow came down hard last night. It has barely been two days and already everything is coated in a thick layer of fresh snowfall as Finch pulls into the school carpark, so it's hard to miss Blue's lump of curls amongst the blinding white.

"They're here, they're in Franklin," she says before I've even closed the passenger door. Ginger stands behind her, his eyes red and his face sickly. Blue's in no better shape.

"What are you guys doing here? You said you were coming back this weekend..." It's hasn't even been forty-eight hours since I last saw them at the hospital. Finch grabs his bag off the back seat, his attention elsewhere.

Ginger nods to his sister. "Cece sensed them nearby when we left the hospital, so we followed her feeling like we did to find you," he points to Finch as he slings his bag strap over his shoulder, "but they were leading us in circles. They're back here now."

Blue blows out a dramatic breath. "They had us chasing our damn tails."

"So there *are* two of them?" Finch steps closer to me as he glances around. A lot of people are staring. News spread like wildfire that I had my ass handed to me after the game, and everyone's made sure to get a good look every time I limp past. Thankfully, my eye isn't swollen anymore, but there is no concealing the ugly puke-green bruises that make up almost every inch of my face.

People whisper around us, and I catch someone say, "You think the Mayor did that?"

I don't correct them, even when I know I should.

Blue shrugs, her bleary eyes drooping. "I'm still not sure. It's all very weird."

Everyone in the carpark and those lingering around the entrance starts to filter into school. I tug on Finch's sleeve. "Hey, classes are about to start. Can we talk about this later?"

Blue narrows her eyes on me, her nostrils flaring. "*We* don't have to talk about this later." Her finger swings between my chest and hers. "Don't keep involving yourself further, Mister Hero. You got pretty beaten up after you went looking for this guy the last time."

"Who cares?" I turn to Finch and find him already giving me a stern look. He doesn't look like he's about to argue in my favour. "I'll do what I want to, Finch."

"Don't you have *any* sense of self-preservation?" Ginger pipes in, his eyebrows furrowed. My teeth grind when my jaw clenches.

"Don't you guys have *school*?" I bite out.

Blue and Ginger shrug their shoulders. "We're home-schooled."

"Of course you are," I mutter. Trudging off, I wave my hand over my shoulder. "Whatever. I'll get lost then."

You're ruining everything.

"Liam—" Finch tries, but I wave my hand at him again.

Don't follow me. I will say something I'll regret later if you do.

I don't take notice of the day as it passes. I don't see Finch between any of my classes. *Maybe he went off with the other two and now they're all searching for Mole.* I tap my pencil against my open notebook, my eyes flickering between the black page and the snowfields. It looks fluffy outside, like piles of cotton instead of ice. The tapping draws the attention from the person next to me, their head turning in my direction for a short moment, before turning back to the teacher without a word.

Tilting my head towards the window, I watch as the snow falls in flurries. The cold seeps through the glass pane, sending shivers up my spine. *I hate sitting this close to the damn windows.* Even through my hoodie, the cold bites at my skin.

You hate the cold.

He's so stupid. Why would he even remember that?

The entire football field is covered in white powder. I can barely see the guy sitting on the stands. His hair's the same colour as the snow, that for a moment I think he's bald. He perches on the stands lining the sides of the barely visible football field, but I know it's the same guy from the Championships. Snowy hair like that isn't common, not in this town at least.

I raise my hand to ask for a bathroom pass, my fractured rib tweaking.

I'll catch him this time.

Trudging through the ankle-high snow coating the field, I don't bother trying to be discreet or sneaky. This guy wanted to be seen. I'm sure other student's will see me, but I'm past caring at this point. *This is all getting a bit too dramatic.*

"What brings you to Franklin High?" I call out when I'm close enough for him to hear me. I might not have an internal radar like Blue does, but I know a creep when I see one. And a mole that size has its own gravitational pull.

My shoes are soaked through, the snow chilling my toes. He continues to glare at the white field like he can't figure out what it could possibly be used for, replying, "You're not stupid."

"Aren't I?" This guy is giving me chills. His eyes are vacant as his hands rub together over his bent legs. He doesn't look comfortable, yet he also seems unbothered. As if I pose no threat whatsoever. I'm sure I don't.

"You aren't who we're here for." His empty eyes flicker in my direction.

But you aren't who we're here for.

I shrug. "Maybe I'm all you're gonna get."

Mole's creepy eyes narrow, his eyelids fluttering, before his lips pull up at the side. "You're gonna be a pain."

"Afraid so."

He stands, his eyelids shuttering again, before he slowly makes his way down from the stands. Snow falls from the benches as he descends, dropping to the ground in white slush piles. My feet stay grounded as he approaches me, my spine achingly stiff. I don't know what the hell this guy can do, and my skin tingles with anticipation. His blank stare sparks an unsettling emptiness in my chest. The dark circles under his eyes emphasise his ghostly skin and hair, his mole drawing all attention to it. His head tilts to the side when he stops in front of me, like he's looking through me.

Wait, is he blind? I wave a hand in front of his face, but he snags my wrist with ease. My heart leaps in my throat. He's much closer now. I try to tug my arm from his grip but his hold is tight, his nails digging in through my sleeve. I don't show him that it hurts, or how my ribs ache from the sharp movement.

"I'm only half blind," he grinds out, his blank eyes narrowing on me. *How did he walk down the stairs so effortlessly?* "Why is he so worried about you all the damn time?" he mutters. I'm not sure he's even talking to me.

I purse my lips. "No idea who you're talking about." When I try to tug my wrist again, his nails cut in deep through my sleeve. *Is this his superpower? Super long freakin' nails or something?*

"Of course you don't," he muses. Mole suddenly drops my wrist, taking a step back. His shoes crunch in the fresh snow as my arm seizes, resisting the urge to clutch at the sensitive marks in my forearm. "Let's go for a walk."

My eyes flicker back to the school building. *I shouldn't leave the school, Finch will have no idea where I've gone if I do, but I don't think this guy is actually giving me a choice.*

He drops his hold and turns away, walking off towards the school gate. My heart races and despite the frigid cold, my palms are sweaty. I know if I let this guy out of my sight, I won't find him again. Or maybe he'd find Finch before I can warn him. So I follow.

"What's your name?" he asks when he hears my footsteps crunching through the snow behind him.

I shrug my shoulders even though he's ahead of me, and I study him closely. "You can just call me Mister Hero."

"I'm not calling you that." He laughs. It's a creepy, quiet

laugh, something I'm not sure he does often. He seems unsettled by it himself. He guides me out of the school gate without a stumble.

"How about I call you Mole, and you can call me Mister Hero." My hands are shaking so damn hard. I tuck them into my hoodie pocket, clenching my jaw. The air is arctic as it passes through my chattering teeth.

"You could very well be the most annoying Normie I have ever met."

Normie? "Is that what you call people who don't have weird powers?" I walk fast to catch up, even though the stiffness in my body is warning me to keep my distance from this guy.

His smile widens, wrinkling his nose. He would look a thousand times creepier without that colossal mole on his face—I can't stop staring at it. "You say 'weird powers', we say 'unlimited opportunity'." His voice takes a darker tone, almost hissing at me. My skin blisters from the crackling air. *He said 'we' again.*

"Doesn't mean they aren't weird."

He laughs again, the sound slow and freaky as hell. "You like to talk a lot of shit for a Normie." His fingers start strumming the air by his thigh.

What the hell am I doing here? Why would I come here without Finch or Blue or Ginger? I can't keep this guy busy, and he knows it. All I can do is talk his damn ear off and hope that one of them finds me before he does anything that could hurt me.

We're both silent for a long time as I follow him into town, the snowplough trucks clearing the main roads. I follow behind him as he leads us towards Cook's diner. *Why*

315

are we going to the diner? As we walk past the windows, I see a lot of people inside. Happy spots me as she sets a plate down onto a table, and waves like crazy. My chest tightens when I see Mole reaching for the door, my throat seizing. *No, not here.*

Please not here.

My hand shoots out and latches onto his coat sleeve. My skin immediately crawls with a sickly shiver, but I grip tighter. "This place isn't that great. The burger joint around the corner—"

"But I've heard so many good things about this place. Apparently Maurie's has the best Pumpkin Pie money can buy. He's gonna love the pie." His smile morphs from pleasant to sinister in the blink of an eye, and my stomach rolls.

He? Is he talking about Finch? Finch doesn't like pumpkin. Mole's eyes stare directly into mine, but they aren't seeing me. Or maybe they are.

"*Please*..." the beg slips out. I don't mean for it to.

He sighs, scratching the back of his head. "Alright, I guess we can—"

The door flies open, the bell ringing as Happy makes an appearance. I quickly drop my hold on Mole's shirt. "Liam, what are you doing wandering around in the cold? You'll catch your death out here! And shouldn't you be at school?" When she sees my face, her eyes blow up. "Sugar, what happened to your handsome face?" She steps closer, cooing over my bruised face before waving me towards the door as her eyes drift over to Mole. "Hey there hon. Haven't seen you around town before. You just passing through?"

Mole nods, his smile seemingly genuine. "You could say

that." He grabs onto my sleeve. "*Liam* here was just helping me around town. My cane is quite difficult to use in snow this deep."

My stomach, my chest, my throat, they're all clenching so damn tight I can't breathe. Glancing back to Happy, I watch as she melts at his lie, her smile broadening but her eyes drooping at the corners.

"Oh you poor thing! Both of you get inside right now!" She ushers us into the warmth of the diner.

No. Please not here.

I catch the mischievous smile on Mole's face when she turns her back to us.

This asshole...He never had any intention of going anywhere else.

"You both sit wherever you like, and I'll fix you something to warm your bones!" The warmth seeps through my hoodie, chills rushing over my skin. My fingers immediately start to thaw, but they don't stop shaking.

I shake my head, my jaw tight. "No, don't—"

"I'm *craving* a steak right now. That wouldn't be too much trouble, would it?" Mole beams at her, his smile giving me the creeps. *Why does he remind me of a shark? Shark's don't have moles that size.*

"'Course not, sugar! I'll have Maurie whip that up lickety-split!" She squeezes my arm before she rushes off, shouting something to Cook in the kitchen.

"Walk me to the booth in the middle, would you?" Mole mutters, his smile slowly falling. The muscles in my neck tense as I walk him between the tables, his grip on my sleeve deathly tight. "Go on," he says as he releases his hold and waves me into the booth. I slip into the bench seat, my spine tightening when he slides in next to me instead of across from me. He pretends to feel around the table, but I know he's aware of where everything is. This guy is telling me a lot without saying anything at all.

"You never said why you're here." I know he's here for Finch, but I don't know why. Sitting this close to him has my stomach twisting in every direction.

Mole flicks his pale hair out of his eyes with a shake of his head. "We're here to take Finch to Chicago with us."

Us.

We're here to take Finch to Chicago with us.

I think I heard a voice...in my head...

It was telling me an address, I think.

It's some random building in Chicago.

I could have just imagined it...

My eyebrows furrow as my lips tighten. "Not gonna happen."

His vacant grey eyes light up as he turns in my direction. "You can't *stop us*, Normie."

My entire body is shaking now, my rib aching with the vibrations. "I don't have to stop you, he won't go."

"Because of you?" His eyebrows rise, and my throat tightens from the look.

"No, he—" I try, but shakes his head with a small smirk on his lips.

"You're not a very good liar, Liam," he mutters, folding his hands on the table in front of him. "I can't understand what he sees in a Normie like you."

I cough to clear my throat, but the lump that's swelling lingers. *A Normie like me*...I don't want that to hurt, but something stings from those words. Mole's face crumples and his eyes narrow. "You have no idea what you're getting involved in, but I suggest you take a step back from all of this, before you sink in any deeper."

"I'll do whatever the hell I want," I snap out reflexively. *I don't let Finch tell me what to do, there's no way I'm letting this guy*.

Mole shrugs his shoulders, his creepy eyes even thinner than before. "Don't say I didn't warn you." He curls his hand around my wrist, jerking it towards him. His skin is icy against mine, rougher than I assumed it would be.

The air thickens, suddenly heavier than before. My lungs start to heave and my skin prickles. My throat burns like I'm trying to swallow barbed wire. The hairs on the back of my neck stand straight, my skin raw and my muscles aching.

What the hell? Is this him? My eyes lock on his fingers, still thrumming against the table. *How is he doing this?*

I grip my throat with my hand, trying to ease the pressure with each breath. Mole just smiles as he watches, his fingers strumming against the tabletop and the other clenched tight around my bare wrist. When his fingers tap faster, the pressure in my chest becomes heavier. It's almost suffocating. *Is this his power? What the hell is he doing to me?*

"What...you...I..." My voice scrapes up my throat, my face burning. *Holy crap, how do I breathe?* My vision blurs, the colours of the diner shifting between bright and brown. When it's brown, everyone in the diner is gone. Even Mole. I glance around, but there's no one here anymore. *Cold. Empty.*

The pressure suddenly disappears, and the air rushes in through my teeth, the bright colours back. Everyone is back. But Mole isn't touching me anymore.

"I'm getting Maurie to whip you up something to eat," Happy says as she appears at the end of the table with a massive smile on her face. I choke as I try to take in as much air as possible, but it's like I've been held under water too long and just broken through the surface. Happy frowns and leans in close, her eyes wide. "You alright, Sugar? Would you like some water?"

I shake my head quickly. "I'm fine," I strangle out, blinking hard until my vision clears again and locking my gaze on Mole. He looks worried as he gazes off, his eyebrows pulling down in the middle as he rubs my back. My shoulders hunch away from the contact.

"Alright, I'll be back with some drinks." She disappears again and any customers that had turned to see what was happening return to their conversations. My eyes narrow on Mole as he hides his smirk behind his hand.

"I can't kill you. At least not until I speak to Finch." I barely hear what he says past the blood pounding in my ears.

"What the hell did you just do?" I rub my temple as a headache starts to form.

"You seem to figure shit out quickly, so you tell me. What *did* I do?" He folds his hands in front of himself again, pursing his lips as he turns my way. My fingers rub at my arms as I scrunch my forehead. *I have to assume that anything is possible with these guys. When you know a small girl with blue hair that can transform into a freakin' gorilla, not a lot should surprise you.*

"You can do two things." My teeth chatter, despite the warmth that encompasses the diner. I think I'm still in shock. *Did I almost die just now?*

His eyebrows rise, but his stoic face gives nothing away.

"Can I?"

He might think he's some big macho guy, but he's transparent as hell. I clear my throat and sit up straight, my shoulders touching the back of the bench seat, the material squeaking with my movement. "You *are* blind...but you can see a different way."

He rubs the back of his neck, his eyes gazing past me out the large window. Almost no one is wandering around town and the snow is falling slowly. "And how could I do that?"

I bite at the inside of my cheek. "I don't know whether you can see the future, or if it's to do with premonition, but you can see things before they happen. That's how you were able to grab me earlier." I want distance between us, but he's got me trapped in the booth. "You realised that someone could sense you when I came after you that night at our basketball Championships." *Of course he did. That's why the creep smiled at me that night. He must have seen Blue would follow him as well.*

He hums, but he doesn't tell me I'm wrong. He's trying to play it cool, but he's bothered by the fact that I have figured things out quicker than he thought I would.

"And the second thing?" he prompts, his fingers flexing. My heart thumps at the movement, ready to have the air snatched from my lungs at any second.

My tongue is numb in my mouth. "It's something psychological. Or maybe it's real, I can't tell. You *create* things in someone's mind." I watch him closely. The way his shoulders stiffen confirms my theory.

"You're half right there." He leans in close, his unseeing eyes gazing back into mine. My stomach rolls again, sweat dripping down the back of my neck. "Do you want me to tell you what I did?" The air is hard to breathe, but I make a point of not showing any discomfort despite the fact that he can't see me. But his lips quirk up as if he's seen it anyway.

I purse my lips. "Sure." *I just need to keep him talking, until I figure out how to get the heck out of here. Or at least until I figure out how to get him out of this diner.*

"If I touch your skin," he mutters quietly, his eyes sharp as they stare off ahead of us. "I can show you glimpses of your future. And sometimes the vision is so strong, you can *feel* it." His eyes snap to me, his teeth flashing in my direction. "I can't pick what I show you, but it's usually something pretty immediate."

"But it was..." I don't know what I saw. But it was cold and dark. *How could he—*

"It's about time," he mumbles, glancing away. My eyes sweep the icy roads outside the diner, my heart joining the lump in my throat. No one drives by, but the hairs on my arms stand on end and my skin crawls. A couple minutes of silence pass before I see it.

Finch's car comes roaring down the icy road, sliding into one of the vacant spots in front of the diner. Finch, Blue and Ginger all climb out, Blue seemingly on the verge of hurling. Ginger's eyes sweep the snow-covered streets, but Finch and I lock eyes through the windowpane. His forehead creases when he spots Mole sitting beside me.

That idiot. Why the hell would he come here? Why did he leave school? His chest heaves as he rushes towards the door, nearly slipping on the icy pavement. The other two follow behind him at a distance, Ginger gripping Blue's elbow.

Finch enters the diner, bypassing Happy without a word as he approaches our booth. Blue and Ginger slow their strides, their eyes wide when they realise I'm here with someone. Finch doesn't hesitate when he's close enough, grabbing Mole by his collar and pulling him up. I'm not sure why he allows Finch to manhandle him, and my heart jumps in my throat.

"Who the hell are you? What the hell are you doing here with Liam?" Finch spits out, his voice rough He sounds feral and vicious. His eyes are half black, that beast inside him teetering on the edge. Mole's white hair flops over his eyes as he smiles, but the air starts to thicken again.

I reach around and latch onto Finch's wrist, digging my nails in. My ribs flare, but I do my best to ignore it. He doesn't know what this guy is capable of. *He needs to calm down.* "Finch, *don't.*"

He stares back. I saw him just this morning, but it feels like years have passed since he last looked at me. "Liam, what are you—"

"*Please,*" I bite out through my clenched teeth. "*Don't.*"

323

CHAPTER 33

Mole brushes Finch's hands away and leans back into the bench. "Take a seat, guys. We've been waiting for you."

Blue and Ginger look to each other, but Finch keeps his eyes on Mole. His jaw is tight as he speaks. "Why are you here?"

The tension crackles between them. When Mole tilts his head, I grit my teeth. He turns and raises an eyebrow at me, gazing blankly out the window.

I nod to the three of them. "Sit down, Finch. I'm alright." I don't know why that slips out. But Finch's pupils pulse. His eyes glance between Mole and me, his lip curling back from his teeth. He takes a seat at my request, sitting directly across from me.

"Why are you in Franklin?" Finch's tone is strangled. His fists clench on top of the table and his shoulders shake, but not from the cold. Mole's mouth pulls up in a loopy smile, his teeth flashing between his lips. Ginger slides into the booth first, leaving Blue on the end of the bench.

"You both ask questions you already have answers for. Why don't you ask me what you *really* want to know?" His head tilts the other way, and the light hits his mole in a peculiar way that has my nose scrunching. *I can definitely see some hairs.*

When Finch hesitates, Blue lurches forward, slapping a hand over her mouth as she heaves. I lean back into my seat. *She better not hurl across this table.* When she swallows, she locks her dizzy, tired eyes on Mole. "Why do you want us to go to Chicago?"

Why do you want us to go to Chicago?

Us.

Have they heard the same voice as Finch?

My head snaps in Mole's direction, my eyes watching as he leans back, raising his hand to her. Not a moment later, Happy appears with two drinks and two plates perched on a tray. Her eyes take in the now full booth, her smile broadening. "Hey honey buns! It looks like we have a full-house today!" Her eyes take in the other two, her eyes widening at the sight of Blue's hair. "Darlin', your hair is gorgeous!" She places the plates in front of Mole and I, then the drinks, our cutlery wrapped in a napkin. When she turns to touch a lock of Blue's hair, her eyes are warm and shiny.

Blue covers her face, her cheeks flushing. "Thank you."

Happy nods before pointing her finger at the three across from me. "You all want burgers?" She waves her hand at us with a laugh. "Of course you do! I'll be right back, sugars!"

"God, I'm hungry," Mole mutters, unravelling his cutlery and cutting into his steak. We all watch him, growing more agitated as each second passes. He hums to himself as he bites into the first piece of meat, resting his wrists against the edge of his plate. "I'm just doing what the big guy asks me to. And he wants you *all* to come back to Chicago with us."

What big guy? What the hell is in Chicago?

"I'm not going anywhere with you," Finch bites out, his eyes narrowed. I feel his foot touch mine under the table, and his shoulders drop the smallest inch. My eyes watch him swallow again, but he's struggling with something. His eyes flicker between Mole and me, his fingers twitching in front of him. Heat rises in my skin from his brief glimpses.

Mole tilts his head back, nostrils flaring and his eyes light up, the dullness dissipating. "Blurry," he mutters, only loud enough for me to hear. "It's never blurry." He cuts another piece from his steak and takes another bite, his forehead creasing. "Is that ugly monster inside you coming out to play?"

My eyes bulge out of my sockets. *How does he know about that? He called it a monster...*When I glance at Ginger and Blue, I can tell they are equally as surprised. Finch shakes his head, lowering his chin to his chest. His shoulders shake violently now, his breath hisses through his teeth.

"Finch," I say as I reach for him, but Mole throws his arm in front of me, keeping me back. I curl away from him, desperate not to let his skin touch me. I won't let him do something like that to me again. He lowers it, but the warning still hangs in the air.

Ginger turns and pins Finch back against the seat. "Hey man, get control of it."

"Finch," I try again. He peeks up through his bangs, his eyes almost completely black. My lips twitch. "If you hurt anyone in this diner, I will *never* forgive you." I don't know if it will work. But it's all I can try do.

Mole takes another bite of his steak. The sight of him eating right now has my stomach clenching.

Finch shakes his head like a wet dog, right as Happy wonders back with more drinks. Ginger slowly pulls back, checking on his sister over his shoulder. Happy's eyes lock on Finch. "You alright there, honey buns?"

Blue quickly nods her head for him, her blue curls bobbing and her eyes swirling, "There was still some snow in his hair." She quickly covers, shrugging her shoulders as she wraps her arms around her stomach. Happy laughs at that one, setting the glasses down.

Mole reaches forward, as if searching for her. Happy leans in close, taking his hand in her plump fingers. "Everything alright, darlin'?"

Mole smiles sweetly at her, making my skin crawl. "Absolutely! I was just wondering if I would be able to try a slice of your famous pumpkin pie I've heard so much about?"

Georgie squeezes his hand. "Of course! I'll go grab you a slice right now!" She's gone and back with a slice in under a minute, winking at us before disappearing again. It takes a few long moments before Finch is breathing somewhat normally again.

When Finch finally lifts his head, he stares back at me. His forehead is sweaty, and his eyes are misty, but it's him again. He nods to Ginger in thanks, before combing his hair back from his face.

"You've all been hearing his voice in your head, haven't you?" Mole asks, his gaze sweeping over the three of them. Ginger and Blue look to Finch, but he's still keeping a watchful eye on me. The two of them nod, whilst Finch offers no visible reply. Mole shrugs his shoulders. "I'm here because you didn't follow orders. At least you two coming here saved me the trip to Maverick."

Blue and Ginger visibly stiffen, their eyes wide and their shoulders hunching. He seems to know a lot for a guy we're only meeting for the first time.

"We're not going with you," Finch barks. His lips are pinched, but he's in control now. He's not shaking as much anymore. His fingers curl into fists again, resting beside his fizzing glass. No one has touched their drinks. Even though the three of them have weird powers, they seem just as anxious as I am.

Mole shakes his head. "Sorry, but you don't really have a choice. The boss asked, so I have to deliver." He finishes off the last bite of his steak, pushing his plate away. He keeps his knife in one hand as he picks his napkin up with the other. He dabs at his mouth, his blank gaze wandering above Ginger's head.

"You can't force us to go with you." Blue doesn't sound certain as she says it.

Mole's lips purse in an awkward smile, his eyes blinking slowly. "We are well aware of your pressure points. We aren't afraid to exploit it to get what we want."

"Don't make us your enemy," Finch grinds out. Pressure builds behind my eyes. *He's not listening. Damn it, he's not listening.*

Idiot. He's not talking about you.

That's why he brought me here. I walked right up to him and offered myself with no resistance.

Mole's smile doesn't change, but his eyes brighten. "We aren't your enemies, Finch. We're the same."

"You don't know me," he hisses out, his eye's smaller

than normal. A vein pulses on his forehead; the 'monster' is sneaking forward again.

Mole's fingers loosen around his knife, but he doesn't drop it. My eyes watch his hands closely, my palms sweating. "You have a cosy little life here in this cosy little town. You three have no idea what making an enemy *really* entails."

"Doesn't matter. We won't let you hurt anyone." Ginger pipes in, his frown casting a dark shadow over his usually light eyes.

Mole chuckles, but the sound is forced and throaty. "You're all new to this. You have no idea what's going on in the *real world*."

"*I don't care.*" Finch punctuates every word, leaning forward. "You have our answer, so get the fuck out of my town." If I wasn't so freakin' anxious, my face would be bright red. Finch doesn't sound like himself right now. He sounds *deadly*.

Everything happens too quickly for my mind to keep up. My eyes catch Mole's fingers tightening around his steak knife right before he swings it at me. I throw my arm up, but he's already latched onto my wrist like he knew I would block with it, keeping my forearm pinned to the table. The dirty knife rests at my throat before I can move my other arm, the serrated blade nipping at my skin. The three of them all reach forward, but Mole presses the blade closer, pricking my skin. "Do you care now?"

Finch immediately leans back in his seat with his hands up, his eyes wide and his mouth presses into a thin line. "I'm sorry, just...*don't hurt him*."

My heart pumps hard in my chest. *Is he going to kill me now? Here, in front of everyone?*

No, he won't. He'll lose his leverage if he does.

"You're done with your little tantrum, then?" Mole sounds older now. Tired. Like he's had this conversation many times before. *Maybe he has.* These three might not be the first they've strong-armed into whatever it is they're doing in Chicago.

"We'll listen. Please...put the knife down." Finch's eyes follow the small trickle of blood that I feel race down the column of my throat. My insides are shaking, and my tongue is still numb in my mouth, but I won't let this guy know how scared I am. *When the hell did my life become this weird series of dangerous situations?*

Mole hesitates a moment longer before he lowers the knife, keeping his hold on my wrist. My other hand rushes to my throat, wiping away the trail of blood as I drag every breath. Finch watches me with clenched fists and a tight jaw, but he keeps quiet. Blue's eyes shimmer, and Ginger's face is grim. They finally realise the reality of the situation.

"Am I late to the party, then?" A deep voice says from the end of the table.

When I turn my head, I find Mole standing at the end of the table. Or rather, someone who looks just like him. But the giant mole on his cheek isn't there anymore.

It's above his eyebrow.

CHAPTER

34

I look between the Mole sitting next to me and the Mole standing at the end of the table, my mind struggling to keep up.

"I take it these are the three we're here for?" the guy that's standing mutters.

"Yep." Mole pops the 'p', rubbing his lips together as if he hadn't been holding a knife to my throat just moments ago. "Hey, they claim to have the best pumpkin pie here, so I ordered you a slice."

"Of course you did." The new guy laughs, sliding in beside Mole. He slides the plate of pie in front of him, spooning a slice. The four of us all watch him with cautious eyes. Finch's foot starts to tap against mine, drumming up my own anxiety.

As if finally noticing me, the guy leans forward to get a good look around his twin. "Who's the Normie?" he says around a mouthful of pie. This guy seems a lot more laid back, but we're all well aware of the threat he poses. The others don't know what Mole can do, but *none of us* know what this new guy is capable of.

Who's the Normie?

No one important. Apparently, I'm leverage.

*Is this how damsels in distress feel? Cause it freakin'
sucks. I'm surrounded by normal looking people with freaky
weird powers.*

He nods his head at me. His hair the same snow white
as Mole's, but his eyes are different colours—one a dark grey,
one a light grey. *I've never met someone with heterochromia
before. Maybe that has something to do with his powers.* His
top lip has a thick white scar through it, causing a small divot
in its shape. "What's your name, Normie?"

Blood swims in my ears, my throat swollen as I try to
answer. "Mister Hero."

The new guy, Lip, throws his head back and laughs. Even
Mole chuckles under his breath. When Lip's eyes land on me
again, there's a dark glint. "Careful, no one saves the hero."

I shrug, tugging my wrist free from Mole's talons. "Guess
it's a good thing I don't need saving." I narrow my eyes on
Finch as I shove my hands into my hoodie pocket. I curl my
fingers into my palm to stop them from shaking, but it
doesn't help much, the bandage around my hand restricts a
lot of the movement. My fractured ribs throb from the blood
rush.

Lip looks at his twin, his eyebrows raised. "Is there a
reason you brought a Normie into this conversation?"

Mole's lips pinch, but his gaze lingers off to the side.
"Only way I could get this guy's attention." He throws his
thumb in Finch's direction, even though he can't see him.

Lip nods his head, before turning back to face the three
across from us. He sends a wink at Blue, that she returns
with a pinched nose.

"Alright, since you're finally here brother, let's get this show on the road." Mole rests his forearms on the table as he leans forward, his eyes empty as they shift around the room. "It's a long drive ahead of us."

Finch leans forward again, his eyes hard. "We already gave you our answer."

Mole breathes out a long, tired sigh, rubbing his hand over his head. "What's stopping you, kid? This guy?" He points to me, his head still faced forward. My heart rate spikes and I almost choke. *Don't pull a damn knife on me again.* Finch shakes his head quickly, but his forehead is damp, and his eyes are shadowed again. "If it's dick you're interested in, there's *plenty* of it in Chicago."

I wish I could punch this asshole in his stupid face right now.

Finch shakes his head, his eyebrows furrowing as his gaze flickers to me again. "I don't want anything to do with these powers."

Lip shakes his head, finishing off his pie and dropping his spoon onto his clean plate. "You sound pathetic." He looks over Ginger and Blue, who have been strangely quiet for most of this conversation. "You guys think this is just some game where you develop these strange powers and get to play around with them risk-free?"

Mole claps his hands together quietly, and suddenly everyone in the diner rises from their seats. They slide out of the booths and stroll past us like zombies, heading for the door with glazed eyes and blank faces. I spin around in my seat, watching as even Happy and Cook march out without a backwards glance. In seconds, the diner is empty. My skin crawls as violent shivers race up my spine.

"What the hell..." Ginger mutters as he watches everyone walk down the streets to their cars and drive away. Blue lurches forward again, cupping her mouth. Her skin is even more washed out than normal. I cross my fingers, hoping she pukes on at least one of the freaky twins.

"That wasn't one of you just now." Blue mumbles around her hand, her eyes rolling around in her head. "Someone else...How?"

Wait, that wasn't Mole? How did she know that? Lip raises his gaze and appraises her, his lips pursed.

"You three are just guppies in a much larger ocean. You might have your abilities, but you aren't safe. Not when there are people who can get inside your head," Lip mutters, rubbing his gloved hands together as he wink's at Blue again. His presence seems to grow larger with each passing moment, and the tight feeling in my stomach seizes. I can see the three across from us are starting to worry. They're gonna roll over and give into whatever nonsense these two are feeding them.

Soon, fear is going to start to overwhelm their sense of reason.

"How did you guys wake up?" Lip asks, leaning forward. They glance between each other again, and Blue bites down on her lip.

"What do you mean 'wake up'?" Ginger asks, leaning back in the seat. His eyes narrow on Lip, dancing between the twins every few seconds.

"Your powers. When did they wake up?"

When I meet Finch's stare, I know he's thinking the same thing I am. *The magic bullet.* Well, not a magic bullet exactly, I guess.

"I was shot," Finch says, his tone dull.

Blue swallows loudly, before mumbling, "I drowned in the creek behind our house."

Ginger nods. "And I drowned when I tried to save her."

Glancing between the three of them, my eyes bulge from my head. They all experienced near-death experiences. Different, but yet too similar a connection for it to be a coincidence. Lip and Mole nod their heads, their smiles animalistic.

"That's how it starts. If it's in your genes, it'll only activate when you're on the brink of death. It's like your body's last-ditch effort to survive."

Blue shakes her head, her colourful curls bouncing around her shoulders. "But why us?"

Lip clicks his tongue at her. "That's a question for the big guy, Sunshine. You'll have to come with us to find out." Shivers race down my spine at his tone.

No. They can't go with them. There's something else he's not saying.

I don't know who the twins truly are, whether they're good or bad, but I can't let these three be sucked into their fears. I lean forward, my eyes darting between the three of them. "Don't listen—"

A huge hand reaches over my face before an icy cold rush crashes into my body. My heart is in my throat as I blink, everything suddenly silent.

I'm in the same booth, but everything is darker.

Shadowed.

Alone.

Finch, Blue, Ginger—gone.

Everyone's gone.

335

Everyone except for me.

Twisting in my seat, I glance around the diner. It's dark everywhere, like it's night and the lights have been switched off. There's no sound, not even wind blowing outside. Glancing out the window next to me, everything is white. Like fog, but it's thick. So thick, I can't see anything beyond the diner window.

No sidewalk. No parked cars.

Nothing.

Maybe it's snow. Maybe the diner's snowed in. Yeah, that has to be it. It's snow. It's snow...

"Finch?" I call out, my voice throaty and weak. I slide out of the booth, my skin erupting with goosebumps. *It's so cold. Why the hell is it so damn cold? It was warm just a second ago.* "Blue? Ginger?" My footsteps are slow as they carry me to the kitchen, but there's no one there. Nothing cooking, just the ovens and the grills. I go back out to the front and search around, but there is nothing out front either. No pumpkin pie, no empty milkshake cups.

"Finch!" My heart hammers in my throat. *Did he leave me here? Where is he? Where would he go? Where are Blue and Ginger? They were here—they were just with me. How did they just disappear?*

You're not going anywhere.

I promise.

You're staying right here with me.

This place is so cold. It's so cold.

"Finch?" *Why would he leave me here by myself? What did I do?*

That hand, that touched my face... Did that make everyone disappear? Why? Why would they leave me here? I'm still in the same diner, right? It's the same, but different.

Rushing to the front door, I yank hard on the handle, but it's stuck. *Why's it stuck? My ears a thumping now. They wouldn't leave me here. He wouldn't. He said I would stay with him. He* said.

You're not going anywhere. You're staying right here with me. I promise.

"*Fuck!*" I messed up. I shouldn't have gone onto that field. I shouldn't have gone looking for Mole. *How do I fix this? I just need to figure out how.*

It's so cold. So dark. It's so dark in here. Pain pounds through my entire body, vibrating my bones. My brain goes fuzzy, and my tongue numb. *It hurts...*

Stop. I want it to stop. *It hurts too much. It's so cold.*

I yank harder, but there's still no give. The snow's too heavy. *Why am I the only one here?*

I promise.

"No!" I try to pick up one of the chairs from a table in the middle of the diner and swing it at a window, but it's stuck to the floor. It shouldn't be, but it is. I try to push the table, but it doesn't move. *Why can't I move anything? Why?*

You're not going anywhere.

"*No!*" I pull at the ends of my hair hard. *Wake up! Wake up, damn it! This is just a bad dream. Finch wouldn't leave me. He wouldn't. He said he wouldn't. This is just a bad dream. This isn't real. It can't be real, can it?* My scalp hurts from pulling so hard. *Is this real?*

You're staying right here with me.

My stomach heaves, bile spewing from my mouth. The acid taste burns my tongue and nose like I've swallowed barbed wire, my eyes blurry. Stumbling back until my back hits the front door, I slide down to the floor. My hands slap against my head, my eyes pinching shut. *A bad dream. Just a bad dream.*

I promise.

CHAPTER 35

The air is frosty like ice coating my lungs. I wheeze with every breath, my eyes blankly watching each puff of air leave my mouth. *It's so damn cold.*

Cold, cold, cold...

I don't know how long I've been here. Maybe hours...Maybe days...

Days, days, days...

The silence is deafening. I keep tapping my foot because I can't stand it any longer. It's hollowing out my insides and making my eyes cross.

Taptaptaptaptaptaptaptaptaptaptap.

It's all so much of the same.

I promise.

Promise, promise, promise...

My hands won't stop shaking as I hold my knees to my chest.

Stop shaking. Stop.

I miss things.

His voice. His pretty smile.

You did good, Liam.

Taptaptaptaptaptaptaptaptaptaptaptaptaptap.

Sound. Colour. Voices. Warmth.

I stare at the wall, my back pressed tightly against the front door. The diner is empty.

Empty, empty, empty...

Or am I the empty one?

Empty, empty, empty...

I keep tapping my foot because I don't know when I'm going to hear sound again. The silence hurts so damn bad.

Hurts, hurts, hurts.

You're not going anywhere.

I'm somewhere. I'm where it's the same. I'm stuck in the dark.

Stuck, stuck, stuck...

My ears ring loud as the silence starts to overwhelm the tapping. So I tap harder. I tap both feet. I tap both until they bleed. *Surely they're bleeding.*

Taptaptaptaptaptaptaptaptaptaptaptap.

Has it been hours or days? I can't remember how many times I've fallen asleep. Only when I can't keep my eyes open.

Taptaptaptaptaptaptaptaptaptap.

This silence is going to kill me.

Shapes are changing. Maybe it's in my head, but the next time I notice it, the chair isn't swirly anymore. It's normal again.

And it's red.

Red...

I stare at the chair for a moment longer. Shapes aren't changing anymore. *It's cold.* But it's a *different cold.*

Cold, cold, cold...

My head turns lazily from side to side. The chair isn't the only thing that's back to not being colorless. The diner walls are blue again. There's a clock above the counter that's ticking.

Tick, tick, tick, tick, tick, tick, tick, tick, tick—

The air chokes in my throat as I glance around frantically. My legs stretch out as I drop my knees, and I try to climb to my feet. My rib aches and my legs have no strength, cramped and tight from sitting curled up for so long.

My eyes water as the ticking fills my head, so loud that I can hear it over the roaring of blood in my ears.

A grunt slips between my lips as I force my legs to straighten. *How long as it been?*

My head is woozy and my eyes struggle to focus as the blood rushes to my head. I turn to look out the window, my chest tight. *Don't be snow.*

Don't be snow, don't be snow, don't be snow—

A car drives past, dark green and loud.

Loud, loud, loud...

They keep driving until they're out of sight. My eyes lock on the old man across the road as he unlocks the door to his shop, his *blue* puffer coat keeping him warm from the biting snow.

Blue, blue, blue...

Tick, tick, tick, tick, tick, tick—

My hands struggle with the door handle, flicking the lock and yanking it open. When the door swings towards me, a sob bursts from my dry throat. My eyes are blurry as the ice-cold air seeps through my hoodie, my vision distorting.

When the silence starts to settle back in as I stare up at down the street, I start to run. I *try* to run. But my legs are sore and weak and the snow is cold and it reaches my knees.

My legs give out beneath me, and the thick powder swallows me whole. I lay there for a long time.

Cold, cold, cold...

Get up, Liam. Get up, get up, get up!

Pushing myself up, the ice biting at the skin of my palms, soaking through the bandages wrapped around my knuckles. The skin burns beneath them, but I grit my teeth and ignore the pain.

Climbing back to my feet, my legs sway. But I lock my knees. *I'm not stuck anymore. I won't be stuck anymore.*

Each step is harder than the one before it, but I don't stop. I trudge through the snow because *I can.*

Not stuck, not stuck, not stuck...

I don't know how long it takes before I make it there, but my shoes are soaked and my legs are numb. Sounds filters in from all directions; the random chirping bird, the crunching of the snow beneath my feet, the laboured breaths hissing between my teeth.

The silence lingers on the cusp of the sound, and my ears bleed with dread.

But after walking and wincing and limping and hurting for what seems like so long, I see it.

His car isn't out front. The tree is bare of any leaves, the branches terrifyingly pointed and ghostly. The snow is starting to gather on my shoulders, seeping in and chilling my skin.

Cold, cold, cold...

Glancing up at the house, it's still the same. Both cars

are in the driveaway. The sky is still dark, and there are no lights shining through the windows. Snow covers the rooftop like a thick sheet. I look back at the tree, and my throat constricts.

Where is he?

He's not here. Why isn't he here? He should be here...

Be here, be here, be here...

I drag my feet blindly through the snow, my legs burning t despite the cold. I don't know how much longer I have until they give out from under me, but I have to make it. *I'm so close.*

Close, close, close...

I'm not sure when I started needing his voice...or her warmth...or his strength...

They'll be there. They have to be there.

The snow shifts around my ankles as I slowly shuffle my way towards the front door. My eyes are blurry, my jaw is chattering, and I think I might bite my tongue off at any moment, but nothing matters except getting to that door.

My heart hammers so loud in my ears and the silence is numbing. *What if I'm dreaming? Because what if I'm still stuck in the diner and everything is still colourless and quiet and I'm alone and there's* nothing—

I press my frozen finger against the doorbell, and the shrill noise travels through the house beyond the door, and for a short moment, the silence is truly silenced.

But it creeps back in as my legs finally give up and I fall backwards against the porch pillar and the snow melts into my clothes and touches my skin. It's so cold it burns.

I stare at the door, but the silence is blinding me. *Why did I come here?*

343

My eyes start to droop, the pain fading as quickly as my eyes close. Before they shut completely, a light flicks on, shining on me through the curtains.

Light, light, light...

But I can't keep my eyes open any longer, even when the sound of a door opening creates a devastating break in the silence.

"Be careful with him, Dean."

"I know, I am."

"Put him down gently..."

"Get your bag. He's cold as ice."

Someone's crying...

The first thing I feel when I wake up is how *heavy* my head is.

Heavy, heavy, heavy...

When I find the energy to open my eyes, I'm immediately blinded by the bright sunlight that shines in through the window above me. It's so bright that I have to turn my head. When I do, my eyes land on her.

Alice sits at the side of the bed, her red-rimmed eyes closed and her head slumped forward. I stare at her for a long time as my eyes water and a lump forms in my throat.

Alice, Alice, Al— "Alice..."

Her head snaps up when she hears me, her large blue eyes locking on my face. They're bloodshot, her nose is pink and flushed like her cheeks, but she still looks so pretty.

Why did I come here?

"Liam..." She leans forward and runs her palm over my forehead, pushing back at hair that is stuck to my sweaty skin. She stares down at me, her eyes watering as her lip trembles.

I can't move my body. It's too sore and I don't have the energy, but the silence is thumping so damn loud in my head. My heart clenches. I want to ask her to talk, to just fill the silence, but before I have the chance her face crumples and she bursts into tears.

She falls down onto the bed, her face buried in the sheets beside my hand. I try to reach out for her, but my body won't respond. I can barely keep my eyes open.

Dean comes running into the room, looking first at Alice sobbing hysterically and then to me. I stare back at him, and my own eyes start to burn. He looks rough, his eyes equally as inflamed as Alice's. His hair is a mess, and he has a beard now; I wouldn't recognise him if it wasn't for the fact that his presence immediately made me feel safe.

"Thank god," he says as he falls into the room, rubbing his meaty hand down his rugged face. "*Thank god.*"

It's hard to breathe, but it's just a little bit easier than it was before.

"Where's Finch? Why isn't he here?" I croak out, my gaze flickering between the two of them.

I need to see him...

Dean moves closer, his eyes hazy as he stares down at me. His eyes flicker to Alice for a moment before they're back to me. But I don't like the confusion I see on his face.

"Who's Finch?"

345

Acknowledgments

This book has been a blur, and it's crazy to think of where it first started. The journey that I've been on with Liam and Finch has been beautiful. I have loved every single version of these boys that I have written, and even the storylines running through my head that I haven't put to paper yet. They are such an integral part of my life now.

It's *hard* to write a story with abuse. But abuse *is* hard. Abuse is real, and it happens in front of us all the time. Abuse and anxiety can take on so many different forms, that it can sometimes be hard to identify when someone is suffering from one or both of these. So please, love and support each other.

My goal as an author is to write something that *stays*. Something that roots itself so deeply that you can't get it out of your head. I want to write something that you think about and discuss. And I couldn't have come *close* to accomplishing that without these people to help me.

Whitney (a.k.a. my absolute rock). You have been the biggest support system when it comes to my writing. You have been there from beginning-to-end, and I couldn't have asked for a better critique partner than you. Thank you for always being as excited about the small things as I am.

Gee (a.k.a. my biggest fan of all time). You. Are. Amazing. Positively phenomenal. Quite possibly the most remarkable person I know. You see so much potential in me and this story, and I can't put into words how much I genuinely appreciate that. Any time I start to doubt myself, you're there to pick me up. I'm so incredibly lucky to call you my friend.

Rena Violet (a.k.a. my amazing cover designer). You were the first to give my story a face. You had ideas when I didn't, and a direction when I had no idea where I was going. You have been so incredibly patient, and it has been an absolute pleasure to work with you on this project.

C.M. McCann (a.k.a. my wonderful developmental editor). Thank you for helping to put my story into perspective. Your words helped me realise where the story was lacking and where is was excelling. You helped me change *so much* for the better, and I would not be as happy with how it turned out if it weren't for you.

Sydney Hawthorn (a.k.a. my incredibly patient copy editor). Oh boy, you helped a lot. I'm sorry I'm so bad with grammar – I promise to be better in the future! But you're work helped me to recognise my faults as a writer (a good thing) and where I needed to improve. It was insanely helpful, and I am so grateful for your help.

My beta readers (a.k.a. the poor souls who had to read the original story). Thank you so much for taking the time to read one of the first versions of *A Glimpse of Light & Glory*. The story has come so far since then, and I hope you all enjoy it.

About The Author

From a young age, M.J.'s love for sweet romance and exciting adventure has always drawn her into stories, so it wasn't long until it wasn't enough and she started to write her own. Now she dedicates most of her time to writing, filling any spare moments with anime, books and tea (only ever white with 3 sugars).